TIME TO PLAY THE MURDER GAME

The phone pinged again.

Of course, she couldn't ignore it. Her annoying curiosity wouldn't let her.

She grabbed her phone from the table. Wasn't there a saying about curiosity killing the cat?

Do I have your attention, Bailey? Welcome to the Murder Club.
Your first case begins today.

Bailey scowled, annoyed by the realization that the mysterious club member hadn't given up.

Who is this? She typed the words before common sense could stop her.

Your greatest admirer

Greatest admirer? A strange unease crawled down her spine. They sounded like the words of a stalker.

Leave me alone, she texted back.

I can't. You've been ~~...~~

Unchoose me.

Too late. I have ~~...~~ e ...

Published by Kensington Publishing Corp.

THE
MURDER
CLUB

ALEXANDRA
IVY

ZEBRA BOOKS
Kensington Publishing Corp.
www.kensingtonbooks.com

To the real BERT AND ERNIE,
who bring me endless joy!

Chapter 1

Monday nights weren't exactly bustling with activities in the small town of Pike, Wisconsin.

Okay, there weren't *any* nights that bustled, but Mondays were the worst. The stores along Main Street had locked their doors at five o'clock on the dot, and the teenagers who'd gathered to watch football practice at the high school had long ago headed home for dinner. The only things open on Monday night were Bella's Restaurant, a gas station, and the Bait and Tackle, a small bar squished between the dentist's office and the laundromat.

The lack of entertainment might explain the bewildering question of why the Bait and Tackle was packed.

It certainly wasn't the ambience, Bailey Evans wryly acknowledged, pushing aside her empty beer bottle, which floated on a ring of condensation. The narrow bar boasted a handful of tables and booths at the front with a scruffy wooden bar at the back. The paneled walls were covered with old-time tin signs, and the lights were hidden behind shades that had yellowed with age, creating a murky glow.

The bar wasn't really Bailey's choice for a night out, but her friend Kari Wentz had insisted that she needed something to lift her dark mood. They both worked at the local nursing home—Bailey as a nurse and Kari a part-time aide—and the older woman insisted that Bailey hadn't been her usual bubbly self. After two days of nagging, Bailey had given into the inevitable.

It wasn't like she had anything else to do, right? Ever since her best friend, Lia, had met Kaden Vaughn, a stuntman from Vegas, they rarely had time to hang out. Which was a shame. Lia would never have badgered her into going to the bar. She would have invited Bailey over to her apartment to watch sappy romance movies and eat homemade chocolate chip cookies.

The perfect evening.

"Another round?" Kari asked. The tall, solid woman had chopped her dark hair short after getting married and having kids. She'd also put on several pounds that she was constantly trying to lose by one wacky diet after another. This week was something to do with boiled eggs and spinach. Gross.

"Not for me, thanks," Bailey declined the offer. "I need to get home."

"Home?" Kari held up her sturdy arm, waving her wristwatch in front of Bailey's face. "It's not even eight o'clock."

"I have to work tomorrow," she said.

"Yeah, yeah, yeah. You're always working."

Bailey shrugged. Her friend wasn't wrong. "Someone has to pay the bills. And since I wasn't born with a trust fund and my dogs haven't hit it big on social media, despite being utterly adorable, that someone is me."

Kari scrutinized her, starting at the brown hair that was pulled into a loose ponytail and the thin face that was dominated by a pair of brown eyes. Bailey hadn't bothered to put on makeup, although she did change her usual scrubs for a pair of jeans and a light yellow sweater. That was as fancy as she got.

"Are you sure you're not still upset about old lady Warren?" Kari pressed, her expression genuinely concerned.

Bailey sighed. She'd been devoted to Nellie Warren. The elderly woman had lived in the nursing home for the past five years and quickly become her favorite. Despite being crippled with arthritis, she had a quirky sense of humor combined with a down to earth common sense that allowed her to age with a unique grace that Bailey could only hope she could emulate.

"I'll miss Nellie, but I've worked at the nursing home long enough to know that the residents have a limited time left in this world," Bailey told her friend. "Although it was crappy that her son didn't even bother with a proper funeral. The whole town would have gone to pay their respects, but I heard he had her body burned and tossed her ashes behind his lumberyard."

"Typical." Kari clicked her tongue. "That's what happens when you have a kid when you're in your forties. And an only child on top of it. The Warrens spoiled Gage rotten. It turned him into a selfish jerk."

"A shame, but Nellie's at peace."

"So if you aren't upset about Nellie, then what's going on with you? Oh . . . wait." Kari grimaced. "Please don't tell me you're rushing home to play that stupid murder game?"

A shiver raced through Bailey and she was suddenly glad she was surrounded by a bar full of neighbors. She'd impulsively accepted an invitation to join the Murder Club when she was sitting home last New Year's Eve. She was bored and feeling sorry for herself and in dire need of a distraction.

At first she'd been enthralled by the thrill of searching through cold unsolved cases and trying to figure out whodunit. She might not be a detective, but her cousin was the local sheriff, and God knew they'd had enough murders in Pike to make every citizen a homicide expert. And honestly, she thought she was good at spotting clues that other people overlooked.

"No, I'm done with that. I closed my account last week."

"I'm glad." Kari lifted her beer in a small toast. "It's creepy."

"It was a way to pass the time," Bailey argued. "Plus, the people I met in the chat room were interesting."

"You mean people like Eric Criswell?"

Bailey pretended she didn't notice Kari's derisive tone. Eric was a fellow aide at the nursing home, but he didn't mix easily with the rest of the staff. He was shy and awkward and routinely disappeared to play games on his phone. Most of the locals considered him an oddball, but Bailey felt sorry for the poor guy.

"He invited me to join, but that's the only reason I knew he was part of the club. Everyone preferred to remain anonymous, and honestly, that's what made it fun. You didn't have any expectations or any pressure to try to impress anyone. I could just be myself." Bailey shook her head. "But you're right. It went from fun to creepy over the past few weeks."

"What happened?"

"I started getting weird messages from the chat room telling me that I'd been chosen to play in a private murder club with a mysterious admirer." She wrinkled her nose. "I tried to ignore them, but whoever it was remained persistent. They sent me invitations and links several times a day. In the end, I just wanted to be out of it."

"That means you have nothing but time on your hands." Kari paused, her brows lifting. "You know what you need?"

"A million dollars and an endless supply of dough-nuts?"

"A man."

Bailey rolled her eyes. How many times had she heard that precise phrase over the past five years? She'd just celebrated her twenty-eighth birthday, but the entire town was convinced she couldn't be happy without a husband and a gaggle of children.

"It's not the eighteen hundreds. I'm doing just fine without a man."

"Aren't you lonely?"

Ouch. Bailey flinched. It was a direct shot where she was most vulnerable.

"Sometimes," she grudgingly admitted.

Kari scanned the crowded room, as if hoping a suitable man might magically be drinking beer at a nearby table. Surprise, surprise, she came up empty. Still, her stubborn expression warned that she wasn't going to be deterred. Bailey grimaced. She knew what came next. Kari wasn't the first friend to try to get her hooked up.

"Why don't you try one of those online dating sites?" she demanded.

"Are you kidding? Absolutely not."

"Why? My aunt just married a man she met online."

"Your aunt has been married five times."

"She's not lonely."

Bailey laughed. "Thanks but no thanks."

"Fine." Kari pursed her lips, mentally searching for another way to torment her friend. "Then let me give you the number of my cousin in Grange. Not that he's husband material. I'm not sure how he makes his money, although I suspect it's not entirely legal. But he's been out of jail for over a year and . . ." The horrifying words thankfully dribbled away as something or someone behind Bailey captured the older woman's attention. "Oh. Hello."

"What?" Bailey started to turn her head only to freeze when Kari reached out to grasp her hand.

"No. Don't look."

"What is it?"

"A dream," the woman breathed.

"I think you've had too much to drink." Bailey tugged her hand free and turned to see who was causing her friend to act so weird.

Immediately she located the source of her enchantment. He was taller than most men in the bar, well over six feet and broad through the shoulders. His hair was cut short, but it glistened like gold in the dim light and his eyes were dark. Not dark like Bailey's brown eyes. But the deepest midnight. Or pools of ebony.

He was wearing a flannel shirt to combat the crisp October air and a pair of jeans that clung to his long, muscular legs. He looked at home in the small bar, unless you took into account his deep tan.

Oh, and the fact that he was heart-stopping, mouth-watering, drop-dead gorgeous.

"You're not dreaming," she murmured, her heart skidding until it crashed against her ribs.

"Right? He must be lost. No man looking like that ever comes to Pike." Kari paused before correcting herself. "Not unless it's Kaden Vaughn."

After nearly a year of living in Pike, Kaden Vaughn was still considered an exotic intruder. With his long hair, tattoos, and love of fast cars, he would always be different from the locals.

"You're not wrong," she told Kari. "It's Dom Lucier. He's a friend of Kaden."

"You know him?"

Bailey's gaze never wavered from Dom's face. It was stunningly familiar despite the fact that it'd been several months since she'd last seen him. As if she'd spent the short time they were together memorizing each feature.

The thought was oddly disturbing.

"We met at the wedding," she explained.

"You mean the super-secret wedding no one was invited to?"

It had been a source of unending annoyance to the citizens of Pike that Lia and Kaden had chosen a small, private ceremony on the land they'd recently purchased outside of town. They'd been expecting a lavish Hollywood blowout that would bring in celebrities rushing to the area.

Instead there were less than twenty people invited. Including Bailey as the maid of honor and Dom Lucier as the best man. The only outsiders were a cluster of paparazzi who had obnoxiously jam-packed the road leading to Kaden's property.

"That's the one."

Kari clicked her tongue. "No wonder Lia didn't want to share."

"Lia wouldn't notice another man besides Kaden if he stripped naked in front of her."

"Darling, if that man stripped in front of me, I'd not only notice, I'd go up in flames," Kari admitted.

"What about Martin?" Bailey teased, reminding Kari of her husband, who was currently at home with their kids.

"Martin who? Oh, heavens." Kari released a nervous giggle. "He's coming this way. Be still my heart."

Bailey wasn't worried about her skidding, crashing heart as she met the midnight gaze that locked onto her from across the crowded room. She was far more concerned she might faint as the air was ruthlessly squeezed from her lungs. Kari was right. He was weaving his way through the tables.

Directly toward her.

Dom Lucier barely noticed the throng of people who were stuffed in the narrow space. Not even when they stopped in unison to watch him walk toward the woman who'd lured him into the bar.

He'd been leaning against the building across the street, impatiently waiting for his dinner, when his gaze was captured by the sign painted on the front window. **THE BAIT AND TACKLE**. He assumed it was some sort of store to buy fishing equipment until he realized the place was filled with customers who were waving around beer bottles. He'd been about to turn away when he caught sight of a familiar face.

Bailey Evans.

Without hesitation, Dom had shoved himself away from the building and hurried across the street. He'd had every intention of looking up Bailey when he arrived in Pike. Not only because she was one of the few people he knew in town but because he hadn't been able to get her out of his thoughts since returning to Vegas.

He'd spent the weekend of Kaden's wedding performing all the traditional best man duties. Thankfully, that included spending time with the maid of honor. First there'd been the combined bachelor and bachelorette party that had been a casual BBQ at Kaden's home. The fact that the sprawling house was still in the process of being built hadn't detracted from the fun of playing yard games and toasting hot dogs and marshmallows over the bonfire.

Then there'd been the wedding rehearsal and dinner, and the actual ceremony, followed by a reception. And through it all Bailey had been at his side.

Warm and charming and completely at ease with herself.

When she was nearby Dom hadn't felt like an outsider. She'd been so welcoming that he'd instantly felt like he was home.

And even after he'd returned to Vegas to run Money Makers, the pawnshop and restoration garage he owned with Kaden, she'd stayed on his mind. Which was only one of many reasons he'd agreed to come to Pike.

At last battling his way through the crowd, Dom managed to reach the small round table. He smiled, barely resisting the urge to push back the stray curl that brushed against her cheek.

They were virtually strangers, but the sensation that he'd known her all his life crashed through him.

"Bailey, this is a nice surprise." He pitched his tone so it would carry over the noise of the bar, but not so loud the gawkers could overhear his words.

Bailey tilted back her head, her wide brown eyes glowing with a velvet softness. Was she pleased to see him? Damn. He hoped so. She was just as beautiful as he remembered.

Maybe not beautiful in the traditional sense. Her features were delicate, almost fragile, but her mouth was too wide for her thin face, and there were several freckles sprinkled over her cheeks. Still, it all somehow combined to create a vision that had haunted him for months.

"Hello, Dom." She blinked as the woman across the table loudly cleared her throat. "Oh. This is my friend, Kari Wentz. We work together at the nursing home."

Dom nodded toward the woman, who appeared to be in her midthirties. "Pleased to meet you, Kari."

Kari flashed a mysterious smile. "Trust me, the pleasure is all mine."

"Are you in Pike visiting Kaden?" Bailey asked, giving him the excuse to return his attention to where he wanted it to be.

"Not this time. We swapped places."

"Swapped places?"

"Kaden is filming a new special for *Do or Die*."

Bailey looked surprised. "Really? I thought he'd retired from his reality show?"

"He doesn't do stunts anymore. Lia would kill him. But he still works on motorcycles. And he has a top-secret client who asked him to restore an antique bike." Dom shrugged. "The specials always bring in a nice flood of customers to Money Makers."

"I sometimes forget how famous he is," Bailey admitted.

"Trust me, Kaden hates to be treated like he's different," he assured her. "But since he's going to be stuck in Vegas for a few weeks and Lia traveled with him to plot an ambitious expansion of Money Makers, they needed someone to house-sit the animals."

She frowned, as if bothered by his words. "They could have asked me. I would have been happy to help."

He didn't doubt her words for a second. He'd watched Bailey during the wedding, constantly moving to assist Lia or the other guests. She was the sort of woman who put the needs of other people before her own.

"I volunteered," he admitted. "I haven't had a break in five years. I needed to spend some time away from Vegas."

"Five years?" She blinked. "You're definitely over-due for a vacation. But . . ." She glanced around the shabby bar. "Pike?"

"It's peaceful."

"Another word for 'boring.'"

"I'm okay with that." Dom pulled out the nearest chair to Bailey and took a seat. "Can I buy you a drink?"

It was Kari who answered. "She'll have a Moss Brothers."

Dom had partied enough to recognize the name of most cocktails, but that was a new one.

He glanced toward Bailey. "Moss Brothers?"

"It's a beer from a local microbrewery," she clarified.

Ah. That made sense. He lifted his arm and motioned toward a woman with hair that she'd bleached to a brittle white. She was darting from table to table with a frazzled expression. He assumed she was a waitress.

As she scurried in their direction, however, he wasn't so certain. Despite the heavy layer of makeup and the low-cut shirt that revealed her lush curves, she didn't look old enough to be out of high school. Of course, he'd just hit thirty-five, he wryly reminded himself. Lots of women looked painfully young to him.

Once the waitress reached the table, Dom glanced toward his companions. "Three Moss Brothers?"

"Naw, just two. I need to get home." Kari abruptly shoved herself to her feet, blowing a kiss in Bailey's direction. "Enjoy."

The older woman disappeared through the crowd and Dom turned his attention back to the waitress. "Two Moss Brothers."

The waitress nodded and hurried away, leaving him alone with Bailey. Or at least as alone as you could be in the middle of a crowded bar.

Angling his chair to the side, he studied Bailey with blatant appreciation.

"It's good to see you again," he said. "I was hoping I'd run into a friendly face while I was in Pike."

She smiled, but her fingers tapped a rapid tattoo on the table. Was she nervous? Dom didn't know if it was a good or a bad thing. He was going to roll with good.

"You'll soon discover that you'll see everyone's face in Pike. It's too small to avoid people," she warned him.

"Sounds cozy."

She wrinkled her nose. "Sometimes too cozy."

Dom had spent the past nineteen years living in cities. First Hollywood and now Vegas. Before that, however, he'd moved from one small village to another in France. He understood what it was like living in a place with neighbors who knew everything about everyone.

There was a loud cheer from the back of the room, no doubt in reaction to the football game that was on the large TV near the bar. At the same time, the waitress arrived at their table carrying a tray with two beer bottles.

"Here you go."

Setting down a beer in front of Dom, the waitress turned toward Bailey even as her gaze remained locked on him in blatant curiosity. Predictably, her distraction led to disaster as she tipped the tray to the side, toppling off the bottle. Bailey managed to grab it before it could shatter, but beer sprayed over the table and into Bailey's lap. The waitress gasped, her face turning beet red as she grabbed the towel she had tucked in her apron and tried to mop up the mess.

"Sorry, sorry."

"No worries, Nicole." Bailey grabbed the towel before the woman could cause more damage and sent her a reassuring smile. "I got this if you want to grab me a new beer."

"Oh. Okay. Thanks, Bailey." Nicole rushed away, obviously mortified by her clumsiness.

Dom's attention remained fixed on Bailey as she calmly wiped up the beer before tossing the towel on the empty seat across the table and pulling a packet of wet wipes out of her purse.

"I can tell you're a nurse," he murmured in appreciation.

Bailey had mentioned her job when they'd been toasting marshmallows at the prewedding party. He'd already suspected that she worked in a career that centered on caring for other people.

She sent him a puzzled glance. "Why do you say that?"

"Dealing with a problem without making a fuss."

She shrugged. "Nicole just started."

"Not everyone is so forgiving."

"Accidents happen." She dabbed at her wet jeans before tucking the wipes back into her purse. Then, settling back in her chair, she sent him a wry smile. "And in her defense, I think she was distracted."

She was clearly referring to the way the waitress had been staring at him. Dom hid a smile. Good. She'd noticed.

"I suppose a stranger is going to attract attention in Pike."

"The attention wasn't because you're a stranger." She wrinkled her nose as she glanced down at her damp jeans. "But I am going to have to take a shower when I get home."

Dom's interest in Bailey Evans had been stirred from the moment they'd been introduced and intensified during the wedding festivities. Still, he'd known there was a chance he would be disappointed when he returned to Pike. People were usually different at parties than their normal, day-to-day self.

But not Bailey. She was the same genuine, kindhearted woman he remembered.

Determined to spend the next couple of weeks getting to know Bailey better, Dom first needed to make sure that she wasn't in a relationship. Lia claimed that her friend was single, but she also admitted that she hadn't had much time to spend with her lately. It was possible that Bailey had started dating someone without Lia knowing.

"I think you mentioned that you live at your grandmother's house?" he asked.

A cloud passed over the delicate features before she nodded. "Yes, she left it to me when she passed away a few years ago."

"Alone?"

It wasn't subtle. But Dom wasn't subtle. His father was a charming, worthless con artist who wouldn't know the truth if it bit him on the ass. Dom prized truth above all things.

"All alone." She paused. "Unless you count Bert and Ernie."

Dom's stomach muscles tightened, as if preparing for a blow. "Friends?"

She snorted. "Two oversize black Labs who rule my life."

He chuckled. "Two? You definitely don't live alone.

I envy you." His words were sincere. When he'd lived in Hollywood he'd had a couple of stray dogs he'd taken in. They'd been great company, but they'd both been elderly and in rough condition when they'd found their way to his doorstep. He'd only had them a few years. "I'm staying in an RV behind the store. It's fine for now, since it's just me. But once I get settled in a real house I'm getting me a dog. I miss having one around."

Nicole came scurrying back with the fresh bottle of beer, clunking it on the table before hurrying off with a harassed smile.

Bailey grabbed the bottle and lifted it to her lips. Taking a deep sip, she lowered the beer and eyed him with a curious expression.

"Are you out enjoying the local sights?"

He shook his head. "Lia insisted I had to try Bella's pizza while I was in town."

"She's not wrong."

"They don't do delivery, so I decided to come in for a quick drink while I wait for my order." Dom lifted his own bottle and took a deep swig. The cold, malty liquid hit his tongue with a refreshing undertone of citrus. Nice. He sent Bailey an appreciative smile. "Now I'm very glad I did."

Bailey nodded. "The Moss Brothers brew a good beer."

Dom leaned forward. "I wasn't talking about the beer."

Chapter 2

It was no surprise to Bailey when she struggled to sleep. It'd been forever since she'd enjoyed a casual evening out with a guy. And never with a guy who made her feel . . . giddy. That was the only word that captured the breathless, dizzying excitement that bubbled through her like champagne. The last time she'd felt like that she'd been sixteen years old and Billy Roberts had invited her to the Homecoming dance.

Dragging herself out of bed at the shrill sound of her alarm, Bailey stepped into the shower despite the fact she'd washed off the sticky beer last night before going to bed. She needed something to wake her up and she didn't drink coffee.

Once she was dressed in her scrubs, she pulled her damp hair into a messy knot on top of her head and moved into the kitchen to feed Bert and Ernie. The large dogs barked their approval, dancing circles in the small kitchen until they threatened to knock her down.

The house really was too small for such large dogs, but Bailey was willing to endure a few bruises. She adored the ridiculous duo.

Once she'd finished a quick glass of orange juice and the dogs had wolfed down their breakfast, Bailey opened the front door to send the pair to her next-door neighbor for the day.

In the beginning she'd tried to keep the exuberant beasts in her yard, but Dorinda Lyle was an elderly widow who assured her that she enjoyed having company. And to guarantee they made a mad dash to her house every morning, she kept an abundance of stuffed toys, treats, and beds that were specifically designed for aging dogs. Bailey counted her blessings they could spend the day being spoiled rotten.

Waiting until the beasts were safely tucked inside, Bailey grabbed her keys and headed out of the house. She got to the sidewalk as a sharp breeze cut through her scrubs. Crap. The October air had gone from crisp to cold. Returning to the house, she grabbed a cardigan sweater her grandmother had knitted for her shortly before she died and pulled it on. It was several sizes too large and starting to fray at the cuffs, but she loved it. She headed back out of the house only to spin around and rush back to the kitchen. She'd forgotten her phone.

It was her usual morning routine. Bailey told herself that she wasn't scatterbrained, she was simply focused on more important things. Scooping the phone from the counter, she glanced at the screen, surprised to see she had a message. It was too early for a casual chat. It had to be something important.

She pulled up the text as she hurried out of the house.

The club is officially open. Ready or not.

Bailey frowned, reading the strange message a dozen

bic vibe that wasn't helped by the line of fluorescent lights that constantly flickered. Bailey was convinced that one day they were going to induce a seizure.

As expected, Eric Criswell was slumped on the couch, his phone in his hand. He had thin, black hair that was roughly chopped, as if he cut it himself, and pale skin that had a jaundiced tint. His eyes were gray and deeply sunken into his thin face. He looked like a man who didn't venture into the sun, preferring the shadows.

Bailey headed to her locker, pulling off her sweater to hang it inside along with her purse, then snapping it shut, and she turned to casually stroll toward the couch.

"Eric," she murmured.

The boy—and as far as Bailey was concerned he was still a boy despite the fact he was twenty-two years old—abruptly lifted his head and blinked in surprise. He'd been so engrossed in his phone he hadn't even noticed her entering the room.

"Oh." His face flushed with pleasure. "Hey, Bailey."

"Do you have a minute?"

"For you?" His lips stretched into a smile. "Always."

"You didn't text me this morning, did you?"

"Text you?" He blinked. "No. I don't even have your number."

Bailey narrowed her eyes. Her number was listed in the employee handbook in case of emergencies. Why was he lying?

Deciding to confront him directly, she held out her phone and turned it so he could see the screen.

"I got this."

"'The club is officially open. Ready or not,'" he read

out loud. Glancing up, he shook his head in confusion, his thin hair flopping. "What's that supposed to mean?"

"I don't know." She slid her phone in the front pocket of her scrubs. "That's why I was asking you."

"Why would you think I sent you the text?"

"The only game I've ever played is the Murder Club."

Eric pinched his lips, as if she'd said something offensive. "It's not technically a game, it's a—"

"Whatever," she interrupted his chiding. Eric was shy and awkward most of the time, but when he was discussing his favorite hobbies he could go on forever. "I've been getting strange invites to a new game. That's why I deleted my account a couple of weeks ago."

"I noticed you scrubbed your profile. A shame." He sounded genuinely disappointed. "You're really good at spotting clues that the rest of us miss."

"Thanks. It was fun for a while, but I'm done." She paused. "It wasn't you, was it? Sending the invites to a private murder club?"

He gave a sharp shake of his head. "I don't know anything about them. If I wanted you to join a private club, I'd just ask you. We see each other every day."

He had a point. So, if the text wasn't from Eric, who'd sent it?

"Do you happen to know the other members of the club?"

"Just by their online profiles."

"Do any of them live in Pike?"

"I doubt it." His expression made it clear that was a stupid question. "These sorts of clubs have people from all over the world."

"Okay."

Bailey turned to leave. There was no point worrying

about who sent the text. Or how they'd gotten her number. If they continued to be a pest, she would simply block them. Problem solved.

At least one problem.

Now she had to find out why she'd been commanded to make an appearance in the pit of doom.

She'd reached the door when Eric suddenly called out, "Hey, Bailey. Sorry I couldn't help."

"No problem."

"I play lots of other games," he continued. "You know . . . if you're interested."

She paused to glance over her shoulder. "I think I'm done with online games."

He flushed, as if embarrassed he'd asked. "Yeah. Gotcha."

Feeling a pang of guilt, Bailey left the break room and headed to the office at the end of the hall. She hadn't meant to hurt Eric's feelings, but she had to know if he'd been the one harassing her.

Dismissing the strange text from her mind, she tapped on the closed door, waiting for a woman's voice to call out for her to enter before pushing it open and stepping inside the room.

It was nicer than the rest of the nursing home. The desk and high-back leather chairs were worn, but they were obviously well-built, and there was a new gray carpet on the floor that matched the drapes. The walls were painted a sterile white with framed oil paintings that were created by local artists with more enthusiasm than skill and a couple floor lamps added a much needed warmth.

It wasn't fancy, but this was Pike, and people would be suspicious of anything too flashy.

"Good morning, Ms. Donaldson," Bailey said, her gaze landing on the short, rail-thin woman who approached her with the crisp confidence of an army general.

Her face was long, giving her the unfortunate appearance of a horse, and her hair was dyed a dark red and sprayed into the shape of a helmet. She was wearing one of her favorite power suits in a bright green that matched her eyes and she wore a cross hanging on a gold chain.

Lorene Donaldson was a formidable woman who treated her employees like trash and refused to pay one penny above minimum wage. She did, however, have the redeeming quality of actually caring about the elderly residents who were in the home.

"It's about time," the older woman snapped.

Bailey resisted the urge to look at her watch. She knew she wasn't late.

"Is something wrong?" she asked.

The woman's lips pursed into a tight circle. "That has yet to be determined."

Bailey frowned. It wasn't unusual for Lorene to call her into the office to lodge some complaint. Any problem with the nursing staff or aides was somehow Bailey's fault, regardless, whether she was on duty or not. But she wasn't usually vague about her chastisement.

"I don't understand."

"I'll let Mr. Bennett explain." Lorene's lips remained pursed. Like she was about to whistle for a dog.

It wasn't a dog, however, who rose from one of the chairs facing the desk. Instead it was Ward Bennett, a large, barrel-chested man with thinning black hair and shrewd brown eyes. He was wearing a suit with a crisp white shirt and a tie that was so tight it looked like it was about to choke him.

On cue, he cleared his throat.

"Forgive me, Bailey," Ward murmured, moving toward her to shake her hand. "I intended to conduct this meeting in my office later this afternoon."

Bailey's state of confusion deepened. Ward Bennett was a local lawyer, but Bailey had never used his services. Mostly because she'd never needed a lawyer. She'd been hoping to continue that trend.

"What meeting?" she demanded.

He cleared his throat again, tugging at his tie. Bailey wondered if his wife had knotted it for him. And if she was pissed.

"You are a beneficiary named in Nellie Warren's will."

Bailey was jerked out of her silly imaginings. "Sorry. What did you say?"

"You are named in Nellie Warren's will." He spoke slowly, as if realizing he'd blindsided her with his announcement.

"Seriously?"

"I never joke about legal matters."

"I just . . ." Bailey shook her head, telling herself that the strange prickles of premonition were nothing more than a figment of her imagination.

So Nellie had left her a small gift. Big deal. It was a nice gesture of gratitude, nothing more.

"I had no idea," she told the lawyer. "She never said anything about leaving me a memento."

"This is more than a memento." The older man lifted

his hand, as if he intended to tug on his tie again, then perhaps realizing he was making Bailey nervous, he gestured toward the nearby chair. "Perhaps you should sit down."

Bailey shook her head. She didn't like the sound of "more than a memento." "I'd rather stand, if you don't mind."

"Very well." The lawyer cast a quick glance toward Lorene, who was watching them with a sour expression, before returning his attention to Bailey. "Let me start at the beginning."

"Okay."

"I've been the Warren family lawyer since I first opened my law firm," he told her. "They entrusted me with their legal needs, including their will, which had never changed from the first day John and Nellie had it notarized thirty years ago."

"I'm not sure what this has to do with me."

He held up a broad hand. "It hadn't been changed for thirty years." He deliberately paused. "Until ten days ago."

"Who changed it?"

"Nellie, of course. She called and asked to come to the office to amend her will. I was shocked, honestly; as I said, it's been thirty years since the first will was written, but I told her to come as soon as possible. At her age any legal matters need to be tended to in an expedited fashion. Not that I ever dreamed she would die less than two weeks later. We're all quite devastated by her loss."

Bailey ground her teeth together. She'd always heard the lawyer was in love with his own voice. Now she believed it. Why else would he make such a production out of a simple explanation?

"Why would she change her will?" she asked, forced to play his game if she wanted answers.

"Apparently Nellie became very attached to you and wanted to be sure she expressed her gratitude."

Bailey shrugged. "She didn't have to do that."

"That's what I said. Repeatedly. But she insisted."

The lawyer looked annoyed that he hadn't been able to sway the older woman. Bailey could have warned him that Nellie Warren was as stubborn as a mule.

"So what did she leave me?" Bailey demanded.

Ward squared his shoulders, as if preparing for an unpleasant task. "You are the sole beneficiary of her private savings account. A little over twenty thousand dollars."

Twenty thousand dollars? Twenty. Thousand. Dollars.

Bailey silently repeated the words over and over, trying to process what was happening. To a woman who'd lived on the edge of poverty most of her life, that was a fortune. Like winning the lottery.

Except it made no sense.

Sure, she'd been close to Nellie. But only as a nurse and a favorite patient. It wasn't like they were best friends. And they weren't related. It would be understandable if she'd left Bailey her favorite scarf. Or a few trinkets that she'd collected over the years. But twenty thousand dollars . . .

"No." Bailey instinctively took a step back, as if to remove herself from the preposterous conversation.

"Yes," Ward insisted. "I personally made the changes and it was notarized by my secretary."

Bailey tried to imagine being handed a check for twenty thousand dollars. Just yesterday she'd sent off the final payment for having her roof replaced and wondered if she should take out a new loan to update her plumbing, now . . .

She shook her head. "This is madness."

"I couldn't agree more," Lorene retorted, her voice sharper than usual.

Bailey ignored her, her gaze locked on the lawyer. "You said you were going to invite me to your office today."

"Yes, I don't usually conduct my business in this manner."

"What happened to change your mind?"

Genuine annoyance tightened the man's broad features. "I was unfortunately out of the country when Nellie passed. I didn't return until late last night, but I assumed that the funeral would be held today, and I planned to arrange the reading of the will after that. That was my normal process." He glanced toward the door, as if ensuring it was closed. "Instead, Gabe Warren unexpectedly had his mother cremated just a day after she died and even more unexpectedly arrived at my house before the sun rose this morning. He was in a hurry to get his hands on—" He halted, clearing his throat. "I mean, to claim his inheritance."

The disbelief that had wrapped Bailey in a strange sense of numbness was shattered by Ward's grim tone. She'd been so shocked by the thought of Nellie leaving her a small fortune, it hadn't crossed her mind that the inheritance might affect anyone else. Now her stomach twisted with an intense dread.

"And you told him that his mother had left me her life savings?"

"Yes. He was unhappy." Ward grimaced. "To say the least."

Lorene sniffed. "He was so unhappy he arrived here an hour ago, warning that he's going to the sheriff with a complaint that you coerced his mother into altering her will."

Bailey stiffened. Gage Warren was a large, aggressive man who'd managed to argue with every citizen in Pike. Which no doubt explained why the lumberyard that had been so successful when Nellie was in charge had declined into an empty shell.

"That's ridiculous," she breathed.

"I'm not done," Lorene snapped. "He also warned me that he wants an investigation into his mother's death."

Bailey shuddered. The last investigation into a death in Pike had been the start of a killing spree.

"Why?"

"He wants to know if there was anything . . . unnatural in his mother's death," Lorene said.

"Unnatural?" Bailey was momentarily baffled. Nellie had died of a heart attack, so why would he . . . The breath was squeezed from her lungs. "Oh my God, he's suggesting she was deliberately killed?"

Lorene glared at her. "That's exactly what he's suggesting."

Bailey pressed a hand over her racing heart, feeling

sick to her stomach. She didn't think for a second that Gage actually cared what happened to his mother. The only time he showed up at the nursing home was when he needed her to write a check to keep the lumberyard out of bankruptcy.

"I don't believe this," she breathed.

Lorene sniffed, her pale skin flushing with a rare display of emotion. "Believe it or not, you've created a very unpleasant situation."

"I didn't do anything."

"Whether you did or didn't, I can't allow people to fear that their loved ones are no longer safe at Pike Nursing Home."

Bailey jerked, her horror at the thought of Gage blaming her for his mother's death replaced by a stunning realization that her life was being turned upside down.

"Are you firing me?"

"Until the investigation is finished—"

"Wait," Bailey interrupted. "There's actually going to be an investigation?"

"The sheriff will have to follow up on Mr. Warren's allegations of exploitation of an elderly person in my care. Not to mention the internal review from our board members and the state officials." Lorene folded her hands, her chin-tilted so she could peer down her long nose at Bailey. "Until that is all completed to my satisfaction, you will be on unpaid leave."

"But—"

"Please gather your belongings and leave the premises."

Bailey stared at Lorene, a surge of anger blasting

through her. She'd worked for this woman for ten years, putting in overtime hours even when she was exhausted, taking on duties that had nothing to do with nursing, and pleading with the staff not to walk out after enduring one of Lorene or her sniveling son's rampages.

She wanted to tell the woman that she could shove her job up her ass. That she wouldn't return to the nursing home if Lorene got down on her knees and begged her. But the words lodged in her throat. She'd been raised by her elderly grandmother, who had drilled into her the importance of being polite. Even when you wanted to punch someone in the face.

"Fine."

Spinning away, Bailey stormed her way toward the door, blinking away the threatening tears. She told herself they were tears of fury. She'd done nothing wrong, but she was the one being punished.

Deep inside, however, she knew that she wasn't about to cry because of anger. She was hurt. It horrified her to think Gage was accusing her of manipulating his mother, and even potentially killing her, to get her hands on twenty thousand dollars. And instead of having her back, the woman who'd depended on her to keep her business running was throwing her under the bus.

She was headed out the door when Ward unexpectedly called out, "I'll be in touch, Bailey. The will is being contested, but Nellie's personal savings weren't a part of the trust fund left for Gabe, or the lumber business. She could give it to whoever she wanted. I'm sure it will all be settled very soon."

"Not soon enough," Bailey muttered, not bothering to glance back as she slammed shut the door.

It was the closest she could come to telling them all to go to hell.

Intending to storm out of the building in a full-blown huff, Bailey was distracted as a door across the hallway was pulled open to reveal a man a few years older than her.

Logan Donaldson was the assistant administrator of the nursing home and the son of Lorene Donaldson. Having a mother as the owner was the only explanation for his position. As far as Bailey knew, he didn't do any actual work.

He had thinning brown hair and a round face that didn't have any similarity to his mother. Neither did his dark eyes and ready smile. He was average height and average size, with a fake tan that made his teeth too white. She'd once heard someone say that he had the personality of a used car salesman. She thought that was an insult to used car salesmen everywhere. Still, the elderly residents seemed to find him charming.

Go figure.

At the moment he was wearing a silk shirt that was left open to expose his chest and a pair of black slacks.

"Can I have a moment?"

Too polite to ignore his request, Bailey came to a sharp halt, folding her arms defensively over her chest.

"Your mother has said enough."

He clicked his tongue. "Bailey, we feel just terrible about this, we truly do. But I hope you understand our position?"

She narrowed her eyes. "Your position of treating me like a criminal?"

"A criminal?" He tried to look shocked, glancing toward the door that Bailey had just slammed shut. "I was afraid Mother would be too harsh, but I can't believe she would say something like that."

"She accused me of coercing Nellie into giving me her money before killing her."

"She didn't." He heaved a sigh as Bailey glared at him. "I'm so sorry. I hope you won't take her seriously. She's talking nonsense because she's upset. No one would ever believe that," he protested. "Certainly I don't."

Bailey snorted. She wasn't going to fall for his faux sympathy. He liked to play the good guy to his mother's bad guy, acting as if he actually cared about the staff members. Bailey had never been fooled.

"No?"

"Absolutely not. This is all the fault of Gage Warren and his nasty accusations." He clicked his tongue. "Let me have a word with Mother once she calms down. I'm sure I can make her listen to reason and you'll be back here." Without warning, he reached out to grab her hand, giving her fingers a squeeze. "Where you belong."

With a shudder, Bailey snatched her hand out of his grasp. His words felt more like a threat than a promise.

Chapter 3

Dom Lucier woke up early and made the fifteen-minute drive into Pike. He didn't really have a reason. Lia had left the freezer overflowing with homemade meals, including a breakfast casserole, and Kaden had stocked the bar with Dom's favorite whiskey. He could easily stay in the new, sprawling house for a month without needing to leave.

But after feeding the two stray dogs that Lia had taken in, he'd found himself unable to settle down. He wasn't in the mood for a long walk through the rolling hills that surrounded the house. Or fishing in the nearby pond. And he certainly didn't want to spend the day sitting in front of the massive television.

Approaching the outskirts of town, Dom slowed to a snail's pace as he checked the railway crossing. When Kaden told him that he was going to settle in the remote area, Dom had thought his friend had lost his mind. Even if he spent at least part of his time in Vegas dealing with their mutual business, Money Makers, and taking lavish vacations overseas, Dom was certain

Kaden would be bored out of his mind in less than a year.

Last night had proved that there were benefits to living in a small town. Not only had the pizza been the best he'd ever tasted—and he'd tasted a lot—but he'd spent one of the most pleasurable evenings he'd had in years doing nothing more than drinking beer in a tiny, overcrowded bar.

Okay, his pleasure hadn't actually been in the tiny bar. It'd been chatting with Bailey Evans. They hadn't spent nearly as much time together as he wanted. His phone had pinged with a message that his pizza was ready and Bailey had immediately risen to her feet, bringing an end to their brief encounter. It'd been long enough, however, for Dom to be convinced his stay in Pike was going to be just as interesting as he'd hoped.

He was across the tracks when he caught sight of a familiar woman stomping down the street like she was marching into battle. She was wearing a lumpy sweater over her scrubs, and the stiff breeze had tugged several strands of hair from her ponytail, but Dom smiled in pleasure at the sight of her.

Suddenly he understood exactly why he'd gotten up early and gone into town. He'd been hoping he'd run into Bailey Evans. Just like when he was seventeen and hanging around a pawnshop in L.A. to catch a glimpse of the owner's daughter, Ashley Haines. Eventually the owner had decided it was easier to hire Dom than continue to try to run him off.

Parking his Land Rover next to the curb, Dom jumped out, his brows lifting as Bailey swept past him as if he was invisible.

"Bailey?" he called out.

He watched her jerk to a halt before slowly turning to face him. "Oh." Something that might have been relief crossed her face. "Hi, Dom."

Dom stepped forward, his gaze tracing the lines of her face. Her skin looked pale in the watery morning sunlight and there was an unmistakable dampness on her cheeks.

His excitement vanished as concern rushed through him. "Have you been crying?"

She reached up, angrily wiping away the tears. "I'm fine." She pinned a smile on her lips. "Are you back for more pizza?"

Dom had a mother and three older sisters. He recognized that tight-lipped smile. It meant she was upset, but she didn't want to talk about it.

With an effort, he resisted the urge to press for an explanation for her tears and searched for a way to lighten her dark mood.

"Actually I'm on a rescue mission," he said, not lying. At least not entirely.

She stared at him in confusion. "Rescue?"

"Last night I was playing ball with the dogs and there was a tragic accident with one of the lamps in the living room," he confessed. There really had been a broken lamp. "Elmer and Nanny are wracked with guilt and I promised them I would find a replacement. I don't want the dogs to be in the literal doghouse."

Her smile softened, a portion of her tension beginning to ease at his teasing. "I hate to break the news, but it's doubtful that Lia bought the lamps in Pike. There really are no stores in town unless you count the local thrift shop."

He shrugged. "No worries. I'll—"

His words were cut short as a white van with **WARREN LUMBERYARD** painted on the side rounded the corner and then screeched to a halt. Parking in the center of the road, a large man with a shaved head and a reddish-blond goatee jumped out and headed directly toward him.

"There you are," he snarled toward Bailey. "I've been looking for you all over town."

"Hey. Slow your roll." Dom moved to stand in the man's path, his gaze skimming over the stranger. He was several inches shorter than Dom and several inches wider, although Dom was willing to bet it was more flab than muscle beneath the work shirt he was wearing with the name "Gage" stitched over the pocket.

The man glared at him with pale blue eyes. "I don't know who you are, but stay out of this," he growled before turning his gaze back to Bailey. "You killed my mother."

Dom ignored Bailey's sharp breath, his focus locked on Gage. It didn't look like the stranger was carrying a weapon, but there was no way in hell he was letting the bastard get anywhere close to Bailey.

"Gage, you know that's not true," Bailey protested.

"What *I know* is that my mother died without warning," Gage snapped, his face ruddy and the stench of alcohol on his breath.

"She was ninety-one years old."

"She was perfectly healthy," Gage hissed, spittle collecting on the corners of his lips. He was foaming at the mouth like a rabid dog. "Then suddenly she decides to change her will to leave her life savings to the devoted nurse who's been whispering in her ear like the serpent in the Garden of Eden and a couple of days later she's dead and you're about to inherit a fortune."

"I had no idea she changed her will."

Dom frowned. He was vaguely aware of the conversation. It had something to do with Gage's mother dying and naming Bailey in her will. Probably something that happened quite frequently at a nursing home. His only concern at the moment was making sure the bastard didn't act on his obvious frustration.

"Don't give me that garbage," Gage snarled. "You and that weasel of a lawyer have obviously been plotting this since I put my mother in that home."

"I took care of your mom because it was my job and because I loved her." There was a throb in Bailey's voice that revealed she was mourning the older woman. Unlike her son, who appeared more concerned with the money Bailey was given in the will than the passing of his mother. "She was a wonderful woman."

"A wonderful *rich* woman. It was bad enough that her emerald ring went missing. Now this."

"What are you talking about? What emerald ring?" Bailey demanded.

"The one my father bought her on their thirtieth wedding anniversary. I went through her things to get . . ." Gage flushed, as if revealing more than he'd intended. "It wasn't there."

"I don't know anything about an emerald ring."

"Right. Just like you didn't manipulate her into getting into her will. Don't think you're going to get away with this," Gage blustered. "I've already been to the sheriff's office. And I don't care if Zac is your cousin, he's not going to be able to save your ass. If he won't investigate this as a murder, I'll go over his head." Without warning, Gage shoved his way past Dom, headed directly toward Bailey. "That money belongs to me and I'll see you in hell before you get your—"

Dom didn't hesitate. He'd survived the streets of Los Angeles when he was a teenager. He understood how to deal with a bully. You immediately proved that you were stronger, tougher, and willing to use whatever level of violence was necessary to stop the abuse.

Dom towered over the male, giving him one last chance to back off. "Touch her and I'll break every bone in your body."

The idiot glared at him, his eyes narrowed. "I told you to stay out of this."

Okay. He'd warned him. Striking too fast for the man to react, Dom grasped Gabe by the throat and, with casual ease, dragged him across the road to slam him against the side of the van.

Gage grunted as the air was knocked from his lungs, his eyes suddenly wide as he belatedly realized his danger. With a cold smile, Dom leaned forward until they were nose to nose, his fingers digging into the spongy flesh.

"You might be the tough guy who gets to terrorize the locals, Gage," he said, his voice soft. "But you don't scare me. You come near Bailey or try to contact her again, I will make you understand the meaning of regret. Got it?"

Gage grunted something that Dom couldn't catch,

but it didn't matter. He could see the fear in the man's eyes. He wasn't used to anyone standing up to him. It was going to take a couple of days and probably a bottle of booze to regain his false sense of bravado.

Slowly unlocking his fingers from the man's throat, Dom stepped back and folded his arms over his chest. In silence, he watched as Gage inched along the van, keeping a wary eye on him before he jumped inside and squealed away.

Dom watched the van until it turned at the next corner and disappeared. Only then did he walk back to study Bailey's pale face.

"What did you say to him?" she demanded.

"I gave him the same advice my mother used to give me."

"What's that?"

"If you don't have something nice to say, then don't say anything."

Her lips tightened until they were white with tension. "Gage has never kept his mouth shut. It boggles my mind that he could be related to sweet Nellie."

"Nellie is the woman he's accusing you of killing?"

She abruptly turned away. "I need to get home."

Dom reached out to touch her arm. He hadn't meant to spook her. "I'll drive you."

"That's not necessary." Her back was rigid, her head turned away as she started walking. "It's just down the street."

Dom used his long strides to easily catch up to her. "I'll go with you."

She glanced over her shoulder, as if checking to make sure Gage wasn't lurking in his white van.

"Okay."

Sensing she was in no mood for small talk, Dom took in his surroundings as they quickly made their way down the crumbling sidewalk. The houses that lined the block were small and faded, like the wilted flowers in the clay pots on the porches. A couple looked abandoned, with plyboard over the windows and "For Sale" signs in the overgrown yards.

It wasn't the nicest neighborhood, but in such a small town he doubted Bailey had to worry about crime.

Reaching the end of the block, Bailey cut across the yard and onto the porch of a house that was larger than the others. It was also in better condition than the rest of the block. The gabled roof had been replaced recently and a fresh coat of light blue paint with dark blue shutters added a splash of color that gave the aging home a unique charm.

She reached into her purse and pulled out a heavy keyring, fumbling to find the right key before she shoved open the door. Together they stepped into the square living room, which was painted a pale silver with a dark gray carpet. There was a wooden shelf along one wall that was loaded with books and dozens of family pictures scattered on the low coffee tables and the back of an upright piano. It should have felt cramped, but instead it was . . . homey. Dom nodded. That was the word.

A long-forgotten memory of watching his mother setting out their few belongings in the latest hovel they were staying in flashed through his mind. No matter how ratty or uncomfortable the place might be, his mother always found a way to make it feel like home.

"This is nice," he murmured.

She glanced around, her expression softening with pleasure. "It's not fancy."

"I'd rather have comfort than fancy any day," he assured her, cautiously cupping her elbow in his hand to direct her toward the couch. "Sit down. I'll get you something to drink."

Clearly shaken by her encounter with Gage, Bailey collapsed onto the soft cushions, wrapping her sweater tightly around her body. As if trying to protect herself from unseen enemies. Dom clenched his teeth, belatedly wishing he'd done more than just running off the spineless bully. He wasn't usually a violent man, but seeing the shattered expression on Bailey's face was stirring primitive emotions he didn't even know he possessed.

Moving across the room, he stepped through the arched opening into the kitchen. The cabinets looked original to the house, with worn countertops, but the appliances were new and the floors were freshly tiled. Bailey appeared to be dragging the old house into the current century. Not an easy task.

Finding a kettle on the stove, he quickly heated the water while he prepared a mug with the tea he found in a copper cannister. Once it was ready, he dumped in several teaspoons of sugar. He returned to the living room, finding Bailey still huddled on the couch, her face so pale she looked like one of the Dresden dolls his sisters loved.

"Tea," he murmured as he stopped next to the arm of the couch.

She reached up with hands that trembled. "Thanks." She bent her head to take a sip and promptly coughed. "Good Lord. How much sugar did you put in?"

"You're in shock," he told her. "I think sugar is supposed to help."

She blinked. "Where did you hear that?"

"On the Internet." He offered a rueful grin. "Where all the best medical advice comes from."

Before she could give her opinion of his medical resources, there was a sharp knock on the door.

Bailey sucked in a sharp breath, her expression stricken. "I don't want to see anyone."

"I'll get rid of them."

Dom was moving before she finished speaking. He didn't think Gage Warren had the balls to continue his harassment, but the lust for money could make men do crazy things. Halting at the front window, he took the precaution of checking out the unwanted visitor. If Gage was stupid enough to come to the house, he was stupid enough to bring a gun.

It wasn't Gage. Surprisingly, Dom recognized the slender man dressed in a brown uniform with a sheriff's badge on his shirt.

"It's Zac," he told Bailey.

"I . . ." She set aside her tea, her expression tense. Almost as if she didn't want to see the man who was not only sheriff of Pike but her cousin. "Let him in," she at last muttered.

Dom pulled open the door and moved back to allow Zac to step over the threshold. He was several inches shorter than Dom and lean rather than muscular, but there was no mistaking the air of authority he carried with him. It wasn't the uniform. Or the weapon holstered at his side. It was a part of him.

"Hey, Bailey," he said, pulling off his hat to reveal dark blond hair that was cut short. His piercing green gaze rested on Bailey's hunched form before moving back to Dom with a lift of his brows. "Dom. I didn't know you were in town."

"I got in yesterday."

Zac nodded, then, crossing the room, he perched on the couch next to his cousin. Dom remained near the door. It gave him a perfect view of Bailey's expression.

"How are you, Bailey?"

She wrinkled her nose. "I've been better."

"I get that." Zac reached out to squeeze her hand. "I suppose you know why I'm here."

"Gage Warren thinks I tricked his mother into giving me twenty thousand dollars in her will and then killed her to get my greedy hands on the money."

She was still hurt, he could see it in her soft brown eyes, but there was a hint of defiance as she spit out the words. Dom was relieved. He hated seeing her look so crushed. But at the same time, unease snaked down his spine.

He suddenly understood Gage's desperation to intimidate and threaten Bailey. Twenty thousand dollars was a lot of money. Especially for a man who was driving a van that was older than Dom and wearing a work shirt that was frayed and worn.

It made him even more dangerous than Dom had first feared.

"I know it's complete nonsense," Zac assured Bailey.

"Of course it is. I loved Nellie." The defiance was more pronounced as the color returned to her face. "Which is more than Gage can say. Do you know how many times he visited her at the home? I could count his visits on one hand. And she was there for over *five* years." She sniffed. "All he wants is her money."

Zac squeezed her fingers. "We all know that Gage Warren is a loudmouthed jackass who drinks too much and has run his parents' lumberyard into the ground. Unfortunately, he's determined to be a pain in my ass and I'm going to have to ask you a few questions."

Dom took an impulsive step forward. "Does it have to be right now?"

Zac sent him a suspicious glance, clearly wondering why he was in his cousin's house when she was at her most vulnerable.

"No, I'm okay," Bailey assured both men. "I want to get it over with."

Zac held Dom's steady gaze for a moment. Perhaps a silent warning he would do whatever was necessary to protect his relative. Then, turning back to Bailey, he withdrew his hand and pulled a small notebook and a pencil from his shirt pocket. He'd gone from sympathetic cousin to a sheriff doing his job.

"The most obvious question is whether you ever asked Ms. Warren for money," he started.

"Never."

"And she didn't mention her intention to change her will?"

"Not once."

Zac nodded, as if that was exactly what he expected. "Do you remember the day that Ms. Warren died?"

"Of course," Bailey said without hesitation.

"Were you working?"

"No. I was scheduled, but I got a call early that morning that a friend from nursing school was in a car crash. I drove down to Madison to spend the day in the hospital with her."

Zac jotted down the information. "That will be easy enough to check. What time did you get home?"

Bailey wrinkled her nose as she considered her answer. "I didn't leave the hospital until after eight that night and I swung through a fast-food place before heading home. Oh." Her lips stretched into a tight smile. "The receipt is probably still in my glove compartment if you need it. After that I drove home." She paused to consider the return trip. "It had to be after ten when I got back. My neighbor could probably tell you the exact time. She was taking care of Bert and Ernie."

Dom released a silent breath of relief. Not because he thought for a second that Bailey could be in any way responsible for an old woman's death. But her airtight alibi meant that Gage's wild accusations would be swiftly smothered. This was a small town where rumors could be just as damaging as a physical blow.

Especially to a person who was as sensitive as Bailey.

"Good." Zac appeared equally relieved as he rose to his feet and pocketed the notebook. "That's enough for now."

Bailey reached up to grasp her cousin's hand. "Zac."

"I know." He leaned down, brushing a kiss over her forehead. "We're going to get this cleared up."

Dom waited for Zac to head to the door before he shared his concern for Bailey's safety.

"What are you going to do about Gage?"

Zac sent him another suspicious glance. "Should I be doing something?"

"He attacked Bailey in the street less than half an hour ago."

Zac's eyes widened as he turned back to his cousin. "Are you hurt?"

"No, he didn't touch me."

"It might have been a different story if she'd been alone," Dom insisted, knowing he was overstepping the line. As far as Bailey was concerned, he was barely more than a stranger. But he was genuinely concerned. He wanted the law officials in town to understand that Gage Warren was a threat. "Plus, I'm sure he was drinking."

Zac's jaw tightened. "Do you want to press charges?" he asked his cousin.

Bailey shook her head. "No."

Zac hesitated, as if wanting to insist that Bailey give him a reason to haul the man into his office and give him a stern warning. Then he grimaced. Bailey knew what she wanted. And she'd said no.

"Call me if you need anything," he finally said, heading out of the door with a glance toward Dom that warned he would be swinging by Dom's temporary residence to discover why he was hanging around his cousin.

Dom shrugged. That was okay with him.

Shutting the door, he turned to discover Bailey regarding him with a resolute expression.

"Thank you for your help, but you don't have to stay."

It was politely stated, but Dom sensed she wanted him to leave. No doubt she needed some privacy to process everything that had happened.

"Do you have someone I can call to check on you?"

She shook her head. "No, really, I'm—"

"Fine. I know," he interrupted with a teasing smile, studying her with a lingering concern. The color had returned to her face and she was sitting with her back straight, but he was reluctant to abandon her. "I still don't like the thought of you being alone."

"I won't be," she assured him. "Bert and Ernie are next door. As soon as they realize I'm home, they'll be back."

"That's not the same as having someone here with you."

She shrugged. "I'm used to it."

It wasn't a complaint, just a simple statement of fact. Dom got it. He had friends who were important in his life, but at the end of the day he was alone. Some days that was great, other days . . .

Not so much.

"Okay. You have my number if you need it." Lia had set up a group chat when she was organizing the wedding to keep everyone up-to-date. "I'll be back later."

Chapter 4

Pauline Hartford watched her grandson pace across the carpet of her elegant living room. Kevin Hartford was a tall, heavyset man with bald spots peeking through his pale hair and a round face that was marred with a petulant expression. He was wearing a pair of dress slacks and a sweater that were at least one size too small, as if he'd had to dig them out of the back of his closet. Which was probably right. He hadn't had a job in months. No doubt he spent his days in sweatpants.

"Why are you being such a pain about this?" he abruptly whined, glaring in her direction.

Pauline rose to her feet. Unlike her grandson, her expensive pantsuit fit her slender form to perfection and her silver hair was pulled into a smooth bun. She might be eighty-three years old, but her career as superintendent of the Grange School System meant she understood the importance of maintaining the proper appearance. Even if she did spend most of her days alone in her house. A gift that had been lost on Kevin.

"Don't take that tone with me," she chastised.

Kevin pinched his lips, as if holding back his angry outburst. "All I'm asking is for a few bucks to get me through the month," he finally muttered.

"I gave you more than a few bucks in August. In fact, it was over five thousand dollars. What happened to that?"

"What do you mean, what happened to it? Shit is expensive. Do you know what it costs to put braces on my kids?" he demanded. "You'd think they were wearing gold grills studded with diamonds."

Pauline sniffed. "If you can't afford braces, then why did you have them put on?"

"You want your grandkids to look like trash?"

"*Great*-grandkids, and I've been supporting them since they were born."

"That's what family is supposed to do. Help each other out, right?" he repeated the words he used every time he showed up at her door.

"It's your family. It's your duty to pay the bills."

He hunched a shoulder. "You know I got laid off."

"Then you shouldn't have braces on your kids' teeth. And if I remember correctly, you told me you were using the five thousand dollars to rent a bigger space for your wife's photography business. You promised that her career was about to take off."

Another hunch of his shoulder. "It did help, but the wedding season is over. There's not that much work for a photographer during the winter."

Pauline tilted her chin. She'd made her decision when she'd gotten the call from Kevin that he was stopping by. The only reason he came by was for another handout.

"Then find another job. I'm done."

Kevin's eyes widened. "What do you mean, you're done?"

"It's not a difficult concept." She spoke slowly. He wasn't the brightest guy. He never had been, sad to say. "I will no longer be handing over money whenever you come here with some new sob story about your children's braces or paying the mortgage on a house you can't afford or expanding your wife's business because you can't be bothered to hold down a job."

His mouth opened and closed, making him look like a fish who'd been left to flop on the riverbank.

"You can't cut me off," he finally managed to protest.

"Of course I can. It's my money."

"I'm your only relative. Without me, you'd be alone."

Pauline clicked her tongue. "Trust me, it would be a blessing not to have you showing up to embarrass yourself like a common beggar. If you need money, get a job."

Kevin's face flushed. She'd like to think it was from embarrassment, but it was more likely anger.

"The money is yours until you die," he hissed. "Then it's all mine."

"Don't be so sure. I can change my will anytime I want."

Abruptly his features twisted into an ugly expression. "Don't push me, old lady. You won't like what happens."

A sensation that felt remarkably like fear pierced Pauline's heart. "Get out of my house."

Kevin pointed a pudgy finger in her direction. "Fine, but you won't get away with this. I have rights."

Pauline watched her grandson storm out of the house, slamming the door shut behind him. Sucking in a deep breath, she calmed her racing heart. Kevin wasn't dangerous. He was just a bad-tempered, sullen child. Just like his father.

This was why she hadn't wanted to have children. After working as a teacher, she'd discovered she didn't really like kids that much. That's why she'd gone into administration. The pay was not only better but she could avoid the screeching chaos of the classroom. But her husband had insisted they needed an heir. Someone to carry on his name. As if anyone cared about that nonsense these days.

"Good riddance," she muttered, heading to the liquor cabinet to pour herself another gin and tonic. It was her third of the day. Or maybe her fourth. It was increasingly difficult to remember.

Her doctor would bitch when she went back for her continuous round of bloodwork. The man was worse than a vampire. He would squawk about her liver and claim she was taking years off her life. Who cared?

At her age, if she wanted to enjoy a drink or two, that's exactly what she was going to do.

Plopping a slice of lime into her full glass, Pauline wandered toward the kitchen. She had been deciding what she wanted for dinner when Kevin interrupted her. Now her head was starting to feel woozy from too much alcohol on an empty stomach. She needed to eat something.

Deciding on a grilled cheese sandwich, she entered the large space that was decorated in the French country style, with white cabinets and a tiled floor. The appliances were stainless steel that gleamed in the overhead light, and across the room a glass sliding door revealed a patio that surrounded the in-ground pool.

Pauline came to a sharp halt as she realized the outside lights were switched on.

She hadn't turned them on. Why would she? She hadn't been out there since she'd had the pool drained and covered weeks ago. Maybe the neighborhood kids had been messing around her property.

With a click of her tongue, Pauline crossed the kitchen and unlocked the glass doors to step onto the patio. She hadn't bothered with a security camera back here. The yard was surrounded by a fence and at one time that had been enough. Her neighbors had always been upper class. Just like her. The past few years, however, had seen a tragic decline in the sorts of people moving in. Tomorrow she would call the security people and have one installed, she decided as she noticed the cover on the pool had been pulled to the side.

Stupid creatures. How dare they come on her private property and mess with her things?

Obviously she would not only have to call the security company but the police department as well.

Kids these days had no respect for their elders. She blamed the parents, who treated them like they were fragile babies rather than reckless delinquents. In her day she was beaten with a switch when she misbehaved. Now they got a cuddle and a new video game so they wouldn't feel bad.

Cautiously she moved to peer into the pool. She wanted to make sure there wasn't any damage, but she had enough sense to realize she wasn't quite steady on her feet. She halted a few inches from the edge and leaned forward. She couldn't see any obvious destruction, but it was already dark. It was impossible to see the bottom. She would have to check in the morning.

On the point of turning around, Pauline thought she heard the soft tread of footsteps, but with her mind fogged with gin, she didn't fully comprehend her danger. Not until she felt strong hands plant themselves against her back. And even then, she assumed that her grandson had returned to spinelessly plead for her forgiveness.

More annoyed than concerned, Pauline was parting her lips to chastise Kevin for daring to enter her home uninvited when she was roughly shoved forward, sending her stumbling over the edge of the pool. A scream was wrenched from her lips and the gin and tonic flew from her hand as she tried to break her fall. A futile effort, as she plummeted downward at a terrifying speed. She screamed again as she smashed into the concrete bottom with shattering force.

Pain exploded in the top of her head, sweeping through her like a tsunami. Thankfully, it lasted a mere second before it was replaced with a numbing darkness. With a moan, Pauline gave in to the inevitable.

Her last thought was that she hadn't had the opportunity to change her will. Her worthless grandson was going to end up with her money after all.

A damned shame.

Bailey slept remarkably well considering her crappy day. Or maybe that's why she slept well, she conceded as she hopped in the shower and then later pulled on a pair of jeans and a Green Bay Packers sweatshirt. She'd been emotionally exhausted by the time she'd tumbled into bed. It was no wonder she'd slept like a log.

Entering the kitchen, she opened the door to let out Bert and Ernie. She'd put up a fence after getting the dogs, despite the fact there was nothing but an empty field behind her. Unless they were visiting Dorinda next door, she wanted them securely locked on her property. The railroad tracks were close enough to give her nightmares. Once they were inside and hoovering down their food without bothering to chew, she squeezed a fresh glass of orange juice and grabbed a muffin.

Not the healthiest breakfast, but she wasn't really hungry. She'd just finished the muffin when her phone pinged. Just for a second, she considered ignoring the incoming text. Yesterday had been a shit show. She wanted to spend today pretending that none of it had happened.

The phone pinged again.

Of course she couldn't ignore it. Her annoying curiosity wouldn't let her.

She wrinkled her nose as she grabbed her phone from the table. Wasn't there a saying about curiosity killing the cat?

Do I have your attention, Bailey? Welcome to the Murder Club. Your first case begins today.

Bailey scowled, annoyed by the realization that the mysterious club member hadn't given up.

Who is this? She typed the words before common sense could stop her.

Your greatest admirer

Greatest admirer? A strange unease crawled down her spine. They sounded like the words of a stalker.

Leave me alone, she texted back.

I can't. You've been chosen.

Unchoose me.

Too late. I have created our first case. Solve it quick or else . . .

Or else what? Was he—or she—talking about losing the game? Or threatening her?

Bailey's mouth was dry, but she shook her head. The nasty confrontation with Gage Warren was making her overreact. This had to be a fellow member from the Murder Club. A few might be eccentric, but they'd never been hostile.

I'm not interested.

You will be.

A link to a newspaper article in the *Grange Express News* popped up. Grange was a town fifteen miles away. It was larger than Pike, but still small when compared to Madison or Green Bay.

Bailey hesitated, telling herself to put down the phone and walk away. Instead, she clicked the link. She had no intention of joining a private club with anyone, let alone a stranger from the Internet, but she couldn't deny she was curious.

> The Grange Police Department have revealed that eighty-three-year-old Pauline Hartford, longtime superintendent of the Grange School System, was found dead in

her empty swimming pool. Her body was
found this morning by her cleaner, who
arrived to find the back door left open and
Mrs. Hartford lying in the pool. Her death
is currently being ruled an accident.

Bailey read the story twice. It was certainly the sort
of case they would investigate in the old Murder Club.
A tragic death that had been ruled an accident. There
didn't seem to be anything special about it.

Whoever was pestering her was obviously hoping to
create an intimate relationship using their mutual interest in solving crimes. It was only her raw nerves making
it feel ominous.

Busy reassuring herself that her life hadn't somehow gone completely into the gutter, Bailey dropped
her phone on the table when it loudly pinged with another text.

Crap.

Bracing herself for some new disaster, Bailey nearly
cried with relief when Dom's name popped up.

Good morning. If you're not working today I would be eternally
grateful if you could bring out Bert and Ernie to play with
Nanny and Elmer. They are missing their owners and have spent
the morning moping by the front door.

Bailey didn't hesitate. She desperately needed to get
out of the house. Otherwise she'd spend the entire day
pacing the floor. Worse, she'd probably bake a thousand
sugar cookies and shove them in her face.

That's what she did when she was upset.

On cue, her stomach rumbled in warning. The muffin
wasn't going to last forever. She sent back a text.

I'll bring pizza.

Perfect. I have the wine.

Feeling better, Bailey shoved herself to her feet and headed into the spare bedroom. She'd been putting off a deep clean of the house. Something her grandmother had always insisted had to be done before the hard winter set in. This morning was a perfect opportunity to get it accomplished.

Four hours later she pulled her aging Ford-150 through the gates, using the electric opener that Lia had given her. She'd bought the truck when she graduated from high school and used it only when necessary. It was going to be a long time before she saved up for a new one.

She shut down the voice in the back of her mind that whispered she was about to inherit enough money to upgrade her vehicle. From the bottom of her heart, she hoped Gage got the will overturned and she never had to hear another damned thing about the twenty thousand dollars.

Bumping up the driveway that hadn't been paved yet, she admired the clean lines of the sprawling brick home. At Lia's insistence it was only one floor, but it was built in a U-shape, with an inner courtyard that framed an in-ground pool. On one side was a sturdy, fenced-in area for the two strays who'd appeared shortly after they'd started construction on the house. And in the distance she could see the roof of Lia's private office that was near the lake, as well as the long garage where Kaden stored his collection of motorcycles, rare cars, and even an airplane.

But it wasn't the expensive house or outbuildings

that was the showstopper. It was the amazing view of the rolling hills and clusters of trees that made it such a special property.

Parking in front of the house, Bailey opened her door and hopped out before the dogs could scramble over her. She also grabbed the pizza box and the sugar cookies she ended up baking despite her best intentions.

The dogs bounded toward the side of the house, and Bailey watched a gate open as Dom stepped out and moved just in time to prevent getting run down by the two eager Labs. The excited yips filling the air assured Bailey that Nanny and Elmer were already outside and eager to play.

Shutting the gate, Dom strolled toward her with a grin. Bailey froze in place, the breath being ruthlessly squeezed from her lungs. He wasn't beautiful like Kaden. His features were bluntly carved and his large body moved with purpose rather than elegance, but there was something irresistibly charming about him. At least as far as Bailey was concerned. And when he smiled . . . it felt as if something inside her was melting, altering her until she'd never be the same again.

Bailey cleared a strange lump from her throat, suddenly wishing that she'd taken more care with her appearance. As usual, she'd coiled her hair into a messy knot on top of her head and pulled on a pair of casual jeans and a sweatshirt. She hadn't even bothered to put on makeup.

Thankfully, Dom didn't seem to care as he halted next to her, his smile widening as if he was pleased that she'd agreed to join him.

"You're a lifesaver."

The awareness remained, sizzling through Bailey, but thankfully, weird awkwardness dissipated with his teasing words.

"Because I brought you dogs or pizza?"

"For the company," he clarified. "It's nice to have the privacy. Especially since I live behind the pawnshop and hundreds of Kaden's fans show up to take pictures of Money Makers day and night. And this is a beautiful place." He grimaced. "But this morning I found myself asking Elmer if he'd read any good books lately."

"Did he answer?"

"He was more interested in the bacon I was cooking."

"Ah. Well, you can't blame him. It's hard to concentrate when bacon is involved."

"True." Dom leaned toward the cardboard box in her hands, sucking in a deep breath. "Speaking of not being able to concentrate. That pizza smells amazing."

"I also brought some sugar cookies I baked this morning."

"You're killing me." He nodded toward the double glass doors in the center of the house. "The dogs will be fine. Let's have some lunch."

Bailey followed him inside, crossing through the living room that was lined with windows that overlooked the distant lake, and into the kitchen that was twice the size as Bailey's entire house. Not that she envied her friend such a large house. After hours cleaning, the thought of scrubbing such a vast space was daunting.

Still, she wouldn't mind having the gleaming,

professional-grade appliances and the handcrafted cabinets, she silently acknowledged.

She moved to set the pizza and cookies on a table arranged in the middle of the ceramic-tiled floor, suddenly aware of a strange scent in the air.

"Have you been painting?"

"Sorry, yeah." Dom moved to shove open a window over the sink, allowing in the crisp air. "Kaden hasn't had time to finish a couple of the spare bedrooms. I thought I'd give him a hand."

"That's nice."

Bailey took a seat at the table, relieved to have a distraction from her troubled thoughts. Although calling Dom Lucier a distraction was like calling a hurricane a stiff breeze. Just being this close to him short-circuited her brain in the best possible way.

Dom collected the bottle of wine that had been left to breathe on the marble counter and two glasses before joining her. There were already paper plates and napkins on the table.

"We've been friends for a long time," he said, pouring them both a glass of the wine.

Bailey took a sip, appreciating the fruity sweetness. "How did the two of you meet?"

Dom grabbed a slice of pizza and consumed it in three large bites. "Like a lot of people, Kaden arrived in LA without much money or a place to stay. He had no idea how expensive it was to get an apartment, so he came to the pawnshop, where I was working, to trade in his motorcycle for some quick cash." Dom took a drink of wine before grabbing another piece of pizza. "I told him to keep the bike and gave him the number of a buddy of mine who was looking for a stunt driver. He made the call from the shop and the rest is—as they say—history."

Bailey reached to claim one of the pizza slices. Dom was drop-dead sexy and being with him made her feel as giddy as a teenager with her first crush, but Bella's pizza was amazing. There was going to be hell to pay if she didn't get her share.

"You started his career," she said.

"No. I offered a suggestion," he insisted. "It was Kaden's talent that made his career."

Bailey suspected that Kaden considered Dom's contribution to his career more than a mere suggestion, but she didn't press him. Instead, she chewed her pizza as she dredged up the few tidbits that she'd discovered about this man.

"Lia mentioned that you moved to LA from France," she finally murmured.

"I did. I left home when I was sixteen."

She blinked. "Alone?"

"Yes. My mother passed away and I wanted a fresh start."

"That's . . . amazing." Bailey grabbed her glass of wine and took a deep sip. She'd considered herself daring for taking off at eighteen to go to college in Madison. It was the first time she'd ever been away from her grandmother for more than a sleepover with a friend. The mere thought of packing a bag and going halfway around the world to start a new life was terrifying. "I would never have had the courage to immigrate to a new country," she confessed. "Especially when I was sixteen."

His expression was impossible to read. "I didn't want to be in France."

Bailey grabbed another slice of pizza, her curiosity overcoming the good manners her grandmother had drilled into her.

"Why not?" she demanded.

He paused, his gaze moving toward the window that overlooked the yard where the dogs were busy playing.

"My sisters were older than me and they'd already moved away when my mother died. And Remy, the man who fathered me . . ." He shrugged as his words trailed away.

The man who fathered me.

Bailey didn't need to be a psychologist to recognize the difference between saying the "man who fathered me" and "my father."

"Sorry. Lia probably warned you that I'm incurably nosy. You don't have to talk about it if you don't want to."

"No, it's okay," he assured her, his voice tense, like he was forcing out the words. It was obvious he disliked talking about his past. Bailey felt oddly pleased that he was willing to make the effort with her. "Remy is what Americans call a grifter," he explained. "He runs scams, he borrows money he has no intention of repaying, and he sleeps with any woman who is willing to invite him into her bed." His jaw tightened. "Most of my childhood was spent running from the law or an angry husband with a gun."

"You immigrated to get away from him?"

"From his baggage." Dom polished off his wine in one large gulp. "Remy can be charming and childishly impulsive, and when I was young I worshipped him. It wasn't until I was old enough to see his constant manipulations and betrayals that I accepted he was a vain, self-centered jerk who would always do what was best for Remy Lucier." He reached for the wine to refill their glasses. "I'll always love him, but I have no respect for the man."

Bailey nibbled at her second slice of pizza. "I get that."

There must have been something in her tone that assured him that she really did understand.

He leaned back in his seat, studying her with an intensity that sent flutters through the pit of her stomach.

"You told me that you'd been raised by your grandmother."

Bailey nodded. She'd been nervous when they were seated together at the rehearsal dinner. He was just so . . . gorgeous. And when she was nervous she chatted like a maniac. She had no idea what all she'd revealed during the long wedding weekend.

"I lost my mother when I was just five," she said. "At that time my dad was a truck driver, and my grandma offered to look after me when he was on the road."

"He was fortunate to have family who was willing to help."

"Nana was wonderful." A smile curved her lips. Nana had been a gruff, no-nonsense woman who took in a grieving five-year-old without blinking an eye. It didn't matter that she barely had the money to support herself, or that she'd lost her husband just a few months before her daughter died. She was the strongest woman that Bailey had ever known. "I missed my mom, of course, but I still had a home where I was loved."

"That's easy to see," he told her. "Your grandmother would be proud if she could see her house today."

Bailey flushed with pleasure. She didn't make a great salary at the nursing home, but what little didn't go to bills was invested in updating the house and adding her own touches. It made her happy to think her nana would be proud.

"It's a money pit, but it's home."

"Is your father still in Pike?"

"No. He met a woman in Tennessee and moved there to be with her and her kids. He invited me to the wedding, but honestly, by that time he'd become pretty much a stranger."

He frowned, as if he was bothered by her words. Bailey wasn't. Her dad had never been around much, even when her mother was alive. The fact that he'd faded into a shadowy memory was inevitable.

"Do you ever hear from him?" Dom demanded.

"Not really."

He placed his wineglass back on the table and snatched a cookie from the plate. "We do have a lot in common."

Bailey snorted, resisting the urge to grab one of the cookies. She'd eaten half the dough before getting them in the oven.

"Except for the multimillion-dollar company and the glamorous lifestyle."

"My lifestyle consists of work, sleep, and more work. Nothing glamorous about it."

Bailey believed him. She'd heard Kaden griping about

Dom working long hours even after they'd hired extra help. Was he trying to prove to himself he was nothing like his father? Probably. It was odd how children could carry the burden of their parents' sins without even realizing what they were doing.

Bailey knew a portion of her inability to form a serious relationship was because of her fear of abandonment. Nothing mysterious about that.

"Do you enjoy owning a pawnshop?" she asked, genuinely curious.

"I do. It's kind of like being a bartender. Some people are there to browse for hidden treasures and other people are there because they've hit bottom and are hoping to turn things around. Sometimes I can help them out."

Bailey had never been forced to pawn her belongings, but she'd known what it was like to worry that one bad stroke of fortune could steal everything.

"What's the coolest thing that ever came into the shop?"

"A fossilized dinosaur egg."

Bailey arched her brows. "How did someone end up with a spare dinosaur egg lying around?"

"His grandfather was an archaeologist in the days when it was acceptable to travel around and dig up treasures to bring home. He claimed he had a dozen of them in his basement."

"I suppose that makes sense. Did you buy it?"

"I did." His smile widened with genuine pleasure. "I later donated it to the University of Nevada to use in their research."

"That was generous."

He waved aside her admiration. Bailey was learning that he was amazingly humble despite his success.

"I do a job I enjoy and have been fortunate enough to make a lot of money." He nodded toward her. "Nothing like what you do. I would never have the patience."

"I always knew I wanted to be a nurse, but I didn't expect to stay in Pike after I earned my degree," she admitted.

"So why did you?"

"I like having residents instead of patients," she said, trying to ignore how boring her life must sound to a man who'd immigrated when he was sixteen and created a small empire with a famous stuntman. "Most of the people at the home I've known my entire life and were friends of Nana. Plus, I'm not always rushing from one room to another." She fidgeted with her wineglass. She loved gossiping and chatting with people, but she never felt comfortable discussing her personal life. Probably because she didn't have a personal life. At least nothing worth talking about. "I can actually take time to listen to the residents and make sure everything is okay with them. It's going to be hard—" Bailey snapped her lips shut.

Dammit, she didn't want anyone to know that she'd been kicked out. Especially not this man. She didn't want pity.

He studied her with a puzzled expression. "What's going to be hard?"

"Nothing." She grabbed the box and held it toward Dom. "More pizza?"

There was a brief silence, as if Dom wanted to press her for an explanation. Then, accepting she wasn't in the mood to reveal what had happened, he grabbed the last slice.

"The answer to that question is always yes."

Chapter 5

Two hours later, Bailey parked her car next to the curb, cracking the window for the dogs, who were sleeping in a tight pile on the floorboard.

She'd fully intended to head home as she waved goodbye to Dom. For the first time in hours the dark sense of doom had been forgotten, replaced with a delicious tingle of anticipation as they'd sat side by side on the outdoor swing, watching the dogs play. Each casual brush of his hand and lingering glance had created dizzying sparks in the pit of her stomach.

It'd been an eternity since she'd been attracted to a man. And never with this sort of intensity. She'd be an idiot not to savor the rare sensations.

Once she was alone, however, the memory of Gage Warren and his vile accusations crashed into her. As if it'd been hovering just out of sight with the intention of punishing Bailey for having the audacity to enjoy her lunch. With a grimace, she'd realized there was no way she could go home and watch television. Not when she'd be wondering if Gage was going to show up at her door, or if Zac was busy checking out her alibi so he didn't have to arrest her for murder.

Besides, as annoyed as she might be by the persistent person trying to include her in a private game, she was genuinely interested in what had happened to Pauline Hartford. She might have quit the online group, but that didn't mean she wasn't still fascinated by unsolved crimes.

It'd been easy to find the house. It was located in the most expensive part of town. Of course, the worst part of town was just a couple of blocks away. There were no such things as suburbs in this area of Wisconsin.

Climbing out of the truck, Bailey shoved her hands into the pockets of her light jacket and studied the house. It was the sort of split-level, brick home that had become popular in the fifties and sixties. The roof was made from wooden shingles and there was a screened-in porch that hid most of the front of the house. The yard was twice the size of its neighbors, and Bailey assumed it'd been built before the other properties were divided in half to maximize profit.

It had almost a fortress feel to it, she acknowledged, her gaze moving to the high fence that surrounded the backyard. A house that stood defiantly against the encroaching tide of change.

"If you're here for the open house, it's been canceled."

Bailey flinched, belatedly realizing she was no longer alone. Turning her head, she discovered a young woman with a mass of curly brown hair and a heart-shaped face standing next to her. The stranger was holding onto a leash that was attached to a small, wiry dog who was busy sniffing Bailey's shoes.

Forcing a smile, Bailey held out her hand, trying to look casual. "Hi, I'm Bailey Evans."

The woman shook her hand. "Janet Stone."

Bailey glanced toward the house next door, where a large FOR SALE sign was planted in the front yard.

"Why was the open house canceled?" she asked, willing to latch on to the excuse to explain why she was standing on the sidewalk.

Janet waved a hand toward the split-level home. "Poor Mrs. Hartford was found deceased this morning. She fell into her pool."

"Oh, how awful. Did she drown?"

"No, she busted her head." Janet shuddered. "Tragic."

Bailey knew she should get in her truck and drive away. She didn't even know why she was there. But she sensed that Janet was eager to discuss the terrible event. Why not discover what happened? It would give her something to think about besides her current troubles.

"Is it your house for sale?" she asked.

"No. I live on the opposite side. The one for sale is empty." Janet clicked her tongue. "Well, not really empty. For the past week there's been construction workers and people mowing the yard and trimming hedges, not to mention the real estate agents who were out taking pictures of the entire neighborhood to put on their website." Janet nodded toward the dog, who had moved to pee on a nearby bush. "My poor Tina has been barking nonstop for days. Now I suppose it will go on for another week because they rescheduled the open house." Janet abruptly cut off her complaints. "Oh, that sounds horrible, doesn't it? Old lady Hartford . . . I mean." She shook her head in resignation. "Never mind. I'm just making it worse."

"I understand," Bailey assured her, glancing toward her truck, where Bert and Ernie were watching her with fierce intensity. "My neighbor had renovations done last year and those two beasts barked from dawn to dusk."

"Right?" Janet smiled, as if relieved that Bailey didn't think she was a horrible person. "And it really is a shame about Mrs. Hartford," she added.

"Did you know her well?"

"No. My husband went to school in Grange, so she was the superintendent, but as far as I know she stayed mostly to herself since she retired. I don't think I've seen her leave the house more than a handful of times since we moved in last year."

Having worked with the elderly for years, Bailey knew the most logical reason a person withdrew from society.

"Was she in poor health?"

"Not that I know of," Janet said, pointing toward the two-storied house with white siding and black shutters. "I can see into her backyard from my upstairs and she looked fine when I saw her walking around the patio. And she swam every morning when the weather was decent."

"Interesting." Bailey revised her initial assumption. There had to be another reason the older woman chose to remain a recluse.

Busy sorting through the various possibilities that ranged from a general aversion to people—not unusual in the elderly—all the way to dementia, Bailey was unprepared when Janet abruptly narrowed her eyes.

"Hey, you're not a cop, are you?"

"No."

"A reporter?"

Sensing the woman was about to put an end to their conversation, Bailey turned to face her.

"Can I tell you a secret?"

There was a long pause before Janet slowly nodded. "Okay."

"I'm in an online murder club." It wasn't a lie. Not exactly. She had been in the club.

"What's that?"

"We're average citizens who investigate cold cases." Bailey nodded toward the Hartford house. "Or suspicious deaths."

Janet's mouth fell open, but it wasn't shock that shimmered in her dark eyes. It was excitement. "Oh my God. You think . . ."

Bailey held up a hand. She didn't want to start any rumors. "I'm just getting some preliminary information to see if it might be something we would be interested in pursuing."

"I've heard about those clubs. Have you solved any murders?"

"A couple." Bailey shrugged, hoping Janet wouldn't ask for details. She didn't want to admit that they didn't have actual evidence to prove their various conjectures and that they'd never brought a criminal to justice.

Thankfully, Janet seemed more interested in the potential of being involved in solving a case than worrying about Bailey's sketchy credentials.

"Cool." She turned to stare at the house where

Pauline Hartford died just hours ago. "What are you looking for?"

Bailey took a second to consider her answer. It was one thing to do this sort of thing on the computer. They looked at reports and images that were available to the public, as well as chatting online with witnesses who were willing to answer their questions. It was completely different to have someone staring at her as she scrambled to think clearly.

"Did Mrs. Hartford have any enemies?" she finally asked.

Janet shrugged. "She wasn't very friendly, but I can't imagine that she left the house often enough to have enemies."

Bailey assumed that meant she hadn't had a feud with anyone in the neighborhood.

"She lived alone?"

"Yes. She had a maid who came in once a week, but her only family was a grandson who showed up on occasion." Her eyes widened as she sucked in a sharp gasp.

"Did you think of something?"

Janet eagerly nodded. "Yesterday."

"What happened?"

"I saw Kevin . . . . Kevin Hartford, that's the grandson. He showed up at the house."

Bailey felt a small thrill of excitement. It might be weird, but she enjoyed playing detective. It was like solving a puzzle.

"Do you know what time he was there?"

Janet considered the question. "It had to be around five o'clock," she told Bailey. "I was in the kitchen cooking dinner when I glanced out the window and saw his car in the driveway."

"You're sure it was his?"

Janet rolled her eyes. "You can't miss it. He drives a silver BMW with fancy wheels, even though my husband claims he hasn't held down a job in years."

Bailey understood the woman's reaction. It was annoying to see people living way beyond their means when you were pinching pennies. But Bailey had been raised to take pride in earning things, not having them handed to her.

"If he was the only family, then I assume he was the heir," she murmured, assuming that Mrs. Hartford was handing out money to fund her unemployed grandson.

"Probably. Unless she left her stuff to charity." Janet snorted, as if she found the mere thought amusing. "Which I very much doubt. She wouldn't even buy a box of Girl Scout cookies from my daughter."

"Do you happen to know what time he left?"

"I know exactly what time," Janet surprised her by admitting. "I was glancing at the clock because I was waiting for my casserole to be done. It was 5:25 when I heard him slam the front door. It was really loud. I glanced out to see him jump into his car, and a few seconds later he squealed away like he was mad about something."

Bailey arched her brows. Now, that was the sort of information that captured her attention. Why would the grandson be angry? The most obvious explanation would be Pauline withholding the cash that he presumably needed if he was unemployed. There was nothing like money to rip a family apart.

"And then Mrs. Hartford presumably went outside and fell into her pool?"

"Yep."

"Did you see her after he left?"

Janet shook her head. "The fence is too high to see into her backyard from my kitchen. I have to be upstairs."

So, there was no actual proof that Mrs. Hartford was still alive after her grandson left. He could have killed her and then staged his dramatic exit for everyone to notice him leaving. They would assume they'd argued and Mrs. Hartford had been upset enough to have accidentally stumbled and end up at the bottom of the pool. Then again, revealing they'd been in a fight might make him a prime suspect if her death hadn't been labeled an accident.

"What are you thinking?"

Janet's question interrupted her musings, and Bailey shoved aside suspicions of Kevin Hartford. There was still no proof it was murder.

"Last night was pretty chilly. Why would she be out by the pool?"

Janet leaned forward, as if she was about to share a secret. "I don't like to speak ill of the dead, but the woman was a drinker," she said in low tones. "I'd often see her out late at night, wandering around her backyard with a glass in her hand."

"An alcoholic?"

"I can't go that far," Janet corrected her, obviously uneasy at sharing her suspicions. "But her maid also cleans for my sister, and she told her that the old woman went through two or three bottles of gin every week. And the few times we spoke I could smell the alcohol on her breath. That's why I wasn't surprised when I heard that she'd fallen."

Bailey nodded, forcing herself to concede that it was increasingly likely that this was nothing more than an accident. She was an old woman who was no doubt upset from her argument with her grandson. Add in alcohol and it was a recipe for disaster.

"That makes sense," she murmured, unable to shake the feeling that she was missing something. Something obvious.

"What's bothering you?" Janet asked.

She tried to imagine the old woman heading out to the patio, a drink in her hand, as she fumed over her annoying relative. Was she headed toward one of the chairs? It was too cold for a swim . . .

Abruptly, Bailey realized exactly what was troubling her. "The newspaper article mentioned that she died in an empty pool."

Janet nodded. "Yeah, I saw the van for the pool guys in front of her house a few weeks ago."

"It seems odd that she would have her pool emptied but not covered."

"Wait." Janet's brow furrowed, as if she was searching through her memories. "I'm not one hundred percent certain, but I would swear that I saw the cover on the pool when I glanced in the backyard a couple of days ago."

"So, did something happen that she had to take it off?" Bailey shrugged. She'd never had a pool. Honestly, she didn't know anyone who did. She had no idea if the wind could blow off a cover, or if there might be some other reason to remove it. "Certainly something to think about." There was a loud bark from Ernie, who was clearly impatient with being trapped in the truck. Time to move along. "Has there been anything else unusual in the neighborhood?" she asked, realizing she wasn't as good at being a detective as she'd assumed.

So far all she knew was that Pauline Hartford may or may not have had an argument with her grandson, that she may or may not have been drunk, and that the cover hadn't been over her pool.

Zac didn't have to worry about her taking over his job as sheriff anytime soon.

"Not really." Janet glanced toward her house. "Between you and me, it's pretty boring around here."

"Trust me, boring isn't a bad thing," she assured Janet.

Climbing into the truck, she put it in gear and drove back to Pike. She parked in the attached garage and herded the dogs into the fenced-in backyard to do their business. A part of her knew that she was avoiding the moment when she had to step into the empty house.

She never missed her grandmother more than she did now, she acknowledged with a small sigh. Normally she kept herself too busy to notice that she lived alone. She had her job, her friends, and the Murder Club to keep her occupied. It was only when she had endless hours stretching before her that she realized she wasn't overly fond of me time.

Trying to shake off her dark mood, she forced herself to concentrate on the dogs, who'd immediately raced to the back porch to sniff something near the door.

"No," she called out, hurrying toward the house.

There was a stray cat in the neighborhood who took inordinate pleasure in tormenting the dogs. The last encounter ended with Ernie nursing a scratched ear and Bailey's favorite flowerpot smashed beyond repair. She was hoping to prevent any more damage.

Leaping onto the porch, she breathed a sigh of relief when she discovered it wasn't a cat but a large envelope near the door. Her next-door neighbor must have put it there while she was gone. There wasn't much crime in Pike, but it was better to avoid temptation, and Dorinda would often grab any deliveries that had been left for Bailey and store them out of sight.

It was one of the upsides of living in a small town.

Unlocking the door, she grabbed the envelope and herded her dogs into the kitchen. Then, flipping on the lights, she wandered toward the table as she ripped open the package to reveal a small jewelry box. Bailey frowned. She didn't remember ordering anything, but it wouldn't be the first time she'd agreed to buy something from one of her resident's grandkids. She had a whole freezer filled with Girl Scout cookies, candy bars, and pizzas.

Pulling off the lid of the box, she felt a stab of surprise at the sight of the pearl necklace that was nestled against the black velvet. Okay, this wasn't anything she'd ordered. She might have forgotten a box of cookies or even a T-shirt, but a necklace? And it looked expensive. Even in the dim light, the pearls glowed with a luminous beauty.

Placing the box on the table, she grabbed the envelope and turned it over. The address was hers, but there was no name. And the return address was too smudged to read. Obviously it was a mistake. Like the package of seeds that had randomly arrived in her mailbox last year or the magazine subscription that she was still trying to cancel.

With a shrug, she left the box on the table. She wasn't worried about the necklace, but it was weird. She'd recently seen pearls. But where?

She had the dogs watered and nestled on their beds in the spare bedroom when she at last recalled where she'd seen the pearls. With a muttered curse, she rushed to the kitchen where she kept her laptop on the table. It was the only place she could work without the dogs jumping on her.

Settling in one of the wooden chairs, she opened her computer and typed in the search engine. A second later the news report of Pauline Hartford's death popped up, along with a picture of a silver-haired woman with hard gray eyes. It was obviously a professional photograph, perhaps taken during her days as a superintendent, but Bailey wasn't interested in the older woman's stern expression or the arrogant tilt to her chin.

It was the pearl necklace hanging around her neck that had Bailey reaching for her phone to send a quick text.

I don't suppose you could come over, could you?

The answer came back in less than a second.

I'm on my way.

Unlike his friend and business partner Kaden Vaughn, Dom wasn't an impulsive man. Even when he'd immigrated from France, it was a decision he'd made when his mother first was diagnosed with cancer. He'd known when she was gone there would be nothing left for him there. And during those awful, grinding months, he'd worked and saved every penny he could scrape together. Evenings he would sit next to his mother's bed and read from English books she'd collected during a rare trip to London. When the time came he'd grabbed the bag he had packed and walked away.

Actually, the only truly impulsive thing he'd ever done was agree to Kaden's proposal to quit his job in LA and join him in Vegas.

Until today.

As soon as the text from Bailey hit his phone, he was grabbing his keys and sprinting toward the door. He didn't bother to ask what was wrong. It didn't matter. If she needed him, then he was going to be there. ASAP.

Traveling at a speed that caused his Land Rover to fishtail on the loose gravel, he reached her house in less than ten minutes. He parked in the driveway, halting to glance around for anyone who might be lurking in the area before he headed toward the door.

It opened the moment he stepped onto the porch, revealing a pale-faced Bailey, who motioned him inside with a tense expression.

"Are you okay?" he demanded, a strange tightness clenching his chest. As if a vice had been wrapped around him. "Did Gage come back?"

"No, this doesn't have anything to do with him."

She turned to hurry through the living room into the kitchen. Dom followed behind her, his gaze searching for any hint of trouble. Everything appeared to be neatly in place. There was nothing broken or turned over. Even the dogs were curled on a rug next to the fridge as he entered the kitchen, regarding him with a sleepy lack of concern. If there'd been an intruder, they would be on full alert.

"Tell me what's wrong," he urged.

Bailey moved to grab an object from the kitchen table. "I want you to look at this."

Dom frowned as he glanced at the pearl necklace that dangled from her fingers. It didn't look in need of repair. In fact, it was in perfect condition.

"Did it belong to your grandmother?"

"No, she never wore jewelry except for her wedding band. And it didn't belong to my mother. She hated pearls."

"I'm not sure what you want from me."

She swallowed, as if she had a lump in her throat. "Can you tell me if they're real?"

Dom took the necklace from her extended hand. His years working in a pawnshop had made him an expert in determining the value of any piece of jewelry. A mere glance was enough to tell him all he needed to know.

"They're real pearls, not plastic, if that's what you're asking," he told her.

Bailey leaned toward the table, turning the open laptop until he could see the picture of an older woman fill the screen. She was wearing a strand of pearls.

"Is this the same necklace?"

He bent forward, quickly shaking his head. The image had been enlarged and was clear enough to make out the details.

"No. Pearls are like diamonds. They're graded by size and type and quality. I'm not a professional jeweler, but

I'm certain that the necklace that lady is wearing is one you could buy in any department store." He returned his attention to the string of pearls spread over his palm. "This necklace came from a high-end store with a hefty price tag."

"You're absolutely certain it's not a fake?"

Dom was confused. The answer was obviously important, but he had no idea why.

With a shrug, he held the necklace so it would reflect in the light. "There's a luster to the pearls that's unmistakable, as well as the fact they're perfectly symmetrical." He brushed his thumb over the clasp. "And look here. This is silver filagree studded with real emeralds."

Bailey released a shaky breath. "Thank God."

He handed her the strand of pearls. "Are you worried someone tricked you into buying imitation jewelry? Or that it's stolen merchandise?"

"I didn't buy the necklace," she muttered, dropping the pearls on the table. "It just showed up."

"What do you mean, it showed up?"

"I found it in an envelope on the back porch when I got home."

"You don't know who left it?"

"No."

His initial concern returned with a vengeance. Gage Warren might not be pounding down the door, but she was frightened.

"Tell me what's going on."

She wrapped her arms around her waist. "I don't know and it's scaring me."

Dom nodded toward the couch. "Sit down. I'll make us some tea."

She obediently dropped in the nearest chair, but she sent him a warning glare. "No sugar."

"Got it."

In silence, he heated the kettle, covertly studying her tense profile as she chewed her lower lip. Once the tea was brewed, he returned to the table, placing the cup in front of her before taking a seat.

"Start at the beginning," he requested, sensing Bailey hadn't been fully prepared to share her troubles with him.

"Okay." She took a sip of tea as she squared her shoulders. As if she needed to gather her courage. "About a year ago I joined a group called the Murder Club."

"Murder Club?" Dom arched a brow. "Like a mystery dinner with actors?"

"No, it was all online and the cases are real," she explained. "I figured that anyone who lived in Pike is an expert in murder. Plus, I have my nursing degree. It comes in handy with any medical questions."

Dom nodded. "Kaden mentioned there was more than one serial killer who passed through Pike. And that the town was compared to the murder capital of the United States," he agreed. "And I don't doubt that you would be fantastic. While we were preparing for the wedding it was obvious you have a rare attention to detail and an incredible memory. I was just thinking that an online game doesn't seem like your kind of thing."

"It isn't really." She shrugged. "But I was bored. Lia was spending her time with Kaden and the winters in Pike can be brutal. There was nothing to do but stay home. The Murder Club seemed like a fun way to pass the evenings."

"What did you do in the club?"

"Someone would present a crime that was unsolved or had been classified as an accident and we would search through the clues to try to solve the case."

Dom had a vague memory of a documentary that focused on regular people who combined their various expertise to study unsolved crimes. Obviously it was more common than he realized.

"Did you have any success?"

She took another sip of the tea, a hint of color returning to her cheeks. "Not officially, but I think we managed to come up with a few reasonable conclusions."

"So what happened?"

"A couple of weeks ago I started to get strange DMs in the chat room."

Dom's jaw tightened. Being pestered with unwanted attention was the bane of every woman who just wanted to be in a public space, whether virtual or online.

"Were they sexual invitations?"

She shook her head. "They said I'd earned an invitation to a private murder club."

Which Dom assumed was another way to lure Bailey into a vulnerable situation.

"You refused?"

"I tried to ignore them, but the messages kept coming." She set down her empty teacup, her hand not quite steady. "So I closed my account. I hoped that would be the end of it."

"But it wasn't?"

"Yesterday morning I got this text."

She grabbed her phone from the table and scrolled through her messages. Once she found the one she wanted, she turned the screen for him to read.

"'The club is officially open. Ready or not,'" he read out loud. "Do you recognize the number?"

"No."

"Did you respond?"

"Not to that one."

"You got another text?"

"This morning." She turned the phone around and did more scrolling before turning it back for him to read through the messages.

A sharp fear pierced his heart as he reread the texts a dozen times. "A different number," he pointed out, his unease spiking. "There's more than one person harassing you. Or the person is using burner phones when they contact you. I don't like either scenario."

She shuddered, obviously troubled by the messages. "Neither do I."

"Did you check out the link?"

She pointed toward the computer. "It goes to a newspaper story about Pauline Hartford from Grange who fell into her pool and died last night."

"Is that Pauline Hartford?"

"Yes."

Dom sorted through the information Bailey had shared. It wouldn't be suspicious that one of the members of the murder club would hope to lure Bailey into a private game. Lots of people hooked up on the Internet. But once she shut down her account, the person should have accepted her blatant rejection. The fact that they insisted on continuing with a game she'd refused to play changed the vibe from a little weird to dangerous stalker.

Add in her recent trouble at the nursing home and Dom's inner alarms were blaring.

Someone was going to a great deal of effort to screw with Bailey's life.

"And you thought the pearls she's wearing somehow ended up on your back porch?"

She grimaced, as if trying to convince herself she was overreacting. "It could be nothing, but I was feeling a little skittish when I got back from Grange today."

"Today?"

"Yes. I went to see where Mrs. Hartford died."

Dom's brows lowered at the realization she must have gone from his house straight to the nearby town. It was aggravating that she hadn't bothered to share her worries or to let him know where she was going.

It didn't matter that he had no right to expect her to share everything that was happening in her life. And that she was perfectly capable of driving wherever she wanted without his permission.

The thought that she might have been in danger crushed any rational reaction.

"You went alone?"

She blinked, predictably confused by his sharp tone. "I had the dogs with me. I just wanted to see . . ." She shook her head in frustration. "Actually, I don't know what I wanted. I guess I wanted to reassure myself her death really was an accident."

Dom sucked in a deep breath, regaining command of his emotions. Typically he was an even-tempered guy who could pacify the most outrageous customers.

A skill he'd developed as a child to deal with the angry bill collectors, neighbors, and even family members who Remy had managed to piss off.

But there was something about Bailey that stirred his most primitive passions.

"Did you reassure yourself?" he asked.

"Not really. Her neighbor admitted that the older woman had a habit of drinking, maybe heavily. That could obviously have caused her to fall into the pool."

"You don't sound convinced."

"The neighbor also admitted that workers had been there to drain and clean the pool for the winter. So why wasn't it covered?"

"Good point," he murmured.

It was a question that would never have entered his mind. When he was in France he never knew anyone with a pool. And since coming to America he'd lived in areas where it was never a concern.

"Plus, the neighbor said that the grandson who was her only heir was there around dinnertime and stormed away as if they'd had a fight."

Dom fisted his hands. He admired her obvious talent in seeing clues most people would have missed, but the fact that her mysterious stalker had forced her to try to solve the case was sending chills down his spine.

"I don't like this," he repeated.

"Neither do I." She shuddered, glancing toward the back door. "Especially after the pearls showed up. It feels like someone is playing with me."

"Could it be Gage?" he asked the obvious question.

The belligerent man had already tried to frame her for the murder of his mother. Maybe he'd discovered

Bailey had an alibi and was trying to implicate her in the death of Mrs. Hartford?

"I doubt that was a member of the Murder Club," Bailey retorted, her tone dubious. "My friend Trish works at the lumberyard taking care of the paperwork, and she once told me that Gage couldn't even turn on the computer without her help. How would he use the direct messages in the chat room? Or figure out how to send texts from different numbers?"

"True. None of this seems to be his style," Dom readily agreed.

"His style is slashing tires or throwing bricks through windows. He's not subtle."

"Who else was in the Murder Club?"

She shrugged. "The only person I know for sure is Eric Criswell."

"Who is that?"

"He works as an aide at the nursing home," she explained. "He's the one who suggested I join."

Dom placed his hands flat on the table as he leaned toward Bailey. "He's an aide at the nursing home? And he was the one to convince you to join the Murder Club?"

Bailey nodded. "He's big into online gaming."

A computer nerd who would know all about burner phones. Dom added the information to the growing list of damning evidence.

"Does he have your phone number?"

"Anyone who works at the nursing home would have my number," she said. "If I'm not working, I'm always on standby in case of an emergency."

Dom stared at her in confusion. "It seems obvious that he must be the one harassing you."

"That was my thought when I got the first text," she conceded. "But I confronted him with the message and he pointed out that if he wanted us to play a private game, he could just ask me. There was no point in using the chat room or sending me creepy messages."

"What would you have said if he asked?"

"I would have said no."

"There you go. He knew you wouldn't play his game, so he hoped he could tempt you by creating a secret identity. Some men just can't accept rejection. Especially if they think you are somehow destined to be together."

She took a minute to consider his words. "But you said the pearl necklace is expensive?"

"Very."

"Then it can't be Eric texting me," she stated in firm tones. "He makes minimum wage and lives with his mother. I doubt he has more than a few dollars in the bank."

Dom was reluctant to give up their most promising lead. "Could he have taken it from his mother?"

"As far as I know, they've always been poor. In fact, the church used to take turns buying groceries and leaving them on their porch." She held up her hands. "Unless Mrs. Criswell came into some unexpected money in the past few months, it didn't come from Eric."

Dom shook his head. "I would guess by the style of the clasp that it's a vintage piece. Probably sold in the late nineteen fifties or early sixties . . ."

His words trailed away as Dom was struck by a sudden thought. Not about Eric Criswell or the pearl necklace, but by the nagging unease he'd felt since coming to Pike.

"Is something wrong?" Bailey demanded, staring at him in confusion.

"Elderly women."

"I don't understand."

"What if the two deaths are connected?" he abruptly demanded.

She stared at him as if he'd spoken a foreign language. "What deaths?"

"Gage's mother and the woman in Grange."

Chapter 6

Bailey stared at Dom, an odd whisper of apprehension sweeping through her as she moved to toss the necklace back on the kitchen table.

She should have laughed at the mere suggestion that the deaths were connected. Just because Nellie Warren and Pauline Hartford were approximately the same age and died within a week of each other didn't mean they had anything else in common. It was a sad truth that people in their eighties died on a regular basis.

But she didn't laugh.

Instead, she slowly turned back to stare at Dom with a vague sense of dread.

"Why would you think the two deaths are connected?" she demanded.

He studied her with a sympathetic gaze, as if he sensed the anxiety gnawing deep inside her.

"Someone has gone to a lot of effort to link your name with two recently deceased women."

"What are you implying?"

He shrugged. "Honestly, I don't know. I just don't think it's a coincidence that Gage Warren tried to implicate you in his mother's death and then a day later you received a text that lured you to Pauline Hartford's home. If the cops were investigating the case, they might have asked you some awkward questions about why you were there. Plus, that necklace left on your back porch has to be a warning."

Bailey shivered, wishing she'd never joined the stupid Murder Club. So what if she'd been bored? She should have opened a bottle of wine and watched porn on her computer like every other single woman alone on New Year's Eve.

"A warning for what? To join the private club? To solve Pauline's death?"

"To play his sick game." His jaw tightened.

Her lips parted to tell him that she didn't understand the game when the dogs abruptly jumped to their feet and charged into the living room, barking loud enough to make Dom wince. Bailey pressed a hand to her quivering stomach, releasing a shaky breath. Her nerves felt as if they'd been rubbed raw, but she wasn't worried about who had caused her dogs to gallop around like drunk wildebeests. Only one person besides herself could cause such spasms of joy.

Ignoring Dom's frown of suspicion, she hurried to push Bert and Ernie away from the door. Then, pulling it open, she revealed her neighbor, Dorinda Lyle.

The woman was in her early seventies and had lived next door for as long as Bailey could remember. She was a short, square woman with a wide face that was emphasized by the headband she wore to keep back her brassy, blond hair, and she spent her days volunteering around town and bluntly informing whoever would listen how they should be running their life. Including Bailey.

Bailey didn't mind. The woman might be bossy and intrusive, but her heart was always in the right place.

"Hi, Dorinda." Bailey stepped back to give the woman room. "Come in."

Dorinda stepped over the threshold, her pale blue gaze skimming the living room as if she was searching for a hidden danger. Her brows arched as Dom stepped out of the kitchen and crossed to stand next to Bailey.

"I saw a strange car in the drive and wanted to make sure everything is okay," the older woman said, an edge of warning in her voice as she stared directly at Dom.

"No worries," Bailey assured her.

Dom leaned forward, stretching out his hand. "I'm Dom Lucier."

"Dorinda Lyle." Dorinda shook Dom's hand, her expression relaxing as she accepted that Bailey wasn't in imminent danger. "You were here for Lia's wedding, right?"

"I was." Dom straightened. "Kaden and I run a business together in Vegas."

With a nod, Dorinda wagged a finger toward the dogs, who continued to dance and whine in an effort to gain her attention.

"Settle down, you brutes," she chided with a fond smile.

"Dog approved, I see," Dom murmured, his own tension visibly easing. Obviously he assumed that Bert and Ernie had a talent for sensing the difference between good and bad people.

He wasn't wrong.

Dorinda pursed her lips. "Like any males, you just have to know how to talk to them."

Bailey glanced toward the man standing next to her. "Is that true?"

His eyes darkened with a blatant invitation. "Absolutely."

A fuzzy warmth spread through her. "Good to know."

Dorinda cleared her throat, as if to remind them that they weren't alone. "Sorry to intrude. I was just checking that you were okay."

"I'm fine."

Dorinda started to turn, only to halt, as if she'd been struck by a sudden thought. "And if you need any money, you just let me know. I have a nice nest egg stashed away."

Bailey felt Dom stiffen at the offer. "You need money?"

She flushed. "No, of course not."

"Now, don't let your pride get you in trouble, sweetie." Dorinda clicked her tongue. "I was at the nursing home today to help organize the bingo game and I heard that you'd been fired."

Dom muttered a curse as he studied her with a fierce expression. "Really?"

"I wasn't fired," she protested. "I'm on leave without pay."

"Same thing." Dorinda shook her head. "Bunch of idiots, if you ask me. They won't be able to run that place without you, mark my words. Soon enough they'll come crawling on their knees, pleading for you to come back."

"I'm not sure I will, even if they do come on their

knees," Bailey retorted, catching herself by surprise. Until the words left her lips she hadn't even realized she was thinking about a change of jobs. She'd been happy with her work until this week, but she was starting to suspect that it was more about her being comfortable in what she was doing than finding actual joy in her work. "It was bad enough to have Gage accusing me of swindling his mother out of her money without them taking his side," she said in defensive tones.

Dorinda leaned forward to pat her arm. "Don't worry, I had a chat with Lorene before leaving today."

Bailey frowned. "A chat about what?"

"About Nellie's decision to change her will."

Bailey's eyes widened as she tried to absorb what Dorinda was saying. "You knew Nellie was going to change her will?"

"Yes. I had lunch with Nellie a few weeks ago and she told me then that she was going to call her lawyer and set up an appointment as soon as possible."

The words were casual, as if Dorinda had no idea that the stupid will had turned Bailey's life upside down.

"Seriously?" she demanded.

"I'm quite serious."

Bailey licked her suddenly dry lips. "Did she tell you why?"

"Oh yes." Dorinda folded her hands together, her expression tightening with obvious disapproval. "She caught Gage stealing her belongings when he last visited."

Bailey was shocked. Gage Warren was exactly the sort of man who would steal from his own mother, but she couldn't believe that he'd visited the nursing home.

"I didn't know that he'd been to see his mother."

"It wasn't actually a visit," Dorinda corrected her. "He crept into her room while she was sleeping. It was his bad luck that she woke up and caught sight of him searching through her drawers. By the time she could fully come to her senses he'd darted out of the room, but not before he'd taken her cash and a very expensive emerald ring."

Bailey shared a quick glance with Dom. That was why Gage had so loudly accused her of stealing the ring. She returned her attention to Dorinda.

"Did Nellie contact Zac?"

"No, she told Logan Donaldson." Dorinda's disapproval deepened. "You can imagine how he reacted. He warned her not to make a fuss and promised that he would take care of it."

"Who's Logan Donaldson?" Dom asked.

Bailey wrinkled her nose. "His mother owns the nursing home. I don't know what he actually does, beyond walking around trying to look important." She sent Dorinda a puzzled glance. "How was he going to take care of Gage stealing from his mother?"

"He wasn't going to do anything." The older woman sniffed in disdain. "Nellie knew that. So did Gage. The Donaldsons don't care about anything but the reputation of the nursing home. That's when Nellie decided to take matters into her own hands."

"By changing her will?"

"Yes. She told me that she couldn't take away the lumberyard or the house. Her husband had been adamant that their property be kept in the Warren family, but she had her own money that she intended to leave to the one person who had shown her kindness since her move to the nursing home."

Bailey was silent as she processed the realization that there was proof that she hadn't coerced Nellie into giving her money. Even if Nellie hadn't called Zac and given an official report, she'd publicly shared the information that—

"Wait." Bailey sucked in a sharp breath, her eyes narrowing. "If Nellie told Logan that Gage had been stealing her belongings, Logan would have told his mother what was happening. She probably even knew Nellie was going to change her will." Anger blasted through Bailey as she recalled the humiliating scene she'd endured as Lorene Donaldson pretended she couldn't be sure whether or not Bailey had been tricking old people into leaving her money. And then Logan acted as if he was the good guy who was going to convince his mother that she was being hasty. "Those . . . assholes."

"She swore that she hadn't known anything about Gage stealing from Nellie. And she promised she'd take the information into consideration." Dorinda rolled her eyes. "Whatever that means. But I agree. They're both assholes."

Bailey struggled to regain control of her raw sense of betrayal. It wasn't like she was surprised that the Donaldsons were willing to trash her reputation rather than let the scandal threaten their business. But she couldn't believe that Lorene would ignore Gage's abuse of his mother. If she truly cared about her residents, she would have called Zac and made an official report of the theft.

Sensing the older woman's concern, Bailey forced a smile to her lips. She didn't want Dorinda regretting her decision to share what she'd discovered.

"Thank you, Dorinda," she murmured. "It was awful to be accused of abusing someone in my care."

"No one would believe such a thing," Dorinda assured her. "Not in this town."

Bailey wasn't nearly so certain. "Thank you for letting me know."

As if sensing her tangled emotions, Dorinda gave the dogs a pat on the head, her gaze moving to Dom.

"I see you're in good hands. I'll talk to you later."

Dorinda was stepping onto the porch when Bailey realized the older woman might be able to offer even more help.

"Wait."

Dorinda turned back. "Yes?"

"Did you happen to notice anyone in my backyard today?"

"In your yard? Did something happen?" Dorinda scowled, looking ready for a fight. "Was it that Gage Warren? I heard that he attacked you yesterday. On a public street in broad daylight too. That boy has no shame."

"No, it's nothing like that." Bailey hastily attempted to calm her neighbor's fierce temper. She wouldn't put it past the older woman to track down Gage and slap his face. "There was a package left on my back porch."

"Was it damaged?" Dorinda's anger vanished as she

glanced toward the dogs still pleading for her attention. "You might ask these two." She leaned down to rub their ears. On cue, Bert and Ernie melted into puddles of bliss. "Have you been playing with packages?" she asked the dogs.

"I'm sure you're right," Bailey said. "But if you do happen to see anyone hanging around, I would appreciate you letting me know."

"I'll be keeping my eyes peeled," Dorinda promised. "Take care."

Dom waited for the door to close behind the neighbor before he turned to study Bailey's distracted expression.

"That was interesting," he said as the silence stretched.

She blinked, as if she'd forgotten he was in the room. And maybe she had, he acknowledged, his jaw tightening. She'd neglected to share that she'd been suspended from her job. Okay, she didn't owe him any explanations. They were barely more than strangers. But it bothered him to accept that she hadn't felt comfortable telling him what had happened.

As if he needed to be the one she turned to when she'd been hurt.

"More than interesting," she insisted. "Dorinda has proof that I had nothing to do with convincing Nellie to change her will."

With an effort, Dom squashed his unreasonable response. This was about Bailey, not his snowballing fascination with her.

"No one needed proof."

Her jaw tightened. "I was let go from my job."

He shrugged. "As your neighbor pointed out, they're idiots."

"They are, but they wouldn't be the only ones to think I'd done something sneaky to get that kind of money."

He reached out to cup her cheek in his palm. "No one who matters."

"Easy for you to say."

He stared down at her, shuddering at the memory of being chased down the street by angry neighbors, or being awakened in the middle of the night to sneak out of town.

"Actually, it isn't easy at all. I spent a lot of years being judged by villagers because of my relationship to Remy." His voice was harsh when he spoke his father's name. He wasn't bitter about his past, but he'd never forgotten the pain his father had caused. "I learned to appreciate the people who took the time to get to know me, instead of leaping to the conclusion I couldn't be trusted because my last name was Lucier."

Her expression softened as she sent him a smile of wry regret. "I'm sorry. I'm being silly, aren't I?" She shook her head. "I have a terrible need to be liked by everyone. My grandmother warned me that it was a losing game. That there were always people out there wanting to think the worst of others."

He brushed his thumb over the lush curve of her lower lip. "You have a big heart that's easily wounded. Don't change because of a few nasty gossips."

She blushed, as if suddenly realizing how close he was standing. "I'm sorry. I keep interrupting your vacation."

"It's never an interruption." He held her gaze, accepting

it was time to take the plunge and confess what had lured him to Pike. "Coming here wasn't just about getting away from work, but an opportunity to spend time with the new friends I met during Kaden's wedding." He paused, his thumb continuing to brush over her lips. "One friend in particular."

Her lips parted as she sucked in a sharp breath. "Me?"

"Yes, you. I thought about you every day."

"I . . . you can't be serious."

"Why not?"

"I'm not very memorable."

She eyed him warily. He shouldn't be surprised, he told himself. He'd arrived in Pike without warning and instantly started to instigate himself into her life. She had to wonder if he was the sort of guy who found a woman in whatever town he happened to be visiting and made her the focus of his attention before moving on.

"You are to me." He lowered his head to brush a light kiss over her lips. "And I hope to convince you to return my interest."

He felt her stiffen in shock. Damn. Had his risk backfired? Then, thankfully, she melted against him, her hands lifting to grasp his shoulders.

"You are a dangerous man, Dom Lucier," she whispered against his mouth.

"No, Kaden is dangerous," he argued, nibbling a path along the line of her jaw. "I'm a simple, uncomplicated man who has no use for games. You'll always know what I'm thinking and what I'm feeling."

She arched back, regarding him with a strange expression. "That only makes you more dangerous."

He claimed one last kiss before reluctantly stepping back. He'd pressed his luck far enough.

"We can take this as slow as you want," he promised. "I'm a very patient man."

She reached up to brush back the hair that had come loose from her bun, her hand not quite steady. Dom hid a smile. He would gloat later at the fact that his touch had so obviously shaken her.

"I'm still sorry I made you rush over here for nothing."

Dom felt a pang of regret as she deliberately diverted the conversation from what had just happened between them, but he didn't protest. He'd assured her that he would be patient. He was a man of his word.

"It's not nothing," he argued, his unease bubbling to the surface. Dorinda's visit had changed his original hypothesis, but it didn't erase his concern. If anything, he was more worried than ever. "And I'm glad you did ask me over. The sooner we figure out who's harassing, you the better."

"I'm not even sure that it is harassment," she said, stubbornly attempting to minimize her danger. "I might be overreacting to a couple of text messages."

"You're not overacting, but I'll admit that I'm reconsidering my theory that the same person is responsible for the deaths of Nellie Warren and the woman in Grange," he conceded, speaking his thoughts out loud. "Your neighbor mentioned Nellie, telling her that she caught her son stealing from her. Gage Warren might not be overly bright, but he had to realize she wasn't going to be happy with him. And that he was in danger of losing everything."

Bailey widened her eyes. "Are you suggesting that Gage killed his mother?"

"That's exactly what I'm suggesting."

There was a long silence as Bailey processed his theory. Her expression was troubled but not shocked.

"You know, a week ago I would have said it was crazy to think that Nellie could have been murdered by her own son," she admitted. "Now I don't know what to think. I mean, Gage has always been a jerk. And everyone in town knows that he would be bankrupt if it wasn't for his mother's financial support. But . . . murder?"

"He was very eager to imply you were responsible for her death," he reminded her.

She nodded. "And the theft of her ring."

"It would have been easy to have slipped something into her food or drink if he wanted to get rid of her."

"Plus, he had her cremated as soon as possible." Her hands clenched into fists. "What was his hurry unless he was afraid someone might question her death?"

"Exactly." He paced across the cramped living room, his mind churning as he tried to imagine Gage's panic when he feared that his mother might cut him out of the will. It would have been a murder of desperation, he silently concluded, not a cold-blooded plan. Which meant that he didn't fit the mystery person stalking Bailey. "But I doubt he had the capability or the interest in becoming a member of an online murder group or send you texts," he added.

She pursed her lips, her brow furrowed. "No."

He came to an abrupt halt. "You thought of something."

She held up her hand, as if trying to lower his expectations. "I agree that Gage wouldn't have any reason to be involved in Pauline Hartford's death, but if—and it's a very big if—Gage did kill his mother to get his hands on his inheritance, it's remarkably similar to what we suspect happened between Pauline and her grandson." She waited for his brows to slowly rise in understanding. "Both women might have argued with their heirs and even potentially cut them out of their wills and within days they're both dead."

"You're right."

"It's possible whoever sent the texts saw the connection between the two deaths and simply assumed that it would make an interesting investigation," she said, something that might have been relief shimmering in her eyes. "Nothing sinister about it."

Dom studied her in silence. He understood her desire to pretend that they'd solved the mystery. Who wanted to accept they'd attracted the sick fascination of a stalker? Or that they were in danger? But as much as he wanted her to feel safe and secure in her own home, he would never forgive himself if she let down her guard and something terrible happened.

"And the pearl necklace?"

"They could be nothing. Lots of packages end up at the wrong address."

"Or they could be something." He folded his arms over his chest. "I think it's interesting that whoever left them there chose a time when your neighbor happened to be away from home."

She flinched, as if his words had caused her a physical pain. "You think they were watching my house?"

"That. Or they were at the nursing home and saw Dorinda there. They would know that your observant neighbor wasn't around to witness them leaving the package." A knot formed in the pit of his stomach. "Either possibility means that someone in Pike is responsible. You need to tell Zac about the texts."

"I will." She heaved a heavy sigh of resignation. "Tomorrow. For now, I want a hot bath and an evening of mindless reality shows."

Dom reluctantly accepted her less-than-subtle hint to leave. "Lock the door. And call me if you need anything." He held her gaze, a slow smile of invitation curving his lips. "And I do mean *anything*."

Her eyes darkened with an awareness that made his heart pound. "I'll keep that in mind."

Chapter 7

Gage waited until he heard the rattle of his secretary's car driving away from the lumberyard before he opened the bottom drawer of his desk and pulled out the bottle of vodka he'd stashed there during lunch.

Usually he forced himself to wait until he was in the privacy of his home to pour his first drink. He'd been banned from the Bait and Tackle last year when he chucked a mug at a waitress who wasn't serving him fast enough. And even the Roadhouse, outside of town, had asked him not to return. He'd warned himself that it was bad enough to be the town drunk without continuing to make a public spectacle of himself.

Tonight, however, even his home was off-limits. He'd paid a damned fortune to hire a maid service from Grange to come over and clean the house. The Realtor had warned him that it had to stay spotless if he wanted to sell as quickly as possible. He wasn't going to risk getting drunk and trashing the place.

Not when he had a mountain of debts from his unfortunate string of bad luck at the poker tables and was in dire need of some quick cash.

It was a need that shouldn't have been necessary. Not if he'd gotten the money that was supposed to be his when his mother finally had the decency to die. Gage took a swig of vodka straight from the bottle and flopped back in the worn leather chair, allowing the bitterness to bubble through him.

He'd known that bitch of a nurse was worming her way into his mother's affections. Whenever he forced himself to visit the nursing home, all she could talk about was "sweet Bailey," and how she'd baked her favorite cookies or played a stupid game of bridge. Like Bailey wasn't paid a salary to take care of the old farts. But it wasn't until his mother was dead that he realized she'd changed the will. Now he was in a frantic scramble to get his hands on some cash until he could prove that Bailey Evans had stolen his inheritance.

Taking another swig, Gage brooded on the bad luck that had plagued him since he was born. Everyone assumed he was so lucky to have parents who could hand him the family business. As if he'd ever wanted to work in a stupid lumberyard. Or listen to his dad's nagging every second of the day. Nothing he did was ever right, whether it was helping customers or sweeping the floors. As if anyone gave a fuck. This place was destined to become a molding pile of shit. With him trapped inside.

Was it any wonder he needed a drink or two to make his life bearable?

What he needed was a stack of money and a one-way ticket out of this hellhole.

Imagining the pleasure of loading up his van and

disappearing, Gage was interrupted when he heard the sound of the outer door closing. Dammit. His secretary was supposed to lock it on her way out. Now he was going to have to deal with some stupid yokel looking for a couple of screws or a cheap piece of plywood. No one ever wanted anything that could bring actual profit to this miserable business.

Shoving himself to his feet, Gage crossed the office and opened the connecting door. He was vaguely aware that his balance was already sketchy. Maybe he should run to Bella's and pick up a pizza before he continued with the vodka.

Eager to get rid of the intruder, Gage stepped into the public area, frowning at the darkness. Even when the lumberyard was closed there were emergency lights near the exits.

Cautiously shuffling forward, Gage struggled to peer through the gloom. He couldn't see anyone. Had he imagined the sound of the door? It wouldn't be the first time. Once he thought his dad was sitting next to him, despite the fact that he'd been dead for years.

Still, he forced himself to move forward. The thought of a pizza had made his stomach rumble with hunger. Trying to decide between pepperoni and sausage, Gage never saw the shadow that moved in behind him. Or the two-by-four that was swinging through the air. It wasn't until a shattering pain blasted through his head that he realized he wasn't alone after all, and that he was about to leave Pike sooner than he expected. Only not in the way he always dreamed . . .

* * *

It was after seven the next morning when Bailey crawled out of bed. Plagued by nightmares of being chased by an unseen intruder, she'd tossed and turned most of the night leaving her feeling lethargic and she dragged herself to the shower.

Thankfully, by the time she was dressed in a fresh pair of jeans and a flannel shirt with her damp hair pulled in a ponytail, she'd managed to clear the fog from her brain. It helped that the sun was shining and the dogs were dancing around her feet with their usual goofy enthusiasm.

Even when they charged toward the front door, yapping with a deafening greeting, she didn't allow the dark clouds to return. Whoever was approaching the house was someone they recognized. Not that she was going to do anything stupid. She moved to peer out the front window to see who was there before opening the door.

Her breath hissed between her lips as she caught sight of Dom standing on the porch, the morning sunlight adding a sheen of gold to his hair and his green Henley clinging to his broad chest with spectacular devotion. Excitement blasted through Bailey as she recalled the searing heat of his fingers, which had brushed over her cheek, and the taste of his kiss.

It had been so tempting to melt into Dom's arms. When he touched her the passion blasted through her with a shocking hunger. She didn't have to think about Gage's ugly accusations, or the fact that she didn't have a job, or the mysterious stalker. There was nothing but sheer pleasure.

So why was she so hesitant to give into temptation?

After all, she'd urged Lia to leap into an affair with Kaden. Who cared if he was only going to be around for a few days? Or that he wasn't the sort of man to settle down? He was sexy and fun and Lia was happy when he was around. Why not enjoy what short time they had together?

When it came to taking her own advice, however, she wasn't nearly so casual about a temporary relationship. Probably because when she thought of being with Dom there was nothing casual about what she wanted. He'd haunted her thoughts from the second she'd met him, and even when he'd returned to Vegas she'd replayed the time they'd spent together over and over. What would happen if she gave into the desire that sizzled through her like magic?

The past had taught her that there was a cost to caring about someone who was destined to leave. Was she prepared to pay it?

Belatedly realizing that she was leaving him standing on her porch while she daydreamed about an affair that hadn't happened yet, Bailey shook her head and hurried to pull open the door.

"Dom," she murmured, awareness blasting through her as she caught the scent of his warm, male scent.

A slow, devastatingly sexy smile curved his lips. "Am I too early?"

With an effort, Bailey forced her gaze from his mesmerizing eyes to focus on the pink package he was holding in his hands.

"That depends on what's in the box," she informed him.

"An assortment of doughnuts from the local diner."

She stepped back to wave him in. The local diner was famous for their apple pie, but their doughnuts ran a close second.

"Then it's not too early."

His smile widened. "Good. I . . ." His words dried on his lips as he turned to squeeze past her. Coming to a halt, he nodded across the street. "Do you recognize that car?"

With a frown, Bailey leaned forward to follow his gaze. She easily spotted the old, rusty vehicle that was parked near the railroad tracks.

She wrinkled her nose. Even from a distance she could see the hubcaps were missing and the back window was covered with duct tape. It made the vehicle easy to identify.

"It looks like Eric Criswell's car."

"The Eric from the nursing home? The one who got you involved in the Murder Club?"

"Yes."

Dom scowled. "His name keeps popping up. Does he live in the neighborhood?"

A chill inched down Bailey's spine. Dom was right. Eric's name kept popping up. And now he was parked outside her house. This wasn't just a coincidence.

"No, he stays with his mother," she said. "Her home is near the nursing home."

Dom shoved the box of doughnuts into her hand. "I'm going to have a word with him."

Bailey dropped the pastries on the table next to the door. "Me too."

Dom frowned. "Bailey."

She placed her hands on her hips. "Yes?"

He sighed. "Never mind."

Muscling the dogs back, Bailey managed to slip outside and close the door. Then, keeping pace next to Dom, she jumped from the porch and headed directly toward the rusty car.

They'd crossed the empty street when there was a loud bang as Eric started the old engine.

"He's going to take off," she warned.

Dom jogged forward, planting his hands on the hood of the car. "I'll block him, you find out what he's doing here."

Bailey nodded. "Be careful," she warned him. "Eric has a habit of panicking if he's confronted. He might run you over before he can stop himself."

"Noted," Dom assured her, his hands remaining on the hood.

Trusting he had enough sense not to get squished, Bailey moved to the driver's door. She could see Eric clutching the steering wheel as he stared at Dom, no doubt battling back the urge to take off.

Tapping on the window, Bailey waited for it to be rolled down. A moment later, Eric reluctantly turned his head to meet her frown.

"Hey, Bailey."

He looked paler than usual with his black hair tousled, as if he'd been running his fingers through the thin strands. His gray eyes, however, glittered with a barely suppressed emotion.

Embarrassment? Excitement? Some gross combination? It was impossible to say.

"What are you doing here, Eric?"

"Oh, you know. Just hanging out." He released a nervous laugh. "I didn't have to work today."

Bailey arched her brows. "You're hanging out in your car?"

"There's not a lot to do in Pike."

She allowed her gaze to sweep down his thin body, taking in the wrinkled shirt and worn jeans. He looked as if he'd slept in his clothes. Just how long had he been sitting out here?

"Boredom doesn't explain why you decided to park in front of my house."

"Your house?" He widened his eyes in faux surprise. "I didn't even know you lived around here."

Anger seared through Bailey. The past few days had been a nightmare. And after a near sleepless night she wasn't in the mood to be jerked around. Especially by someone who was partially responsible for her current troubles.

"You picked me up and dropped me off from work for an entire week when my truck was in the shop last year," she snapped. "Tell me what you're doing here before I call Zac."

"Okay, okay." Eric held up his hands, a muscle twitching next to his eye. "I heard that Gage Warren had threatened you and I was worried. He's been violent to other women and I didn't want you to get hurt."

Any other day it might have been a plausible explanation. Since they'd started working together, Eric had been protective of her. Sometimes to the point she had to ask him to back off. But there was a nervous energy buzzing around the younger man that warned her that he wasn't being entirely honest.

"If you were worried, why not come to the house?"

He licked his lips. "I didn't want to bother you. I knew I could keep a watch from here and—"

Eric swiveled his head toward the passenger door as Dom abruptly jerked it open so he could slide into the car. Then, before Eric could stop him, he grabbed the phone that was balanced on Eric's lap.

"You were doing more than just keeping watch. Weren't you?" he demanded.

"Hey, that's mine." Eric made a futile grab for the phone.

Dom easily slapped his hand away, turning the phone to show Bailey the screen. "He has ten pictures. All of you."

Bailey's stomach clenched as Dom scrolled through the images. Two of them had been taken when she was standing on her porch, a couple were when she was walking down the street, and some were of her standing in front of Pauline Hartford's house in Grange. Those had been zoomed in to reveal her pale face in intimate detail.

Bailey had no idea where Eric had been hidden to take the clandestine pictures, and right now she didn't care. The mere idea that he'd been sneaking around—spying on her—was enough to make her feel sick.

"Why?"

Eric turned back with a pleading expression. "It's not what you think. I'm not a creeper, I swear."

"Then why are you parked outside my house taking pictures of me?"

There was a tense silence, as if Eric was going to

refuse to answer. Then Dom leaned toward him with a grim expression.

"I wanted a new phone," Eric burst out, pressed against the driver's side door as Dom loomed next to him.

"A new phone?" Bailey shook her head. Was that some sort of slang? "What are you talking about?"

Eric scrubbed his fingers through his hair. "You know I don't make crap at the nursing home. And my mom says she'd not going to give me any more allowance unless I start doing more chores around the house." His features twisted into a petulant expression. "Like she does anything but sit on her ass. Why should I have to do everything?"

"What does any of this have to do with you stalking Bailey?" Dom broke into the shrill whining.

Eric huffed out a harsh breath. "How many times do I have to tell you? I wasn't stalking her."

Dom narrowed his eyes. "Answer the question."

Eric sniffed. "I'll answer, but not because you're threatening me." He glanced back at Bailey. "It was the day you were fired—"

"I wasn't fired," she instinctively denied, only to wrinkle her nose as she realized that her job status was the least of her worries. "Never mind. Go on."

"I left work at the usual time, but when I reached my car I found Ford Smithson waiting for me."

Bailey didn't recognize the name. "Who's that?"

"He's renting the old hunting lodge."

"Oh. Right." Bailey had seen the strange man in town over the past few months. He was a tall, thin man with a mop of dark curls that were rarely combed. He was usually wearing a long trench coat with a scarf wrapped around his neck no matter the temperature and a pair of reflective sunglasses. She assumed he was trying to look bohemian, but most people in Pike weren't impressed by his style. It didn't help that he was living outside of town in an empty building. The lodge hadn't been used for anything beyond an occasional party event for years. "He's an artist or something, right?"

"Yep," Eric agreed.

"Why was he waiting for you?"

Eric glanced toward Dom's hand. "He wanted to show me that brand-new phone. I watched as he pulled it fresh out of the box." His tone lowered, as if he was discussing a rare book or a priceless gem. "It was released less than a month ago and no one around here has it yet."

Bailey sent a worried glance toward Dom. If someone wanted to manipulate the naïve young man, a new piece of technology would be the perfect bait.

"Why would he have a phone for you?"

Eric hunched his shoulders, almost as if expecting a blow. "He said that he was working on a new painting."

"And?"

"And he needed a muse."

Bailey stared at him in disbelief. Was this a nasty joke? Muses were beautiful, exotic women who captured the imagination or inspired lust. She was grindingly normal. The girl next door with a heart of gold . . . in other words, boring. With a capital B. She wasn't feeling sorry for herself. It was the truth.

"And you thought I should be the muse?" she demanded in accusing tones.

"No, no. Not me. It was Ford who decided he wanted you."

Bailey stepped away from the car, thoroughly unnerved. "You didn't think it was creepy that some stranger wanted you to take pictures of me?"

Eric flinched at her harsh tone. "He explained that he never asked models to sit for him because they were stiff and unnatural. He wanted . . ." Eric waved his hands as he struggled to recall what he'd been told. "What did he call them? Candid. Yes, that's it. Candid shots that showed the real person."

Bailey stared at him in disbelief. "If it was so innocent, why didn't he take the pictures himself?"

"Because he'd heard that I. . ." Eric halted, clearing his throat as if he almost revealed more than he wanted to. "He'd heard that we were friends and he assumed I could get closer to you without you knowing what I was doing."

Bailey didn't believe the excuse for a second, but she wasn't going to argue. "And it didn't occur to you that I might not want to have my picture taken? Or to be the muse for some weirdo artist?"

Eric scrunched his face, sending her a wounded glare. "I didn't think it would hurt anyone. And I intended to keep an eye on you anyway. Just in case Gage tried to bother you. It seemed like fate." With an unexpected speed, Eric swiveled to snatch the phone from Dom's hand. "And I really wanted this phone."

Dom shrugged. "I already deleted the pictures."

Eric scowled. "Hey. I needed those."

Dom leaned close enough to force Eric to squeeze tight into his worn seat. "If I see you near Bailey again, those missing pictures will be the least of your worries. Got it?"

"He's not going to bother me, are you, Eric?" There was an edge of warning in her tone.

Eric scowled. "Who is this guy?"

"A friend."

"A friend who is ready and willing to protect her from anyone who I think is a threat," Dom growled. "Got it?"

"Bailey," Eric whined.

Bailey shook her head. "Please don't come back, Eric. And no more pictures."

"You know I'll do anything for you," Eric insisted. "Anything."

"Just go."

Eric waited for Dom to crawl out and slam the passenger door, then squealed away. Bailey watched him turn at the nearest corner and disappear.

"His interest in you isn't healthy," Dom said as he moved to stand next to her. "He's at the top of the list of suspects."

"He's a little odd," she agreed.

"There's nothing wrong with odd. Or being socially awkward. Some of my best friends are both," he said, his hands planted on his hips as if deciding the level of threat posed by the younger man. "But none of them would sneak around taking pictures of women without their permission. That goes beyond eccentric."

"Okay, he's more than odd," Bailey agreed. It pained her to admit that her trust in Eric had been misplaced. "But I'm more worried about the strange artist who wanted the pictures in the first place."

"Yeah, assuming Eric wasn't making up a story to cover his ass, I think we should have a chat with the mysterious Ford Smithson." Dom's brows abruptly snapped together. "But first it looks like you have company."

Bailey turned her head to watch the brown SUV with a sheriff's star painted on the side pull into her driveway, her brief moment of relief that Eric was gone quickly replaced with dread.

"I have a feeling this isn't good news."

Chapter 8

Dom watched as Zac Evans climbed out of his vehicle. He was wearing his sheriff's uniform, and even at a distance he could make out the lawman's grim expression. Bailey was right. This wasn't a social visit.

Scurrying across the street, Bailey halted directly in front of her cousin. "What's going on?"

Zac cast a quick glance toward Dom before returning his attention to Bailey. "I wanted to check on you."

"Why?"

"Can we go inside?"

"Sure."

Bailey turned to lead her guest into her house and Dom silently followed them, his gaze locked on Zac's rigid posture. He didn't know what had happened, but he was certain they weren't going to like it.

Entering the living room, Bailey waved a hand toward the sofa. She waited for Zac to take a seat, her expression wary, as if she was preparing for a blow.

"Can I get you some coffee?"

Zac grimaced. "Yeah, I'm going to need it."

Bailey hesitated, obviously torn between finding out

what Zac was doing there and wanting to put off the bad news. In the end she reluctantly turned to head into the kitchen, leaving the two men alone.

Zac barely waited for her to disappear before he was staring at Dom with blatant suspicion. "What are you doing here?"

"I brought doughnuts." Dom strolled to grab the cardboard box from the table next to the front door, then, flipping open the lid, he crossed to stand in front of the lawman. "Want one?"

Zac leaned forward to gaze at the assortment of pastries, muttering a curse as he pulled out a glazed doughnut.

"Don't tell my wife," he pleaded. "She's pregnant and on a health-food kick. I haven't had real sugar in weeks."

"Harsh," Dom murmured.

"You have no idea." Zac took a large bite, groaning in sugary bliss. "God, that's good." Two more bites and the doughnut was gone. Casting a regretful glance at the apple bear claw, Zac settled back in the cushions of the couch and studied Dom. "Now tell me why you're really here."

Dom set the box on the coffee table, meeting Zac's steady gaze. "I liked Bailey when I was in Pike for Kaden's wedding," he admitted. "And honestly, I couldn't get her out of my mind. There's something about her . . ." He struggled to put his attraction toward Bailey into words. Nothing truly captured her essence.

"Decency?" Zac offered.

"There's that," Dom agreed, "but it's much more. She captivated me from the moment we first spoke. I wanted to see if it could be something more than a temporary attraction."

Zac narrowed his eyes. "She's special to me."

Dom wasn't offended by the warning. "I'm discovering that she's special to a lot of people."

"True."

Before Dom could assure Zac that he had no intention of hurting Bailey, she reappeared from the kitchen.

"Here you go." She handed Zac a mug of coffee before she perched on the couch next to him. "What's happened?"

Zac took a sip before he answered the question. "Gage Warren was found dead this morning at the lumberyard."

There was a stunned silence as both Dom and Bailey tried to process the abrupt announcement.

"Dead?" Bailey shook her head as if trying to clear it. "You're sure?"

"Very sure."

"What happened?"

"It looks like he was reaching for a box of shingles he had stored on a top shelf and accidentally fell off his ladder," Zac said. "His skull was cracked by the impact."

Bailey pressed a hand to her mouth. "Oh my God."

Dom was less concerned with Gage's unexpected death than the manner it had happened.

"You said it *looked like* he fell off his ladder. Is there a question about what happened?"

"We'll do an autopsy." Zac had on his cop face. "It's possible he had a heart attack that caused him to fall. Or he might have been drunk."

"Or he might have been pushed," Dom suggested.

Bailey gasped, but Zac merely nodded. He'd obviously had the same thought.

"Hopefully, the autopsy will give us some answers."

"When did he die?" Bailey asked, her face pale as she clenched her hands together in her lap.

"He was found last night just after midnight by Anthony."

"Who's Anthony?" Dom demanded. Wasn't there a theory that the person who found a dead body was often the murderer?

"He's one of my deputies," Zac explained. "He was on patrol last night when he drove by and noticed that the lights were on at the lumberyard and the front door was wide open. He wanted to make sure nothing was wrong. When he went inside he found Gage on the floor with the ladder next to him."

So, not the killer then, Dom silently acknowledged. A shame.

"Did the deputy have any idea how long Gage was dead?"

"No, but we have a witness who saw Gage alive at five o'clock."

"In between five and midnight. That's a fairly small time frame." Dom tried to think like a detective. It wasn't the first time. Owning a pawnshop was more than determining the worth of an item, although that was obviously an important part of the job. He also needed background information on the customer to certify that the item hadn't been stolen, and that it had the proper paperwork to prove it was authentic. A signet ring that had a trail of official documentation to prove it belonged to George Washington was worth a lot more than a ring that was found in an attic with a story from an aging grandma that it'd once belonged to a president. "Is there a security camera?"

Zac made a sound of disgust. "Gage was too cheap to install any sort of security. He expected my deputies to be his personal guards. He was constantly calling to complain that we weren't doing enough to protect his property."

"Then there's no way to know if he was alone." Dom shoved his hands in the pockets of his jeans. Why couldn't anything be easy? Like a crystal-clear video of the killer committing the crime?

Zac shrugged. "We'll check any security footage in the area, but it's doubtful they'll have anything useful."

Bailey wrapped her arms around her waist, as if she was battling back a cold chill.

"I'm sorry that Gage is dead. No matter what ugly accusations he made about me, it's tragic that he died so young," she said, eyeing her cousin with a wary gaze. "But I'm not sure why you came to tell me."

Zac shifted on the couch, as if prepping himself to share bad news. "We searched his office at the lumber-yard to make sure nothing was missing or out of place."

"Was something wrong?" Bailey demanded.

"His secretary couldn't see anything unusual." Zac reached into the pocket of his jacket to pull out a clear baggie. He held it up to reveal the small black object inside. "Except for this."

Both Bailey and Dom leaned forward. The item was about the size of Dom's palm and looked like it was made from cheap plastic.

"Is that a phone?" Bailey asked.

Zac nodded. "A burner. It was found on a desk in Gage's office."

Bailey shook her head. "I still don't understand."

"Gage had a far more expensive phone in the pocket of his jeans when we found his body." He jiggled the baggie. "This appears to be an extra one."

"Is it for the lumberyard?" Dom demanded. He had separate numbers for his business and his personal life. Otherwise he'd never have any peace.

"No." Zac sent him a grim glance. "This phone didn't make or receive any calls. In fact, it didn't have any activity beyond sending one text a couple of days ago."

A troubling unease spread through Dom, drying his mouth as Bailey studied the phone in the baggie with a frown.

"Was it new?" she asked.

Zac pursed his lips. "I don't know yet. I'll have to do some research."

Dom wasn't interested in where the phone came from or when it'd been purchased. There was only one thing that mattered.

"What was the text?" he abruptly demanded.

"Yes." Zac nodded toward Dom, as if in approval of the question. Then he glanced back at his cousin. "It was sent to your number, Bailey. And it said . . ." Pausing, Zac once again reached into the pocket of his jacket, this time pulling out a small notebook. He read from the top page. "'The club is officially open. Ready or not.'"

Bailey sucked in an audible gasp. "Gage sent the message? Seriously?"

Dom was equally shocked. Hadn't they already decided Gage didn't possess the intellect to be the cyberstalker? Obviously they sucked at this detective thing.

"All I can say is that the phone was in his office," Zac said, implying he wasn't fully convinced about the origin of the phone or the text. "I'll have to check it for prints and try to trace where and when it was purchased. Do you know what the message means?"

Bailey sent Dom a quick glance before rising to her feet and hurrying into the kitchen. She returned with her phone, handing it over to Zac.

"There are more messages."

Bailey explained about the Murder Club as well as the direct messages she'd received, as Zac silently scrolled through the texts, reading them with a grim expression. Dom didn't have to point out that Bailey was obviously being stalked. Zac was well aware his cousin was in danger.

"The second time you were contacted was from a different number," Zac said, catching the same discrepancy that had troubled Dom.

"Yes," Bailey agreed.

"Maybe I should check Gage's house." Zac handed Bailey's phone back to her and rose to his feet. "Make sure he doesn't have another phone hidden away."

Bailey wrinkled her nose. "It just doesn't seem like him," she muttered. "He hated technology and now he's playing computer games and texting me from two different phones? I would bet good money he didn't know his number popped up when he sent a message."

"In my job I've discovered you really never know a

person," Zac warned. "It's possible he pretended to be incompetent to cover his tracks." Zac held up his hand as Bailey's lips parted to argue. "But I intend to keep an open mind. Not only about Gage's death but about whether or not this burner phone even belonged to him."

Dom clenched his teeth as Zac's words clicked inside his head. *Whether the burner phone even belongs to him . . .*

That was the answer, of course. Gage didn't write the messages. Whoever had pushed him off the ladder had left the phone on his desk. And Dom had no doubt why it was left there. It was a message to Bailey. The only question was whether it was a clue for her to follow. Or an attempt to connect her once again to a murder.

"Is there anything else I should know about?" Zac asked his cousin, his tone hard. He didn't need to be a genius to suspect that whoever was sending the text messages was playing a nasty game with Bailey.

She hesitated, as if she was reluctant to reveal the harassment she'd been enduring. Dom understood. She was the sort of person who was used to offering support and sympathy to others. It made her visibly uncomfortable to accept that she needed help. Clearing her throat, she reluctantly revealed the fact that she'd gone to Grange to discover what had happened to Pauline Hartford, along with her conversation with the neighbor who'd implied there'd been an argument between Pauline and her grandson shortly before her accident. Zac's expression hardened as Bailey continued with her story, revealing the pearls that had been found on her back porch and her suspicion that they had been left there by someone who wanted her to connect them to

Pauline's death. When Bailey at last fell silent, Zac rose to his feet, shoving the baggie with the phone into his jacket pocket.

"Why didn't you come to me?"

Bailey scowled at his sharp tone. "I was going to."

Zac sucked in a deep breath, as if trying to control his burst of temper at Bailey's reckless disregard for her own safety.

"Is that it?" he demanded.

"Yes," Bailey said.

"No," Dom intruded into the conversation.

She sent him a startled glance. Had she forgotten he was there? That was a humiliating thought. Then she wrinkled her nose as she realized why he'd said no.

"Oh, right."

Zac planted his fists on his hips. "Tell me."

"Eric Criswell was parked across the street this morning."

Zac looked confused. "I think I met him when I was driving here. Hard to miss that piece of crap he drives. Why was he here?"

"He was taking pictures of me."

Zac narrowed his eyes. "Repeat that."

"He claimed that Ford Smithson traded him a new phone in return for sending him my picture. It's supposedly for a new work of art or something."

"Dammit, I knew there was something odd about him," Zac growled.

"Which one?" Dom asked.

"Both. I'll deal with them." Zac reached out to grab Bailey's hand, his expression worried. "Bailey, you need to be careful."

"I am."

"I mean really, really careful," the lawman insisted. "I've been through this before and it feels like you're a target."

Bailey parted her lips as if she intended to offer a flippant retort, but seeing the blatant concern on her relative's face, she heaved a frustrated sigh.

"How can I be careful when I don't know who's doing this?"

"Come stay with me." The words left Dom's lips before he could consider the wisdom of his offer. Not that he was sorry. The thought of having Bailey living beneath the same roof as himself felt extraordinarily right. Probably because he'd already accepted that their future was meant to be together.

Bailey, on the other hand, looked shocked by the mere suggestion. "What?"

"Kaden and Lia's house has top-of-the-line security, plus it's remote enough to keep away any casual visitors," he said in light tones, as if living together was no big deal. "Not to mention the fact that four dogs under one roof are better than two."

"He's not wrong," Zac surprisingly added.

"There are a dozen bedrooms to choose from," Dom continued. He wasn't trying to force Bailey into staying with him, but it was unbearable to consider her alone in this house when there was some crazed stalker roaming the streets of Pike. "You'll have all the privacy you want, I promise."

Zac moved to grasp Bailey's shoulders, gazing down at her with a somber expression.

"It would ease my mind."

She heaved a resigned sigh, accepting it was the best solution for everyone.

"Okay. I'll pack a bag."

Pulling away from her cousin, Bailey turned to disappear into the narrow hallway that led to the back of the house.

Zac turned to stab Dom with a warning glare. "Take care of her."

Dom didn't hesitate. "It will be my greatest honor."

Chapter 9

Bailey sat next to Dom in the Land Rover as they pulled away from her house. Any other time she would have admired the sleek elegance of the expensive vehicle. She wasn't a person who cared about designer clothes or fancy jewelry, but she did appreciate the soft-as-butter leather seats and the dashboard that looked like it belonged in a spaceship. This morning, however, she was too distracted to do more than sigh as she sank into the seat and allowed Dom to drive them out of town.

"Are you okay?" he finally asked, breaking the thick silence.

Bailey glanced over her shoulder, making sure the dogs were snuggled on the blanket she'd tossed in the back seat. Both of them were used to riding in her truck, but they'd never been in a strange car. Thankfully, they had curled up and promptly fallen asleep.

They were obviously adjusting to the rapid changes in their world a lot better than she was.

With a grimace she turned to sweep her gaze over the chiseled lines of Dom's profile. She hadn't allowed herself to consider the fact that she was going to be alone with this man. She had enough on her mind without adding in a fear that proximity might prove that she was as boringly ordinary as she'd tried to warn him.

"Right now I'm just . . ." She shook her head as the trite words dried on her lips. "I'd say I'm trying to process what's happened over the past couple of days, but I have no idea what actually *did* happen," she confessed, shivering as she forced herself to consider the questions that still gnawed at her tired brain. "Nellie Warren might or might not have been murdered. Pauline Hartford might or might not have been murdered. And now Gage Warren might or might not have been murdered. I feel like I'm trapped in a hideous nightmare with no idea how I got there."

Dom's fingers tightened on the steering wheel as if he was struggling to control a strong emotion.

"What we know for sure is that you've been connected to each death," he said in dark tones. "First from you working at the nursing home and then by the texts from the mysterious stalker."

Bailey flinched, but she didn't try to deny the truth of his words. There *was* someone out there forcing her to become involved in the deaths.

"I can't believe Gage was the one sending them," she muttered.

"Probably because he wasn't."

"I agree." Bailey nodded. As soon as Zac told her about Gage's death, she'd suspected that it was more than an accident. Which meant that the phone had to have been planted there by the killer.

"If Gage was murdered, why leave behind the burner phone?"

Dom slowed as he reached the graveled road. Or the road that had once been graveled. The heavy trucks that had brought supplies to build Kaden and Lia's new house had churned the rock into mud, leaving behind a goopy mess that had dried into solid ruts.

"My first guess is that the phone was left to prove to you that Gage's death wasn't an accident. Just like the pearls being planted on your back porch proved Pauline Hartford's death wasn't an accident." He shrugged, keeping his gaze locked on the narrow pathway as he tried to avoid the worst of the potholes. "Plus, each clue had the benefit of tying you to both crimes."

Bailey heaved a frustrated sigh. She understood that Dom was trying to help, but his words weren't answering her questions. Why was the mystery person sending her texts? Was she supposed to be investigating the suspicious deaths? Or were they hoping to implicate her in the crimes as some sort of revenge for refusing the numerous invites?

But that would mean that the person texting her wasn't just interested in the deaths, but actually . . .

"Oh my God," she breathed.

Dom flashed her a worried glance. "Bailey?"

"I thought it was a game."

"You thought what was a game?"

"The Murder Club. None of it felt real. I mean, I knew logically that we were discussing the evidence of a person who'd died. And even when I hoped we might expose the person guilty for committing murder, it was more like winning a challenge than revealing a coldhearted killer."

"It's human nature to enjoy a mystery," Dom tried to reassure her. "There are entire networks devoted to true crime."

Bailey pressed her hand against her stomach. She felt nauseous. She didn't know if it was from the anger that suddenly churned in her gut or sheer fear. Probably a toxic combination of both.

"It might be human nature, but when I started getting the strange messages I should have realized the person was dangerous," she muttered. "Instead, I treated them like they were just another annoying jerk who couldn't let a woman be on the Internet without harassing her." She clenched her teeth, her gaze locked on Dom's profile as she considered the possibility that the deaths had been carefully planned and executed by a lunatic. A lunatic who was obsessed with her. "But that's not what this is, is it?" she spoke her fears out loud. "Whoever sent those texts isn't trying to solve the murders, are they?"

"No."

"They killed Nellie and Pauline and Gage."

Dom's knuckles turned white as he clutched the steering wheel, revealing he'd already come to the same conclusion.

"It seems possible."

Bailey muttered a curse. A part of her wondered why she'd been so blind, while another part realized that she was more resigned than shocked to accept she was being stalked by a killer. As if she'd sensed there was something ominous about the strange messages from the very beginning, but her mind had refused to believe it was possible. After all, how many times could lightning strike in the same spot?

"How could this be happening again? Is Pike cursed?"

"I don't believe in curses," he said with a certainty that eased her apprehension that bad things were fated to happen in Pike. "But it's very likely that the history of this town would attract someone fascinated with death and violence."

Bailey shuddered. "That's a disturbing thought."

He shrugged. "If you're a sun lover, you go to the beach. If you love the snow, you hit the mountains."

"And if you love murder, you go to Pike?"

"Something like that."

His words made sense, as much as she hated to admit that her beloved town was forever stained with blood. And more importantly, if he was right, it would narrow down the possible list of suspects.

"Then we need to look at anyone new to Pike," she said.

He sent her a wry smile. "Or the history of murder in Pike might have inspired a current resident who isn't completely stable."

"Great." She rolled her eyes as he squashed her hope they could quickly track down whoever was committing the crimes. At the same time she pointed toward the dirt pathway that branched away from the main road. "Let's go that way."

Without hesitation he followed her direction, not even grimacing when the expensive vehicle swayed and rattled over the bumpy track.

"Do you have a particular destination in mind?" he asked.

"The old hunting lodge is a couple of miles from here," she told him.

He sent her a startled glance. "That's where Ford Smithson is staying, right?"

"Yes. I want some answers."

He paused, as if choosing his words with care. "Me too, but are you sure we shouldn't wait for Zac? He's the professional, after all."

"I can't just sit around waiting for the next horrible thing to happen. I need to feel like I'm doing something."

"Yeah, I get that, but—"

"Turn here," Bailey interrupted his protest. She wasn't in the mood to be sensible. She was in the mood to pretend she had some control over her spiraling life. "This path will take us to the back side of the lodge."

Dom obediently took a sharp right onto the road that had overgrown with weeds to the point it was barely distinguishable, but his jaw was clenched with frustration. He might have accepted there was no talking her out of her reckless plan, but he didn't like it.

They drove the remaining few miles in silence, the SUV slowing to a mere crawl as they approached the two-storied log building with massive windows and a patio that wrapped completely around the structure.

Pulling to a halt in the thick line of pine trees that framed one side of the empty parking lot, Dom switched off the engine and leaned forward to peer through the windshield.

"This is the place?" he demanded.

Bailey nodded, understanding his confusion. Even at

a distance it was easy to see that the heavy logs were weathered with age while the tin roof had long ago rusted. Even the heavy stone chimney was covered in moss.

"I haven't been out here in a long time," she admitted, unhooking her seat belt.

"I thought it was going to be a hotel."

"My grandmother told me that the original owner ran it as sort of a B-and-B for out-of-town hunters, but eventually he moved away and the new owners boarded up the upstairs and opened the ground floor as a place to rent for wedding receptions and charity events." Bailey was struck with a sudden memory. "We had our senior prom out here."

"Did you go?"

"Of course." A reminiscent smile curved her lips. Her gaze moved to the patio where she had stood along with her classmates to have a thousand pictures taken by the gathered crowd of parents. "My grandmother made me the most beautiful gown and my date was my high school crush." Her smile widened. She'd been so giddy with excitement she hadn't been able to sleep for a week. "It was supposed to be the perfect night."

Dom unhooked his seat belt and swiveled to face her. "Not so perfect?"

"Nope." Her tone was light, although at the time she'd been furious. More at herself for allowing the prom to become the most important event of her young life than the boy who'd disappointed her. Honestly, nothing could have lived up to her expectations. "I was dancing with a bunch of my friends when I realized that my date had slipped out the back to drink from a keg the boys had hidden in the woods. He passed out halfway through the dance and I had to call my grandmother to pick me up. I couldn't look at Billy again without thinking about him in his fancy tux with his face in the mud."

He chuckled. "The destruction of young love."

"Exactly," she said, not adding that it had also been an important lesson in judging the worth of a man by how he treated others rather than his shallow popularity. It was a rite of passage for most teenagers. "The only good thing was that Zac had already left Pike to go to college. He would not have been happy."

"I can imagine," Dom murmured.

Bailey returned her attention to the building that appeared tired and depressed despite the morning sunlight.

"This place has definitely gone downhill since my high school days. Why would anyone want to stay here?"

"Let's find out."

Dom exited the Land Rover and waited for her to join him. Then, walking along the edge of the decaying parking lot to stay in the shadows of the trees, they made their way around the lodge and climbed onto the front porch. The boards creaked beneath their feet, but the wood was solid. The lodge might be shabby, but it was still sturdy. It had been built when things were meant to last.

Dom crossed the porch, rapping his knuckles against one of the double doors. A minute later it was pulled open to reveal a man with messy black curls and a pale, thin face. He was wearing a pair of silk pajama pants and nothing else.

Had he been sleeping? Certainly he didn't look pleased to see them. "Yes?"

"Ford Smithson?" Dom asked.

"Yes."

"I'm Dom Lucier."

Ford's features tightened, revealing faint wrinkles that fanned out from his green eyes. Bailey found it impossible to guess the man's age. He could be anything from twenty-five to thirty-five.

"Okay." Ford glanced toward Bailey, pretending he didn't recognize her.

"I'm Bailey Evans," she forced herself to offer her name.

There was an awkward pause, as if Ford was waiting for them to reveal why they were bothering him. Then, with a less than subtle sigh, he stepped back and waved them inside.

"Please, come in."

Dom stepped through the entryway and Bailey was close behind him. Once inside, however, she halted in the middle of the cavernous space and glanced around in surprise.

Nothing had changed. The faded paneling still lined the walls, the floor was still bare wooden planks, and the staircase that led to the upper floors was still boarded closed. Overhead, the open beams were studded with a few bare light bulbs and a ceiling fan that moved the stale air. The only additions had been a stack of empty cavasses and tripods stacked in a corner and a couch that had been pulled out to provide a rumpled bed near the back wall.

"You live here?" she asked in surprise.

Ford strolled to grab a T-shirt from the bed and pulled it over his head. "It's not fancy, but it makes a perfect artist's studio." He shoved his fingers through his loose curls, exuding the confidence of a man who knew he was irresistible to most women. Not Bailey, of course. She preferred large, dependable men who didn't bother with foolish games. "The light in the afternoon pours through the windows. And the sunsets are magnificent. I've spent weeks trying to capture their beauty."

Bailey wasn't an artist, but she could understand Ford's obvious enthusiasm. The large windows would not only let in tons of natural light but they offered a stunning view of the rolling meadows in one direction and a swath of towering pine trees in the opposite direction.

"You're an artist," Dom murmured, casually strolling around the empty room.

"You don't sound impressed." Ford's lips twisted into a mocking smile. "I don't blame you. I tried several times to settle down and get a regular job. Unfortunately, the attempts ended up with everyone involved being miserable. I've at last accepted a life of being a nomad, without friends or roots."

Bailey watched Dom study the stack of canvases before moving toward the empty bookshelves built into the wall. Was he searching for something?

Stepping forward, Bailey deliberately placed herself in front of Ford, blocking his view.

"You have at least one friend," she said.

Ford arched a brow. "Do I?"

"I assume so." She forced herself to smile. "You gave Eric Criswell a new phone. It's a very generous gift if he isn't a friend."

Ford frowned, almost as if he was having difficulty

remembering the name Eric Creswell and why he would give him a phone.

"Oh. Right." Ford snapped his fingers. "The computer guy."

She allowed her smile to disappear. "He also told me that you asked him to take pictures of me."

"Of you?" Ford held up a hand. "Wait a minute. That's not what happened."

"Then what did happen?" she demanded, keeping him distracted to give Dom the opportunity to look around.

"A week or so ago I was having trouble with my laptop and someone suggested that I ask Eric Criswell to come over and get it straightened out." He glanced toward the computer that was precariously balanced on a pile of dirty laundry. "While he was here, he happened to notice the phone that had just come in the mail. It was a present from my parents." A sneer touched his lips. "A less-than-subtle dig that I don't stay in contact like they want me to. Anyway, Eric mentioned how much he wanted one."

"And you just gave him the phone?"

"Not then." Ford lifted his head to meet her suspicious gaze. "I was finishing up a series of landscapes when I decided I wanted my next painting to include a local person." He shrugged. "That's when I decided to offer the phone to Eric in return for taking a few candid shots around town. It must have been a couple of days ago."

"Of me?" Bailey demanded.

"Of anyone he thought might stir my muse."

"Anyone?" Bailey's self-righteous anger faltered. "You didn't ask Eric to specifically take pictures of me?"

Ford cleared his throat, suddenly looking uncomfortable. "I don't mean to be rude, but honestly, I have no idea who you are. I mean . . . I might have seen you around town, but I don't think we've ever spoken. And I certainly didn't know your name. Not until you showed up at my door this morning."

Bailey studied him, frustration bubbling inside her. His arms were folded over his chest, but he appeared thoroughly relaxed as he stood in front of her. Too relaxed? Bailey liked to think she was intuitive when it came to people, but she wasn't trained to read body language.

She knew someone was lying. Either Eric or this man. But how the hell was she supposed to know which one?

"I found Eric parked in front of my house taking pictures of me. He claimed you wanted them."

"Seriously?" The green eyes narrowed. "I swear, I would never have asked him to become a stalker. I just wanted a few candid shots. I'll tell him to stop."

"If you wanted pictures of people, why not take them yourself?" Bailey pressed, far from convinced this man was as innocent as he wanted her to believe.

"I had to finish the landscapes and have them delivered to a gallery in Minneapolis before the owner canceled my showing, I was running late as usual and I hoped to start the new project when I returned." He wrinkled his nose, looking ridiculously charming. "And to be honest, I wanted to do something for Eric. He seemed kind of pathetic and lost when he was here."

"You didn't think it was creepy to take pictures of people without their knowledge?"

"No." He glanced toward the empty canvases in the corner. "I'm an artist. The people in my paintings aren't individuals to me. They're a mixture of light and shadows that blend into the background." He glanced back at Bailey. "There would be no way anyone could be recognized in my paintings."

"Then why do you need a muse?"

He looked shocked by the question. "Every artist needs inspiration."

Without warning, Dom appeared next to Bailey, his arm resting over her shoulders with a comforting weight.

"Bailey is no one's muse," he growled, proving he'd been listening to their conversation.

Ford held up his hands, taking a step backward. "Hey, that's fine with me. I'll get my phone back from Eric and make sure he understands my request wasn't an invitation to spy on women. Is there anything else?"

Dom didn't look satisfied. "How long do you intend to stay in the area?"

"As long as my creative juices are flowing." Turning, Ford moved to the door and pulled it open. A less-than-subtle hint that the impromptu meeting was over. "Once they dry up I'll pack my things and move on."

Dom and Bailey exchanged a glance before they grudgingly headed out of the lodge. The door shut behind them—not a slam, but hard enough to rattle the windows.

"I don't trust him," Dom muttered as they climbed

off the porch and headed around the corner toward the parking lot.

"Do you trust anyone in Pike?"

"No."

"Neither do I." Bailey glanced up at the building that loomed over them with a decaying threat. She heaved a sigh. "It's awful."

They didn't speak again until they were back in the Land Rover, driving away from the secluded lodge.

"See if you can pull up any information on Ford Smithson," Dom abruptly requested.

Bailey dug into her purse and grabbed her phone, typing Ford's name into a search engine. Surprisingly, dozens of links popped up, along with various images of paintings that featured bleak landscapes and stormy skies.

"I think he must be famous," she murmured, pressing one of the links. "Here's the latest news article." She read it out loud. "'Ford Smithson is a modern American artist who rose to fame with his conceptual interpretation of the rural Midwest. Ford is a renowned recluse who has transformed postmodernism. His latest show will open at the Signs of the Times Art Gallery in Minneapolis on Halloween and run through the new year.'"

"Is there a picture?" Dom demanded.

Bailey scrolled through the various articles and biographies, finding nothing. She hopped over to social media, hoping for better luck.

"There are thousands of photos of his artwork but not of Ford," she muttered in frustration. "I can't find anything personal beyond the fact that he was born in Oregon, Illinois, in 1986."

"He's about the right age," Dom grudgingly conceded.

"And he mentioned traveling to Minneapolis."

"He still feels sketchy," Dom insisted. "It would be easy to pass yourself off as a reclusive artist who doesn't allow any public pictures."

"Plus, he's slick."

Dom sent her a baffled glance. "Slick?"

She shrugged. "You know . . .slick. Handsome and charming. And he had an answer for everything."

Dom's brows drew together. "You think he's handsome?"

She rolled her eyes as he missed her point. "What I mean is that if this was a movie, he would be my first suspect."

Dom snorted, returning his attention to the sorry excuse for a road. "If this was a movie, I would have found a clue while I was searching the room and solved the case."

"You didn't see anything out of the ordinary?"

He shrugged. "There was sawdust near the bookcases. I'm guessing that place is riddled with termites. But that's it. No hidden weapons or detailed plans of mayhem and murder."

She dropped her phone back into her purse. She didn't have the skills to do the sort of online snooping that would reveal if the man staying at the lodge was the true Ford Smithson.

"Hopefully, Zac will run a background check on him."

"I'm sure he will, but unfortunately, it might be a while before he gets around to it. I think Zac has his hands full."

"True." Bailey hadn't forgotten the strain etched on

her cousin's face. Not only had he been up all night investigating Gage's death but the rash of deaths was no doubt forcing him to recall the serial killer who had nearly taken his beloved wife. Bailey shuddered. "It's one horrible thing after another."

Dom's jaw tightened. "And they're all connected."

Bailey shuddered again. "To me."

"We're going to find out who's behind this, Bailey." Dom reached out to squeeze her fingers, his voice hard. "That much I promise."

Chapter 10

It was almost eight the next morning when Bailey strolled into the massive kitchen to discover Dom standing next to the stove. He was wearing a pair of jeans and a flannel shirt that was stretched tight over his broad shoulders. His golden hair was damp, as if he'd just stepped out of the shower, and Bailey shivered at the knowledge she'd no doubt been showering at the same time. The thought was obscenely erotic.

A flare of wry humor raced through her. She was obviously in a bad way. What would happen if they really did shower together? She'd probably self-combust.

Thankfully unaware that she was currently picturing him naked with hot water pouring over his hard muscles, Dom turned to send her a welcoming smile.

"Good morning. How did you sleep?"

"Like a log," she admitted, not sure if it'd been exhaustion that had allowed her to collapse into the bed in a spare bedroom and pass out or if it'd been the knowledge that for the first time in forever, she wasn't alone. More than likely it was a mixture of both. "I don't think I moved all night."

It was obvious by his smug smile that Dom assumed it was his presence that was responsible for her deep sleep.

"Good." He turned back to the stove. "I'm making us some breakfast."

Bailey wandered across the floor to lean against the counter. Close enough to catch the scent of the soap still clinging to his warm skin. Delicious.

"A man of many talents," she murmured.

"Not really. I can scramble a few eggs and put bread in a toaster. That's about the limit of my culinary skills."

She didn't tell him that she wasn't talking about his cooking. "Later today I'll run over to Grange and pick up a few things to make for dinner," she offered.

He cracked the eggs into the skillet that was sizzling with butter. "That's not necessary. Lia left the freezer loaded with food."

"I know, but I like to cook." She turned her head to glance out the window, not surprised to find the four dogs dashing around the enclosed yard. They were like giddy kids enjoying a sleepover with their bestie. "And it's not as if I have anything else on my agenda. At least not until I decide what to do with my future."

"You don't plan on returning to the nursing home?"

She turned back to discover him staring at her with an unreadable expression.

"That depends on what happens during my meeting."

"What meeting?"

"I had a voice mail from Logan Donaldson when I woke up this morning asking for me to come to the nursing home today at nine o'clock."

"Are you going?" His gaze slid over her casual

sweatshirt and jeans before lifting to take in the messy bun on top of her head.

"Yes." There was a hint of defiance in her voice. She hadn't bothered with makeup or fancy clothes because she didn't care what the Donaldsons thought about her. Not anymore. "I'm still technically an employee at the Pike Nursing Home. But more importantly, I have several questions I want answered."

He hesitated, as if he wanted to ask her not to go. Then, accepting she couldn't avoid the place forever, he squared his shoulders.

"I'll go with you."

It was the relief that flooded through her that warned Bailey she was treading dangerous waters. It was one thing to lust after this man. Who wouldn't? He was not only drop-dead sexy but he was genuinely kind and scrupulously honest. The sort of man a woman could lean on in times of trouble.

Bailey, however, had long ago decided that she was never going to depend on anyone.

"I'll be fine," she forced herself to say.

"Yes," he agreed, reaching out to cup her face in his hands. "Yes, you will."

She tried to ignore the pleasure tingling through her at his soft touch. "Dom, you came here to relax, not to be my personal bodyguard."

His thumb brushed her lower lips. "I did say I wanted to spend time with you, remember? The more time the better as far as I'm concerned."

His voice was low and husky with the same desire that burned inside her. Bailey lifted her hands, but she didn't push him away. Instead, she rested her palms against his chest and tilted back her head to meet his smoldering gaze. She'd spent years erecting her protective barriers, but they were no match for this man.

He was smashing through them with outrageous ease.

She heaved a wry sigh of defeat. "I still don't get it."

"Get what?"

"Why you would be interested in me." She pressed her fingers against his lips, refusing to let him speak. "I'm not begging for compliments, but I'm a realist. I am the typical small-town girl. There's nothing special about me."

He gazed down at her, waiting for her to remove her fingers, before he answered.

"Remy was a successful con artist because he was handsome and persuasive and people allowed themselves to be fooled by his image of respectability," he said, referring to his father. "They wanted to believe in his get-rich-quick schemes and his shallow seductions. Just as my mother wanted to believe his assurances that he was going to change. But his promises were empty."

Her hands smoothed over his broad chest, offering comfort for the past that would never fully heal.

"I'm sorry."

"Don't be. It was a painful lesson for anyone unfortunate enough to cross Remy's path, but his cruel games taught me to watch what people do, not what they say." He deliberately paused, gazing down at her. "And what you do is make this world a better place every day you're in it."

Her eyes widened, her heart forgetting to beat at his

outrageous claim. "That's . . ." She was too flustered to speak.

His hands skimmed down the curve of her neck, his dark gaze focused on her with an intensity that sent chills shivering through her.

"You genuinely care about your friends and neighbors and the residents at the nursing home." He chuckled. "Lia calls you 'her bundle of sunshine.' What could be more special than bringing happiness to others?"

His words touched her more deeply than she wanted to admit. What woman didn't want to be a bundle of sunshine?

"I could be rich and beautiful and sexy," she tried to tease.

"You've got beautiful and sexy covered," Dom growled. "And if you were interested in money, you wouldn't have become a nurse."

"I'm not beautiful," Bailey protested, a flush staining her face. Compliments always made her feel awkward.

"It's all in the eye of the beholder," he insisted. "And to me, you are exquisite."

Bailey curled her fingers into his flannel shirt as the world seemed to tilt beneath her feet. There was a stark sincerity in his voice that assured her that he wasn't mouthing words he thought she wanted to hear. He truly thought she was beautiful.

"It's still a mystery," she breathed. "But at least it's a nice mystery."

As if sensing she'd accepted there was no fighting against the desire smoldering between them, Dom released a low growl of anticipation.

"I think we can do better than nice."

Still holding her gaze, he plunged his fingers into the damp strands of her hair and lowered his head. He skated his lips over hers. The kiss was a soft promise, like the brush of a butterfly's wing, but it created pure chaos as her heart thundered and her stomach clenched with sweet anticipation. He stroked his lips back and forth, the delicate friction setting off tingles of erotic pleasure.

Bailey wrapped her arms around his neck, arching her back to press against his large body. Her breath caught in her throat. His muscles were rock hard, offering a direct contrast to her feminine curves. Yin and yang fitting together with amazing perfection.

Lost in the dazzling pleasure that swirled through her, Bailey wanted to forget the troubles that plagued her. Just for a few minutes she wanted to be young and carefree, with nothing on her mind but the shattering pleasure of Dom's kisses.

Unfortunately, the world had no intention of cooperating.

Even as her lips parted to invite the sweep of his tongue, she caught the acrid scent of smoke. Pulling back, she blinked in confusion.

"Something's burning."

"Me," he rasped, his fingers gliding up her back. "I'm on fire for you . . ." Belatedly realizing she wasn't talking about the heat smoldering between them, he turned to shove the smoking skillet off the stove and into the sink. "Hell," he muttered. "Looks like the scrambled eggs are off the menu." His gaze moved to the toaster, where the bread had long ago finished cooking. "Along with the cold toast."

"No problem," she assured him. "We can run by the diner before we go to the nursing home."

"Good plan."

She stepped back, her gaze moving toward the glass sliding doors that led to the backyard. Her lips twisted into a wry smile at the sight of four furry faces pressed against the glass.

"But first we have a pack of very hungry dogs who are desperate for our attention."

"Not nearly as desperate as I am," he murmured, brushing a kiss over her forehead. "Later."

Bailey desperately hoped it wasn't too much later. Now that she'd accepted that a relationship with Dom Lucier was inevitable, she was anxious to lose herself in his sensual spell.

The sooner, the better.

Nearly two hours later, Bailey was using the side door to enter the nursing home. Dom was reluctantly waiting for her in the parking lot after losing the battle to join her inside. She'd pointed out that there was no way anyone would hurt her in front of a full staff and fifty residents. It was far more likely a stalker would be waiting in the shadows, maybe hoping to sabotage the SUV while they were inside.

Now she moved through the kitchen and laundry rooms that were empty this time of day before slipping into Logan's office. As she'd hoped, she was early enough that he wasn't there yet. Logan Donaldson took full advantage of the fact he was Lorene's only child. Pure nepotism meant he could come and go as he pleased. She'd rarely seen him there before nine o'clock.

If she was there waiting for him when he eventually

strolled in, she would have the advantage. Or at least that was her hope.

Crossing the soft cream carpet that contrasted with the dark paneled walls and heavy wooden furniture, she was about to take a seat near the glossy desk when she caught the sound of voices.

"What do you mean you invited that woman to come to the nursing home?" Lorene was demanding in a shrill tone.

"Exactly what I said."

That was Logan's voice, Bailey realized with a stab of surprise. Obviously he could pull himself out of bed when he wanted. Tiptoeing forward, Bailey pressed herself against the wall next to the door that connected the two main offices. It was open less than an inch, but she could easily hear the conversation.

Bailey smiled, not at all bothered by the fact that she was eavesdropping. The Donaldsons had lied and manipulated her to save their own asses. They didn't deserve the good manners her grandmother had instilled in her.

"I told you to let me deal with her," Lorene was insisting.

"I did let you deal with her. And what happened? You kicked her out of here and exposed us to legal retaliation," Logan retorted in sharp tones.

Bailey clenched her hands. They were discussing her. Unless they'd suspended someone else.

"She wasn't kicked out," Lorene protested. "I quite reasonably requested that she take time off until Gage Warren had calmed down and stopped accusing her of murder."

"You put her on leave with no pay."

"I'm not going to spend money on someone who's not working. She should be happy that I didn't fire her on the spot."

Bailey rolled her eyes. Lorene Donaldson was nothing if not predictable.

"Mother, this isn't the good old days when you could treat employees like your personal servants and fire them without due cause. Especially in front of a lawyer. What if Ward Bennett had urged Bailey to sue us for wrongful dismissal?"

Lorene snorted. "That girl isn't suing anyone. She doesn't have the backbone."

"It's not just the worry she might demand money that made me invite her here this morning," Logan admitted. "I'm sick and tired of listening to the complaints from the residents. Christ, you'd think we'd murdered a baby when they learned Bailey was suspended."

Despite the nerves that were causing her pulse to race and her mouth to feel weirdly dry, Bailey felt a smile curve her lips. It was nice to know that the residents missed her. She considered them her family.

"They'll get used to the new nurse."

"Are you kidding? They hate her," Logan groused. "And so do I. She refuses to work weekends, she demands double pay if she's on call, and last night she informed me that scheduling the staff wasn't in her job description. Not to mention the fact that she refuses to help handing out the breakfast trays. She told me that if I wanted it done, I could do it myself. Me."

"Fine, we'll find someone else."

"In Pike?" Logan made a sound of disgust. "Do you think that qualified nurses grow on trees?"

"There are always staffing problems. You know that, Logan."

"Well they're a pain in the ass," he snapped. "And honestly, I'm not in the mood to deal with it. In fact, I'm not in the mood to be in this shithole at all. If I had a damned dollar to my name, I'd be out of here."

"And who's fault is it you don't have any money?" Lorene shot back. "I never dreamed you could be so stupid."

There was a sharp silence, as if Logan was blindsided by the attack.

"Oh yeah? You want to know whose fault it is?" Logan at last managed to find his voice. "It's yours."

"Mine? All I've done is try to protect you."

"No, what you did was steal my legacy," Logan accused in harsh tones. "If you hadn't abandoned my father, I would be living a life of luxury. Instead, I'm wasting my life in this crappy town, running a crappy nursing home."

Bailey felt a pang of shock. She'd thought Logan's father was dead. A car accident or something.

"Your legacy? I have always hoped this nursing home would be your legacy. Especially now that we're on the brink of expanding the business," Lorene informed her son with a loud sniff. "Unfortunately, your recent behavior suggests you have no respect for what I've created."

"I'm happy to walk away," Logan snarled.

Bailey froze at the sound of footsteps approaching the connecting door. Crap. There was nowhere to hide.

And even if she ran full speed, she wouldn't be able to reach—

"Wait, Logan." Bailey's frantic thoughts were interrupted as Lorene called out, a startling edge of pleading in her voice. "You know I need you here. I can't manage the home without you."

The footsteps stopped. Thank God.

"Then stop nagging me," Logan commanded. "And for God's sake, stop fighting my decision to bring back Bailey Evans. She's the only decent staff member we have."

Bailey inched her way down the wall, back to the door that would lead to the corridor. Damn. That was too close for comfort.

"Having her back isn't without risk, you know," Lorene said, the words oddly clipped. As if she was afraid Logan would be pissed. "She might start asking uncomfortable questions."

Bailey frowned as she continued to inch her way out of the office. What questions? The fact that Gage Warren was stealing from his mother and they'd tried to hide the truth? The cover-up had certainly come back to bite them when Gage accused her of manipulating and then potentially killing his mother. Or was it something else? Some nefarious business dealing? Some creative accounting? Logan was certainly capable of Medicare fraud.

"Why would she?" Logan demanded. "Unless you give her a reason to suspect that something is wrong."

"I have always done my part. No matter what the cost to myself."

Logan made a sound of disgust at his mother's bitter retort. "God save me from martyrs," he rasped. "It's almost nine o'clock. Bailey should be here any minute."

Bailey darted into the corridor just as the door to Lorene's office was pulled open to reveal Logan in a pair of black slacks and an expensive cashmere sweater. His fake tan was darker than usual, contrasting against his blindingly white smile. Just the sight of him made her flesh crawl.

"Ah, Bailey." He motioned her forward. "Right on time."

Bailey walked past him to enter Lorene's office, her back stiff. "I've never been late to work." She flashed a humorless smile. "Unlike some people."

As usual, Logan allowed the insult to bounce off his thick skin. If anything, his smile widened.

"True. You've always been a model employee. I can only wish that the rest of our staff was as dependable as you." He led her across the room to where a chair had been arranged next to the large desk where Lorene was seated, glaring at her with blatant disapproval. As if Bailey was the one who'd demanded this meeting. "Please have a seat," Logan murmured.

"No, thanks." Bailey halted in the middle of the room, her head tilted to a defiant angle. "I prefer to stand."

"Don't be rude, Bailey," Lorene chided.

"Mother, let me handle this." Logan's gaze never wavered from Bailey's face. "I understand that you are unhappy with the situation."

She narrowed her eyes. "I'm not unhappy. I'm pissed."

"Language, young lady," Lorene sputtered in outrage.

"Mother," Logan snapped before deliberately softening his sharp tone as he tried to soothe Bailey with his slimy charm. "Of course you're pissed. It's been an unfortunate incident for all of us."

"For all of us?" Bailey shook her head in disbelief. "You weren't the one who was falsely accused of stealing money from an elderly resident in your care and being a potential murderer. If you were a decent employer, you would have had my back."

Logan's smile never faltered. "I'm sorry you feel that way, Bailey, but in all good conscience we had to investigate the claims."

If Dorinda hadn't revealed Nellie's confession about catching Gage stealing from her and the fact that she'd told Logan what had happened, she might have swallowed his lies. They were said with such sympathy.

"No, you didn't."

He flinched at her cold rebuff. He'd expected her to back down. Like she had so many times before.

"Excuse me?"

She took a step toward Logan. "You didn't have to investigate the claims because you already knew I was innocent, didn't you?"

The smile faltered as the dark gaze darted toward the silent woman behind the desk. Logan could act like he was in charge, but in the end it would always be Lorene who was the driving force of the duo.

"Well, of course we believed in your innocence, didn't we, Mother?"

Lorene pinched her lips, as if she'd caught a bad smell. "Certainly."

Bailey released a sharp laugh. "You didn't have to

believe in me. You had proof that Nellie confessed that she'd caught Gage stealing from her." She stabbed a finger toward Logan. "You, in turn, begged her not to call the sheriff, so she felt she had no choice but to change her will to punish her son."

A nerve twitched beside Logan's eye, but he waved his hand in a gesture he probably assumed was calming. All it did was make her want to kick him.

"As I said, it was never about your innocence, but Gage was creating such a fuss. What else could we do?"

"You told me you were investigating his claims when you knew they were false," Bailey growled. "You let people in this town think it was possible I had conned an old woman out of her money."

Logan shook his head. "We did what was right for the nursing home. As well as you."

"For me?" Bailey made a sound of disbelief. "What would have been right for me is you admitting that Gage had been stealing from his mother and that was why she'd changed her will."

"Okay, okay." Logan reached up to smooth his thinning strands of hair. "In retrospect I can see it was a mistake. At the time I was worried about a scandal. You know how people in this town can talk. It's vital that our residents and their families are confident they will be looked after with all the care and consideration we can offer."

"And now that Gage is dead you assume that the scandal will be forgotten?"

In the blink of an eye, Logan had conjured an expression of grief. "Poor Gage. Such a tragic loss. First Nellie and then her son."

Had Logan taken acting lessons or was he a natural? Bailey wasn't fooled for a second. "But his death is why I'm here, isn't it?"

Logan pressed a hand to the center of his chest. "I'm wounded you would think that, Bailey. I asked you to come here today because we've missed you. And more importantly, the residents have missed you. There's not a day that goes by that one of them isn't asking when you'll return, isn't that right, Mother?"

Lorene pinched her lips tighter, refusing to admit she might need Bailey.

Bailey shrugged. "And what do you tell the residents?"

Logan's phony smile made a return. "I assured them that Nurse Evans will be back soon where she belongs."

Bailey scowled. "You shouldn't say that."

"Why not? It's time to put this unfortunate incident behind us."

"Being accused of murder isn't an *unfortunate incident*. And I'm not about to forget how easily I was thrown under the bus after dedicating myself to this place for nearly a decade." She tilted her chin an inch higher. "And honestly, I haven't decided if I'll be back at all."

Silence greeted her warning. A heavy silence that pulsed with disbelief. The Donaldsons' obviously expected her to leap at the opportunity to return to her old job even after they'd treated her like trash.

"Is this about money?" Logan abruptly demanded. "Do you expect a raise?"

"Absolutely not," Lorene protested.

Bailey sent the older woman a cold smile. "I will

certainly expect a raise if I return, but that won't be the deciding factor."

"What do you want?" Logan demanded.

Bailey turned toward the door. She didn't know what she'd expected to happen. Embarrassment at being caught outright lying to her? Guilt for allowing Gage to harass her with ugly accusations? Admitting they'd been wrong to suspend her? Whatever she'd hoped for, it was obvious she was never going to get it. Not from the Donaldsons.

"What I want is respect." She paused at the door to give the two one last glare. She was never going to work for either of them again. "Something you'd never understand."

Chapter 11

Dom ignored the icy breeze as he leaned against the side of the Land Rover and waited for Bailey to return. Logically, he knew that she wasn't in physical danger. Not that something bad couldn't happen, but it was extremely unlikely in such a public setting in the middle of the day. But he was worried about her emotional well-being.

He'd seen the devastation in her eyes when she feared that people might believe she'd coerced an old woman into handing over her money. And the shame of being suspended from the job she loved. He very much wanted to have a word with the Donaldsons.

Only the fact that she'd specifically requested to speak with them alone kept him where he was. This was her fight. And the only way to purge her anger was to confront them face-to-face.

Thankfully, his nerves weren't tested beyond the limit of endurance. Less than a half hour after they'd pulled into the parking lot, Bailey was storming out the front door, her face flushed with an intense emotion.

He was guessing it was anger.

Shoving himself away from the SUV, he reached out to grasp her hand. Her skin was chilly despite the fact that she'd been inside.

"Is everything okay?" he demanded, then he grimaced. "Sorry, I'm asking that a lot."

"I'm fine." Her voice was low, as if she was struggling to keep it steady. "And really, I think I needed that meeting. It opened my eyes."

He studied her upturned face, trying to judge whether she was fine or not. "Is that a good thing?"

"Hopefully. If nothing else, it forced me to realize that I've accepted being used and taken for granted for the sake of comfort."

"I assume you're talking about the Donaldsons?"

She nodded. "I love the residents, I truly do, but I've stayed here because I was too scared to take the risk of trying something new."

"A new job?"

"A new anything." She ground out the words, as if her anger wasn't just directed toward the Donaldsons. She was mad at herself. "A new job. A new house. A new life. Being in a rut was better than exposing myself to disappointment." She paused, her gaze unfocused, as if she was trapped in her inner thoughts. "Or loss."

He lifted her hand to press it against his lips. It was understandable that she'd been eager to create a sense of stability. She'd lost her mother when she was a young child and her father had all but abandoned her. Then her grandmother died. A part of her would always be expecting her loved ones to disappear from her life.

"I get that," he assured her.

"Do you?" She arched her brows in disbelief. "You're not scared of anything."

"Ah." He released a sharp laugh even as he allowed his gaze to skim around the parking lot in search of a stalker. Since realizing that Bailey was in danger, he'd been plagued by a fear that she would be hurt. The unease buzzed through him like an electric current, scraping his nerves raw. "If only that was true."

"You traveled to America when you were sixteen," Bailey insisted. "That seems pretty courageous to me."

Dom hesitated. When he left France he liked thinking he was daring, a risk-taker who was off on an adventure. It took years of soul-searching before he accepted that he wasn't searching for a fresh start. He was fleeing the world that was crashing around him.

"It wasn't courage that brought me here," he reluctantly admitted, returning his attention to her puzzled expression.

"Then what was it?"

"I was running so I didn't have to remember." His lips twisted. "Trust me, trying something new just for the sake of trying something new is the same sort of avoidance as staying in a rut."

"Were you running from your father?"

He didn't know why he was caught off guard by her question. Most people would assume he'd want to put as much space as possible between himself and his criminal father.

"No, Remy is . . . Remy. He's a shallow, selfish bastard who's never going to change. I didn't have to leave France to get rid of him. As soon as he got his grubby hands on my mother's life insurance he packed his bags and headed out. He didn't even bother to attend the funeral."

"Then why did you leave?"

He shook his head, ridding himself of the memory of his worthless father. "I left because of my mother."

She blinked in confusion. "She'd already died, hadn't she?"

"Yes. And I don't know how many years I've spent being angry with her."

"I don't understand."

He hadn't either. Not for a very long time. "I told myself it was because she refused to leave my father," he told her. "Remy treated her like shit, but she refused to stand up to him."

"That wasn't why you were angry?"

"No." He released a heavy sigh. "I was angry because she died when I still needed her."

She winced, as if his words hit an exposed nerve. "Yeah."

He pressed the palm of her hand against his cheek, gazing down at her with a fragile hope filling his heart.

"We've both been alone a long time. Now we have each other."

A tentative smile touched her lips. "That sounds nice."

"Nice again," he teased. "We're going to have to work on that."

"Is that a promise?"

Her lips parted in silent invitation, and Dom slowly lowered his head. He'd been aching to kiss her since they'd left the house. Hell, he hadn't wanted to leave at all. The need to hold this woman in his arms and explore every satin inch of her was a ruthless hunger that was becoming painful in its intensity.

The fierce desire, however, didn't blind him to the fact that they were in a public space and that Bailey was being hunted by a crazed stalker. It was that awareness that forced him to abruptly jerk away as he detected a flash of movement out of the corner of his eye.

"What's wrong?" Bailey demanded.

Dom frowned as he tried to pinpoint what had distracted him. He couldn't see anyone in the parking lot or near the nursing home. Then there was another flicker, and he realized it was coming from the window of an old building on the adjoining lot.

He nodded toward the three-story brick structure with large terraces on the front and a sagging roof. It looked like it had been a school at one time. Or maybe a hospital.

"What is that place?"

"When my grandmother was young she said it was the local poorhouse," Bailey explained. "Then it was used as the county nursing home until the Donaldsons opened a new one."

Dom continued to survey the building. The bricks had faded to the color of mud and the paint had peeled from the windowsills, but it looked like someone had recently replaced the gutters, and there was a newly paved pathway that led to the parking lot.

"Is it still used?"

"Just for storage. Why?"

He turned back to meet her curious gaze. "I thought I saw someone in the window."

"You probably did," she assured him. "We have

equipment in there, along with most of the cleaning supplies. The maintenance staff is always complaining when they have to go in there during the winter. The building has electricity, but it's not heated. The night janitor, Kyle, claimed he got frostbite when he came over to get a mop and bucket."

Dom judged the distance between the two buildings. It wasn't a large gap, but winters in Wisconsin could be brutal. It wouldn't be much fun to have to dash through the snow and ice to get a mop.

"It does seem inconvenient."

"It is, but the county owns the building and allows the nursing home to use it for free. That means the Donaldsons don't have to pay to add on storage rooms." Bailey rolled her eyes at her employers' stinginess. "And for every employee who complains, there are two who want it kept open so they can sneak over and have a cigarette there without getting caught." Bailey wrinkled her nose, visibly shivering as she glanced toward the aging structure. "I think it's creepy."

"Let's get out of here," Dom abruptly suggested.

As an answer, Bailey hurried to crawl into the SUV, revealing her eagerness to be away from the nursing home. Or, more precisely, to be away from the Donaldsons.

Dom hurried to join her, pulling out of the parking lot and zigzagging his way through the small town until he at last found the road that led to the highway. Still, it wasn't until they were several miles away from Pike that Bailey sent him a startled glance, as if belatedly realizing they weren't on the road to Kaden's house.

"Where are we going?"

"Away," he told her, his gaze sweeping over her pale face before returning to the road.

She'd claimed that she was happy she'd confronted the Donaldsons, but he sensed the meeting had left her feeling emotionally drained and questioning her future. Right now she needed a break from any mention of stalkers or mysterious deaths.

Bailey heaved a soft sigh and settled back in the soft leather seat. "Away sounds perfect right now."

Switching on the radio, Dom headed north as Bailey closed her eyes and allowed her body to relax. He smiled, strangely pleased with the knowledge she trusted him to keep her safe.

It was over two hours later that he finally veered off the highway. They'd had breakfast at the local diner, but he'd chosen a piece of apple pie that Kaden had assured him was the best in the state. He hadn't exaggerated. It was delicious, but it was long gone. Now his stomach was rumbling for nourishment.

Following the wooden signs, he stopped at a local orchard that offered farm-to-table luncheons and fresh apple cider. The air was crisp, but the sun was shining, and it was a perfect day to eat outside at the tables that were arranged near the apple trees.

By mutual consent they kept the conversation light, discussing their various tastes in reading and sharing stories of Dom's early days at the pawnshop and Bailey's college years. It was exactly what they both needed: a few relaxing hours to simply enjoy each other's company.

It was late afternoon when he pulled through the

heavy iron gates and parked in front of Kaden and Lia's house.

Bailey unbuckled her belt and sent him a genuine smile. "That was . . ." Her words trailed away as he arched a brow. "It was wonderful."

He chuckled as she managed to avoid the word "nice." "Better."

They slid out of the vehicle and together strolled around the edge of the house to enter the fenced-in backyard. Immediately Bailey was surrounded by dogs who wiggled and yapped in an effort to capture her attention. With a laugh, she bent forward, giving each of them a scratch on the back that only intensified the wiggles until Dom was nearly knocked off his feet.

"I think they missed you," he pointed out the obvious.

"It wouldn't matter if I walked to the end of the driveway and back, this is how they would react."

"Pure, unconditional love."

She straightened, holding up her hand with a rueful grin. "With lots of slobber."

Dom stilled as he gazed down at Bailey, something monumental shifting inside him. It wasn't just that she was beautiful, with her eyes shimmering with flecks of gold in the sunlight and the wind tugging at her satin brown hair. Or that she looked happier than he'd seen her since he'd returned to Pike. It was in the absolute certainty that his life would be an empty shell without this woman at his side.

The emotions were shocking, complex, and yet completely uncomplicated.

Whatever sorcery the universe used to concoct the perfect companion, it had waved its magic wand and created Bailey Evans for him. Now he had to discover a way to make sure she was equally enchanted.

Stepping forward, he intended to wrap her in his arms when a low chime destroyed the moment. The sound was muffled, but there was no mistaking the sound of an incoming text.

Bailey's smile faded as she reluctantly reached into her purse to pull out her phone.

"Oh," she breathed as she gazed at the screen.

"Is it from the stalker?" Dom glanced around, sensing that the bastard had to be close. Perhaps even watching them now.

"Yes." She tilted the phone so he could see the screen. "This time he sent a picture."

Dom was momentarily baffled as he took in the image of a bedroom. There was no one in the picture. Just a bed with a wooden headboard and a matching dresser. Then he noticed the open window with blue-and-silver-striped curtains that were blowing in the breeze.

Striped curtains he easily recognized.

"Shit," he muttered. "I'm going to search the house."

Bailey grabbed his arm before he could turn away. "Take Ernie with you."

He glanced toward the dogs, who had easily sensed his tension and gone from goofy to vigilant as they pressed near Bailey. Touching the larger of the two Labs on the head, he murmured the word "Come" and headed toward the back door.

Tapping the code into the keypad, he entered the house and made a quick investigation of the downstairs before heading up to the spare bedroom Bailey had chosen to use when she arrived yesterday. Ernie dashed forward, jumping on the bed and regarding him with a curious expression. Obviously the dog didn't sense an intruder. Still, Dom wasn't satisfied until he'd searched through every closet and bathroom and under each bed. He even crawled into the attic to make sure no one was hidden among the empty boxes and leftover building supplies.

At last satisfied that whoever had been in the house was gone, Dom returned to the backyard.

"Nothing," he assured Bailey.

Her features were tight with fear. Or maybe it was annoyance. "How did they get in?"

Dom considered the question. There was a fence around the large property, but it would be easy enough to climb it. And it was isolated enough that no one would notice if they were sneaking around. No, wait. It might be isolated, but it wasn't unprotected.

"We can find out," he assured Bailey, turning to lead her into the house. "Kaden had security cameras installed everywhere."

Walking through the kitchen, they battled past the dogs, who continued to vie for Bailey's attention as they entered Kaden's office. The room was as large as the kitchen, with a row of windows that overlooked the lake and cabin that they were building to serve as Lia's private office. As if Kaden needed to be able to see where his wife was spending the majority of her time. Dom suddenly understood his friend's obsession. Being with the right person filled a void he hadn't even known he possessed. He didn't doubt it was exactly the same for Kaden.

Moving toward the desk near the windows, Dom opened the laptop. Then, logging on with the password his friend had used for years, he pulled up the security footage, rewound it back seventy-two hours, before pressing fast forward.

Bailey pressed next to him as they studied the small squares where the images from the various cameras flickered on and off. Most of the cameras were motion activated, with only the front and back doors recording 24-7. They watched as deer and racoons strolled around the empty pastures along with the dogs and occasionally Dom roaming in and out of the house. Two deliveries arrived at the front gate and the trashman drove past, reminding Dom he hadn't remembered to set out the cans. Something he'd deal with later. And eventually Bailey arrived with Bert and Ernie.

"There's no one," Bailey muttered in confusion.

Dom was equally confused. "I suppose a talented hacker could have erased any evidence of their trespassing."

She furrowed her brow, obviously sifting through the various possibilities. "Or maybe there was no trespassing," she slowly suggested. "At least not today."

Dom released a breath that hissed between his clenched teeth. Of course. Why hadn't he noticed it when he first looked at the picture?

"You're right. This was taken before I came to Pike," he said, his voice sharp with annoyance.

She looked surprised at his absolute conviction. "How can you be sure?"

"Lia mentioned they'd been late in getting into

Vegas because a painting had arrived that she'd bought when she was in Paris and she wanted to hang it in a spare bedroom before she left," he explained.

"Oh. The one of the Champs-Élysées over the bed. I noticed it when I was unpacking my case," Bailey said, fumbling to pull out her phone to study the image sent in the text. "You're right. The painting isn't there."

"The question is, how did anyone get a picture of this room before either of us arrived?"

It wasn't the only question on Dom's mind. He was far more worried about *why* the stalker had sent it, not *how* he'd gotten it. But it was easier for them to figure out the how.

"Lia and Kaden have both been fanatical about avoiding all social media," Bailey agreed. "But it's possible that someone else might have posted pictures of the property. There were dozens of workers around here during the construction of the house, plus, there were a couple of interior decorators. And then they hosted the wedding here. It wasn't large, but there were caterers and florists."

Dom slowly nodded. It might have been bizarre to suspect random construction workers or caterers of taking pictures of a client's place and posting them online, but Kaden was famous. It would be human nature to want to brag that they'd been working for him. Or just to share the inside of the beautiful home that very few people ever got to see.

"There was also a photographer," he reminded her.

"Lia will have a list of who she paid, both for the building of the house and the vendors for the wedding."

"True." He'd only known Lia for a few months, but he'd already discovered that Kaden's new wife was not only a financial wizard, she planned and organized everything down to the smallest detail. It was a trait he admired. "And each file will be color coded in alphabetical order with names, dates, and the amount they were paid and their eye color and birth date."

Bailey managed a faint smile. "She is thorough."

"Meticulous," he agreed, his hands clenching as he realized they might have answered one question, though dozens remained.

"What is it?" Bailey asked, easily sensing his burst of anxiety.

"We might be able to explain how someone could have gotten pictures of the interior of this house, but how did the stalker know which room you're using?"

"I—"

They both stiffened as another chime sounded. His brows snapped together as Bailey glanced down at her phone, the color draining from her face.

"The stalker?"

She gave a sharp nod. "A text this time." She stepped to stand next to him, allowing him to see the screen. "'Do I have your attention?'" she read out loud.

Dom could see her fingers tighten on the phone. "Do you want me to call Zac?"

"Later." She squared her shoulders. "I have to play his game. At least for now."

Dom wanted to argue. Hell, he wanted to take her phone and throw it out the window. Nothing good could come from giving into the stalker's manipulations. Then again, there were potentially three people dead. Could they risk turning Bailey from the stalker's obsession to his enemy.

He grudgingly nodded and Bailey quickly typed in the words.

Yes, you have my attention.

Good. I will offer you one warning . . .

They waited. And waited. At last Bailey typed in the question the stalker wanted her to ask.

A warning?

Our private murder club has started. I don't like having you distracted.

Bailey glanced at Dom, her expression puzzled. "What's he talking about?"

Dom shrugged. "I don't have a clue."

Trust me. I'm not distracted, Bailey typed.

There was another long pause before a picture popped up. This one wasn't of the house. Instead, it was a fuzzy image of him and Bailey in the nursing home parking lot. They were standing close together, both oblivious to the world around them.

Dom easily recalled that precise moment. He'd been desperate to sweep Bailey into his arms and claim her lips. He also recalled what had shattered the moment.

A movement out of the corner of his eye.

"This picture was taken from the old building next door," he said, not surprised when Bailey nodded, no doubt recalling his claim that he'd seen a figure in the window.

"Quite possibly."

Returning her attention to her phone, she hesitated, as if considering the best way to respond to the stalker.

I had a meeting with my boss at the nursing home.

The text came back at lightning speed.

Lucier isn't a part of our club. Why is he with you?

Bailey made a sound of surprise. "He knows your name."

"And he's not a fan," Dom growled, the dread that pulsed through him suddenly edged with a fierce anger. "I'm no expert on stalkers, but I'm guessing he sees you as his private property. He's angry that you would be giving me attention when you should be concentrating on his sick game."

Bailey shivered but, clenching her teeth, she responded to the creep.

Dom Lucier is a friend.

You don't need a friend. You have me.

Who are you?

There was a pause, as if the stalker hadn't expected the blunt question.

You know who I am.

Bailey sucked in a sharp breath. "'You know who I am,'" she read out loud. "Does he mean from the Murder Club? Or does he mean I actually know him? Like in real life?"

Dom nodded toward her phone. "Ask him."

If I know you, why can't you give me a name?

You have to earn the privilege. Solve the case, Bailey, and stop wasting time.

Bailey sent Dom a worried glance. "He sounds annoyed."

Dom agreed. It was impossible to be certain with a text, but the stalker wasn't asking Bailey to join him in the game. He was demanding it.

Bailey typed in her response.

Which case? Nellie or Pauline or Gage?

Clever, clever girl. I wasn't sure you'd managed to connect them. But hurry. You're already behind.

Then help me, Bailey typed back.

I have. The clues are all around you.

Bailey and Dom shared a worried glance. Was the stalker referring to the pearls left on her back porch and the phone left on Gage's desk? Or were there more clues they were missing?

Where? Bailey asked. *If we're in this game together, why won't you tell me where to find the clues?*

You would see them if you weren't with Lucier. Perhaps you're bored with the cases I have offered. Would you like a new one?

Bailey cursed as she hurriedly typed in the word, *No.*

The seconds ticked past. Then the minutes. Bailey sent more texts.

Hello? Please. I'm not bored. I need your help.

There was no response. At last Bailey gave up, glancing at Dom with a worried expression.

"That was a warning."

"Yes," he agreed. "Why else would he ask if you want another case?"

She shoved the phone back into her purse. "We need to find Lia's files."

Chapter 12

They located Lia's files stacked in a closet of Kaden's office. Lia had mentioned that she was anxious to have her first private space to run her financial empire. She'd spent the past decade working out of the back of her family's grocery store. But they were still waiting on the plumbing to be finished and the furnishings she'd special ordered from a local craftsman to be delivered.

For now she was forced to share this office with her new husband.

Settling on the floor, they spread out the files, separating them into local contractors Bailey would recognize while Dom concentrated on the construction crew that was based in Madison.

Bailey patiently shifted through the stacks of invoices and receipts, struggling to concentrate.

You know who I am . . .

The text from the stalker whirled through her mind, like a hamster on a running wheel, spinning and spinning while going nowhere.

Did she know the stalker? Was it someone she'd gone to school with? Or someone at the nursing home?

A neighbor? She wanted to believe it was a stranger. Just a random weirdo who'd become obsessed with her when she was a member of the Murder Club. It didn't make the danger any less real, but it was horrifying to think she could be smiling and chatting with the creep and not even know it.

Clearing the lump that settled in her throat, Bailey forced herself to concentrate on the files. There was no use in dwelling on the fear that knotted her belly. The only way to stop it was to uncover the identity of the stalker.

"Anything?" She at last broke the silence, glancing toward the man sitting on the floor next to her.

Dom continued to read through a stack of invoices, his jaw clenched. He hadn't said anything about the most recent texts she'd received from the stalker, perhaps sensing her nerves were too raw for her to discuss the danger that was closing in around her. But there was a tension humming around him that revealed he was well aware that things were escalating.

"Yeah. I think I might have found something," he abruptly announced, pulling a sheet of paper out of a file. "This is a bill from Warren Lumberyard. I'm assuming there's only one in town."

She nodded, surprised to discover that Lia had hired Gage. Her friend had never hidden her dislike of the town bully.

"Did he do some work here?"

"No work, but he did deliver a load of bricks for the pizza oven on the back terrace," Dom said. "It would have given him access to the property at a time when there was pure chaos happening around here. It would have been easy for him to slip in and take a few pictures."

Bailey considered the possibility. "I doubt he had any social media, but the stalker could have gotten the photos from Gage's phone after he was. . ."

"Yes," Dom agreed as the word "murdered" stuck on her lips.

"Is that all?" she asked, anxious to divert her thoughts from Gage Warren.

"Not really." He held up a bright red file. "This is a running account of the expenses for the house. Most of the building supplies were brought in by the construction crew out of Madison. Plus, I'm guessing Kaden was adamant that there was a limited number of people allowed onto the property."

"That should narrow things down."

"It does. I have the names and addresses of the full construction crew, including electricians and plumbers," he said. "We can start combing through their social media accounts later. What about you? Anyone stand out?"

"The caterers are all local," she told him. "I know them all and it seems doubtful they would have broken Lia's trust by taking pictures and posting them online." Bailey glanced toward a file she'd laid on the floor. "And the flowers came from a shop in Green Bay. I picked them up the day before the wedding and her mother arranged them."

"I remember. The entire house smelled like daises," Dom murmured. "What about the photographer?"

Bailey grabbed the last file and flipped it open. "'Images by Lisa,'" she read the name from the top of the invoice. "It's a shop in Grange." She skimmed over the various expenses that were itemized until she reached the bottom, where it was signed by the actual photographer. "Oh."

"What?"

"The photographer was Lisa Hartford."

"Lisa Hartford?" Dom frowned before he realized what had captured her attention. "Hartford. A relation of Pauline Hartford?"

"A good question," she retorted.

Without warning, Dom rose to his feet, his brow furrowed. "You know, I remember the photographer. She spent a few days around here, taking pictures of the bachelor party and the rehearsal dinner before the wedding and reception."

Bailey dredged through her memories of that weekend. It was more difficult than it should have been. Partly because she'd been preoccupied helping Lia with the copious details that went into organizing even the smallest wedding and partly because she'd been gloriously distracted by her fascination with the best man, Dom Lucier.

At last she managed to form the image of a short woman with a plump face and a tangle of blond curls that gave her a childish appearance that was at odds with her militant habit of ordering people around to make sure she got the shot she wanted. She'd bustled around the house and yard from the crack of dawn until Kaden demanded that she leave.

"You're right," she told Dom, abruptly recalling that the woman hadn't been alone when she'd packed her equipment into a van. "There was also some guy with her. He was big, with an angry expression."

Dom nodded. "She introduced him as her assistant, but they bickered like they were married."

Bailey dropped the file and surged to her feet, heading to the laptop that was still open on Kaden's desk.

"We should check them out," she said. "If the man was Pauline Hartford's grandson, then we have a direct connection to Pike."

Dom joined her, standing close enough to wrap her in the warmth from his body. Bailey breathed in his clean male scent, savoring his unwavering strength. She was trying to pretend that she was in control as she focused on the latest clue, but inside she was freaking out.

It was bad enough to have the creepy stalker texting her as if they were old friends. But realizing that he'd been lurking around the nursing home when she was standing in the parking lot was terrifying. Had he followed her there? Did he work there? And what about his warning of more cases?

With an effort, Bailey leashed her rising panic. Fear wasn't going to keep her safe. Discovering the identity of the killer was her best hope.

Pulling up a search engine, she typed in Images by Lisa and pressed Enter. A list of links appeared.

"There's no website, but she's on Facebook." Bailey clicked on the page and studied the collection of photos she had posted, along with the address for her photography shop. Scrolling down, Bailey searched for any mention of Lia or Kaden or pictures of their private property. "Nothing on here," she muttered. "Let me check for a personal page." A minute later she located a Lisa Callum Hartford from Grange, Wisconsin, and pulled it up. "Here we go," she said, instantly recognizing the profile picture of a woman with a round face surrounded by blond curls. She glanced through the info page. "'Lisa Hartford,'" she read out loud. "'Thirty-three years old. Making the world a prettier place to live. Mom of three. Hobbies include photography, baking cookies, and scrapbooking.'" Bailey frowned as she scrolled down. "No mention of her husband."

"And no pictures of him," Dom murmured.

"Lots of kids and cookies."

He pointed toward the image of two white poodles with matching bows tied around their necks.

"Even dogs."

"Says a lot about the marriage," Bailey murmured, closing the laptop and turning toward Dom. "The photography shop is close to the grocery store," she told him, not bothering to mention that Grange was bigger than Pike but still small enough that everything was close together.

He arched his brows. "Two birds and one stone?"

She wrinkled her nose. "Yeah, although that's kind of disgusting."

"Noted." He glanced toward the door of the office, where the four dogs had curled into a pile and fallen asleep. "Let's leave the beasts inside. They can keep an eye on the place."

After double-checking the locks, they returned to Dom's Land Rover and drove the fifteen miles to Grange. As Bailey had predicted, Images by Lisa was just a couple of blocks from the grocery store. They parked along the street and crossed the sidewalk to stand in front of the shop. Bailey skimmed her gaze over the photographs that were artistically arranged in the large windows. Weddings, graduations, and a family all wearing overalls and flannel shirts. Was that a thing? With a shake of her head, she reached out to push open the front door only to frown when it refused to budge. Belatedly, she noticed the handwritten sign that was taped to the glass.

Closed for a death in the family.

"She has to be related to Pauline." Bailey turned to find Dom peering between the photographs inside the darkened shop. "There can't be that many Hartfords dying in Grange."

"It's a reasonable hypothesis," he agreed, his jaw tight. "And it would implicate Kevin Hartford as your stalker. But how is he connected to Nellie and Gage?"

"It's possible there's a family relationship," she conceded. "I could ask Dorinda. She knows everything about everyone in the area."

"Or they could have a connection through the lumberyard. Or even the school where Pauline Hartford was superintendent." He made a sound of frustration. "If we could discover how the three of them fit together, we might be able to figure out if Kevin is the one behind the deaths."

"We need to let Zac know what we've found out," Bailey announced, heading back to the SUV. She didn't want to admit she felt exposed standing on the sidewalk. As if the stalker was lurking just out of sight. "But first the groceries. I'm in need of a distraction."

"Will there be cake involved?" Dom teased, as if sensing her need for a distraction.

"If you want." She halted near the curb. "What kind?"

He sent her a glance of pure disbelief. "There's only one kind of cake. Chocolate."

She rolled her eyes. "I suppose that can be arranged."

"With chocolate frosting?"

"Greedy."

"For you?" He moved to stand a breath away, his eyes smoldering with a hunger that had nothing to do with chocolate cake. "Yes."

Dom drove through the narrow streets of Pike with a back seat overflowing with ingredients that promised a delicious dinner and a decadent dessert. They'd already stopped by the courthouse, where the sheriff's office was located, only to be told that Zac was at the Warren Lumberyard.

"There's Zac," Bailey abruptly broke the silence as she pointed toward the uniformed man standing next to his vehicle as if he was on the point of leaving.

Dom pulled to a halt next to him and rolled down the window. "Anything new?"

"Nope." Zac cast a disgusted look toward the lumberyard, which was draped with yellow police tape. "I'm spinning my wheels here, but I don't know what else to do. I keep hoping I'll find a clue I overlooked."

Bailey suddenly leaned across him to hand Zac her cell phone. "I don't know if this will help or not."

Zac glanced at the screen, his body jerking as if he'd taken a blow. "Shit. These are from the stalker." He lifted his head to reveal his troubled expression. "Gage wasn't the one sending you the texts."

"Nope," Bailey agreed.

Zac glanced back down at the phone, scrolling through the messages. "Wait." He turned the phone to flash it toward his cousin. "Is this picture from Lia and Kaden's house?"

"It is, but it was taken before I arrived in town," Dom answered.

Zac shifted his attention to him. "Why would he send this?"

Dom shrugged. "Another question to add to the list."

Zac handed the phone back to Bailey, who settled back in the passenger seat, her expression weary.

"Who would have access to the house?"

Dom took command of the conversation as Bailey shook her head. It was obvious she was still trying to process the suspicion that Kevin Hartford might be involved in the murders. Or maybe she needed a moment to sort through the confusing mess of emotions that darkened her eyes.

He desperately wanted to pull her into his arms and assure her everything was going to be okay. But they both knew that was a lie. He couldn't promise her anything but the fact that he was going to do his damnedest to protect her.

"There's not many," he told Zac, forcing himself to concentrate on the lawman, who was eyeing him with a worried expression. "The most obvious was the construction crew that built their house. We went through Lia's files, but no one stood out except for Gage Warren, who delivered a load of bricks."

Zac glanced toward the police tape surrounding the building. "A shame he's no longer a suspect."

"No, but he might have taken pictures of the house and shared them with his friends," Dom suggested.

"I'll check on his phone." Zac grimaced. "Both of them."

"We also looked through the vendors Lia hired for her wedding," Dom continued.

"Good idea. Did you find something?"

"Yes. A Lisa Hartford."

"Who's that?" Zac dug into his shirt pocket to pull out a small notebook and pencil, jotting down the name.

"She's a photographer in Grange. She has a business called Images by Lisa."

Zac continued to write down the information. "And?"

"We suspect she's married to Pauline Hartford's grandson, Kevin Hartford."

Zac jerked up his head. "The woman who fell into the empty pool?"

"Yes. We drove over there this morning, and Images by Lisa is currently closed due to a death in the family."

Zac arched his brows, tucking the notebook back into his pocket. "Grange is out of my jurisdiction, but I'll do some checking." He shook his head. "This just keeps getting more complicated."

Dom silently agreed. They had gone from no clues to a confusing jumble of them. None of which offered them a clear trail to follow.

Was that the point? he silently mused. Were the texts and vague threats of more deaths done on purpose to blind them to something obvious?

Swallowing a sigh of resignation, Dom was on the point of rolling up his window when he abruptly recalled something that had been gnawing in the back of his mind.

"Did Gage leave anything behind?" he abruptly demanded.

Zac looked confused. "Like what?"

"Cash or jewelry?"

"Not that we could find. In fact, his house was almost empty. Like he'd sold off everything that had any value."

Dom tapped his fingers on the steering wheel. It'd been obvious when Gage accosted Bailey on the street that he was desperate for money. And the fact that he'd sold off his belongings only emphasized his need to steal from his own mother.

"So no emerald ring?" he insisted.

Zac studied him with a searching gaze. "Why would you assume he had an emerald ring?"

"Nellie Warren told Bailey's neighbor that she woke up at the nursing home and spotted Gage going through her belongings," he explained. "Gage ran off, but when she checked her stuff, she discovered she was missing some cash and an emerald ring."

"Wait. What?" Zac moved to grip the frame of the open window, peering past him to study Bailey's pale face. "Why wasn't I told?"

"Logan Donaldson."

Zac made a sound of disgust. The name clearly was enough to explain the lack of a police report.

"Of course." He glanced back at Zac. "No. We didn't find a ring. And certainly no cash."

"Interesting," Dom murmured.

There was a static crackle before a voice floated through the walkie-talkie Zac had attached to his jacket.

"Sheriff, you're needed back at the office."

Zac reluctantly stepped away from the SUV, pointing his finger at his cousin.

"Bailey."

"I know. I'll be careful," she promised.

Dom rolled up the window and pulled away. "Christ, I hate this," he growled.

"I hate it too," Bailey agreed.

"It's time for cake."

"And dogs," she added.

"The perfect combination."

Bailey glanced in his direction, a small smile curving her lips. "Perfect."

Dom gripped the steering wheel, resisting the urge to slam his foot on the gas and zoom to the house at top speed. As much as he wanted to get Bailey naked, he wasn't going to rush into an intimate relationship. When the time was right they would both know it. And it was going to be explosive.

They'd reached the edge of town when Bailey broke the comfortable silence. "Why did you ask about Nellie's ring?"

"If Gage did steal it from his mother, it should have been hidden in his belongings."

"Unless he sold it to someone."

"Exactly. Gage was obviously in need of money, and the quickest way to get his hands on some cash would be to sell the ring to a local pawnshop." He sent her a wry smile. "Thankfully, that's my one area of expertise."

She took a second to consider the idea of Gage hocking his mother's belongings.

"I don't think there's one around here," she finally told him. "He'd probably have to go to Madison or Green Bay."

Dom made a mental note to check out the nearest pawnshop. "There's also the possibility that he still had the ring and it was stolen after he was dead," he suggested, refusing to close his mind to any possibility.

"The killer?"

"Something to consider."

She nodded. "We should check out the pawnshops. Just in case."

"I agree." He turned onto the narrow dirt path. "Would you recognize it?"

"Absolutely."

Dom felt a small flare of hope. If they could locate the ring, the owner of the pawnshop would have a name and address of whoever sold it. They might even have video footage of the transaction, if he could convince them to share it with him. He wasn't sure what it would prove beyond the fact that Gage was a lowlife who stole from his aging mother, but he wanted concrete proof the stalker wasn't involved.

The thought of the stalker had Dom bypassing the private drive that would lead to the house and instead continued down the rough road that curled a path through the thick layer of trees that framed the large property.

"Where are we going?" Bailey asked.

"I'm taking the back road."

"This goes behind the house, but there's no way to get through the fence," she warned.

"I want to check something out."

"What?"

The expensive vehicle rattled over the rapidly deteriorating road. It was no wonder the locals avoided driving back here, and that was exactly how Kaden wanted to keep it.

"The night before the wedding Kaden and I walked down to the lake to talk about the future of Money Makers," he said. It'd been a bittersweet night for Dom. He'd been pleased as hell for his friend. It was clear that Kaden had found his true love. But Dom knew there was going to be a huge hole in his life where his friend used to be. At the time he'd been fiercely attracted to Bailey, but he hadn't yet realized she was destined to fill the emptiness in his heart. "It was dark, but there was enough moonlight to catch sight of someone standing next to the back fence."

"Back here?" Bailey glanced out the window. There was nothing to see but a bunch of pine trees. "Who was it?"

"Kaden, being Kaden, took off chasing them, but by the time he could reach the fence whoever it was had jumped in a vehicle and driven away."

"You all never said anything."

Dom shrugged. "Kaden assumed it was one of the paparazzi sniffing around and didn't want to worry Lia."

Bailey visibly shuddered. "They were everywhere."

She wasn't wrong. The small town of Pike had been overrun with journalists as well as the tabloid press. Not only because Kaden was getting married but he'd been at the center of an old, unsolved murder case. It was hard to walk down the streets without being harassed.

Dom slowed to a mere crawl, at last pressing on the brakes when he spotted the gap in dense branches.

"This is the place," he said, putting the vehicle in Park and unbuckling his belt. He left the engine running, however. He wasn't going to be caught anywhere without a quick getaway.

Leaving the Land Rover, they squeezed their way through the opening to discover a low wire fence directly in front of them, and beyond that were the rolling pastures that surrounded the large property. To the left they could see the lake and the new office for Lia, and to the right was the main house. Standing on the ridge of a hill, they were perched high enough to easily see over the back fence Lia had demanded be built for the dogs.

"There's a clear view of the back of the house," Bailey said in surprise. "And it's a lot closer than I expected."

Dom nodded. "With a pair of binoculars it would be easy to see inside the house."

Bailey wrapped her arms around her waist as if she was suddenly cold. "I stood at the window last night. I would have been visible from here."

"And it's hard to miss those curtains," Dom added, his voice hard. He was trying to concentrate on solving how the stalker had known to send Bailey the picture of that particular bedroom. Now he knew that she'd been exposed to the sick bastard while he stood in this exact spot. "If you'd been inside the house, you would know which one it was."

"It would explain how the stalker knew which room is mine." She easily followed his line of thinking.

Turning away from the house, Dom walked back to the SUV, studying the sorry excuse of a road. "Where does this go?"

Bailey stood next to him, glancing down the road that disappeared through the trees. "I haven't been out here much, but I think it eventually goes past the old rock quarry and ends up at the access road that runs next to the highway."

"Remote?"

"Beyond."

"So no one would notice someone driving back here and parking?"

"No."

Dom silently considered what he knew about the security system Kaden had installed.

"The cameras around the edge of the property are motion activated. If someone was here last night, they were either incredibly lucky or they knew exactly where to stand to spy on the house without being caught."

A strangled sound was wrenched from Bailey's throat as she glanced over her shoulder. "It's horrible. I mean . . . I knew I was being stalked, but to think that the creep was so close. Just standing there watching me."

Dom moved to drop a kiss on top of her head. "We need cake."

"Immediately."

Chapter 13

Kevin Hartford unlocked the back door of his grandmother's house and shoved it open. Oddly, his feet remained glued to the patio that framed the empty pool.

For as long as he could remember, his grandmother had criticized and belittled and humiliated him on a regular basis. She'd used her money as a weapon, trying to control him as she tried to control her own son. At least until he'd put a bullet in his brain just to get away from her. And while he'd resented their love-hate relationship, she'd always seemed larger than life.

Was it any wonder that he was afraid she might be standing inside with a gin and tonic in her hand, waiting to steal another chunk of his manhood despite the fact that he'd been at her funeral less than an hour ago?

"Dammit, she's rotting in the ground," he muttered. "She can't hurt you. Not anymore."

Annoyed by the realization he continued to let the bitch live rent free in his head, Kevin forced himself to step over the threshold and enter the shadowed kitchen. He grimaced, resisting the urge to tug open the shutters.

He'd gone to the effort of parking his car a block away and climbing over the back fence, nearly ripping a hole in his last decent pair of slacks. He wasn't going to risk being spotted by one of the nosy neighbors now that he was finally inside.

The house belonged to him, of course. Or it would once the stupid lawyer got off his ass and completed the paperwork. He still didn't understand why his grandmother would use an attorney from Pike. And worse, why she would have made the lawyer the executor of her will when Kevin could have done it all himself. He assumed it was to make his life as difficult as possible. That seemed to be the only thing that gave her pleasure.

But while the house would eventually be his, along with a sizable life insurance policy, he wanted to empty out the most valuable contents before his wife could come in and do her own inventory.

Kevin might be down on his luck but he wasn't stupid. He knew that Lisa intended to divorce him, that the only reason she'd hung on for this long was to wait for Pauline Hartford to die. She wasn't going to miss out on her half of the considerable inheritance. And there wasn't a damned thing he could do about it.

A humorless laugh was wrenched from his lips as he headed into the master bedroom. It was his grandmother who'd warned him to have a prenup in place before he got married. He should have listened. Just as he should have listened when she warned him about speeding around town on his motorcycle. Five years ago he'd run the damned thing into the back of a semitruck.

The wreck had left him bedbound for two weeks, but while he'd eventually healed, he hadn't managed to get rid of the painkillers he'd been prescribed like they were candy. He was well and truly addicted.

Since then he'd lost everything. His job, his self-respect, and soon his family. The only thing he had left was the sweet oblivion when he was stoned out of his mind.

And for that he needed cash.

Immediate cash.

Crossing to the far wall, he tugged on the frame of the cheap landscape that looked like it'd been painted by one of his grandmother's students. The picture swung outward, revealing the safe. Pauline Hartford was nothing if not predictable, he wryly acknowledged. This would be the first place any thief would search for valuables. Her predictability also made it easy for him to guess the passcode. The date she'd been the grand marshal of the Dogwood Parade. She had a massive picture of herself riding on a float, wearing a ridiculous cape and tiara framed in the living room. She told anyone who would listen it was the happiest day of her life.

Punching the numbers onto the keypad, Kevin smiled as the steel door swung open. As he'd expected, there was a stack of folded documents. They were no doubt important but of no use to him. At least not now. Instead, he grabbed the stack of hundred-dollar bills he knew his grandmother kept on hand in case of an emergency, along with her pearl necklace and wedding ring. He could try to pawn those later. Slamming the safe shut, Kevin turned to leave.

His body was starting to shake with a hunger that consumed him. The gnawing, bottomless pit of need was an old friend now, but it warned of worse things to come.

"Why am I not surprised to find you here?"

Busy stuffing the money in his pocket, Kevin was distracted by a voice that destroyed the welcome silence. He froze, his mouth sucked dry, as he tried to determine whether the voice was a product of his imagination. Very likely, he tried to reassure himself. Just last week he was sure he could hear church bells ringing. When he complained about them his bitch of a wife had told him that he was losing his mind.

Forcing his feet to turn him toward the door, Kevin felt another jolt of shock when he caught sight of the shadowed form. There *was* someone in the house. He didn't know whether to be relieved he wasn't losing his mind or worried that he'd been followed. It was possible he owed more than one dealer some serious cash.

"Who the hell is there?" He narrowed his eyes, trying to peer through the gloom. At last he recognized the face that was partially obscured by the heavy hood of his sweatshirt. "Oh, it's you. What are you doing here?"

"I like this location." The intruder strolled forward, looking wildly out of place in the bedroom, with its fake marble paneling and Louis XIV–style furniture. The bed was draped in a gold comforter that sparkled when the overhead chandelier was switched on. It was no doubt intended to be classy, but it was a gaudy mess as far as he was concerned. Nothing in the room had any substance. Like his grandmother, it was all about surface impressions. "It reminds me of a tomb."

"You're right." Kevin released a humorless laugh.

"I should have had the old bat buried here and saved myself a few thousand dollars on her funeral."

"You're not grieving for your grandmother?"

Kevin shoved the necklace and wedding ring into his pocket, telling himself that the pang in the center of his chest had nothing to do with Pauline Hartford or her unexpected death. He wasn't going to miss her. He wasn't, dammit.

"Why should I grieve?" he scoffed. "She wouldn't have given a shit if I died. I don't think she cared about anything but her reputation. If they knew her like I did . . ." He allowed his words to trail away with a restless shrug.

The intruder took a step closer. "Did she tear you down, Kevin? Maybe make you feel less?"

"She was a ruthless nag." Kevin squared his shoulders as the words reminded him of the price his grandmother demanded for her love. "Just like my wife."

"Yes, women are the bane of men's existence," his companion purred.

"Can't live with 'em, can't kill 'em. Am I right?"

"No."

Kevin frowned. "What?"

"You said, can't live with them, can't kill them. But you can live without them and you most certainly can kill them."

Kevin replayed the words in his head, trying to decide if he'd misheard them. When he finally accepted that's what the intruder had said, he forced out an uncomfortable chuckle.

"Is that a joke?"

"Who would joke about murder?"

Kevin was abruptly aware of the heaviness in the air. As if some sort of evil had crept in when he wasn't looking. Was it his grandmother's ghost? It would be just his luck to have the bitch crawling out of her grave to make his life a misery.

"Well, it takes all kinds, I guess," he muttered, moving forward only to come to a sharp halt when the intruder refused to move. "Look, I gotta get out of here."

"I thought we might have a chat."

"Now?" A tremor raced through Kevin. His stomach was curling with a familiar sickness. He needed to get to his dealer. "I got stuff to do."

"You're in a hurry?"

"I hate this place. Like you said. It's like a tomb in here."

"Probably because it is."

"What is what?" Kevin struggled to concentrate. Had the intruder moved closer? It felt as if he was being crowded.

"This place is a tomb." An eerie laugh floated through the room. "At least for you."

"I don't know what's going on, but—" Kevin's words ended on a shriek as there was a blur of movement and the intruder was behind him, circling his arm around Kevin's neck to put him in a choke hold. He hadn't considered the possibility that he might be in danger, but it seemed he wasn't the only one who wanted the cash and jewelry left behind by his grandmother. "Shit, just take the stuff," he rasped, a darkness closing in as his throat was painfully being crushed.

He felt a stir of air next to his ear before there was a

sharp jab of a needle plunging into the inner flesh of his arm.

"Say hello to Pauline for me."

The next morning Dom was showered, dressed, and seated at the kitchen table consuming a large slab of cake when Bailey made her entrance. She was wearing a pair of faded jeans and a Pike High School sweatshirt with her hair pulled into a ponytail. She did nothing special to attract his attention, but Dom felt as if the world had transformed the moment she appeared.

Suddenly, the morning sunlight was a bit brighter. The chocolate on his tongue tasted a bit richer. And the caffeine from his morning coffee was racing through his blood a bit faster. Then she smiled and he melted.

Just like that.

The only thing that was marring her intoxicating beauty were the shadows beneath her eyes. They revealed her night had been as restless as his own.

Reaching the table, she gazed down at his plate with a lift of her brows. "You can't be serious."

"I'm always serious about cake," he assured her, licking his fork.

"For breakfast?"

"You eat doughnuts," he pointed out. "And pancakes."

She considered his perfectly reasonable response before giving a nod of her head. "True. I'm a convert."

"That was easy," he murmured as she headed to the counter to grab a plate.

"It's cake," she said, cutting a large slice before grabbing a fork and joining him at the table.

"Not just cake. A celebration."

She scooped up a large bite. "What are we celebrating?"

"Being here. With you."

A hint of color brushed her cheeks as she tried to pretend she wasn't pleased by his words.

"Hmm. I suspect you would find any excuse to eat cake."

Shoving aside his plate, Dom folded his arms on the table and leaned forward.

"Actually, I always had a very specific purpose," he confessed. "When I was young my mom would bake a chocolate cake when my father took off with another woman. She thought we were missing him and she wanted to give us a special treat."

She took another bite. "I'm guessing you weren't missing him?"

Dom prepared himself for the usual discomfort in discussing his past. He'd rather walk over hot coals than reveal anything about his childhood, but with Bailey it was easy to share. Probably because she was studying him with genuine curiosity and not the condescending pity that set his teeth on edge.

"Not only did I not miss him but for me, the cake was a celebration of freedom. Without Remy around I didn't have to worry about some new disaster forcing us to flee our home." He paused, recalling the nights he would lay in his bed, dreading the sound of pounding on the door. "The only disappointment was when he returned and my mother welcomed him back with open arms." He grimaced at the harsh edge in his voice. "That sounds terrible when I say it out loud."

"It sounds honest."

Dom shoved aside the painful memories. He wasn't going to ruin this moment.

"It's also honest when I say that chocolate cake will no longer remind me of my life in France. It will now forever be connected to Bailey Evans dancing around this kitchen with frosting on her chin."

The color in her cheeks deepened as she sent him a chiding frown. "That's a lie. I might have been dancing, but I didn't have frosting on my chin."

"You did." He reached out to scoop a glob of frosting from her cake and smeared it on her chin. "It was right here."

"Hey."

The word had no doubt been intended as a protest, but it came out as a breathy invitation.

"You have no idea how much restraint it took not to lick it off." Dom leaned forward, holding her gaze as he closed the space between them. "Like this."

Swiping his tongue over her chin, he captured the frosting, savoring the rich chocolate before he nuzzled a path of kisses along the line of her jaw. He groaned. Her skin was just as sweet as the cake. And twice as decadent.

Bailey swayed toward him, her lips parting as she released a soft sigh of pleasure. "Dom."

Accepting her silent invitation, Dom captured her lips in a soft, searching kiss. Raw pleasure scorched through him and he eagerly deepened the kiss, reaching out to stroke his fingers along the slender curve of her throat. He could feel the rapid beat of her pulse and catch the scent of soap that clung to her skin. It helped assure him that she wasn't a fantasy that had escaped his dreams.

Everything about her was real. And he was on fire to finally have her wrapped in his arms.

Dom cupped his fingers around the back of her neck, considering the pleasure of seeing her lying naked on the kitchen table. There was leftover frosting in the fridge that he could spread—

The delicious image was abruptly shattered when a sharp buzz echoed through the kitchen, closely followed by a deafening chorus of barking from the dogs, who'd been sleeping off the massive breakfast they'd consumed at record speed.

With a groan, Dom broke off the kiss. Even if he could ignore the sound of someone buzzing at the front gate, the dogs were creating enough chaos to destroy the mood.

"I have to be cursed," he breathed, watching as Bailey jumped to her feet and hurried across the kitchen to peer at the security monitor set into the wall. "There's no other explanation."

"It's Zac," Bailey announced, pressing the button beneath the monitor to open the gates. Then she slowly turned to send him a rueful glance. "The day started out so promising."

Dom squashed his aching desire and rose to his feet so he could cross the room and brush a kiss over Bailey's forehead. Right now she didn't need a lover; she needed a friend to stand at her side and confront whatever new disaster was about to descend on them.

"I'll let him in," he murmured, leaving the kitchen and crossing the foyer. He pulled open the door just as Zac was parking in front of the house.

Neither man spoke as Dom led him into the kitchen, where Bailey was brewing a fresh pot of tea.

"Good morning, Bailey," Zac said, his expression grim. "Sorry to interrupt your . . ." His brows arched at the sight of the plates smeared with the remains of chocolate cake. "Breakfast?"

"There are a couple of slices left." Bailey handed Zac a mug, nodding toward the pan on the counter. "Do you want some?"

"Don't tempt me," Zac protested, heaving a regretful sigh. "I swear, Rachel can smell chocolate on my breath a mile away."

Dom leaned against the kitchen table, folding his arms over his chest as he prepared himself for a fresh catastrophe. Zac wasn't there to deliver good news.

"What brings you out here?"

Zac took a gulp of his tea, blinking as he realized it wasn't coffee with the kick of caffeine he needed.

"Kevin Hartford was found dead this morning," he announced, setting the mug on the counter.

"Oh my God," Bailey gasped.

Dom swore beneath his breath, wondering if he really was cursed. They'd just managed to move Kevin Hartford to the top of the suspect list and now he was dead? How bad did their luck have to be?

He grimaced. Obviously, he sympathized with the family who'd lost a loved one, but he was focused on how Kevin's death affected Bailey and their fumbling attempts to unmask the stalker. It was almost as if the killer was deliberately leading them in one direction only to taunt them with yet another murder. Was it possible? Dom shuddered, horrified by the suspicion that someone was evil enough to play such a sick game.

"What happened?" he forced himself to ask.

Zac looked grim. "The official cause of death is an overdose."

It wasn't the answer Dom was expecting. "Kevin Hartford was a drug user?"

"That part doesn't seem to be in dispute," Zac informed him. "His wife admitted that he'd been struggling with an addiction to painkillers since he had a motorcycle accident five years ago."

Dom narrowed his eyes. Zac's expression was set in cop mode, but there was an edge to his tone that suggested he wasn't entirely happy with the official report.

"You aren't convinced it was an overdose?"

"I have questions." Zac drained his mug and set it on the counter. "Starting with the fact that his body was discovered at his grandmother's place."

Bailey sucked in an audible breath. "Pauline's house?"

Zac nodded. "A neighbor called the Grange police station this morning to say that the back door to Pauline Hartford's house was left open and that she was afraid there might be a thief inside."

Dom silently tucked away the suspicion that the door had been deliberately left open. If Kevin was killed, the murderer wanted the body to be discovered.

"Do you know what Kevin was doing there?" Dom asked.

"The current theory is that he went to steal the cash Pauline had in her safe."

"Why would he have to steal it?" Bailey looked confused. "I thought Kevin was the only heir."

"The will hasn't gone through probate, so technically it isn't his yet," Zac explained.

"Are they sure he was trying to steal anything?" Bailey was obviously resisting the urge to leap to conclusions.

"He was found with a thousand dollars in cash stuffed in his pockets, along with Pauline's pearl necklace and wedding ring."

Dom shared a quick glance with Bailey. "Pearl necklace?"

"Yes. They suspect it'd been left in the safe with the money," Zac answered.

Dom returned his attention to the sheriff, reminding himself that Bailey was right not to jump to conclusions. It seemed beyond belief that Kevin's death could be a coincidence, but stranger things had happened.

"It's not illogical to assume that Kevin would be looking for some easy cash if he was a drug addict," he forced himself to point out.

"True, but he overdosed there. Which means he already had the drugs he needed. Why not get the cash before you meet with the dealer to get a larger supply? Or go steal the cash after you'd used up what you had?" Zac's jaw tightened. He was a man who'd already endured the horrors of a serial killer. He understood the dangers of turning a blind eye to potential clues. "It seems odd that he would go there to steal the contents of the safe and then risk exposure by leaving the back door open and staying around long enough to shoot up."

"You're expecting reasonable behavior from a drug addict," Dom said.

Zac refused to back down. "There's also the fact that his car is missing."

"The BMW?"

Both men glanced at Bailey in surprise. It was Zac who asked the question on both their minds.

"How did you know he drove a BMW?"

"The nosy neighbor."

Zac paused, as if considering her explanation. "I wonder if she's the same one who called in the open back door. It might be interesting to talk to her."

"Could he have sold it?" Dom stubbornly demanded, still determined to keep an open mind.

"That's the opinion of the Grange police chief," Zac conceded. "He believes that Kevin sold his car to get his drugs, then walked to Pauline's house to search for more cash. While he was there, he decided to get high and accidentally overdosed."

"He didn't think it was more than a little weird that Pauline died of an accident just a few days before her grandson overdosed in her house?" Bailey asked in disbelief.

"Two unfortunate incidents are easier to accept than a convoluted game of murder," Zac retorted. "And honestly, I don't blame them. Grange is bigger than Pike, but the police department still runs on a shoestring budget. It's hard to sacrifice manpower and resources to follow vague suspicion when you have a backload of crimes that need your attention."

Dom understood that Zac wasn't making excuses for his fellow law officers; he was just stating the hard truth. Plus, the police chief of Grange didn't have full access to all the facts.

Not like Zac . . .

Dom abruptly frowned. "How did you get involved? It's out of your jurisdiction, isn't it?"

Zac glanced toward Bailey. "I contacted the Grange Police and told them about the texts you received after Pauline died. I didn't mention you by name, just said I was looking into a case that involved a potential stalker and possibly worse." Zac reached into the pocket of his jacket to pull out a baggie with a familiar object inside. "He came to the office this morning to bring me this."

Bailey stiffened. "A phone?"

"Kevin had two phones on him when his body was discovered. One that appeared to be his primary phone and this one."

Dom clenched his hands as a furious realization blasted through him. There was no way Kevin's death was an accidental overdose. This was another twist in the ugly game the stalker was playing with Bailey.

"Let me guess. It's exactly like the phone you found at the lumberyard," he growled. "Nothing but texts to Bailey."

"Exactly," Zac conceded in grim tones. "The chief was happy to assure me that my stalker was revealed when he found the texts and pictures sent to Bailey. He also assured me that I no longer had to worry about him bothering my citizens."

"He was murdered," Bailey breathed.

Zac shoved the baggie into the pocket of his jacket. "I'm going to have the phone dusted for prints, although I have no idea how many people have handled it since it was found. And I'll try to trace where it was purchased and, hopefully, who bought it."

"That's going to take time," Dom complained.

Zac nodded. "Yeah."

Bailey wrapped her arms around her waist. "At least we know that Kevin isn't the stalker."

"True. A damned shame, considering he was the most likely suspect. Just like Gage was the most likely suspect before he turned up dead . . ." His words died on his lips as Dom realized what he was saying. "Wait. Maybe we're overlooking the obvious."

"The obvious what?" Bailey asked.

"He's *still* the most logical suspect," Dom said, holding up his hand as Bailey parted her lips to remind him that Kevin Hartford was dead. "He had access to Kaden's and Lia's house during the wedding. He had reason to want his grandmother dead. And the drugs would have affected his mental health."

"So who killed him?" Bailey demanded. "Or do you think his death was accidental?"

"It's possible he overdosed." Dom's tone made it clear that he didn't believe that for a second. "Or there might be more than one stalker."

Bailey gasped in horror. "No."

Dom flinched, regretting his blunt words. He was thinking out loud, but he should have known he would cause Bailey even more stress.

"I'm sorry, Bailey. I'm just trying to consider every potential explanation." He held her worried gaze. "What if Gage was involved and that's why he had a phone? And Kevin was also involved and that's why he had a phone."

"They were both texting me?"

"Yes."

"If I follow your line of thinking, it's possible Gage

killed his mother for her inheritance and Kevin killed his grandmother for the same reason," Zac added.

Dom nodded. "Then there would have to be at least one more out there who killed both of them."

Bailey shook her head in disbelief. "A group of stalkers who are also killing their relatives?"

"It wouldn't be a huge stretch," Zac protested. "People with all sorts of fetishes find it easy to create groups in chat rooms or on social media."

"Like the Murder Club," Dom added. "Only they didn't want to solve crimes; they came together out of their desire to kill someone who could leave them a fortune."

"But why include me?" Bailey stubbornly demanded. "And why would one of the group suddenly decide to kill Gage and Kevin?"

"Enough. This is driving me crazy." Zac moved to give Bailey a hug. "I need to go spend some time with my wife and clear my mind. Maybe then I can figure out what the hell is going on. Until then . . ." He kissed the top of Bailey's head. "You be careful."

With a nod toward Dom, the sheriff exited the kitchen, and a minute later they heard the sound of the front door closing.

"That must be nice," Dom murmured, not bothering to keep the envy out of his voice.

"What?"

"To have someone you can be with to ease your worries."

A wistful smile touched Bailey's lips. "Do you think it's really possible?"

Dom moved to pull Bailey into his arms, savoring the warmth of her slender body as it pressed against him.

"I didn't. Not until my best friend convinced me to attend his wedding in Pike," he confessed.

She tilted back her head, her expression somber. "Now you're caught up in a murder investigation. Not the best way to ease any worries."

He gently brushed a kiss over her forehead. "I'd rather be here investigating a murder than anywhere else in the world."

Chapter 14

Bailey opened the passenger door of the Land Rover, not surprised when Dom made a sound of frustration. He'd held his tongue during the drive to her house, but she'd known he wasn't happy at her insistence that she needed to take care of a few things. And he'd been even more unhappy when she insisted she needed to do them without him around. Not that he was foolish enough to try to stop her, she wryly acknowledged.

"I don't like you being alone," Dom abruptly burst out.

Bailey glanced over her shoulder to the dogs, who were impatiently waiting with their noses pressed against the back window.

"I won't be alone. I'll have Bert and Ernie with me. And once I've cleaned the fridge and taken out the trash I'll be over at Dorinda's house."

He snorted. "That's not much protection. I should be with you."

Bailey didn't disagree with his logic. But she couldn't have a bodyguard 24-7. Not unless she was willing to give up every ounce of freedom. She wasn't going to take unreasonable risks, but she was going to do everything in her power to discover who the hell was stalking her.

"Dorinda won't feel comfortable gossiping in front of you," she insisted.

"Then I'll wait here."

She reached out to run her fingers along the stubborn line of his jaw. "You said you had stuff to do," she reminded him. "Go do them."

He growled low in his throat before he leaned forward and claimed a scorching kiss.

"The stuff I want to do includes you," he muttered against her lips.

Her fingers stroked through the lush softness of his hair. "Maybe we should grab a pizza and a bottle of wine for lunch."

He nuzzled a path of kisses over her cheek. "I can do that."

Bailey shivered, suddenly wishing they were in the privacy of Lia's house. Why had she been in such a hurry to leave? The trash would've lasted another day. And there'd been cake and Dom and, if she'd been smart, Dom covered in cake . . .

She forced herself to lean back, but her gaze remained locked on Dom's mouth. It was baffling how he could create such delicious chaos with a simple brush of his lips.

"This won't take long," she assured him.

"Promise me you'll be careful," he demanded, peering deep into her eyes.

"I'll be careful."

"And you'll hurry."

"As fast as possible."

"Faster."

"Okay. Faster than possible," she swore.

Pressing a quick kiss against his lips, Bailey jumped out of the vehicle before he could wrap her in his arms. She was already regretting her decision to spend even a minute away from this man. Obviously she needed an hour or so to clear her mind.

Opening the back door, she let out Bert and Ernie and headed for her house. She barely got the door open before the beasts were rushing inside, scampering from one room after each other, as if they'd been away for a year, not a couple of days. Bailey waited for them to prance back into the living room before she leaned out the front door and waved toward the waiting SUV. If there'd been anyone hidden inside, the dogs would have alerted her.

She waited until Dom drove away before she grabbed the mail from her letter box and closed the door. She plucked out the bills from the junk flyers as she headed into the kitchen. Might as well take care of them while she was there. She had no idea how long she was going to be staying at Lia's.

Within a half an hour she'd finished the bills, cleaned out her refrigerator, and folded the clothes she'd forgotten in the dryer. Then, gathering the trash, she retraced her steps through the living room. She didn't want to miss the garbageman, who would be by any time. She was grabbing the door handle when Bert and Ernie burst into the room, loudly barking at the window.

Bailey came to an abrupt halt at the sight of the man who was peering through the open curtains, the air squeezing from her lungs. Grabbing the phone from the pocket of her jacket, she was pressing 911 when she belatedly realized she recognized the trespasser.

Ward Bennett. The lawyer dealing with Nellie's estate.

Cautiously, she pulled open the wooden door, leaving the screen door locked.

"Yes?"

The large man was attired in another suit that was a shade too tight and a tie wrapped around his thick neck. With a practiced smile he moved across the porch to stand directly in front of the screen.

"Sorry. I was just about to knock. I couldn't tell if you were home or not."

Bailey narrowed her gaze. It was hard to imagine this man was a threat. He was not only standing on her front porch in broad daylight but he'd parked his black Mercedes directly in front of her house. The entire neighborhood would be gawking out their windows trying to figure out who the car belonged to.

Only an idiot would be that conspicuous if he was there to hurt her.

Then again, he had been peeking in her window. She kept the phone in her hand as she patted Ernie's head. The dog was leaning protectively against her, growling at the intruder.

"What are you doing here?"

He held up a manila folder he was holding. "I have some paperwork I need you to look over."

Bailey remained wary. "There was no need to bring it yourself. I could have come to the office."

"I'm afraid I didn't have your cell phone number."

His smooth response reminded Bailey that she still didn't know how the stalker had gotten her number. It also suggested that Ward Bennett wasn't the killer.

"Come in."

She reached to push on the screen door, allowing it to stay open as Warren stepped into the house. Turning to face him, Bailey remained next to the threshold, prepared to run at the least sign of danger. At the same time the dogs moved to stand in front of her. Did they sense her tension? Certainly Ward did. He was eyeing her with a puzzled expression.

"You said you had some paperwork?" she prompted.

"Yes." He cleared his throat, reverting to lawyer mode. "I suppose you've heard that Gage Warren died in an unfortunate accident?"

Bailey's mouth was suddenly dry. There'd been so many things happening, it was a shock to be reminded that Gage was dead.

"I did."

"That, of course, changes Nellie Warren's will since he was the primary beneficiary."

Bailey felt a sharp flare of relief. It wasn't that she couldn't use the money. Or that she didn't believe Nellie truly wanted her to have it. But everything about the inheritance had been tainted by Gage Warren's ugly accusations.

"Oh, well, if I'm no longer included, that's fine," she assured her companion. "In fact, it's great."

"Oh no." He held up the file, as if she could provide all the answers. "The provision that included your legacy remains the same. Nellie was very specific about that. But now that Gage is . . ." The words faded, as if in grief for Gage's unexpected death. Bailey hid a grimace, fairly confident that it was an act the lawyer had developed when discussing wills with heartbroken families. "Now that he's gone, the bulk of the estate will be split between Nellie's favorite charity and the nursing home." His practiced smile returned. "You'll be happy to know that they've already agreed that the will can proceed without being contested."

"Wait." Bailey didn't try to disguise her shock. "The nursing home is going to get Nellie's money?"

He nodded. "Nellie made a provision that if her heir was to die before her, or within a year of her death, his inheritance would revert and be split between Crossroads Food Bank and Pike Nursing Home."

Bailey tried to process what he was saying. Nellie died. And then Gage. And now the Donaldsons were going to inherit half of a lumberyard and who knew how much in life insurance? Was it connected? Did it have anything to do with her stalker?

She shook her head, realizing that Ward was waiting for her to speak. "Is that unusual?" she blurted out.

"Which part?"

All of it. She didn't allow the words to leave her lips. Ward was beginning to look uncomfortable.

"Having the will revert if the beneficiary dies within a year of inheriting?" she clarified.

He shrugged. "I can't say it's common, but it's not wholly unusual."

"Why?"

He took a moment, as if deciding how to explain why Nellie would have deliberately made sure the inheritance was rescinded if Gage died within a year without giving away his confidential conversations with his client.

"Well, for instance, someone might be concerned that their loved one might be taken advantage of because of their inheritance," he finally explained. "Or perhaps placed in danger when they have a sudden influx of assets."

It was vague, but Bailey didn't have any trouble in figuring out that Nellie was worried someone might marry Gage for his inheritance and then get rid of him or, more likely, that the shady people who'd loaned him money might threaten to kill him if he had some extra cash.

"So the money will go to the Donaldsons?" She wanted to make sure her suspicions were right.

"Half the estate, yes." He studied her, as if trying to analyze her concern. "But I'm the executor and Nellie left concise instructions on how she wanted the money used to improve the lives of the residents," he added.

"Then I'm sure it will be used wisely."

The words came out stiffly, and Bailey wasn't surprised that Ward pressed his lips together, as if offended by the implication that she didn't trust him.

"Here is your copy of the will." He handed her the file. "Please feel free to have your own lawyer look it over. Once you're satisfied it's all in order, stop by the office and we can finalize the details so you can get your money."

"No, I don't need a lawyer," she assured him, not about to explain that she was more worried at how Nellie and Gage had died and not what was going to happen to the money.

She didn't doubt for a second that the Donaldsons would find a way to slip a portion of the inheritance into their own pockets.

"Good." Ward touched the too-tight tie, as if suddenly anxious to be on his way. "I'll be in Grange today dealing with yet another unexpected death, but if you call my secretary—"

"Kevin Hartford?" Bailey abruptly interrupted.

Ward jerked, as if blindsided by her ability to guess the identity of his client. "How did you know?"

She waved a dismissive hand, smoothing her expression into one of mild sympathy. "Word gets around. Poor Lisa."

"Yes, well, it's quite tragic, and with young children, she'll need the legal work settled as quickly as possible." He shifted his feet, obviously uncomfortable with the thought that he'd revealed more than he wanted to. "I should be on my way."

"Thank you for bringing the paperwork."

Bailey stepped aside, allowing the lawyer room to scurry through the open door and off the porch. Then, as he drove away with a soft purr of his car's expensive engine, she glanced down at the dogs, still pressed against her legs.

"What are the odds of Ward Bennett being the lawyer for both Nellie and Pauline?" She abruptly moved to drop the file onto the coffee table. She'd deal with her inheritance later. For now, she had more important matters on her mind. "We need to talk to Dorinda," she muttered. "Come on, boys."

* * *

Dom parked in a corner of the lot that offered an unobstructed view of the old building next to the nursing home. He hadn't told Bailey he intended to come here, mainly because he knew it was probably going to be a waste of time. But with nothing better to do, he'd decided to take a chance.

Amazingly, he'd only been there ten minutes or so when he caught sight of the young man in blue scrubs strolling from the nursing home into the side door of the nearby building. A grim smile curved Dom's lips as he left his Land Rover and jogged across the parking lot.

When he slid into Eric Creswell's car after catching him spying on Bailey he'd caught the unmistakable stench of cigarette smoke. Which meant that he was probably one of the employees that Bailey had mentioned who used the abandoned building to grab a quick smoke during his work hours.

Reaching the door, he pulled it open, pausing to peek inside. He wasn't expecting a trap, but right now he wasn't willing to take any chances. The late-morning sunlight was struggling to penetrate the tall windows, which hadn't been cleaned in years, but it was enough to reveal a large lobby area that was lined with steel shelves loaded with cleaning supplies. In one corner there were several wheelchairs in various states of disrepair and in another was a stack of old mattresses.

Dom's attention turned to the slender man standing in the center of the room, puffing on a cigarette. With a grimace, he forced himself to step inside. Between the combustible chemicals and the flammable material, the place felt like a death trap. All it would take was one spark from the cigarette.

He quietly moved to stand directly behind the man, who was obviously lost in his thoughts.

"Hello, Eric."

"It's about time." Eric didn't seem surprised by the interruption. At least not until he turned to discover Dom standing a few feet away. With a frown, he dropped the cigarette and crushed it beneath his heel. "Oh, it's you."

"It's me," Dom agreed. "Who were you expecting?"

Eric hunched his shoulders, looking more jaundiced than usual in the murky light. "No one."

Did Dom believe him? Nope. But right now he was more interested in getting information.

"Good." He folded his arms over his chest. "I thought we might have a chat."

Eric shook his head. "I'm working."

Dom glanced around the empty space. "Do your employers know that you're on the clock?"

"I get a break."

"So it's a perfect time."

Eric hissed out an annoyed breath. "I come out here to be alone."

"And have a smoke."

"So?" His thin face settled into a petulant expression. Dom was going to guess his mother nagged at him about his smoking habit. "It's not illegal."

Dom didn't bother to point toward the large "No Smoking" sign taped to one of the windows.

"That's debatable, but I don't give a shit," he assured the younger man. "I want to talk to you about the phone you got from Ford Smithson."

"Christ, not that again." Eric shoved a hand through

his roughly chopped hair. "I haven't been taking any pictures of Bailey. Not that it's any of your business."

Dom ground his teeth, reminding himself he wasn't there to punish the creep. Not unless he discovered Eric was involved in terrorizing Bailey. There was, after all, a very real possibility that there was more than one stalker.

"It's very much my business," he warned. "But I'm more interested in the fact that Ford claims he never asked you to take pictures of Bailey."

"What?" Eric's brows lowered. "That's a lie."

"He told me that he asked you to take pictures of random people around town. Nothing else."

"Bullshit. That's not what he said."

"You're sticking to your story that Ford Smithson specifically asked for pictures of Bailey?"

Eric's lips parted, but he hesitated, as if trying to recall the conversation. "I can't remember his exact words, but he said he wanted pictures of 'my friend.'"

"Just your 'friend'? As in any of your friends? Or specifically Bailey?"

The boy hunched his shoulders. "Everyone knows that Bailey is my only friend."

"So he didn't use her name?"

"I told you, I can't remember his exact words."

Dom swallowed a curse. "Has he asked for the phone back?"

"I haven't seen him."

Well, hell. Dom had been hoping to catch one of the men in a lie. There would have to be a reason for that person to deliberately try to mislead him, right? Now it was possible it might have been nothing more than a miscommunication.

Dom ground his teeth in frustration. Time to change the subject. "How did you get involved with the Murder Club?"

Eric blinked. "I got an invite from the club. They were looking for someone who had gaming experience to help with a case."

Dom's disappointment was forgotten as he studied his companion with a narrowed gaze. Was it a coincidence that he'd been invited to the club or had Eric been deliberately chosen because of his connection to Bailey?

"How did they know you had gaming experience?"

"I may be a loser in Pike, but I have tons of fans on Twitch."

Dom arched a brow. He didn't know much about Twitch beyond the fact that it was watched by gamers, but he suspected Eric didn't have tons of fans or he would be getting paid.

He probably had a few followers and whoever had invited him to the club was pandering to Eric's ego to get him to join. Which would imply that they were acquainted.

"You never met any of the group in person?" he demanded.

"No. We have weekly conferences where we discuss ongoing cases, but it's always online," Eric insisted.

"Bailey mentioned a chat room."

"Yeah, we have a private chat room where we can go to post messages about evidence we've found or suggestions to other members." Eric shrugged. "Sometimes we go in and just spend some time talking about random stuff. But we never share names or anything. We like to stay anonymous."

Dom wondered how much time Eric spent in the chat room and how much he'd revealed about himself without realizing what he was doing. It was obvious that he was treated as an outcast in Pike. It would be understandable if he sought companionship online.

"Why did you ask Bailey to join?"

"We didn't have anyone in the group with medical expertise. And I thought she would enjoy it. She's not like most people in this town who are terrified of technology."

The smooth explanation sounded rehearsed. As if Eric had practiced the words before using them to convince Bailey to join the club.

"Did you need medical advice for a particular case?"

"A couple of them."

"And Bailey helped?" he demanded.

"Yep." Eric nodded. "She was great at spotting clues. Probably the best."

Dom didn't think Eric was exaggerating. Being a nurse meant she would have to develop an attention to the smallest details. Plus, she was naturally empathetic. She could sense when something was wrong or out of character.

"Did anyone in the group mention they missed her?"

"Everyone. Like I said, she was the best at seeing stuff the rest of us missed."

"But anyone in particular?" Dom demanded. "Maybe

they asked for her private information? Like her phone number?"

Before Eric could respond the door behind him was pulled open and the sound of footsteps echoed through the building.

"Eric, I don't have much time . . ." The words faded as Dom turned to face the intruder. He was about the same age as Dom, with a round face and hair that was brushed to the side in an effort to hide the fact that it was thinning. His dark eyes narrowed as he came to an abrupt halt. "Who are you?"

"Dom Lucier. And you?"

The man scowled. "Logan Donaldson."

"Logan Donaldson." Dom felt his expression hardening into lines of disgust. "You're the selfish bastard who was responsible for Bailey losing her job."

The man took an instinctive step backward, as if sensing Dom's burning desire to punch him in the middle of his fake-tanned face.

"What are you doing in here?"

With an effort, Dom squashed his violent impulse. Punching the idiot might make him feel better, but it wouldn't do anything to help Bailey. And that was all that mattered.

"I'm just having a chat with Eric," he drawled.

"Well, do it when he's not on the clock." Logan glared toward the silent Eric. "Get back to work."

With visible relief, Eric scurried past Dom and out the door. Dom didn't bother to stop him. Instead, he allowed his gaze to sweep over Logan, taking in the expensive cashmere sweater and black slacks before lowering to the leather shoes that were coated with a fine layer of dust.

This man hadn't come into this derelict building to berate a missing employee. Not when he was wearing shoes that had set him back several hundred dollars. So why was he there? Had he set up a meeting with Eric? A meeting he wanted to keep secret from the rest of the staff?

That seemed the most reasonable explanation. But why?

"This is private property," Logan intruded into Dom's musings.

Dom arched a brow. "Is it? I understood it belonged to the county."

Logan pinched his lips, but he didn't bother to argue. In fact, he started backing toward the door as if he was afraid to be alone with Dom.

"Go away, Mr. Lucier," he commanded, nearly stumbling over the warped threshold. "And don't come back."

For once those words had no power to hurt Dom. In fact, he smiled as he watched Logan bolt toward the nearby nursing home. Eric and Logan had a secret. And Dom had every intention of discovering what they were trying to hide.

Chapter 15

Dorinda was standing in the open doorway as Bailey finished hauling out her trash and climbed onto the porch. No surprise. The older woman had no doubt been peering through the window from the moment Dom dropped her off and impatiently waiting for Bailey to stop by for a chat before she left.

"It's about time you brought them for a visit," Dorinda complained as she encouraged the dogs to dance around with their tongues hanging out and their tails wagging.

"It's only been a couple of days," Bailey retorted, not sure if she was speaking to Dorinda or her ridiculous pets.

"That's too long." Dorinda scratched the dogs in the perfect spot behind their ears. "Isn't it, boys?"

Bailey rolled her eyes as her dogs melted with pleasure. "Bert and Ernie agree."

"Of course they do. They are very smart."

Realizing she was wasting time, she lifted her gaze to meet her neighbor's steady gaze.

"Are you busy?"

"Not unless you count watching old game shows.

Come in." Dorinda stepped back and the dogs darted inside, headed toward the kitchen, where the older woman kept a box of toys. Bailey followed at a slower pace, halting in the middle of the small living room as Dorinda crossed the worn carpet to shut off the television. "Sit down and I'll get us a cup of tea."

Bailey perched on the love seat that was upholstered in the same ugly brocade as the long couch. She adored Dorinda, but the older woman had stuffed the tiny house with heavy furniture and dozens of tables that were cluttered with stacks of old magazines. Bailey struggled against a sense of claustrophobia whenever she spent time there.

Returning with two cups of tea, Dorinda offered one to Bailey before she took a seat on the couch.

"What's on your mind?"

Still uneasy at the realization that Ward Bennett was the lawyer for both Nellie and Pauline, she asked the question on the top of her mind.

"Did you know Pauline Hartford from Grange?"

"The one who fell in her pool?" Dorinda waited for Bailey to nod before she continued. "I wasn't personally acquainted with her, but I know she was the superintendent of the Grange school system." Dorinda sipped her coffee. "She was always in the paper or on the local news. She seemed to like being noticed. Why do you ask?"

Bailey carefully set the cup on a nearby table. She was too edgy to hold the delicate china.

"I was wondering if Pauline Hartford and Nellie Warren were related."

"You mean blood-related?"

"Related in any way."

Dorinda pursed her lips, searching her mind for any association between the women. "Not that I can think of," she at last conceded defeat. "Is there a reason you care?"

Bailey swallowed a sigh. Dorinda knew everything about everyone. That meant there was no obvious connection between the older women.

"Just curious."

Dorinda clicked her tongue. "You didn't leave that gorgeous man alone because you're curious," she chided. "What's going on?"

Bailey didn't want to share what was happening. Not when there was even a vague possibility it would put the older woman in danger. But she knew Dorinda too well to think she would answer her questions without some explanation.

"I was at the nursing home—"

"Have you gone back to work?" Dorinda interrupted in sharp tones.

"No. Logan asked me to come in to try to persuade me to return."

"Of course he did." The older woman sniffed. "Did he beg?"

"Not exactly."

"I'd wait until he got on his knees."

Bailey tried and failed to imagine the egotistical Logan Donaldson on his knees.

"A nice thought, but it's doubtful he'd ever swallow his pride."

"That's true enough." Dorinda leaned forward to shove aside a stack of magazines so she could set down her cup. "If you decided to quit your job, Bailey, you know you could always ask me for help. That's what neighbors are for."

Bailey felt a flare of warmth. It wasn't just the fact that Dorinda would share everything she owned without hesitation; it was the kindness that shimmered in her eyes. This woman had been a part of Bailey's life since she moved in with her grandmother. She'd been a babysitter, a confidant, and a shoulder to cry on when Bailey was afraid to tell her grandmother she'd crashed their only car.

"All I need is information," she assured her friend.

"Okay." Dorinda sat back, her hands folded in her lap. "I have plenty of that."

"True." Bailey deliberately paused to tease the older woman's curiosity. "And you're also willing to overlook the fact that I might have gotten the information by eavesdropping on a private conversation between Logan and his mother."

As expected, Dorinda's eyes sparkled with anticipation. "Eavesdropping is always the best way to get information," she agreed. "What did you hear?"

"They were arguing about Logan endangering the reputation of the nursing home. I'm not sure exactly what they were talking about, but I assumed it had something to do with the fact that he'd refused Nellie's demand to call the sheriff when she caught Gage stealing from her."

Dorinda's expression tightened with disapproval. "Not to mention blaming you when Nellie changed her will."

Bailey grimaced, refusing to dwell on the distress

that the Donaldsons had deliberately caused her. Those two would be willing to sacrifice anyone and anything to protect their business.

"Logan refused to accept the blame and insisted that he wouldn't have to take risks if she hadn't kept him away from his father."

"Oh."

Bailey frowned as she watched a strange emotion soften the older woman's features. As if she'd forgotten why she was angry with the Donaldsons.

"I thought Lorene was a widow when she came to Pike," Bailey said. "I remember someone mentioning a car accident."

Dorinda nodded her head. "That's the story I heard as well."

"So no one knows where she comes from or anything about her past?"

The older woman shifted on the couch, as if she was suddenly uncomfortable with the conversation.

"There were rumors when she first showed up," she eventually admitted.

"Such as?"

"Some people whispered that she had an affair with a married man and that his wife ran Lorene out of town."

Bailey shook her head at the mere idea that the fierce, ruthlessly determined woman who controlled the nursing home and her staff with an iron fist could be frightened into fleeing.

"I don't believe it."

Dorinda shrugged. "She was young and pregnant."

Bailey continued to shake her head. Lorene could

have a gun pointed at her head and she would spit in the person's face. There had to be another explanation.

"Were there other rumors?"

Dorinda glanced away, allowing a long, oddly strained silence to stretch between them. Was she trying to recall the ancient gossip? She seemed tense, as if there was something bothering her.

"Not exactly a rumor," the older woman at last admitted.

"Dorinda, what is it?"

"I've never told this to anyone. Not for over thirty years."

Bailey arched her brows. This woman was an avid gossip. There was nothing she loved more than sharing the tidbits she picked up from her numerous friends. The fact that she'd kept a secret for thirty years was nothing short of a miracle.

"I'm listening," Bailey murmured.

"Back when Lorene first moved to Pike our church group was in charge of bingo day at the nursing home," she said, her gaze locked on her hands, which she'd twisted together in her lap. "Those were the days before the new nursing home was built and it was next door in the old poorhouse. The kitchen was in the base-ment. I hated going down there, but I had to get the cupcakes we'd brought to serve the residents. Choco-late with sprinkles, I think. Or maybe they were the vanilla ones with cream cheese frosting. Yes, it was the cream cheese ones. We left them in the walk-in cooler. Remember, that place didn't have air-conditioning and in the summer it was always unpleasantly hot. . . ." She abruptly lifted her head to send Bailey a wry glance.

"Oh, you wouldn't remember, would you? You weren't even born yet."

Bailey frowned. Her older friend might like to gossip, but she didn't usually babble nonsense. The only time she ever talked in circles was when she was hiding something.

"Dorinda." Bailey narrowed her eyes. "Why are you stalling?"

The older woman blew out a harsh breath. "I don't like Lorene Donaldson. And after what she did to you I like her even less. But I do have sympathy for her."

"Why?" Bailey demanded in surprise. Sympathy for Lorene? It was like having sympathy for a crocodile.

"While I was in the kitchen I heard Lorene talking to someone. She was outside, but the window was open and I could hear them clear as day."

"Do you know who it was?"

"I didn't recognize the voice, but it sounded like an older woman. She was telling Lorene that she had to come home."

"I'm assuming she didn't mean her house in Pike?"

Dorinda shook her head. "She was very specific that she was disgusted that Lorene was working for a living and ruining her grandson's life by keeping him away from his birthright."

"Birthright?" That sounded like something rich people said. "She didn't mention a location?" Bailey asked.

"As far as I know, Lorene has never said where she came from."

Bailey shuffled through her memories, trying to recall whether Lorene had ever mentioned her life before Pike. She came up with nothing. Not beyond the practiced story of arriving at the nursing home with nothing but determination and ending up as the owner.

She shook her head. Where Lorene came from didn't matter. "Did she say anything else?"

"That Lorene had a duty to her husband and family."

Bailey jerked in shock. "Husband and family?"

"Yes."

"Her husband isn't dead. Or at least he wasn't when she left." Bailey thought back to the conversation that she'd overheard at the nursing home. "And Logan knew. Why lie about it?"

"I'm sure she had her reason."

Bailey studied her friend. The older woman was still keeping something from her.

"What did Lorene say about returning home?"

"She said that she would cut her own throat before she went back."

Bailey grimaced. "That's a little dramatic."

"I thought so too," Dorinda agreed. "Until I heard the slap."

"Lorene slapped the old lady?"

Dorinda shook her head. "No, I heard a crack, and then Lorene cried out in pain. I peeked out of the window and I could see she was on her knees with her arms covering her head, as if she expected more blows."

Bailey abruptly understood why her friend felt sympathy for Lorene. "Could the older woman have been her mother?"

"That was my first guess," Dorinda admitted. "Or maybe her mother-in-law. It made me fear that Lorene was running from an abusive situation."

Bailey slowly nodded. Certainly the stranger was

violent if she'd slapped Lorene. But if Lorene had been in danger from her family, why hadn't her husband run away with her? Unless he'd been equally violent? She frowned, struck by a sudden thought.

"You said the older woman mentioned a husband and family. It could mean anything. Parents or siblings, but . . ." She allowed the words to trail away and Dorinda nodded.

"Yes, I did wonder if there were other children." Dorinda bit her bottom lip. "Children she left behind."

Chapter 16

Dom studied Bailey's pale face, sipping the wine he'd found in Kayden's private stash. It was a rare vintage that cost a fortune, but at the moment Dom didn't care. He'd returned to the house after collecting the pizza he'd ordered from Bella's to discover Bailey at the table, eating the last of the cake straight out of the pan. Never a good sign. Scooting aside the cake, he'd divvied out the pizza and gone in search of the best wine he could find.

Thankfully, lunch had visibly eased the tension humming through Bailey to a dull buzz. At least enough for Dom to ask the question that was burning his tongue.

"I know I ask this a lot," he murmured, "but are you okay?"

She wrinkled her nose. "I'm just trying to make some sense out of what's happened today."

"Tell me," he urged.

In clipped tones, she shared the conversation she'd overheard between Logan and his mother, Ward Bennett's unexpected arrival at her house, followed by her conversation with Dorinda and the fact that Lorene might have secrets from her past. In turn, Dom shared his encounter with Eric Criswell and his suspicion he was meeting Logan.

"We went from not enough information to too much information," Bailey muttered, echoing his own frustration. "It's giving me a headache."

"Me too," he admitted in dry tones. "Maybe it will help if we put it in order."

"Okay." She paused, as if trying to organize her thoughts. "This morning we discovered that our latest suspect was found dead in his grandmother's house from an overdose."

"Along with the fact that Kevin was in possession of the phone that sent you texts," Dom added.

"He was also the heir to his grandmother's estate, just like Gage Warren."

"It's certainly interesting that Ward Bennett was the legal representative for both Nellie Warren and Pauline Hartford," he agreed. "The question is whether he had any other involvement in what happened to the older women."

"And even more interesting is that at least half of Nellie's wealth will be handed over to the Donaldsons," Bailey retorted.

Dom dismissed Ward Bennett from his mind. Right now they didn't have enough information about the older man to assume he was anything other than an attorney doing his job. As Bailey said, the Donaldsons were more interesting.

"We haven't really considered Logan as a possible suspect."

She tapped her fingers on the edge of the table,

clearly ready and eager to believe that her employer was capable of murder.

"I wonder if Pauline Hartford's will included a donation to the nursing home like Nellie's did," she murmured. "Pauline's neighbor mentioned that the older woman wasn't exactly charitable, but when I was talking to Dorinda this morning she made a comment that Pauline Hartford was always pushing herself into the news, as if she craved attention. Maybe she left some money to the Donaldsons with the demand that her legacy would be attached to the gift. Like the Hartford Library or the Hartford Butterfly Garden." Bailey shrugged. "Something like that."

The words made sense to Dom. He'd been raised by a narcissist who would love nothing more than to have his name engraved on plaques scattered around France.

"It's a good theory," he agreed. "That would explain why the Donaldsons would want her dead."

Bailey hesitated, then heaved a sigh. "But not what happened to Kevin."

Dom considered the various explanations. They'd been looking at Kevin as a suspect, not a victim. Why would Logan want him dead?

"Maybe he decided to contest the will," he finally suggested. "Or maybe a larger chunk of the inheritance goes to the nursing home if Kevin is out of the way." He paused before adding, "Or maybe they were working together, and Logan decided that Kevin's drug habit was making him a liability to their secrets."

"That would fit. Logan makes a good suspect. He could easily have overheard Eric and me discussing the Murder Club. And he would obviously have my cell phone number and my address along with my work schedule."

Dom narrowed his gaze. He didn't miss the edge of disbelief in her tone. "But?"

"He can barely bother to show up for work," she pointed out. "I can't imagine him with the ambition to plot and murder, then follow through with stalking his victim and doing the deed."

"He wasn't necessarily acting alone," he reminded her. "There's a chance he had help."

"Kevin?"

"Kevin and possibly Gage," Dom added. "Plus, at least one more possibility."

She pursed her lips, trying to dredge up likely partners in crime. "Not his mother." The words were a statement, not a question.

"Actually, I was thinking about Eric Criswell," Dom clarified. "I'm convinced Logan and Eric were meeting this morning. And that they wanted the meeting to be a secret."

"I agree. Why else wouldn't they meet in Logan's office?" She shook her head in disgust. "He spent a fortune having it refurbished a few months ago."

Dom muttered a curse, his head spinning. Then, after polishing off the last of his wine, he leaned forward to place the empty glass on the table. At the same time, he dismissed the worry that was gnawing at him like a cancer. He was going to have an ulcer before this was all over, but for now he wanted to think about something other than the stalker who lurked just out of sight.

"What we need is a break," he announced in firm tones. "It will hopefully clear our brains."

She stilled, as if sensing he had decided exactly how he wanted to clear his brain.

"What kind of break? A long walk? A hot bath?"

With a slow smile, he slid his finger along the edge of the cake pan, scooping out the last of the frosting. Then, holding her gaze, he dabbed the rich chocolate on her lower lip.

"I was thinking dessert," he murmured, shoving himself to his feet so he could lean across the table and claim her lips in a kiss that sent shock waves of hunger blasting through him.

Bailey had returned to the house with a dark cloud of fear hanging over her head. It wasn't just fear for herself, although she could sense the danger like a shadow breathing down her neck. Her greatest fear was that she wasn't going to be able to figure out who was stalking her and they would kill again and again.

Then Dom licked the frosting from her lips, and suddenly the cloud was gone. It wasn't that her troubles disappeared, but they melted to the background as heat blasted through her, creating delicious butterflies in the pit of her stomach.

She parted her lips in invitation as the eager anticipation bubbled through her. From the moment Dom Lucier had appeared in Pike for Lia's wedding, he'd fascinated her. No surprise. He was a strikingly gorgeous stranger and sexy as hell.

But the past week had added depth to her initial attraction. This was a man she trusted, who she turned to when she was afraid or when she needed someone to share her thoughts. The man she wanted at her side when she woke in the morning and who would be there at the end of the day.

This was the man she wanted to be a part of her life. End of story.

"Should I whip up more frosting?" she asked as his mouth moved to explore her features with soft sweeps.

"Tempting, but I'm hungry for something sweeter." He kissed her with a shocking demand before lifting his head to study her flushed face with a wry smile. "Perhaps we should take this upstairs. I'd like some privacy."

"Privacy?" Bailey frowned, the desire fogging her brain. It wasn't until he nodded toward the dogs, who were lined up next to the table as they impatiently waited for their share of pizza that she realized what was troubling him. "Oh. They are nosy," she agreed with a chuckle.

Warm fingers traced the edge of her hairline, intensifying the craving that was no longer fluttering in the pit of her stomach. It was churning with a reckless abandon. Dom's softest touch stirred a need that was drowning her with pleasure. And she'd never been more eager to become lost in the glorious sensations.

"And I'm old enough to desire comfort," Dom added as he moved around the table to stand beside her.

She tilted back her head, her lips curving into a teasing smile. "No kinky experimentations?"

The black eyes smoldered with a sensual promise.

"I'm open to any kink you want. All that matters is pleasing you."

Bailey's smile faded as she allowed him to glimpse the emotions he stirred deep inside her.

"You please me," she said in a husky voice. "Everything about you."

A strange expression touched his features as he bent down to slip his arms beneath her, scooping her into his arms with a graceful ease. Bailey instinctively wrapped her arms around his neck as he cradled her against his chest before he headed out of the kitchen. Bailey released a soft sigh as she studied the face that had become so vitally important in her life. Was it a cliché to be impressed by a man sweeping her off her feet? Who cared? Dom Lucier made her happy. To the depths of her soul. Besides, falling in love was supposed to be a little clichéd, right? Racing hearts and delicious tingles that made her toes curl.

"What does 'everything' include?" he asked as they moved through the living room and down the hallway.

She rolled her eyes. "You don't need me to tell you that you're outrageously gorgeous."

"I wouldn't mind."

She blinked, belatedly catching sight of his vulnerable expression. He truly needed to be reassured that she found him irresistible. Was it because they'd known each other for such a short time? Or because this moment mattered as much to him as it did to her?

Either way, she didn't hesitate to reassure him. Holding his gaze, she ran her fingers through the short strands of hair at the base of his neck.

"I love how your hair shimmers in the sunlight. Like

priceless gold. And it feels like satin." She tangled her fingers in the silky strands. "And I love your eyes. They're as dark and mysterious as a midnight sky." Her hand stroked over his cheek, relishing the scrape of his whiskers, which he hadn't bothered to shave that morning. "And this face . . ." She traced the proud length of his nose before moving to outline his lush lips. "Each feature is perfect." She released a shaky breath as he entered the shadowed bedroom and gently lowered her onto the mattress. The short journey had inflamed her passions until they threatened to explode. Touching him . . . wrapped in his arms as his scent seeped into her skin . . . it was intoxicating. Plus, it had been a long time for her. Nearly two years since she'd dated a guy she'd desired. And it'd never been like this. She was starved for Dom's touch. "I love all of you." Reaching up, she grasped the edges of his flannel shirt and opened it with one determined yank. She smiled in pleasure as the sculpted muscles of his chest were exposed. "And I want to spend my nights exploring every inch."

Dom shivered as she placed her palms flat against his chest, her fingers spreading to explore the steely strength beneath his smooth skin.

"Yes, please," he rasped, his eyes dilated and his skin flushed with anticipation as he leaned over her.

She lightly scraped her nails over his puckered nipples, savoring his deep groan of desire.

"But that's not why I want you in my life," she breathed. "Or at least not the only reason."

"Then why?" His voice was strained, revealing the effort it was taking not to fall on top of her and ease the hunger pulsing between them.

"Because I trust that you would never walk away from me. Not even when it gets too hard." The words were simple, but they came from her heart. Any other man in his right mind would have disappeared the moment they realized she was being stalked by a crazed killer. But not Dom. He'd convinced her to move in with him while he put himself in danger to keep her safe. "You don't see me as disposable."

"Never." It was a harsh vow that echoed through the room as Dom swiftly rid himself of the remainder of his clothing, revealing a body that looked as if it'd been chiseled from stone.

Bailey's mouth went dry as she ran her fingers over the rippling muscles, heat blasting through her as she investigated the broad expanse of his chest. Sucking in a ragged breath, Dom was settled on the edge of the mattress, gazing at her with a fierce intensity.

"You are where I want to be. For always," he assured her, reaching out to cup her cheek in his hand. "Now it's my turn."

Bailey lay back against the pillows, watching him with a delicious sense of anticipation.

"Your turn for what?"

"For sharing how much I adore these freckles." He bent down, brushing his lips over the bridge of her nose.

Bailey trembled with pleasure even as she snorted at his ridiculous words. "That's a stretch."

"Not at all," he insisted. "I sat next to you at the wedding dinner, battling the urge to do this." He pressed kiss after kiss over her face. "I also spent an inordinate amount of time wondering if you had those delicious freckles anywhere else on your body."

She arched her neck as his mouth moved down the curve of her throat. "We'd just met."

"I knew I desired you at first glance," he assured her, expertly grasping the hem of her sweater to gently tug it over her head before tossing it aside. He gazed down at her as he unhooked her bra and smoothed it away. "And spending time together that weekend convinced me you were special."

Bailey gasped as his hand cupped her breasts. His touch was gentle, but there was nothing gentle about the pleasure that seared through her. It felt like lava flowing through her blood.

"I'm not special," she muttered.

He scowled down at her. "I get to decide. And to me you are . . ." He paused, his gaze moving to where his thumbs were stroking her nipples to sensitive peaks. "You are exactly what I need." He once again bent down, nuzzling a path of caresses over her forehead. "This beautiful face." He brushed his mouth down her nose before tracing her lips with the tip of his tongue. "These kissable lips." Bailey released a strangled groan as he continued to explore every inch of her face while his fingers lowered to unzip her jeans and tug them downward. "These eyes that hold a kindness that draws people to you like bees to honey." He kissed her eyes shut as Bailey kicked off her shoes and eagerly helped him dispose of her clothing. As she lay back, she caught him gazing at her with an oddly tender smile before he released her hair from the bun on top of her head and threaded his fingers through the tangled strands. "This hair that refuses to be tamed."

A chuckle was wrenched from her throat. She'd

never been a woman who spent hours on her hair and makeup, and working as a nurse had solidified her appreciation for comfort over fashion.

Thankfully, Dom didn't seem to mind.

"Untamed is one way to—"

Dom claimed her lips in a kiss of sheer demand, silencing her teasing words as her brain shut down and her body ignited with a blast of desire. As if she'd been struck by lightning. Every nerve was shrieking in pleasure, demanding a fulfillment that could only come from one man.

Stretching out next to her, Dom wrapped his arms around her, pressing her tight as the friction of their naked flesh sparked low moans of anticipation.

"I'm obsessed with holding you in my arms and drowning in your scent. Of tasting your sweetness." He swept his lips along the line of her jaw before trailing a path of kisses down her arched throat. "Your breasts . . ." he breathed, stroking his tongue over her nipples as his fingers parted her legs to seek out her most sensitive spot. "Your hidden secrets . . ."

Bailey trembled, wrapping her leg over his hip as her passion spiraled ever higher. "Dom."

He continued to pleasure her as his mouth moved to press between her breasts. "But more than all that, I'm captivated by this."

Bailey tangled her fingers in his hair, moving her body against his in a silent plea for more.

"My heart?"

"Your ability to offer love without manipulation," he clarified, his words unsteady as she reached down to wrap her fingers around his thickening erection. "To care for others without expecting anything in return."

Bailey smiled as she stroked her fingers down his arousal. It was true. They'd both built shields over the years to protect their shattered hearts, but somehow, together, they'd found the means to overcome the wounds of the past and connect in a way that healed them both.

Did that mean they could find a way to forge a future together? That was a conversation for later. Much later.

"That's enough talking," she groaned, rolling onto her back and urging him on top of her.

Dom chuckled, readily settling between her spread legs. "I've always been a big believer in action speaking louder than words," he growled, piercing her with a slow, delicious thrust that brought a cry of bliss to Bailey's lips.

Chapter 17

Dom squeezed Bailey tightly in his arms, her head resting on his chest as he stroked through her hair, troubled by the unease that settled in the center of his heart. The sex had been epic, of course. In fact, it'd been whatever was beyond epic. Each soft stroke of Bailey's fingers, each brush of her lips and each groan that had been wrenched from her lips had torqued his pleasure until he'd shattered in an explosive climax. But he'd already known that sex with Bailey was going to be spectacular. He'd been fantasizing about her for months.

What he hadn't expected was how vulnerable he would feel as they snuggled in the soft bed, the world outside blocked by the heavy curtains and closed door.

Since coming to Pike and spending time with this woman, his soul had been blasted wide open. And that wasn't an exaggeration. Over the years he'd developed a protective shell to keep people at a distance. He was never going to be like his mother, who allowed her heart to be trampled on a regular basis.

But allowing Bailey beneath his defenses left him

feeling exposed, as if his nerves were scraped raw. And it didn't help that Bailey had barely said a word since their last bout of lovemaking. He'd like to think she was speechless with pleasure, but there was a gnawing fear deep inside him that she might regret what had happened between them.

An unbearable thought.

"You're making me nervous," Dom at last broke the silence, telling himself that the truth couldn't be any worse than what he was imagining. "You aren't usually this quiet."

She stiffened. "Are you implying I'm loud?"

"Never loud, but I love the sound of your happy chatter." Dom paused, patiently waiting for her to tilt back her head to reveal her wary expression. "It reassures me that all is right in the world."

She studied him as if seeking some sort of reassurance. "Is it right?"

Unease pierced his heart. He wanted this woman glowing with the same joy that bubbled through him. The fact that she wasn't only added to his profound sense of vulnerability.

"Are we discussing what just happened in this bed?" he bluntly demanded. "Because I'm going to tell you up front that making love to you has turned my world upside down." He stroked his fingers through her hair, his voice raw with emotion. "I'm not sure I'll ever be the same."

A shaky smile curved her lips. "Me too."

"Then what's bothering you?"

"I was waiting."

Dom turned, balancing on his elbow as he gazed down at her in confusion. "Did I leave something out?"

"Nothing." She reached up to brush her fingers along the line of his jaw. "But usually at this point I start to feel awkward." She wrinkled her nose. "I'm not much of a cuddler."

Dom sensed there was more to her words than an aversion to snuggles. "Why?"

"No matter how much I might like a guy, there's this awkward part of me that wants to get dressed and put some space between us."

A portion of Dom's unease faded. Her tension had nothing to do with him or what had happened between them. Thank God.

"A therapist might see that as a fear of intimacy," he murmured, bending down to press a lingering kiss against her mouth. "But I'm going to cling to the hope that it's just because you hadn't found the right man."

She pressed her hands flat against his chest, not to push him away but to smooth her palms over his rigid muscles.

"I'm going to agree with you because all I want to do is snuggle with you."

Dom growled in approval as her fingers teased his hardened nipples. Both of them were going to have to work through the baggage they carried from their past, but the fact that they could openly share their fears was a good start. There was nothing they couldn't work through if they were honest with each other.

And it didn't hurt that her light touch was setting him on fire. Passion like this was rare and wonderful.

"You feel as perfect in my arms as I dreamed," he

assured her, his hand cupping the soft weight of her breast as he hardened in anticipation. "This is paradise." He nuzzled the corner of her mouth, shivering as her hands slid downward. She wanted her fingers wrapped around his arousal, stroking him until . . . His delightful fantasy was rudely interrupted by the buzz of Bailey's phone. Lifting his head, he glared at the offending object. "And that is the serpent," he rasped.

Rolling to the side, Bailey reached to grasp the phone, glancing at the screen before sending Dom a rueful grimace.

"It's Zac."

Dom ground his teeth. Of course it was Zac. That would be the only person with the power to crush their illusion of being secluded from the world. Resisting the urge to take the phone and toss it across the room, Dom sat up.

"What's happened?"

Bailey shoved her hair out of her face. "I'm not sure. The text says he's at his office and he has some information we might be interested in."

Dom cupped her face in his hands, branding her lips with a fierce kiss before lifting his head to regard her with a grudging resignation.

"As much as I want to stay here with you, I have a feeling we should find out what he has discovered," he conceded.

She touched her fingers to the center of his chest, directly over his thundering heart.

"Remember this moment. We'll pick up where we left off later."

"Not later." He stole another kiss before speaking against her lips. "Soon. Very soon."

"Yes."

They climbed out of bed and Bailey headed for the spare bedroom as Dom hopped in the shower. He intended to try to convince Bailey to move into this bedroom, but for now they were both focused on what Zac had to share with them.

Within less than an hour they were across town and entering the courthouse on Main Street where the sheriff's department was located. It was five on the dot, but Dom was still surprised to discover how empty the old building felt as they passed through the wide corridor that was lined with heavy wooden doors. The emptiness was only intensified as they crossed the outer office and through an open door at the back.

They entered a large room with a soaring ceiling and wood-planked floors. The furniture was worn but obviously from a time when it was made by hand and built to last. On the far wall there was a line of towering windows that offered a view of downtown Pike, along with the picturesque park that was framed with trees.

It was the sort of office Dom had seen on movie sets for old-time cop shows. Only the monitors that were mounted on the wall over the old wooden filing cabinets ruined the effect.

Turning his head, Dom discovered Zac seated behind a desk that was stacked with files and empty coffee mugs. He was in his uniform, but his hair was tousled, his whiskers darkening his jawline. He looked like a man who'd had a very long day. And wasn't expecting it to get any shorter.

Glancing up, Zac sent them a weary smile. "Thanks for stopping by. I'm short-staffed, as usual, and I don't want to leave the office unless I have to."

That explained the echoing emptiness, Dom silently acknowledged, walking next to Bailey until they were standing directly in front of the desk.

"What did you find?" he asked.

Zac leaned back in his chair, glancing toward Bailey as if reassuring himself that she was okay before returning his attention to Dom.

"You mentioned that Ford Smithson was the one who gave Eric Criswell a phone to take pictures of Bailey."

Dom shrugged. "He denied it when we talked to him."

Zac scowled. "You talked to him?"

"A friendly chat, nothing more," Dom hastily reassured the lawman. He was going to do whatever he needed to do to protect Bailey, but he preferred not to get on the wrong side of Zac. Not only because he was a sheriff who could throw his ass in jail but he was also Bailey's cousin. He hoped they would eventually be family, and that they could have Christmas together without Zac considering the need to pull his gun. "Ford told us that he wanted random pictures of the locals to use in his art and that Eric misunderstood his request. I doubted his story at the time, but I later confronted Eric about his claim, and he was a lot vaguer about the pictures he was supposed to take," Dom admitted. "It's possible Eric deliberately misunderstood Ford's request."

Zac pursed his lips, tapping his fingers on the arms of his chair. "Or maybe Ford is just a liar."

"He seemed sketchy," Bailey said. "After we left the

lodge we tried looking up information about him, but there's nothing beyond press releases. Not even a picture."

"I had a little better luck." Zac abruptly sat forward, grabbing a file from the top of the stack. "I found out that Ford Smithson, world-renowned artist, is currently living in Hong Kong."

Bailey grasped Dom's hand, staring at Zac with a worried glance. "You're sure? From what I could find online, he's a hermit. And he does have an art show coming to Minneapolis. It would make sense for him to be in the general area."

Zac shrugged. "I guess I can't swear he's in Hong Kong, but I can be confident he's not staying at the old hunting lodge in Pike." Zac flipped open the file and pulled out a photo of a tall man with a bald head and bushy beard who weighed at least three hundred pounds. "This is his picture."

Dom instinctively tugged Bailey closer, realizing they might have been standing mere inches away from a cold-blooded killer.

"So who's staying at the lodge?" he demanded.

Zac tossed the photo back on his desk, his expression frustrated. "I'm not sure."

"Are you going to arrest him?" Bailey asked.

"I don't have anything to charge him with unless he's using his fake identity to swindle people or signing legal documents with a fake name," Zac said. "I'll check with the real estate agent who rented out the lodge to see what name he used on the contract, but even then it would be a stretch to throw him in jail."

Bailey shook her head in confusion. "He can just

call himself Ford Smithson and pretend to be a famous artist?"

"For all we know his name *is* Ford Smithson," Zac argued. "There could be more than one in the world." The lawman lifted his hand as Bailey parted her lips, as if to point out how ridiculous his theory was. "But yeah, it doesn't matter what his name is. You can call yourself Santa Claus and claim to have a bunch of elves in your basement as long as you're not committing fraud."

Dom didn't bother to worry about how a stranger could move to a new town and pass himself off as someone else; it no doubt happened more than anyone could imagine. Instead, he tried to remember exactly what the man had said while they were at the lodge. He couldn't recall the conversation word for word, but he remembered enough to know that the mystery man had gone from a potential person of interest to the number one suspect.

"If he's not Ford Smithson, why did he give Eric Criswell a new phone and ask him to take pictures?" he abruptly demanded.

"I'll run out and have a word with him. When I have a spare minute. Which will probably be . . ." Zac heaved a sigh as he waved his hand toward the towering stacks of files. "When hell freezes over."

Dom wasn't upset by Zac's confession it might be days or even weeks before he could get out to the lodge. The lawman had already admitted he couldn't take legal action against him, at least not without proof that he'd committed a crime.

For now Dom didn't want the pretend Ford Smithson to know they'd found out he was lying. Not when he could slip out of town before they could discover if he was stalking Bailey.

"How long has he been in Pike?" Dom asked.

"I don't have an exact date." Zac hesitated, as if considering the question. "Five. Maybe six months." He narrowed his eyes, no doubt sensing that Dom intended to confront the man. "Long before the stalker started bothering Bailey."

Dom ignored the hint of warning in Zac's tone. "Does he have any friends or family around here?"

"Not that I know of, but . . . shit." Zac glared at the landline that intruded into the conversation with a shrill ring. "I have to get this."

"Thanks, Zac," Bailey said, bumping into Dom in a silent urge to get him moving.

Clearly she was on the same page as Dom in the need to get out to the lodge before Zac could try to stop them. And before the mystery man could hurt anyone else.

"Bailey." Zac lifted the phone receiver as he glared at his cousin. "I don't know what's up with the stranger at the lodge, but let me deal with him, okay?"

Bailey smiled, waving her hand as they headed out of the office. "Tell Rachel I said hi."

They were silent as they headed out of the courthouse, both aware that they were being monitored by the security cameras that fed directly into Zac's office. It wasn't until they were in the Land Rover and pulling away from the curb that Bailey glanced toward him with a grim expression.

"We're going to the lodge, aren't we?"

"Immediately," Dom assured her. "I don't want to piss off Zac, but there's got to be a reason for someone to use a fake name. I intend to find out who he is and what he's up to."

"Don't worry about Zac," Bailey assured him. "He knows what we're doing."

Dom drove down Main Street, not bothering to ask if there was a shortcut to reach the lodge. At the moment the temptation to beat the truth out of Ford Smithson pounded through him with a savage force. He needed a few minutes to gather his composure. The man had lied to them, but that didn't make him a killer. And even if he did turn out to be guilty, they needed proof. Something he wasn't going to get if he went charging over there like a lunatic.

With an effort, he sucked in a deep breath and forced himself to concentrate on Bailey's claim.

"Why do you think Zac knows what we're doing?" he demanded.

Bailey shrugged. "My cousin loves to give the impression he's just a good ol' boy, bumbling along as the local sheriff, but he's a master chess player who is always three steps ahead of everyone else. Including me. And when he's on duty, he never does anything that doesn't have a purpose."

Dom had never been fooled by Zac's laid-back manner. He'd sensed there was a ruthless determination beneath the charming smile. It didn't seem unreasonable to suspect he'd invited them to his office with the intention of manipulating them into doing what he wanted.

"Are you suggesting that he deliberately told us about Ford Smithson so we would confront the man?"

"Zac admitted his hands were tied," Bailey reminded

him. "And that it would be weeks before he could go out to talk to the mystery man."

"True."

"And he knows me well enough to realize I would rush out to the lodge the second I realized the guy had lied to us," she said wryly. "If he didn't want us to figure out what was going on with Ford Smithson, he wouldn't have asked us to come to his office and tell us that he's an imposter. We would never have gotten the information on our own."

Dom nodded. The explanation fit his own suspicions. Zac obviously couldn't ask them to confront a man who hadn't broken any laws. At least none they'd discovered. But he could give them enough information to send them on their way.

"Intelligence obviously runs in the family," he said, sending Bailey a smile.

She wrinkled her nose. "I'm not sure about that."

He was. But beyond the obvious book smarts needed to study and graduate from nursing school, she also had a rare empathy. She could read the feelings of others and offer them what they needed. Comfort, peace, joy, love . . .

"Were the two of you close growing up?" he asked, keeping her distracted as they reached the outskirts of Pike.

"Yes, which was kind of odd."

"Why was it odd?"

"Our fathers were brothers, but our families weren't that close. Probably because they were complete opposites."

"In what way?" Dom was genuinely interested. His

grandparents had kicked Remy out of the house when he turned eighteen and his mother was an orphan. He'd never experienced an extended family.

"Zac's parents were smothering," she explained. "They controlled everything about his life, and even after he married and moved away they pressured him into returning to help on their dairy farm. It didn't matter to them that he wanted to be a cop." She made a sound somewhere between a laugh and a snort. "My dad barely recalled he had a daughter, especially after my mother died."

Dom reached out to grasp her hand, giving her fingers a gentle squeeze. "And yet you both thrived."

She lifted his hand to press her lips against his knuckles before releasing it. "Like you."

Dazzled by the lingering warmth of her kiss, Dom turned onto the narrow dirt path that led to the lodge.

"I'm hoping we can make life easier for our own kids," he murmured, allowing the words to leave his lips without thinking.

Always a mistake.

"Kids?" The word came out as a squeak.

"Sorry, maybe I shouldn't have said that out loud," he admitted. "But I very much hope you want to spend your future with me."

There was a long silence, as if Bailey was adjusting to the thought of having him around forever. Then she shifted in her seat, turning so she could study his profile.

"Have you ever been married before?"

"No. I assumed I'd be single forever," he admitted. "And honestly, I wasn't bothered by the thought."

"You like being single?"

It wasn't a trick question; still, Dom understood that his answer was important.

"It wasn't so much that I liked being single, but I understood that I wasn't ready to share my life with anyone else. Not when I was struggling to figure out who I was. Or, more importantly, who I wanted to be." The memories of his earliest days in America had been a blur of survival. Living on the streets without friends and barely able to speak the language had been a challenge. Thankfully, he'd endured, and the harsh lessons had taught him that he could not only survive but thrive on his own. It also taught him to take pride in his accomplishments. He hadn't cheated or lied or manipulated people to get ahead. He'd earned every penny that went into his pocket. Now that he'd reached a place where he was happy with himself, he was ready to share his life with the woman who'd taught him the meaning of joy. "It took a while, but I concentrated on building my career and surrounding myself with people who were focused on making a better life for themselves."

"Kaden?"

"Yes."

Kaden hadn't been quite as lost as Dom when he first arrived in California, but it was close. He was young and broke and alone. Being able to offer him a helping hand had given Dom a sense of satisfaction. As if he'd realized he had finally reached a point of success in his life.

"It sounds like you know what you want."

"I do." He shot her a quick glance. "And who I want it with."

She heaved a loud sigh. "I'm not nearly so put together. I have no idea if I'm going back to my job or—"

"Do you want to be with me?" he interrupted.

"Yes."

Dom smiled. There hadn't been a second of hesitation in her answer. She might have doubts about what she wanted to do with her career, but she had made the decision to be with him. At least for now.

"Good. That's all that matters," he assured her. "It's just you and me and what makes us happy."

"You and me against the world," she added.

"It feels like that. But we're going to figure this out. I promise. Starting with the pretend Ford Smithson."

His hands tightened on the steering wheel as he turned into the back parking lot of the hunting lodge. He wished Bailey would wait in the vehicle while he confronted the mystery man, but he knew he would be wasting his breath to try to convince her to stay. Besides, there was a part of him that needed to have her in sight at all times. As if he sensed that the moment he couldn't see her, something terrible would happen. Not very logical, but his feelings for Bailey had nothing to do with logic.

"And hopefully ending with the pretend Ford Smithson," she said as she unhooked her belt and shoved open the passenger door. She waited for him to join her near the hood of the Land Rover, glancing around with a small frown.

"I don't see his truck."

She was right. When they were there the first time

there had been a silver truck parked near the steps that led toward the nearby lodge. Today the parking lot was empty.

"It might be parked in the garage." He nodded toward the long structure that ran the length of the lot. It had four bays with heavy steel doors and a tin roof that had long ago rusted. "Last time we were here the first two bays were open. I noticed because there was graffiti spray-painted on the back wall. It seemed out of place around here."

Bailey studied the lodge. "I suppose there's only one way to find out if the mystery man is around."

With a nod, Dom led her up the slope and around the edge of the lodge to the front porch. Reaching the front door, Dom rapped on the wooden frame loud enough to echo through the large building. A minute passed, and then another. He rapped again. Still no answer.

Hissing in frustration, Dom grabbed the doorknob. It refused to budge.

"Locked," he muttered, moving to the nearest window and peering through the glass.

"Can you see anything?" Bailey asked.

"There's no one in the main room."

"He must be gone."

A sudden unease blasted through Dom. What if Ford Smithson—or whoever the hell he was—had already left town? What if he'd managed to discover Zac was checking into his background? Or maybe he got spooked after Dom and Bailey had come out to ask him questions. Either way, they had no way to track him down if he'd decided to slip away.

Jogging down the length of the patio, Dom peered

around the corner of the building. He hoped to find a back door he could force his way through. He didn't care if he was breaking and entering; he had to know if the place had been abandoned.

"Gotcha," he muttered as he caught sight of the wooden stairs that led to an upstairs balcony.

Without hesitation, he started up the narrow steps. The glass sliding doors that opened onto the balcony from the lodge would be the easiest way to enter. He could hear the creak of the stairs as Bailey followed closely behind him, but his attention remained focused on what was ahead. If Ford Smithson was home, he would know they were sneaking around. It wasn't like they were being subtle. And if he was the killer, there was a good chance he was waiting for them to enter the house so he could shoot them. That was what Dom would do. Once they were inside, Ford could claim self-defense, with no one to prove otherwise.

Reaching the balcony, Dom pressed himself against the smooth logs of the lodge and leaned to the side. Cautiously, he peered through the glass door, relieved to discover a narrow loft area that was currently empty. At first glance it appeared to be a bedroom, although the narrow bed had been shoved against the wall and a long dresser was being used to hold four separate monitors. On the opposite wall a small desk was buried beneath books and what looked like stacks of photos.

With a frown, Dom moved to stand directly in front of the glass door, staring at the monitors, which looked as if they were displaying security footage. There was something familiar. . .

"Shit," he muttered.

"What is it?" Bailey moved to stand next to him, pressing her hands against the glass as she peered inside. A second later she gasped in horror. "Oh my God."

"Call Zac," Dom said in urgent tones.

"If you mean the local sheriff, then by all means let's call him," a male voice drawled. "I'd like to make a complaint against two trespassers."

Chapter 18

Dom whirled around, instinctively shoving Bailey behind him as he glared down at the man standing at the bottom of the stairs.

Ford Smithson was wearing a long trench coat over a pair of slacks and a hand-knit sweater. His mop of curls was tousled and his eyes were hidden behind a pair of reflective sunglasses. He looked exactly the way you'd expect a famous, reclusive artist to look. And that was no doubt the point of his deliberate style. Dom felt a stab of annoyance. He should have suspected something was wrong. Ford Smithson was a walking, talking cliché. Which meant it had to be an act.

"I'm going to warn you that having a couple trespassers is the least of your worries," Dom snapped in frustration.

"You're right." The man pulled a cell phone from the pocket of his coat. "It makes more sense to contact my lawyer and sue you for invasion of privacy."

Dom snorted at the empty threat. "Does your lawyer know that you're living here under a false name?"

The man stiffened, his expression suddenly wary. "What are you talking about?"

"We know you aren't Ford Smithson," Bailey said, her tone accusing. "He's currently in Hong Kong. So who are you?"

Without warning Ford was jogging up the steps, and Dom urged Bailey toward the edge of the balcony, keeping himself between her and the approaching man. He had no idea what Ford intended to do, but he was ready and willing to grab the bastard by the neck and toss him over the railing.

"Maybe I decided to leave Hong Kong and travel to Pike." Ford planted himself in front of the glass doors. He was obviously hoping Dom and Bailey hadn't had a chance to figure out what he was doing in there. "Just get off my property and I won't press charges."

"We've seen a picture of the real Ford Smithson," Bailey pressed. "And it's not you."

The man's jaws clenched, as if he was grinding his teeth. Interesting. He appeared more frustrated than afraid that his masquerade had been discovered.

"Are you implying there can't be more than one Ford Smithson in the world?"

"Only one who's also a world-famous artist with a show in Minneapolis," Bailey reminded the fool of his claim he was busy painting for his upcoming exhibition. "So why are you lying?"

His lips pinched as Bailey refused to back down. "It's none of your business."

"It's very much my business when you've been stalking me."

"Stalking?"

"That's what I said."

"How dare you?" Ford bristled with outrage. "Do you go around making wild accusations to everyone or just those people who weren't born and raised in this town?"

Dom studied him with a cold contempt. Ford's reaction was painfully over the top. Just like everything else about him.

"Either you think we're idiots or you're deliberately trying to piss us off." Dom pointed over Ford's shoulder. "We can see from here that you're spying on Bailey's house. Along with Kaden and Lia's property."

The man shrugged. "So I have a few cameras on public property? It's not illegal."

Dom muttered a curse. "I'm done with your lies," he warned, taking another step forward. "You're going to tell us the truth."

"Or?"

"Or I'll find out for myself."

The pretend Ford smiled, tilting his chin to a mocking angle. Dom knew what the other man was doing. He was trying to bait him into taking a swing at his smug face. No doubt he intended to have Dom arrested the second he punched him. Or maybe he was just hoping to sue him. It wasn't a secret that Dom had made a fortune after opening Money Makers with Kaden. Thankfully, Dom wasn't that impulsive. Unless the man tried to harm Bailey, he was going to use his brain, not his brawn, to get the information he wanted.

Shoving Ford aside, he grabbed the handle of the glass door and with one sharp jerk managed to break the flimsy lock. A wry smile twisted his lips. Okay, maybe a little brawn was going to be necessary. Along with a few broken laws.

"Dammit! You're going to pay to replace that lock,"

Ford blustered, following behind Dom as he strolled into the room and turned in a slow circle.

"Send me a bill," he told his companion, glancing toward the monitors that not only showed Bailey's and Kaden's houses but the outside of the lodge. Dom narrowed his eyes at the sight of the truck in the parking lot. Obviously Ford had just returned. The question was whether he had accidentally stumbled across them or had he had some sort of alarm set up to warn him that someone was near his property?

Dom shrugged, moving toward the desk even as he caught sight of Bailey heading toward the monitors, her face flush with anger.

"Tell me why you're stalking me," she demanded.

Ford held up his hands, trying to look innocent. A wasted effort. "Look, I'm not stalking anyone."

Bailey pointed at the monitors. "Then what's this about?"

Dom grabbed one of the books from the desk, grimacing at the sight of a famous actress on the front cover, her cheeks streaked with mascara and her hair a mess. It was one of those tell-all books written by a paparazzi. About to toss it aside, his gaze caught sight of the stacks of photos, his heart stopping as he recognized Kaden and Lia in their wedding attire, gazing at each other in blatant rapture.

"Bailey," he rasped, keeping the book in one hand as he used the other to knock over the stack of photos.

Bailey hurried over, her brows lifting as she studied the dozens of pictures that were now spread across the desk. Most of them were of Kaden and Lia's wedding, along with the reception that included both him and

Bailey, but there were also pictures of Pike and the surrounding area. Predictably, a few of them had been taken next to the railway tracks, where a skeleton had been recently discovered.

"Dammit," the pretend Ford growled. "You can't just paw through my shit."

"Agree to disagree." Dom waved the book toward the advancing man, reading the author's name from the back cover. "Thorpe Curry. That's your real name, isn't it?"

Bailey leaned forward, grabbing one of the glossy magazines that had been stacked next to the books. The front cover had the picture of a famous politician heading out of a courthouse with his lawyer, trying to hide his face.

"You're a paparazzo?" she hissed.

The man glared at them. "I'm a journalist."

"A journalist who sneaks around, making money by spying on people." Dom tossed the book back on the desk. He'd lived in LA long enough to have heard the name. Thorpe Curry was notorious for using outrageous stunts to get pictures of the rich and famous. "That's worse than a stalker."

The man pulled off his sunglasses and shoved them into the pocket of his coat. "When you become a public figure you accept that the fans who made you rich deserve to know what's happening in your life."

Dom made a sound of disgust. "You came to Pike to harass Kaden."

"It's not harassment." Thorpe revealed zero embarrassment at having his secret revealed. As if he'd spent so much of his life lying and pretending to be someone else, it was just another day for him. "When a famous stuntman solves a fifteen-year-old murder in a town that has been plagued with serial killers . . . it's going to be the story of the year. Of course I came here. Like every other journalist."

Dom was shaking his head before the man stopped speaking. "Not like every other journalist. You used a fake name."

"Because not every other journalist is famous," Thorpe argued, his expression faintly smug. "I was afraid Kaden would recognize me."

"Why Ford Smithson?" Bailey asked, handing Dom a pile of eight-by-ten photos that had been hidden in a file folder.

Thorpe shrugged. "He's a distant cousin. I knew he was living overseas and that he'd done his best to avoid sharing any personal information that might be found on the web. He's obsessive about maintaining his privacy."

Dom twisted his lips in a humorless smile. "I'm surprised you haven't outed him and plastered his face across every magazine in the world. Anything for a profit, right?"

Another shrug. "He pays me to keep his identity a secret."

Dom rolled his eyes, glancing toward the photos in his hands. There were more images of Kaden and Lia, but these all had sticky notes attached. On each note was the name of a magazine or newspaper or online site, along with a row of numbers. Kaden assumed it was the buyer for each picture and what they'd paid. It added up to an astronomical sum.

Christ, it was no wonder Thorpe had been willing to skulk around, pretending to be someone else. On the point of returning the photos to Bailey, Dom caught sight of a familiar image. Anger blasted through him and he clenched the picture until it threatened to rip.

"How did you sneak into Kaden's house?"

Thorpe's smug expression faded as he gazed at Dom with a sudden wariness. "I didn't."

Dom held up the picture of the guest bedroom that Bailey had been using. "Then what's this?"

Bailey reached up to snatch the picture from his hand, her face pale as she glared at Thorpe with a sick expression.

"That's the picture that was sent to me by the stalker."

"I've told you. I'm not a stalker," Thorpe protested.

"We have all the proof we need."

"You have nothing."

"Let's ask Zac what he thinks," Dom drawled, reaching into his pocket to wrap his fingers around his phone. "I'm pretty sure he takes a dim view of people who lie about their name, sneak into peoples' homes, and spy on women in his town."

"All right. I'll admit that I came to town to take pictures of Kaden to sell. It's my job," Thorpe ground out. "But I didn't trespass on his property."

Dom pointed toward the picture of the bedroom. "And this?"

"I have no idea . . ." The man's words trailed away as Dom pulled out his phone. "Wait," he snapped. "Most of the photos are mine, but I couldn't get into the wedding, so I bought a few pictures, including the ones inside the house."

"Bought them from who?"

Thorpe's expression hardened, but he forced himself to reveal his source. No doubt he sensed that Dom was ready and willing to call the sheriff.

"Kevin Hartford."

Dom and Bailey shared a shocked glance. It felt as if they were caught in a tangled web. Every time they pulled on a new strand they ended up back where they started.

Bailey dropped the photo as if it was tainted. And maybe it was. So far two men connected with the texts had ended up dead.

"How did you know Kevin?"

"I didn't." Thorpe held up his hands as Dom parted his lips. "I was hanging around the front gates trying to get pictures of the wedding guests when he arrived in the photographer's van and happened to notice me."

Dom wasn't convinced. "There were lots of paparazzi at the front gate. Why would he notice you in particular?"

"I'd watched the van go in and out of the property for a couple of days, so I made sure I was at the front of the crowd on the day of the wedding. When the dude in the passenger seat glanced out the window I flashed a wad of cash. He nodded, and I knew he understood what I wanted. I hung around after the reception ended and the crowd thinned. At last he came to find me. We made a deal that he'd get me copies of whatever photos his wife took and I'd pay him for them. It's an arrangement I've made a thousand times before."

Dom wasn't shocked by Thorpe's confession. He'd spent enough time with Kaden to know that the paparazzi were ruthless when they scented a story. Like flies buzzing around a carcass. And that they'd use anyone to get some sort of exclusive scoop. He wasn't even shocked that Kevin would agree to sell his wife's pictures and put her livelihood at risk for a wad of cash. Drug addicts would sink to any level to get their next high.

And the explanation answered a few of their questions. Like why Thorpe had lied about his identity and how someone had a photo of the guest room Bailey was using. And even who might have been spying on him and Kaden the night before his wedding.

But there were still hundreds more questions churning through his mind.

Starting with who had been texting the picture of the guest room to Bailey.

"Did you sell the pictures you bought?"

"The wedding ones. They were worth a fortune."

No shit, Dom silently conceded. If the numbers on the sticky notes were correct, Thorpe could spend the next few months relaxing on a private beach.

"And the pictures inside the house?" he asked. "Did you sell them?"

Thorpe shook his head. "No."

Dom studied the man's narrow face. He was a master liar, but he seemed sincere when he claimed he hadn't shared the pictures.

"Could Kevin have sold them to someone else?"

Genuine anger flared through the green eyes. "He better not have. I paid a fortune to make sure they were exclusive."

"Then the only people we know for certain who had access to the photos of the guest room were Kevin

Hartford, Kevin's wife, who took the photos, and you," Dom said, his tone hard. "So who sent them to Bailey?"

Thorpe shook his head. "I don't know what you're talking about. Are you saying the photos weren't exclusive? Did Kevin sell them to someone else? If he did, I'll kill the bastard."

There was no point in arguing with Thorpe. He was determined to pretend he knew nothing about the texts. Or Kevin Hartford's death.

"Did you give Eric the phone to take pictures of Bailey?" he instead demanded.

Thorpe scowled, as if considering whether or not to lie; then he gave a grudging nod. "Yes."

Bailey sucked in a sharp breath. "Why?"

"When I came to Pike I intended to stay through the wedding and then head back to Chicago."

"That's where you live?" Dom asked.

"I have an apartment on Michigan Avenue," Thorpe admitted. "Although I'm rarely there."

Bailey stepped closer to Dom, her arms wrapped around her waist. "Why did you want pictures of me?"

Thorpe heaved a sigh, as if he was growing weary of the conversation. "Like I said, I intended to leave after I got the wedding pictures, but then my agent called me with an offer."

"You have an agent?" Bailey asked in confusion.

"I'm a professional. Of course I have an agent."

Dom resisted the urge to point out he was a professional dirtbag. Name calling wasn't going to get him the answers he needed.

"What was the offer?" he demanded.

"A book deal."

Dom was confused. "A book about Pike?"

"On Kaden Vaughn's thrilling life," Thorpe corrected. "According to my agent, the world is desperate to know more about the man who fled home at the tender age of eighteen to escape the brutality of his alcoholic father and landed in Hollywood, where he went from living on the streets to creating a career as a famous stuntman. And if that wasn't enough, he risked his life, nearly dying in his attempt to solve the mysterious case of his brother's missing fiancée." A cynical grin twisted his lips. "And now he has made the romantic decision to settle down with his own personal Cinderella in this remote town famous for producing serial killers."

"That's why you wanted the pictures of his house," Bailey breathed in disgust.

"It's quite a story. I have no doubt it will be a best-seller."

Dom clenched his hands, struggling against the urge to wrap his fingers around the bastard's neck and squeeze.

"You understand that if you're stupid enough to write a book about Kaden's private life he will devote every waking second to destroying you?"

Thorpe yawned. "He'd have to get in line."

Fury blasted through Dom at the man's smug confidence that he was impervious to getting the shit beat out of him. Kaden was his best friend and this sleazebag was willing to worm his way . . .

The sensation of Bailey's slender fingers squeezing his hand pierced through his anger, allowing him to regain command of his composure. He wasn't going to do Bailey any good if he ended up in jail. Besides, Thorpe wasn't worth the effort.

Keeping a tight hold on his hand, Bailey glared at the jerk. "Not to be repetitive, but why would you need pictures of me if you're writing a book about Kaden?"

"Lia is a big part of his life and you're her best friend," Thorpe retorted. "Of course you would be included in the book."

The answer was smooth. Too smooth. "That's not the only reason," Dom warned.

There was a flash of something in the green eyes. Something dark and dangerous.

"Okay." His tone was sharp with annoyance. "I also hoped to get some exclusive information on Lia and perhaps her relationship with Kaden."

"Exclusive?" Bailey looked confused. "You mean things she told me in confidence?"

"Exactly."

"I would never betray her trust."

Thorpe stared at Bailey as if she was some sort of alien being. And she probably seemed like one to the paparazzo. She had an innocent belief in the goodness of her fellow man. A belief that was all too rare these days.

"Everyone has their price," Thorpe informed her.

Bailey grimaced. "Money?"

"It's what makes the world go round."

"Not my world," Bailey assured him.

Thorpe shrugged. "Yeah, I figured that out early on."

"That's why he's spying on you," Dom informed Bailey, not surprised when she continued to look confused.

Her naïveté created a source of wonderment and fear inside Dom.

"I don't understand," she said.

"The bastard was hoping to find some way to force you to give him the information he wants."

"By taking my picture?"

"He was hoping to catch you doing something he could use to blackmail or bully you into giving him what he wants."

Bailey shuddered as she sent Thorpe a glare brimming with revulsion. "You're despicable."

"I'm a businessman." Thorpe nodded toward the books stacked on his desk. "I know what people want and I'll do whatever's necessary to give it to them."

"Did you pay anyone else in town to spy on Bailey?" Dom asked.

"No." Thorpe pressed a hand over his heart, his expression mocking. "I swear."

Dom took a threatening step forward, childishly pleased when Thorpe stumbled back. "Like I would believe a word that comes out of your lying mouth."

As if embarrassed he'd revealed he wasn't as impervious to fear as he wanted them to believe, Thorpe pulled out his phone and held it up in a threatening gesture.

"I've told you everything. Now get off my property before I really do call the sheriff."

Dom wasn't afraid of the man calling Zac. Partially because he didn't believe he was willing to invite the lawman to the lodge. Not when he might snoop around. And partially because he didn't think for a minute that Zac would blame them for demanding answers from the man who was spying on Bailey.

Still, it was obvious Thorpe Curry was done answering their questions. At least for the moment.

"Let's go, Bailey." He squeezed her fingers. "We know where to find him if we have more questions."

"Or if I decide to sue him for invading my privacy," Bailey added. "I know a lawyer who would be happy to get a lawsuit started."

"All my cameras are on public property," Thorpe retorted, but he couldn't hide his hint of unease.

He might not worry about getting the shit beat out of hm, but he didn't want to be sued.

Dom wasn't patient enough to allow the wheels of justice to grind. "A warning, Thorpe," he said between clenched teeth. "Remove the cameras or I will."

Turning, Dom led Bailey through the open glass doors and down the stairs. He picked up his pace as they walked down the grassy slope to reach the parking lot. He wanted Bailey far away from this lodge. And Thorpe Curry.

Chapter 19

As they pulled out of the parking lot, Bailey leaned forward to switch on the heater. The sunlight was fading and there was a distinct chill in the air. Or maybe her shivers were caused by a delayed reaction to the realization that Thorpe Curry had been spying on her for months. What kind of psycho put a camera in front of a woman's house in the hopes of catching her in a scandal?

And worse, he wasn't even the stalker. Or at least he didn't appear to be the stalker. Which meant there was more than one person out there following her around.

It was enough to make her consider packing her things and driving as far away from Pike, Wisconsin, as possible.

"Are you okay?"

The soft question shattered the rising sense of panic, and with a shaky sigh she turned her head to study Dom's profile. Even in the gathering dusk she could make out the stern lines of his face, revealing he was battling his own tumultuous emotions. The knowledge somehow eased her fear. Whatever happened, she wasn't alone.

Dom Lucier would be at her side.

"Not really," she admitted, snuggling back in the soft leather seat as they bumped over the dirt path. "You know, even after all the terrible things that have happened, I wanted to believe that Pike is a good place to live. And that my neighbors are decent people."

"Most of them *are* decent," he insisted. "It's like any town: good guys and bad guys and lots of guys in between."

She shook her head. Dom hadn't been here for the past few years. It'd been one horrible event after another. As if they'd been cursed.

"Pike feels like it's had more than its fair share of bad guys." She wrinkled her nose. "And gals."

"Maybe," Dom conceded, accepting she was the expert on Pike. Then his hands tightened on the steering wheel. "One thing is for certain: Kaden's going to lose his shit when he finds out what that creep has been doing. Assuming I don't kill him first."

Bailey didn't even want to think about Kaden's reaction. Especially when he learned that Thorpe was the one responsible for selling the photos of his wedding and spying on Bailey in the hopes of getting dirt on Lia.

Instead, she concentrated on why they'd gone to the lodge in the first place. "Do you think he was telling the truth?"

"I believe he's a paparazzo and that he came to Pike to make a lot of money off Kaden," Dom said slowly, as if he was considering his answer. "Whether or not he has other motives for being in town is an open question."

"I feel like we turned over a rock and exposed a whole new batch of roaches," she muttered with another shiver.

Dom tapped the brakes as he turned onto the road that would lead to Lia's house. "Unfortunately, we still have no idea which roach has been stalking you."

He was right, Bailey acknowledged with a flare of frustration. No matter how much information they uncovered, they were no closer to finding the truth. Still, they had answered a few nagging questions.

"We at least know where the pictures inside Kaden's house came from," she reminded him.

"True. Either Kevin Hartford sent the pictures himself or he was involved with whoever did."

"That might explain why they killed him," she suggested. "They might have been afraid he would expose who he'd given the picture to. A drug addict isn't the most reliable partner."

Dom nodded. "Possibly."

"And I suppose we also discovered that Eric was telling the truth when he claimed the pretend Ford Smithson asked him to spy on me."

"The question is whether Eric believed he was helping an artist who needed a muse or if he knew that he was helping a paparazzo blackmail you into betraying your best friend."

Bailey winced. Even after everything that'd happened she didn't want to think she could be so wrong about Eric. Not everyone could be horrible, right?

"I refuse to believe he would have accepted the phone if he knew the truth," she stubbornly insisted.

"We'll ask him. Tomorrow." Dom reached up to punch the opener attached to the sun visor. Then, pulling into the drive, he waited for the gates to swing open. "Tonight I want to go home and hold you in my arms."

Bailey allowed the tension to drain away. It'd been another stressful day. And tomorrow wasn't looking any better. Alone time wrapped in Dom's arms was exactly what she needed.

"Yes, please."

After a glorious night of exploring every inch of Dom's hard body, Bailey slept late and then enjoyed a leisurely breakfast in bed while Dom took the dogs on a long hike. At last she forced herself to get dressed in a comfortable pair of jeans and a chunky sweater.

If they wanted to speak to Eric when he was alone, they needed to get to his house while his mother was at church. That was the only time the elderly woman ever left her house. That gave them a limited time frame.

Pulling into the driveway at exactly eleven o'clock, Bailey hopped out of the SUV and glanced toward Dom. Before leaving the house she'd explained that Eric wasn't going to tell them anything if he tried to use intimidation. The only way to get to the truth was for Bailey to coax it out of him. But as her lips parted to remind him of their plan, she caught sight of the golden hair that was ruffled by the breeze and the impossibly beautiful features. An aching tenderness dried the words on her lips, along with a wistful regret that they couldn't have simply met and fallen in love without a dark cloud hanging over them.

Then again, Dom had proven beyond a doubt that he

would always be there for her. Through the good and the bad and the downright scary. She had zero fear that he would bolt at the first sign of trouble.

Swallowing a sigh at the regret they couldn't turn around and head back to the privacy of Lia's house, Bailey climbed onto the narrow porch. The house was a small bungalow set over a full basement with faded green shutters and peeling white paint. It wasn't derelict, but it was bordering on shabby. No wonder Eric's mom was always bitching at him to do more around the property.

Squaring her shoulders, Bailey knocked on the screen door. Now wasn't the time to be distracted. Eric not only worked at the nursing home; he'd been taking pictures for Thorpe Curry. He might not be on the top of her list of suspects, but it was possible he had information that could help them pinpoint the villain.

There was the sound of footsteps before the front door was pulled open to reveal the young man. He was wearing a pair of scrub pants and a wrinkled T-shirt and his hair was limper than usual. As if it'd been a few days since he'd bothered to wash it. His thin face lit up as he caught sight of her.

"Bailey." He leaned forward to shove open the screen door. His expression tightened as he caught sight of Dom. "And you."

Dom stepped forward. "And me."

Eric deliberately returned his attention to Bailey. "What are you doing here?"

"I have a few questions," she said, sending him a reassuring smile.

"From him?" Eric jerked his chin toward Dom

without allowing his gaze to stray from Bailey. "I already answered them."

"These are new ones," she reassured him.

He pressed his lips together, as if torn between slamming the door in her face and spending more time in her company. At last he gave a furtive glance from side to side before stepping back to wave them inside.

"Come in," he ordered. "I don't want the entire neighborhood knowing you're here."

Together, Bailey and Dom stepped into the front room, all of them grimacing at the overwhelming smell of pine. Someone had recently polished the dark wooden paneling, along with the furniture that was almost a duplicate of the couch and love seat in Dorinda's house. Bailey's grandmother had told her there used to be a furniture store in Pike. Obviously they'd had a limited selection.

"No!" Eric called out as Bailey reluctantly moved to perch on the love seat. He flushed as she sent him a startled frown. "My mom doesn't like people touching her stuff. We can go downstairs."

Wondering if Eric's mom understood the basic function of furniture, Bailey was distracted as Dom moved to stand directly beside her.

"Absolutely not."

"We can talk here," Bailey said, heading off any argument. "This won't take long."

"Whatever." Eric hunched his shoulders. "Why are you here?"

Bailey cleared her throat. Before leaving the house they'd agreed to start the conversation with discovering how much Eric knew about Thorpe Curry.

"Tell me what happened when Ford Smithson gave you the new phone."

Eric rolled his eyes. "That again? How many times do I have to repeat myself?"

"At least once more," Dom said, his voice hard.

"I came out of work. The dude was leaning against my car and he handed me the phone."

"And he told you to take pictures of me?" Bailey took back command of the questioning.

Eric did more hunching. "I don't remember his exact words. He might have said your name or he might have called you my friend. Either way, I knew what he wanted."

"And you believed he was an artist in search of a muse?"

"Why wouldn't I?"

Bailey studied his thin face. He looked genuinely annoyed. As if he didn't understand why she was asking the question.

"We've discovered that he's been lying since he arrived in Pike," she informed him.

Eric stared at her, as if waiting for her to go on. "Lying about what?" he finally demanded.

"Everything. He's not Ford Smithson and he's not an artist."

"Who is he?"

"Thorpe Curry." Bailey shrugged. "Or at least that's the professional name he uses. He might have another one," she conceded.

It'd been Dom who'd suggested that the man might be using a pen name to sell his photographs. Ford/Thorpe was obviously fond of remaining incognito. Probably to avoid being smothered in his sleep.

"Professional what?"

"Paparazzo."

Eric's lips parted, as if he was struggling to process what she was telling him. "You're being followed by the paparazzi?"

"Not me. Or not exactly. He wanted a way to get to Lia and through her to Kaden."

Eric remained confused. "Did Ford . . . or whoever . . . want me to take pictures of Lia? She's not my friend. And I've never met Kaden Vaughn."

Bailey risked a quick glance toward Dom. His expression was grim as a visible tension hummed around his body, as if preparing for a surprise attack. But he shook his head in response to her silent question.

He didn't think Eric was involved with Thorpe Curry. Not unless you counted being a clueless accessory.

"It doesn't matter," she reassured Eric again. Time to move on. "I just wanted to warn you that he can't be trusted."

"Thanks." Eric's wary expression softened as he studied her with a disturbing intensity. "You've always looked out for me, Bailey. You're the only one." He reached to grab her hand. "I wish you were still at the nursing home. It's not the same there without you."

Bailey gently tugged her hand free. She had to be careful not to offend Eric. He had the emotional maturity of a child, but she didn't want him touching her. His clammy skin gave her the creeps.

She forced a smile to her lips. "Speaking of the nursing home . . ."

The gray eyes widened with hope. "Are you coming back?"

"I haven't decided."

"Why not? It's not that bad of a place to work."

"I didn't think so." She paused, as if reluctant to reveal her reasons for avoiding her old job. "Not until the Donaldsons accused me of abusing my patients. Perhaps even killing one of them."

Eric was shaking his head before she finished speaking. "I'm sure they never believed that."

"So am I," she agreed. "They knew that Nellie changed her will before she died. And exactly why she'd given me a portion of the inheritance."

"They knew?" Eric furrowed his brow. "Why would they lie?"

"It's a question I've been asking myself. At least until I learned that they will inherit Nellie's estate. Obviously they hoped to make me the scapegoat if anyone started asking questions."

"What?" Eric froze, as if struggling to accept what she was telling him.

"The Donaldsons are about to inherit half of Nellie Warren's estate," she helpfully repeated.

"No. That can't be right," Eric stubbornly insisted. "I heard Gage bragging about the amount of money he was going to have as soon as his mother was dead." He jutted out his jaw. "He was a real jerk if you ask me. And I don't care if he is dead."

"I agree, he was a jerk," Bailey quickly agreed, refusing to dwell on how the man had died. Or who might be responsible. She needed to concentrate on getting answers from the man eyeing her with a wary expression. "And it's because Gage is dead that the money is going to the nursing home."

"I . . ." Eric licked his lips. "Are you joking?"

"I heard it from Ward Bennett. I doubt he would joke about something like that."

"No."

"I'm surprised Logan Donaldson didn't tell you about the inheritance," Dom said.

Eric's brows snapped together at Dom's intrusion into the conversation. "Why would he tell me?"

"I thought the two of you were friends," Dom pressed.

"As if," Eric scoffed. "He's just my boss. I doubt he even knows my name."

Dom looked mildly surprised by the fervent denial. "That's odd. You guys have been meeting in the old building next to the nursing home, haven't you?"

"What?" Eric flushed, opening and shutting his mouth a half dozen times before he could spit out his denial. "I don't know who told you that, but they're liars."

"Seriously? I saw the two of you with my own eyes," Dom reminded him.

The younger man stepped back, wrapping his arms around his thin waist. He looked as if he was feeling attacked and was on the point of shutting down. Bailey needed to distract him.

"Eric, if Logan has done something bad, you can tell me," she said in soft tones. "I'll make sure Zac understands that it wasn't your fault."

Eric shifted from foot to foot, unable to hide his discomfort. "Why do you think he's done something bad?"

"Don't you think it's suspicious that Nellie would die and leave her estate to Gage and then just days later Gage would die, making sure the large sum of money ends up in the Donaldsons' hands?"

"Nellie died because she was old and Gage fell off a ladder."

Bailey squashed her burst of annoyance. She hadn't expected Eric to dig in his heels. It was going to take more than her suspicions to make him question his loyalty to the Donaldsons. Sending out a silent apology to Zac, she leaned forward, revealing she was about to confess a secret.

"Both Nellie's and Gage's deaths are under investigation," she said.

Eric looked skeptical. "No way."

"Yes."

"And those aren't the only deaths connected to the Donaldsons," Dom smoothly added.

"No. I don't believe you."

All right. Time for drastic actions, Bailey silently acknowledged. Eric had some reason for his stubborn refusal to believe what she was telling him. She was going to have to shake it out of him.

She took a step toward him, her expression one of sympathy. "Eric, I'm not trying to implicate you in the murders."

"Murders? Me?" Eric made a strangled sound, looking shell-shocked by the accusation. "No. No way."

"I just don't want you to get caught up in something that might ruin your future," she continued in soothing tones. "Logan Donaldson isn't worth going to jail, is he?"

The color drained from Eric's face, emphasizing the

jaundiced hue to his skin. "The bastard swore I wouldn't get in any trouble."

Bailey released a small sigh of relief. Finally.

"In trouble for what?" she asked.

"For Nellie."

Bailey's relief was shattered as she gazed at her companion in horror. "You . . ." She was forced to clear the sudden lump from her throat. "Did you hurt her? Maybe by accident?"

He gasped at her stumbling words. "Of course not. I can't believe you would even ask me that."

"I'm sorry." Her apology was genuine. Eric appeared deeply hurt by her words. "I was trying to work out what Logan forced you to do," she managed to continue. "And there was something, wasn't there?"

Eric shot a quick glance toward Dom, as if he was wishing the large man wasn't there. Dom folded his arms over his chest, silently warning him that he wasn't leaving. Eric heaved a loud sigh.

"Yeah. Okay," he conceded. "There was something."

"You can tell me," Bailey urged.

"It wasn't my fault. Logan more or less threatened to fire me if I didn't help him out." He waved his hand. "And you know my mom would freak out if I lost my job. She threatened to kick me out the last time it happened. Where would I go?"

Bailey glanced around the living room with a tiny shudder. It was weirdly sterile and lifeless. No pictures, no flowers, not even a television. Just unused furniture and a Bible set on the low coffee table.

Bailey returned her attention to Eric. "I'm sure you had no choice."

"I didn't. Really and truly."

"What did he make you do?"

"He made me steal from the residents."

Chapter 20

Bailey was braced for Eric's confession. She had no idea what he might say, but she assumed it would be something shocking. It wasn't until the words left his mouth that she realized she wasn't surprised. Probably because so many awful things had been happening that a little petty theft didn't seem like a big deal.

How sad was that?

"What did you steal?" she demanded.

Eric hesitated, his expression hovering between defensive and sulky. Like a child forced to admit what he'd done wrong.

"Nothing big." He glanced away, reluctant to reveal the truth. "At least not at first. I'd take their credit card out of their wallet for Logan to use and then return it the next morning. And occasionally I'd take some cash that was lying around. It was harmless."

Bailey frowned, no longer dismissing the theft as petty. The residents depended on Eric, not to mention Logan, to keep them safe. That included their meager belongings. The fact that they would abuse that trust and take what little they had was disgusting.

For now, however, she had to bite back her words of condemnation. She had to know what Eric was involved in.

"You said it was nothing big in the beginning," she reminded him. "What changed?"

"Logan said he needed more."

"More what?"

"Money." Eric glanced back at her, his expression wary, as if he could sense her disapproval. "He told me to start taking anything of value."

Value? Bailey shook her head. Most of the residents were there because they didn't have the money to go to senior housing or the fancier nursing home in Grange. Nellie had been one of the few who had decided to stay local despite her wealth.

"What would they have to steal?"

"Most of them had wedding bands," Eric confessed. "And a few had necklaces and earrings."

"What about an emerald ring?" Dom demanded.

The truth hit Bailey like a slap to the face and she gasped in disbelief. She was so blind. She should have guessed the truth the second Eric revealed he'd been stealing from the residents.

"It was you," she breathed. It was a statement, not a question.

A pained blush of embarrassment stained Eric's face. "Logan was the one who wanted it. He said it would be worth a fortune." He held a pleading hand toward Bailey. "I didn't want to do it. I liked Nellie. I really did."

Bailey stepped back, revulsion rolling through her in waves. "She treated you like a son."

"I know," he muttered. "That made it even worse."

"But you did it anyway." She couldn't stop the accusation from flying out of her mouth. She was just so . . . mad.

Poor Nellie had been such a kind, sweet woman. It wasn't fair she'd been abused by the people she most trusted.

"I'd taken a couple of rings and necklaces from other residents without them knowing, but I must have made a noise when I went to Nellie's room," Eric said.

"She woke up and jumped to the conclusion you were Gage?"

Eric gave a jerky nod. "I didn't know that until later. At the time I hoped she would dismiss me as a bad dream."

"But she didn't dismiss you as a dream," Bailey replied in flat tones. The two men didn't look anything alike, but in the dark, without her glasses, Nellie could easily have mistaken Gage for Eric. Especially if she already was worried about Gage's inability to live within a budget. "And you let her believe her own son had robbed her?"

"Logan told me to keep my mouth shut," Eric whined, refusing to take any blame. "Besides, Gage was always begging his mother for extra cash. It wasn't like she didn't know he was a greedy jerk."

"What did you do with the ring?" Dom demanded, no doubt sensing Bailey's temper was frayed to the snapping point.

Logically, she knew they had to pander to Eric's childish refusal to accept any blame, but her heart wanted to scream at him in outrage. What kind of person abused frail, vulnerable people who had a limited time left in this world?

Eric grudgingly glanced toward Dom. "I gave it to Logan."

"Do you know what he did with it?" Dom asked.

"I know exactly what he did with it."

Dom arched a brow. "Seriously?"

"I'm supposed to have a cut of the stuff I was . . ." Eric's words faltered as he glanced back at Bailey. "Taking."

Did he think "taking" sounded better than "stealing"? It didn't.

"Logan forgot to share?" she asked.

Eric's features hardened with annoyance. "He gave me a few bucks here and there, but I knew he was lying to me about the amount of money he was getting for the jewelry."

Bailey wasn't surprised that Logan would manipulate the younger man into a life of crime and then stiff him when it came time to pay him. The only surprise was that Eric had managed to figure out he was being scammed.

"What did you do?"

"After I gave Logan Nellie's ring I followed him around until he eventually drove out of town." His lips thinned at the memory. "A couple of hours later we ended up in Green Bay at a pawnshop."

"Which one?" Dom asked.

"Brew . . ." Eric struggled to come up with the name. At last he shrugged. "Brew something or other. It was just off University Avenue."

Dom narrowed his eyes, a sudden tension humming around him. "Did you actually see him pawn the ring?"

"Yep. I snuck inside while Logan was bartering with the owner. I couldn't get too close, but I heard how much he got for the ring." The thin face hardened. "Then I came back to Pike and waited for Logan to give me my cut."

"Let me guess. He lied about how much he got," Dom said in dry tones.

Eric nodded in sharp agreement.

"No honor among thieves. Shocking." Bailey rolled her eyes. Both men disgusted her.

Dom sent her a rueful glance, easily sensing her raw need to strike out at Eric.

"I assume you asked for your fair share?" he asked the younger man.

"Of course. I told him that I wanted the money and he promised to get it to me. Finally I had to threaten to go to the cops." Eric glared at Dom. "He was supposed to bring the money to me the day you interrupted us."

Bailey and Dom exchanged a glance. His instinct was right. The two men were meeting.

"Why did Logan need money?" Bailey asked the question that had been nagging at her since Eric confessed his unholy alliance with Donaldson. "I'm sure his mother gives him a generous salary and he still lives at home, so it's not like he has any bills to pay."

"His online girlfriend," Eric revealed without hesitation.

Bailey arched a brow. "Seriously?"

"Yup. Last year he asked me for a way to set him up on a dating site without his mom finding out what he was doing. I guess he met someone he liked and they've been chatting."

"Why would he need money for that?"

"He didn't say. The only thing I know was that he maxed out his credit cards keeping her happy. Including the one that was only supposed to be used for stuff at the nursing home."

"A reason to commit murder?" Bailey muttered. Logan was a weak man who depended on his mother for his basic survival. If that was put at risk, he absolutely would strike out in fear.

"I'm telling you, I don't know anything about that. I swear." Eric glanced toward the window, his finger nervously tugging at the hem of his T-shirt. "My mom's going to be back soon. You need to go."

Accepting that they'd discovered all they could for the moment, Bailey turned to head for the door. Dom, however, paused to deliver a final warning.

"Don't make any plans to leave town."

Eric didn't respond to the threat and together Dom and Bailey stepped out of the house and headed across the lawn. Once they were in the Land Rover, Bailey heaved a frustrated sigh.

"I don't think he knows anything about the murders."

Dom put the vehicle into Drive and pulled away from the curb. "He could be acting."

Bailey agreed with his warning. Eric was proving to possess a genuine skill in pretending to be innocent even when he was lying to her face. She wasn't going to believe anything that came out of his mouth. But there was one reason she doubted Eric wasn't involved in the deaths.

"Yeah, but if the killer murdered Kevin because he thought his drug addiction made him a weak link, they most certainly would have gotten rid of Eric. He would spill every secret he knew if Zac showed up at his front door."

Dom turned at the corner, heading in the opposite direction of the way they'd come to the house.

"We have one way to check to see if he's telling us the truth,"

"How?"

"We can go to the pawnshop to find the emerald ring."

She studied his profile, recalling his response to Eric's confession that Logan had taken the ring to a pawnbroker.

"You know where it is?"

"No, but we have a partial name. It shouldn't be that hard to locate."

"True. I'll look." Bailey pulled out her phone from her purse and typed in pawnshops in Green Bay. A second later she found it. "'Drew's Brew Trading Post,'" she read out loud. "'Pawnshop and Microbrewery. All your shopping needs under one roof.'"

"Is it open today?"

Bailey checked the website. "At noon."

Dom pressed on the accelerator as they reached the access road, picking up speed to veer onto the highway.

"Plug in the directions." He nodded toward the GPS system on the sleek control panel that looked as if it belonged in a spaceship.

She blinked in surprise. "We're going now?"

He turned his head to flash a smile that threatened to

stop her heart. "Unless you have something you'd rather be doing?"

"I do," she answered with blunt honesty, a warmth spreading through her body at the pleasure of returning to the bed she was sharing with Dom. Then, with a sigh of resignation, she settled back in the soft leather seat. "Unfortunately, we need to get to the pawnshop as soon as we can," she reluctantly admitted. "I want to find the ring before someone buys it. That's the only way we can prove what Logan and Eric were doing. Even if it doesn't tell us anything about the murders, we can at least stop them from stealing from those poor old people."

"It will also prove that Logan had a reason to kill Nellie," Dom added.

Bailey grimaced, trying to imagine Lorene Donaldson's reaction to discovering her son was a common thief. And just as bad, using nursing home funds to indulge his online girlfriend. She acted as if they were a step above the common folk in Pike. It would devastate her to have people gossiping about her precious son.

"I'm sure Logan would do anything to keep his mother from finding out what he was doing," she said.

"Maybe she did find out."

Bailey studied Dom's profile. "Why would you think that?"

"You overheard her telling Logan that he was putting the nursing home at risk."

"True." Bailey settled back in the soft leather seat, considering what she'd overheard. There had been something Logan had done to put the home at risk, and something they didn't want Bailey to discover. Vague implications that there was a secret they were hiding. Too vague. "But what did she find out?" She spoke the questions swirling through her mind out loud. "That Logan was using the nursing home credit card for personal pleasure? That he was stealing from the residents? Or that he killed Nellie and then Gage to get his hands on the inheritance?"

Dom was silent as they hurtled northward, the rolling hills and fenced pastures zooming past.

"Let's say she knew it all," he abruptly said. "That would explain why she was willing to kick you out after Gage's accusations even though she knew you had nothing to do with Nellie's change of will. She wanted you to look guilty."

Bailey frowned, struggling to imagine Lorene Donaldson being involved in anything criminal. She was so . . . perfect. Like an ice queen. Was it possible she was willing to cover up Logan's habit of stealing from residents? Or even murder?

Yes. The answer came without hesitation. Lorene Donaldson would do anything for her son. Including murder.

"They probably even goaded Gage into publicly accusing me of killing his mother to get my hands on the inheritance," she muttered, a shiver racing through her. She'd never liked the Donaldsons, but she would never have suspected they might be cold-blooded killers.

"Gage was always an ass, but he acted as if he had some sort of evidence I was involved in his mother's death."

"You're right. They wanted someone to take the blame if anyone questioned it."

"And then they killed him."

Dom's fingers tightened on the steering wheel. "It's just a theory, but right now the evidence points at Logan and his mother."

"I agree." Bailey tapped her fingers on her knees. The evidence did point toward the Donaldsons, but there was something nagging at the back of her mind. Something she couldn't put her finger on. "I'm not sure how any of that connects to the person who's been stalking me," she finally muttered.

"It's possible the stalker isn't the killer," Dom pointed out. "It might be someone who's using the murders for their own amusement."

Bailey's stomach churned with unease. It was almost worse to think there was some sicko out there enjoying the slaughter of their neighbors, and maybe even their friends. When she was a member of the Murder Club the victims were strangers. And she only wanted to help find the truth of how they died. She didn't take pleasure in the fact that they'd been tragically killed.

"What do they want from me?" The words burst out of her before she could halt them.

"To manipulate you. To watch you squirm." Dom sent her a grim glance. "To make you afraid."

Bailey pressed herself deeper into the leather seat. "They're doing a good job."

Dom returned his gaze to the highway. "Or maybe there isn't a separate stalker. It could be Logan who's responsible for killing those people as well as harassing you. He's obviously teamed up with Eric for his crime spree at the nursing home. What if Eric mentioned the Murder Club and the fact that you were also a member?"

Bailey considered the possibility. "Logan knows how to use a computer," she conceded.

"And if he killed Gage and Kevin, he could have left behind the phones that were used to text you."

She made a sound of frustration. When she was working with the Murder Club the group would sift through clues and throw out various possibilities, then poke holes in those theories before coming up with new hypotheses. It was like a puzzle and Bailey could instinctively sense when they'd managed to get a piece of it to fit. It wasn't the same at all in real life. Nothing was fitting together. No matter how hard they tried.

"Again, why?" she demanded, her tone sharp. "All the deaths were being treated as accidental. Why risk unwanted questions by leaving the phones?"

"A sick fetish." He paused. "Or maybe an attempt to frame you as the killer."

Both theories were plausible. And yet . . .

"Or—" She abruptly clenched her hands into tight fists, trying to clear her tangled thoughts.

"Or what?"

She released a slow breath. "I don't want to think it, but what if Logan is the killer as we suspect, but that Eric lied to us. What if Eric *has* known all along that Logan murdered Nellie and Gage? And perhaps Pauline and her grandson?"

Dom abruptly slowed the Land Rover, as if he needed to concentrate on what she was saying.

"Eric did admit he's been following Logan around," Dom murmured. "He could have witnessed the murders."

"Yes." Bailey didn't have any trouble imagining Eric sneaking around, spying on Logan. He'd probably been doing it long before he suspected Logan was cheating him. More than likely from the moment the older man had come to him and asked him to help set up his online account. Eric had a tendency to fixate on anyone who showed him a bit of attention. Whether it was positive or negative. "And he could have planted the phones after Logan left. Plus, he's been stealing from the residents. It's possible he took the pearl necklace and decided to keep it for himself."

"He's also been spying on you," Dom added, clearly warming to her theory. "He would know when you weren't home so he could leave the necklace on your back porch."

The memory of Eric slouched in his car as he secretly took pictures sent a wave of nausea through her. His behavior had been disgusting. And worse, she felt betrayed. She'd been nice to Eric when no one else would bother.

With an effort, Bailey dismissed her hurt feelings. Eric had proved that he couldn't be trusted. The only question now was how far he would go.

"And he went to the hunting lodge to work on Ford . . ." Bailey's words faltered as she recalled that Ford was yet another man lying and hiding secrets. It was like an epidemic in Pike. "To work on Thorpe Curry's laptop. He could have downloaded the pictures of Kaden and Lia's house onto his burner phone and then texted them to me."

"It makes sense," Dom readily agreed.

It did. Bailey heaved a harsh sigh. "I always felt

sorry for Eric and I tried to be his friend, but he's always wanted more."

"Much more," Dom added. "Including having you as a member of the Murder Club."

"Yeah. He was kind of obsessed with having me join." She dredged up the memory of Eric's expression when she'd revealed she didn't want to be a part of the group. "And extremely disappointed when I deleted my account."

"It was a way to manipulate you into a relationship."

Bailey pressed a hand against her churning stomach. "I suppose I should be relieved at the thought that Logan is the killer and Eric is the stalker." She forced the words past her stiff lips. "Logan has no reason to kill me and I can't believe Eric would ever hurt me. At least not physically." She shivered. "But those text messages are just so creepy."

"I wouldn't be so certain about either of those assumptions," Dom abruptly warned. "We've been asking a whole lot of uncomfortable questions. If the Donaldsons are hoping to pin the murders on you, it's very likely they plan to make sure your lips are sealed. After all, you can't defend yourself if you're dead." His voice was grim. "And we have no idea how far Eric will go in his warped fixation with you. He's obviously trying to coerce you into continuing with his twisted game." Dom paused, as if he'd been struck by a sudden thought. "Or maybe he's hoping to frighten you into running to him for protection."

"As if." Bailey made a sound of revulsion. "First off I don't need a man to protect me. And second I have—"

"Me," Dom interrupted.

Bailey chuckled. "I was going to say a cousin who's a sheriff, but I guess you'll do."

Dom flashed her a wicked smile. "I hope to do for a very long time."

Bailey hoped so too.

With an odd sense of contentment, she laid her hand on Dom's arm as he pressed his foot on the accelerator, picking up speed. The traffic was light enough to ensure they would reach Green Bay in a couple of hours. Until then Bailey intended to relax and enjoy being alone with the man who'd stolen her heart.

Closing her eyes, she allowed the smooth sway of the expensive vehicle to lull her into a light sleep.

Chapter 21

Dom turned down the narrow street, allowing Bailey to navigate them through the city as he kept a close eye on the rearview mirror. He didn't think they'd been trailed from Pike, but he wasn't taking any chances. So far they'd caught Eric Criswell parked outside of Bailey's house taking pictures and Thorpe Curry video-taping her. Who knew how many other weirdos were following her around.

"Pull in here." Bailey pointed toward a parking lot on the opposite side of the street. "This is the place."

Dom swerved into the small lot, relieved to find it nearly empty. He didn't want a lot of gawkers hanging around if he needed to question the owner. Then, climbing out of the vehicle, he took a moment to study the L-shaped, red-brick building that had a corner patio with a handful of picnic tables. He assumed that side of the building was used for the microbrewery. Which meant the entrance to the pawnshop was through the double glass doors closest to the sidewalk.

Waiting for Bailey to join him, Dom crossed the crumbling concrete to pull open the door and step inside the shop. It was a long, narrow space that was framed with metal shelves that held a variety of musical instruments, power tools, sports equipment, and used electronics. The larger lawn equipment cluttered the floor of the shop along with the gun cabinets that were stuffed with weapons. At first glance it looked like most pawnshops, but Dom didn't miss the fact that it was ruthlessly clean and the merchandise was precisely arranged. Whoever owned this place took pride in their business.

"Let's find the display case," he murmured, grasping her hand as they headed to the front of the shop. They stopped at the glass cabinet that held dozens of velvet-lined boxes. "Do you recognize anything?"

Bailey leaned forward, carefully studying the various rings and necklaces that sparkled beneath the bright lights installed in the cases.

"The plain wedding bands would be hard to pick out. Most of them look the same," she murmured, keeping her voice low despite the fact that they were the only customers. She pressed her finger against the top of the case, pointing at a pair of gold earrings that were shaped like butterflies. "But those look familiar. I think they may have belonged to Betsy Felton. She wouldn't have missed them. And even if she did, the Donaldsons could have claimed she'd lost them. Her dementia is pretty bad." She slowly straightened. "I don't see any emerald rings."

"There's another case over there."

Dom led her over to the small glass cabinet that was arranged next to the door to an office. As he'd expected, the jewelry was a different quality. The settings were gold or silver and the gems were real.

Once again, Bailey leaned forward, scanning the selection. A minute later she was sucking in a sharp breath.

"This one." She pointed toward the ring at the very center of the display. "That's Nellie's ring."

Dom arched his brows. It was by far the most expensive piece of jewelry in the shop. Including the dozen diamond necklaces on the other side of the case.

"You're sure?" he demanded.

"Positive. Her husband had it handcrafted from a store in Chicago for their thirtieth wedding anniversary." Bailey abruptly straightened, her body stiff as she rapidly blinked back tears. "God."

Caught off guard by her intense reaction, Dom wrapped her trembling body in his arms.

"Are you okay?"

"It's so stupid." She leaned against him, her words muffled as she pressed her face against his chest. "We've been discussing people stealing from Nellie and even someone killing her for days. But it wasn't real. Not until now."

Dom smoothed a hand down her back, regret slicing through him. Bailey was so boldly courageous, he sometimes lost sight of how much she'd endured over the past days. It'd started with the death of her friend and Gage's ugly accusations and quickly spiraled into the grinding fear that she was being stalked by a psychopath.

It was a wonder she wasn't locked in her room, curled in a ball of terror.

"Do you want to wait outside?"

"No. I want this finished." She lifted her head to

meet his worried gaze. "I want it to be just the two of us with no distractions."

An unexpected shudder raced through him, proving his own emotions were scraped raw. He'd never wanted anything more in his life. Including when he was starving on the streets.

"It sounds like paradise," he whispered, his fingers stroking down her back in a comforting motion.

Her lips parted, but before she could speak the door to the office was yanked open and they stepped apart to watch a tall, painfully thin man with long, mousy blond hair and a scraggly beard walk into the store. He was wearing a T-shirt with the sleeves cut off to reveal his numerous tattoos and jeans that hung low on his narrow hips.

"See anything you like?" He halted on the opposite side of the case. Then, without warning, his pale brown eyes widened in shock. "Are you shitting me?"

Dom wrapped a protective arm around Bailey. "Is there a problem?"

"Problem? Hell no." The man placed his hands flat on the glass as he leaned forward. "I can't believe this is real. You're Dom Lucier."

Dom kept a smile plastered on his face. Although he'd been friends with Kaden for fifteen years, it'd only been since the opening of Money Makers that he started being recognized. Usually by people in his industry.

"That I am," he murmured.

"King of Pawn," the man continued.

Dom cleared his throat. He wasn't Kaden. He would never be comfortable with fame.

"I don't know about that."

The man ignored his lack of enthusiasm. "You won't remember, man, but I'm Drew Stroud. I came out to Vegas the week you opened Money Makers. It was epic. The live music, the celebrities just strolling around, and Kaden fucking Vaughn on his vintage motorcycle. Yeah . . . epic."

It had been epic. They'd spent a fortune to make sure the launch of the combination pawnshop and motorcycle restoration would attract attention and they hadn't been disappointed. The crowd had been lined up for days before they'd opened the doors, and by the time the first week was over they'd had over ten thousand customers step through the doors.

"I'm glad you had a good time."

"Look at that." Drew turned to point to a framed photo that was nailed above the cash register. Even from a distance Dom could make out Drew's smiling face as he stood between Dom and Kaden. "Place of honor."

"Awesome."

Drew reached into the back pocket of his jeans to pull out his phone. He held it up, shifting from foot to foot as if he was suddenly nervous.

"Do you mind?"

Dom swallowed a sigh. He might dislike the attention, but he needed this man's help.

"Not at all." Removing his arm from Bailey's shoulders, he bent across the case so Drew could snap a picture of them together.

"I can't believe you're standing here," Drew breathed, taking several pictures before shoving the phone back into his pocket.

Dom straightened, leaning his hip against the edge of the cabinet. "I'm hoping you can answer some questions for me."

Drew lifted a brow. "For real?"

"Yep." Dom pointed toward the middle of the case. "What can you tell me about the emerald ring?"

Drew's dazzled smile was suddenly replaced with a shrewd expression. He might be a fan, but he was also a businessman. And selling the ring would no doubt be a big boost to his bottom line.

Grabbing the keys that were stored in a drawer next to the cash register, Drew quickly unlocked the case and pulled out the velvet-lined box.

"This one?"

"That's it."

"Excellent taste," Drew commended him, tugging out the ring so the stones could glitter in the glow of the overhead lights. Dom silently appreciated his dramatic flair. Selling secondhand stuff took more effort than simply tossing it on a shelf. You had to convince the buyer they were getting the deal of a lifetime. "It's a two-carat, oval-cut emerald with diamond accent stones. Fourteen carat white gold." He tilted the ring to look inside the band. "Size six." He glanced toward Bailey before returning his attention to Dom. "I can give you a great deal on this."

"I'll take it," Dom grabbed the ring, tugging off the price tag before he shoved it in his pocket.

Dom ignored Bailey's startled glance. This ring was evidence that Logan Donaldson and Eric Criswell had been stealing from the residents of Pike Nursing Home. Not to mention the fact that it obviously had a sentimental value to Bailey. There was no way he was going to risk having it disappear.

Drew appeared as surprised as Bailey by his abrupt decision. "No haggling?" he complained. "Where's the fun in that?"

"Next time." Dom pulled out his wallet and tossed his credit card on top of the case. "For now I'm more interested in how the ring came to be in your shop."

Drew pulled out an invoice pad and painstakingly began writing out the information. He obviously preferred to do things old school. Dom approved.

"I'm not sure what you're asking."

Leaning forward, Dom planted his elbow on the glass. "Can I be honest with you?"

Drew finished writing out the details of the ring and Dom's credit card number before glancing up.

"Sure." He studied Dom with a lift of his brows. "What's up?"

"We're trying to discover who's been stealing from the elderly residents in a nursing home. Including a close friend of ours," Dom told him.

Drew's smile was replaced with an expression of outrage. "Hey, there was nothing hinky about the ring. I report all my merchandise to the local authorities. If something was stolen, it would have set off an alarm."

"I'm not accusing you of anything improper, I swear," Dom hastily assured him. "I know exactly how hard it is to run a pawnshop and the amount of red tape you have to wade through."

"No shit. I'm drowning in rules and regulations," Drew groused.

"I hear ya. And you have my full sympathy." Dom

lowered his voice. "The theft of the ring hasn't been reported. We're hoping to avoid the cops until after we track down who stole it. There's always the possibility that it was someone we know. We don't want to cause any trouble until we can be sure what happened," he said, allowing the man to believe it might all be swept under the rug. "Once we have a name I'll get out of your hair," he promised.

"I suppose it doesn't hurt to look at the information of who pawned the ring since you're buying it today," Drew slowly conceded. "And if you happen to see the paperwork . . ."

With a conspiratorial wink, Drew disappeared into the office, and Dom exchanged a glance with Bailey.

"You don't have to buy the ring," she whispered in a harsh voice. "It's expensive."

He reached to brush his fingers down her cheek. "It was important to Nellie. And she was important to you," he said, reaching into his pocket. "She would want you to have it."

Her lips parted as he pulled out the ring and pressed it into her hand. "Dom, I can't accept—"

"It's yours." He pressed a quick kiss against her lips.

Before she could argue that it was too expensive, Drew returned from the office carrying a file folder. Flipping it open, he spread the papers across the top of the case.

"I appreciate this," Dom murmured softly, his gaze scanning the paperwork to land on the photocopy of Logan Donaldson's driver's license.

"It was Logan." Bailey grasped the edge of the case as if her knees were suddenly weak. "That . . . bastard."

Dom wrapped his arm around her waist, his gaze never wavering from Drew. "Is he a regular?"

"Not really. He's been in maybe four or five times that I can remember."

"Recently?"

Sorting through the papers, Drew shook his head. "The last time was over three weeks ago. When he brought in the emerald ring."

Wondering if Logan had put the thefts on hold after Nellie's murder to avoid unwanted attention from the sheriff or if he was collecting the jewelry and waiting to come to the pawnshop when he ran out of money, Dom at last straightened.

They'd gotten the answers they'd come for. Time to get back to Pike.

"Thanks, man." Dom nodded toward his credit card. "If you'll ring us up, I won't bother you anymore."

With a nod, Drew took the card to the scanner next to the cash register, quickly finishing the transaction before returning to hand the card and receipt to Dom.

"You know, it would be awesome if you could keep the shop out of any unpleasant investigations."

Dom nodded. He didn't suspect Drew was doing anything illegal, but pawnshops were always treated as if they were operating on the wrong side of the law. Even Money Makers.

"I'll do my best," he promised, even as he silently acknowledged that it was going to be tough to avoid getting the cops involved. Still, he would do his best to make sure that nothing bad happened to Drew or his pawnshop. "I won't forget your help," he promised.

He was about to turn away when Bailey abruptly pointed toward a shelf above the cash register.

"Do you sell a lot of phones?" she asked.

With a jerk of surprise, Dom glanced up, his gaze landing on the stack of boxes with prepaid phones. He hadn't noticed them. Thankfully, Bailey was more observant.

Drew turned to study the phones. "Not really. They're cheaper at the big-box stores."

"Did the man who brought in the emerald ring buy any phones?" he demanded.

"I don't think so."

Dom's brief surge of hope faded. If they could have pinned the phones on Logan, they would know exactly who was stalking Bailey. For now, however, they could at least hand over the information about Nellie's ring to Zac. It might not be enough for an arrest, but it would point him in the right direction.

"Okay. Thanks again."

Together Dom and Bailey headed across the store. They'd reached the door when Drew suddenly called out, "Wait!"

Dom glanced over his shoulder. "Yes?"

"The dude who sold the ring didn't buy any phones, but another guy bought four of them on the same day."

Dom whirled around, his body suddenly tense. No one bought four phones unless it was for a nefarious purpose.

A terrorist. A drug dealer. A stalker . . .

"You're sure it was the same day?" he asked.

"Without a doubt. I was still cleaning the emerald ring when he came to the counter and asked for four phones." Drew shrugged. "It was weird enough it stuck in my memory."

"Can you describe him?" Bailey asked, her voice unsteady as she pressed her hands together.

They both realized if Drew could identify the man who bought the phones, the nightmare would be over.

"Naw." Drew grimaced. "He was an average Joe. I wouldn't recognize him if I passed him on the street."

Dom bit back a curse. He appreciated the man's honesty, but once again the truth remained just out of reach. A damned shame.

"Did he pay cash?"

There was a long silence as Drew dredged through his memories. "I don't know. I suppose I could check through the receipts, but it'll take a while."

Dom crossed back to the display case, pulling out a business card. Grabbing the pen next to the invoice pad, he used it to write out his cell phone number on the back of the card. "If you find out anything, I'd really appreciate you letting me know."

The man smiled, clearly pleased at having Dom Lucier's private number. "Sure thing."

"Thanks, Drew." Dom reached out to shake his hand. "Great to meet you."

Drew flushed. "This has been epic, man."

Dom strolled back to the waiting Bailey and together they stepped out of the shop. Then, climbing into the SUV, Dom fired up the engine and they headed back to the highway.

"I forget," Bailey murmured.

"Forget what?"

"That you're famous."

Dom snorted. "I'm not. It's nothing but reflected fame from Kaden. Which is just fine with me." He sent her a wry glance. "I'm just plain Dom Lucier."

She stroked her hand down his arm. "Just plain Dom Lucier is pretty special."

Her soft words touched the place deep inside Dom that he had always tried to ignore. The empty place Remy had chiseled out with his callous indifference for the boy who had desperately craved his love.

He sent her a glance that held all the emotions that bubbled inside him. "How did I survive without you, Bailey Evans?"

Chapter 22

Bailey spent the return trip to Pike trying to ease the guilt that gnawed at her like a cancer. It wasn't her fault that Nellie was dead, she told herself over and over. Okay, maybe she shouldn't have stood up for Eric Criswell when the staff complained that he was odd. If he'd been fired, he would never have been able to steal from Nellie and the other residents. Not that it would have stopped Logan Donaldson from getting his hands on the cash and jewelry, she silently acknowledged. He might be a lazy jerk, but he was in a position to force one of his employees to help him. Whether they wanted to or not.

Her dark musings were thankfully distracted as they veered off the highway. Eventually she would look back and put everything into perspective. For now she needed to concentrate on making sure no other resident at the nursing home was put in danger.

"Are we going to have a chat with Logan?" she demanded, straightening up in her seat. "Maybe include Lorene in our discussions?"

Dom shook his head, taking the exit that led directly

to Main Street. "Not until we've had a chance to share what we've discovered with Zac. I don't want the Donaldsons disappearing before they can be locked away."

She scowled, but she didn't argue. They couldn't risk alerting Logan to the fact that they knew he was stealing from the residents. He was cowardly enough to go into hiding and leave his mom to face the consequences.

"Dammit," she muttered. "I want to look Logan Donaldson straight in the eye when I kick his balls."

Dom made a choked sound of surprise at her violent fantasy. "That's very specific."

"Don't make me mad."

"Noted."

His lips twitched as they pulled into the parking lot next to the courthouse. A quick glance revealed that it was empty except for a tan Bronco that no doubt belonged to the deputy on duty.

Dom muttered a curse. "He's not here."

"I'll give him a call." Bailey dug out her phone and pressed her cousin's number. Zac answered after the first ring. "Hey, Zac. Are you at home?" she asked, her heart sinking as he answered her in distracted tones. "Nope. No worries," she assured him when he finished. "You take care of Rachel and I'll see you tomorrow."

She ended the connection and tossed the phone back into her purse.

"Is everything okay?" Dom asked.

"It's fine, but Zac is getting ready to head out of town. He's spending the night with Rachel in Madison. She has a routine ultrasound at the hospital tomorrow morning," she told him.

Dom's jaw tightened, but he knew as well as she did there was nothing they could do about the Donaldsons. Not until Zac returned.

"What now?" he muttered, tapping his fingers on the steering wheel. "We could go back to the house—"

"If we can't confront Logan and his mom, we can at least find Eric and talk to him, right?" she interrupted. As much as she enjoyed having time alone with Dom, she was too on edge to relax. "He followed Logan to the pawnshop. He has to be the guy who bought all the phones."

Dom pulled out of the lot and headed south. "Oh yeah. We need to talk to him. The sooner, the better," he agreed.

It took less than ten minutes to reach Eric's house. They slowed as they neared, but before Dom could pull into the driveway, she reached out to touch his arm.

"Eric's car isn't here," she said, her hands clenching in frustration. "He must be working this afternoon."

"It's Sunday." Dom rolled past the house, stopping at the end of the block. "He might be out enjoying his weekend."

Bailey shook her head. "If he's not home, he's usually at the nursing home. He doesn't have a lot of friends."

Dom grimaced, doing a U-turn to drive the short distance to the nursing home.

"I'd say that was pathetic, but there's an old saying about not throwing stones in glass houses," he admitted in wry tones. "My life revolves around work and work and more work. I collapse in my bed by nine o'clock unless I fall asleep on the couch even earlier. Worse, I live on the property, so I never leave."

Before the past week Bailey assumed Dom Lucier lived a Vegas lifestyle that was filled with late-night parties and glamorous women. Now it was remarkably easy to imagine him cuddling her on the couch while Bert and Ernie battled for the prime spot next to them.

It was a vision that Bailey clung to with a fierce urgency, attempting to banish the heavy cloud of anxiety that threatened to drown her.

"That was pretty much my schedule," she told him. "The nursing home is constantly understaffed, so I had to work double shifts or come in on my days off. Being able to stay home and sleep was better than a vacation."

"Kaden and Lia have made the pledge to work fewer hours and spend more quality time together," he said. "It's worked out pretty well for them."

Bailey nodded. "Lia did hire staff to run her family grocery store. I know that's taken a load off her."

"And Kaden has two full-time mechanics who take care of the routine repairs. A minor miracle considering he's a control freak."

She chuckled at his accusation. If Kaden was a control freak, Dom was a control maniac.

"Like someone else I know," she said.

"Guilty," he readily agreed. "But if they can do it, so can we. There's no reason I can't hire more staff and train a manager to run the day-to-day operations of Money Makers."

We . . . Such a simple word, but it pierced her heart like an arrow. For so long she'd imagined a future where she was alone. It wasn't until Dom that she realized her decision hadn't been made because she preferred not to share her life—a legitimate choice—but a decision created by fear of being hurt. And that those were two very separate things.

"I have nothing but free time," she assured him wryly.

He reached out to grab her hand, raising it to press her fingers against his lips. "You won't be unemployed for long. But I hope when you discover what you want for your future I'll be included in your plans."

"Always."

With a last kiss, he released her hand and turned into the parking lot of the nursing home. The SUV rolled to a halt as Dom glanced around the numerous cars with a lift of his brows.

"It's busy today."

"A lot of relatives visit on Sundays," she told him, a little surprised herself by the crowd. Then she recalled what day it was. "Oh yeah. And it's the first Sunday of the month. The residents host an ice cream social for the town. It's always a big hit."

"Do you see Eric's car?"

Bailey scanned the lot, frustration searing through her as she was forced to accept Eric wasn't working. There was no way to overlook his car.

"It's not here." She clicked her tongue. "Maybe he is off somewhere having fun."

Dom heaved a harsh sigh. "We'll check his house later. For now . . ."

Bailey sent him a confused glance as he seemed to forget what he was going to say. "What's wrong?"

He nodded toward the abandoned building next to the nursing home. "Does anyone drive a silver BMW in Pike?"

"Not that I've noticed." She glanced across the lot, noticing the silver car that had been pulled into a no-parking zone. As she watched, it backed out, offering her a perfect view of the license plate. HARTFORD4. "Dom," she breathed, her mouth suddenly dry. "Kevin Hartford drove a silver BMW."

"Yep," he rasped. "And according to the cops in Grange, it was missing after he was found dead."

"Whoever is driving that car has to be the killer."

"Or a trap," he countered.

She jerked her head around to study his grim expression. "A trap?"

"It seems pretty damned convenient that Kevin Hartford's stolen car would appear in the parking lot of the nursing home at the same time we're here," he pointed out. "Not unless it followed us and pulled into a spot we were bound to notice."

He had a point. It did seem too good to be true for the killer to be in the same place as them, driving a car with a license plate they would be sure to recognize. But as the vehicle headed toward the side exit of the lot, her heart squeezed with fear.

"You're just going to ignore it?" she demanded.

"Hell no." There was a tense pause. "But I want you to wait for me inside."

Her mouth dropped open. "Seriously?"

"Yes."

"Wait." She narrowed her eyes. "Are you saying you can put yourself in danger, but I can't?"

His jaw tightened. "I don't intend to put myself in danger, but if this is a trap, it would be foolish for both of us to get caught in it, wouldn't it?" He held her gaze.

"One of us needs to stay here in case things go sideways. You're going to have to rush to my rescue."

"You're just saying that to get rid of me," she ground out.

"And because it's true," he insisted, his body tensing as he glanced toward the car that was pulling out of the lot. "Bailey."

Bailey removed her seat belt, her movements jerky. As much as she wanted to argue that she deserved to be there when the killer was finally cornered, she wasn't willing to risk having him disappear. Nothing was more important than ending this nightmare.

"Don't die," she muttered.

"I'll be back for you." He leaned across the console to swipe a quick kiss over her lips. "I promise."

Dom waited until Bailey disappeared into the nursing home before backing out of the lot with a spray of gravel.

He hadn't been lying when he warned Bailey that the silver BMW was probably a ploy to attract his attention. His luck hadn't been good enough to randomly stumble across the killer. He genuinely needed someone in a position to call for help if he got caught in a trap. But it was also true that if this was the person stalking Bailey, he didn't want her anywhere near the bastard. Not until he was behind bars.

Shoving the SUV into Drive, Dom scanned the road, cursing at the realization the BMW had disappeared.

No. It couldn't have gone far, he silently reassured himself, driving at a crawl as he glanced from side to side. Pike wasn't big enough for anyone to hide for long.

Less than five minutes later his confidence was rewarded as he caught a glimpse of silver through the neat row of homes. Turning at the next block, Dom halted at the stop sign. If this wasn't a trap, he didn't want the killer to realize he was being followed.

He waited until the BMW had reached the end of the street and was making another turn before he released the brake and rolled forward. Once he reached the corner he stopped again, his brows snapping together. The car had disappeared. If the killer was hoping Dom would shadow him, he wasn't making it easy. Of course, if he made it too easy, Dom would know it was a trap.

Dom muttered a curse.

There was no way to guess the motive of the driver. Not until he had an opportunity to beat the truth out of him.

Turning in the direction he'd last seen the car, Dom zigzagged his way through town, resisting the urge to pick up speed. Not only did he not want to miss the car in case it'd pulled into a parking lot or driveway, he'd discovered since arriving in Pike that the locals had a habit of stopping in the middle of the street to chat with their neighbors. Or even randomly leaving their cars in the road if they were running into one of the stores and didn't intend to be there for long.

Dom didn't want to plow into a couple of old men catching up on the latest gossip.

He made another turn, his brows snapping together when he realized he'd reached the outer road. He'd run out of real estate to search. Dammit. Had the driver doubled back? Was he returning to the nursing home?

Dom's heart squeezed with a sudden fear. It hadn't

occurred to him that the killer might try to lure him away from Bailey.

Pulling out his phone, Dom intended to call Bailey and warn her to stay in a public area of the nursing home when he was distracted by a flash of light. It was the glint of the setting sun against a vehicle speeding away from town.

The BMW.

Dom hit the accelerator; he wasn't going to let the car disappear again. Concentrating on the fading glint of silver, he failed to notice where they were headed until they reached the familiar dirt road. This was the way to Kaden's house.

His fingers tightened on the steering wheel. This was no coincidence. He was deliberately being led away from town and back to the house he was sharing with Bailey. But why?

Only one way to find out.

Maintaining a speed that allowed him to keep the dust trail from the moving vehicle in sight but far enough away to stop if he sensed something sketchy, Dom clutched the steering wheel hard enough to turn his knuckles white. He wasn't like Kaden, who got a thrill out of dangerous situations. He didn't drive his cars at breakneck speed and jump off high buildings. In truth, he wouldn't be chasing the damned vehicle unless it was to end the threat against Bailey. He'd walk into the fiery pits of hell to protect her.

Slowing as he reached the sharp curve, Dom frowned as he pulled into the narrow driveway. There was no sign of the silver car, but there was a dark pile of junk tossed next to the closed security gates.

Dom cursed as he rolled to a halt, realizing the car must have turned off the road and headed into the dense trees on the opposite side. He was going to have to turn back and look for the tire tracks he'd missed. . . .

His thoughts shattered as his gaze absently skimmed over the pile next to the gate. It was only then that he realized it wasn't a bundle of clothes that had been tossed out. It was a body.

Leaning forward, Dom studied the unmoving form with a stunned sense of disbelief. The man was wrapped in a brown blanket, which was why he hadn't instantly recognized what he was seeing, but his face was visible. Dom's breath tangled in his throat as he easily recognized Logan Donaldson. There was no mistaking the pudgy cheeks and thin strands of hair that wafted in the breeze. But that wasn't what captured his attention. It was the wound in the center of his forehead. A wound that was leaking blood.

Yanking out his phone, Dom dialed 911 and quickly gave the address to the operator, along with the fact that Logan Donaldson was injured and lying in the driveway to Kaden Vaughn's house. Then, keeping the call connected, he shoved it back in his pocket.

It looked as if Logan was unconscious and in desperate need of assistance. Which meant he couldn't sit in his vehicle and wait for him to die. But Dom intended to be prepared. This could very well be the bait to lure him into an ambush.

He wanted his phone connected to 911 to capture whatever was happening.

Leaving the engine of his Land Rover running in case he needed a quick getaway, he climbed out and cautiously inched his way toward the motionless body, his gaze scanning the area for any potential dangers.

When he'd started chasing the BMW he'd assumed that Logan was the driver. He was the primary suspect, after all. Now it was obvious the assumption was wrong. So who was behind the wheel? And how had Logan ended up in front of the gates?

When he didn't detect anything but the scurry of a squirrel across the yard beyond the gates, Dom knelt and pressed his fingers against Logan's throat.

No heartbeat. And the skin was cold.

Shock jolted through Dom. Despite the bullet hole in the center of his forehead, he hadn't actually expected to discover a corpse.

Dom straightened, a chill racing through him. He'd seen dead bodies, of course. Including his mother. And he'd even touched them. But there was something outrageously creepy about stumbling across a man who'd been murdered and then dumped like he was garbage.

With a grimace, Dom reminded himself this was a crime scene that shouldn't be disturbed. The ambulance was no doubt on its way and because there was nothing he could do for the dead man it was time to return to his hunt for the silver car.

His decision made, he stepped away from the body, concentrating on the ground to make sure he didn't disturb any footprints that might be near the victim. A commendable effort that was ruined as there was a crunch of wheels on gravel and he belatedly caught sight of the silver BMW that was hurtling toward him at a speed he couldn't possibly outrun.

The distraction of the dead body combined with the

hum of the Land Rover's motor had kept Dom from recognizing the danger until it was too late. Now he could only watch in horror as the vehicle passed the SUV and aimed straight in his direction.

No, a voice sternly whispered in the back of his head. He wasn't going to just stand there and die.

He'd spent endless days on movie sets watching Kaden practice for upcoming stunts. That certainly didn't make him a pro, but it did warn him not to try to run or drop to the ground to try to avoid the oncoming car.

Squaring his shoulders, he spread his legs and sent up a silent prayer. Then, forcing himself to wait until the last possible second, he reached out his arms and jumped as high as he'd ever jumped in his life.

The desperate leap didn't keep the front bumper from smashing into his legs, but instead of dragging him under the car and into the path of the tires, the impact propelled him up and over the hood.

He caught a glimpse of the driver through the front windshield, but before he could process what he was seeing, Dom slammed into that same windshield with skull-cracking force.

Pain splintered through him, the grinding agony so intense he feared that he'd not only cracked his skull but that more than one internal organ was damaged. And worse, he couldn't move his legs. He was completely helpless.

Groaning, he tried to battle back the red mist that swirled through his brain.

Bailey was in danger.

He had to warn her.

He had to . . .

* * *

After Bailey grabbed her purse and slid out of the Range Rover she'd swiftly jogged to the nursing home entrance. She knew Dom well enough to realize he wasn't leaving the lot until she was safely locked inside. Pressing in her password on the keypad, she opened the door and entered the front lobby with a small shiver. She had to trust that Dom wouldn't do anything foolish. And that whatever happened he would keep his promise to return to her.

Yeah, that was gonna happen, she wryly acknowledged.

She was going to be worried sick until Dom was standing safe and sound directly in front of her.

Barely aware of the loud sound of chatter coming from the nearby dining room that was packed with guests eating large amounts of ice cream, Bailey forced herself to take in slow, deep breaths.

How long would he be gone? Five minutes? An hour?

Wishing she was at home so she could pace the floor without attracting attention, Bailey nearly jumped out of her skin when a voice spoke directly behind her.

"Hey, girlfriend."

Spinning around, Bailey released a shaky breath of relief as she caught sight of the dark-haired woman dressed in scrubs. She hadn't seen her friend since their night out over a week earlier.

"Oh . . . hi, Kari."

"Where have you been? I was afraid you'd left Pike."

"Nope, I'm still hanging around."

Bailey kept her voice light. She adored Kari, but

the older woman was incurably nosy. If she suspected Bailey was hiding something, she wouldn't stop digging until she found out what it was.

"It's time for another girls' night out."

"Agreed. How are you?"

Kari stuck out her tongue. "Overworked and underpaid."

"The same as always then?"

"Yep, except I miss your face." Kari glanced toward the central desk where a middle-aged woman with short, bleached-blond hair and a crisp white jacket was surveying the dining room with a pinched expression. "The nurse they hired to replace you might be qualified for the job, but she has the personality of a turnip. I don't think I've ever seen her smile." Kari leaned in, lowering her voice. "You didn't hear this from me, but the staff is about to revolt."

Bailey had to admit she did look like a sourpuss. Still, being competent at her job was more important than her personality.

"I'm sure she's not that bad," she protested.

Kari rolled her eyes. "She's the worst. Thank God she's just a placeholder. When are you coming back?"

"I don't think I am," Bailey said without hesitation. Just walking through the doors made her feel nauseous. She would always love the residents, but the place had been tainted by Logan Donaldson, along with Eric. It would never be the same.

Kari's eyes widened. Bailey understood her friend's surprise. Everyone assumed she would spend the rest of her life working at the nursing home. Including Bailey.

"Do you have a new job?" Kari asked.

Bailey shrugged. "Not yet, but I'm sure something will come along."

Kari's dismay was slowly replaced with a mischievous smile. "Ah. Does that 'something coming along' have the name of Dom Lucier?"

"Perhaps," Bailey admitted. It felt oddly wonderful to openly admit her relationship with Dom.

As if it made it real.

Kari smiled. "Lucky you."

"Yeah." A flush of pleasure touched her cheeks. "I really am."

"Have you told the Donaldsons that you're not coming back?"

Bailey struggled to hide her contempt. "I haven't formally handed in my notice, but they know it's a possibility."

Kari snorted. "That must be why they didn't show up for church. They know you're the reason this place runs so smoothly. They'll be lost without you."

Bailey froze, a niggle of unease inching down her spine. "The Donaldsons weren't at church?"

"Nope. First time I can remember them missing. . . ." Kari thought for a moment before shaking her head. "Actually, I don't remember them ever missing. Not in the almost thirty years I've been going to that church."

That was exactly what was troubling Bailey. Any normal person missing church wouldn't be a big deal. But the Donaldsons?

"Did anyone know where they were?"

"No. I even asked around," Kari admitted. "You know me, I have to know what's going on with everyone in town. But no one has heard from them since they left work on Friday."

"That's odd."

"Really odd." Kari glanced around, making sure no one was close enough to overhear her words. "Lorene is freakishly predictable. She gets to work at the exact same time every morning. She leaves the exact same time every night. And she is always at church on Sunday, sitting in the middle of the third pew with her cross on and her lips pursed in righteous disapproval."

"Hmm."

Bailey struggled not to overreact. Okay. The Donaldsons hadn't missed church in thirty years. But that didn't mean there wasn't a legitimate reason for them not to be there. A death in the family. The stomach flu. A broken-down car.

Or they were fleeing town because Logan had stolen from the residents and murdered at least four people . . .

"Crap," Kari muttered, her gaze locked on the nurses' station. "I'm getting the stink eye from your replacement. I need to get the residents back to their rooms so we can clear out the guests and set up for dinner."

Bailey stepped forward, hugging the woman who'd always brightened her day when they worked together.

"Good to see you, Kari."

"Call me." The older woman squeezed Bailey tight before stepping back. "We'll go out and I can live vicariously through your stories of romance with that gorgeous male."

"You got it."

Bailey watched Kari disappear among the clusters of people filling the dining room. Then, with a nonchalance she was far from feeling, she strolled toward the back of the building. Thankfully, the staff was too busy with the ice cream social to stop and chat, allowing Bailey to turn into the short hallway without any awkward questions.

Once out of sight, she scurried to the end of the hall. She couldn't shake the fear that Logan knew they'd discovered his connection to the thefts and had already disappeared.

Grasping the doorhandle of Lorene's office, she gave it a shove. Locked. Bailey muttered a curse, turning to try Logan's door. She shook the handle, but it refused to budge.

It wasn't unusual. The Donaldsons always locked their offices when they left the building. But it did mean that she couldn't search them. Which was annoying as hell. She had to know if anything was missing. After all, if they intended to sneak out of town, they would surely take their prized possessions, including Lorene's key to the city, which she'd been given by the previous mayor, and Logan's expensive golf clubs, which he kept handy so he could sneak away to play on nice days.

Thwarted for the moment, Bailey turned away, heading back down the hallway until she reached her old office. Pulling out her keys, she glanced around before she let herself in.

It wasn't like she was doing anything wrong, she told herself. She was still employed by the nursing home, and this was still technically her office. Her reassurance didn't slow her racing pulse, but it did give her the courage to cross the cramped space to the bulletin board on the wall behind her desk. Before everything had been computerized, the board was used to display the weekly work schedules as well as any changes in medication for the residents. Bailey had covered the board with various pictures of the residents as they enjoyed special events. The Easter egg roll, the ragtime sing-along, the children's reading hour . . . Reaching the board, she grabbed the picture of Nellie that showed her standing next to a large Christmas tree. It was one of the best pictures she had of the older woman, but that wasn't why she was shoving it into her purse. The picture clearly captured the emerald ring Nellie was wearing as she placed an ornament on the tree. They might need proof that the ring they'd bought from the pawnshop was the same one that had been stolen from Nellie.

With the photo safely tucked away, Bailey quickly left the office and returned to the front lobby. She halted as she realized that most of the crowd was streaming out the door and the aides were assisting the residents back to their rooms. Soon the place would be empty and the staff would start to wonder why she was there. She needed a reason to be hanging around when she obviously wasn't on duty.

She hesitated before she abruptly turned to the left and headed across the lobby. The one place she could reasonably hang around for an extended length of time was the employee break room, she decided. It would, hopefully, be empty this time of day, plus she could always claim that she was there to clean out her locker. She had a few personal belongings she'd left behind.

Entering yet another hallway, she was debating

whether to call Dom and warn him that the Donaldsons were potentially trying to escape when the door next to her swung inward. She moved to the side, not particularly concerned.

It wasn't until an arm reached out and a hand painfully slammed across her mouth that she realized she was in danger. And then it was too late. Yanked into the large room that was lined with washing machines and heavy-duty dryers, she had a glimpse of the long, stainless-steel tables covered by stacks of folded towels before she was lifted off her feet. The world tilted in a dizzy circle as she was turned upside down and roughly shoved into one of the fifty-five-gallon barrels they used for their laundry detergent.

Stunned by the speed of the unexpected attack, Bailey belatedly cried out for help as her head hit the bottom with a painful thud, but the lid was already being snapped shut. Not that it mattered. The sound of the numerous machines running at the same time was loud enough to drown out any other sound.

No one would hear her scream.

Chapter 23

Bailey tried to brace herself as the barrel was tilted onto a dolly and she was wheeled out of the back of the nursing home. It was a futile effort as they rolled over the rough ground, banging Bailey from side to side while her head was pressed against the bottom at an awkward angle.

She had no idea where she was being taken, but each minute she remained locked in the cramped container, the more difficult it was to breathe. Was she running out of oxygen? Or was it fear making her feel as if she was being smothered?

Swaying and jolting over the rough ground, there was a pause before she was rattled over what she assumed was a doorjamb. Bailey felt a faint stir of hope. They had to be in the abandoned building next to the nursing home, right? They hadn't gone far enough to reach anywhere else.

Which meant she wouldn't have to go far for help once she managed to escape.

And she had every intention of escaping.

Clinging to that belief with every fiber of her being,

Bailey ground her teeth as the barrel was abruptly toppled onto the side. Pain jolted through her, but she was bruised, not broken, she tried to reassure herself, ignoring the trickle of blood that streamed from a cut on her brow. She could still put up a fight.

She clenched her battered muscles as the lid popped open, but even as she tried to kick whoever was reaching into the barrel, a pair of hands grasped the waistband of her jeans and dragged her out. Bailey screamed, flailing her arms. Her screams wouldn't be heard from the nursing home, but if someone was in the parking lot, they might come to investigate.

Seemingly indifferent to her cries for help, Bailey was abruptly pinned face-first against the broken tile floor with a knee pressed to the center of her spine. The pressure was hard enough to hold her in place as her arms were yanked behind her back. There was a loud click and Bailey felt a pair of handcuffs being snapped around her wrists.

"Stop that," a male voice commanded. "No one can hear you from here. I made sure the room is soundproofed."

Bailey cut off her screams as she instantly recognized the voice. "Eric?" she rasped, caught between a strange sense of shock and not shocked. "What's wrong with you? Have you lost your mind?"

The hands on her arms gentled as she was turned over. Bailey knew she should be terrified. Instead, she felt more anger than fear as Eric slowly straightened up.

"I needed to talk to you," he said.

"So you attack me, handcuff me, and hold me prisoner

in a room you claim is soundproofed?" Her voice was sharp. "That's not talking, that's kidnapping."

There was the sound of muffled footsteps before a flickering glow suddenly battled against the darkness. Bailey blinked, watching the fluorescent light hum to life before she rolled onto her side to glance around. It looked like an old bathroom, but the stalls had been pulled out along with the sinks, leaving it a cavernous, barren space. The walls that at one time were painted an industrial green were peeling, making it appear as if it was a snake sloughing off a dead skin. It was a setting worthy of a horror film, she acknowledged with a shiver, but her interest at the moment was in the fact that there were no windows. And worse, Eric was standing in front of the only door.

She was going to have to find a way to get past him, she accepted. But how? It was doubtful she could convince him to release her. Not after he'd gone to so much trouble to kidnap her. Her only hope was managing to overpower him.

Easier said than done.

"You wouldn't listen to me. Not unless I forced you to," Eric claimed, thankfully appearing unaware of her dark thoughts. "That man has clouded your mind."

Bailey sat up with a groan. Every muscle ached and there was a throbbing pain behind her right eye. Still, she managed to swivel on her butt until she was directly facing her captor. The position had the added benefit of hiding her hands from his view.

She wasn't a magician. She hadn't practiced escaping handcuffs. But on the other hand, Eric wasn't a professional kidnapper. The cuffs were tight, but they weren't so tight that there wasn't a possibility she could wiggle her hands through them.

Only one way to find out.

"What man?" she demanded.

"Dom Lucier." Eric scowled, his expression more like a petulant child's than a crazy stalker's. "Nothing has been the same since he came to Pike. We never spend any time together anymore."

Bailey studied him in confusion. He was wearing jeans that were too large for his skinny frame and a black windbreaker. His hair was sticking out, as if he'd been running his fingers through it, and his eyes glittered with a hectic glow. Unease pierced her heart.

He looked different, warning her that there was a lot she didn't know about Eric Criswell.

"What are you talking about?" she demanded. "We didn't spend time together before Dom came to Pike."

Eric flinched, as if her words hurt him. "Of course we did. We had lunch together almost every day."

His bold claim caught her off guard. It was true they both ate lunch in the break room at the nursing home when they were both working. But most of the time Eric was seated in a corner by himself, while Bailey sat at the table with a few of the other staff. She might have said hi or even discussed a case from the Murder Club. But they certainly hadn't been besties.

Still, it didn't seem wise to aggravate him by saying that now. Not when she was handcuffed and at his mercy.

"It wasn't Dom's fault that I wasn't at the nursing home," she gently reminded him. "I was told to leave by Lorene."

"Maybe not, but he's the reason you haven't come back to work," Eric insisted.

"No." Bailey shook her head, pressing her shoulders back as far as they would go. She hoped to create slack in the chain that held the cuffs together. It seemed reasonable that it would make it easier to slip a hand free. "The only one to blame for me leaving and staying away from the nursing home is the Donaldsons. When they accused me of coercing Nellie into leaving me money I realized I wasn't staying here because it was my life's dream. I stayed because I was too afraid to take on a new challenge." She shrugged. "It's time to move on."

Eric stuck out his lower lip. "And leave me behind."

"My decision has nothing to do with you."

"Of course it doesn't. Because I'm a nobody, right?"

Bailey forced herself to count to ten. She wanted to scream at her captor that he might have friends if he didn't act like a sulky manbaby. Oh, and if he didn't kidnap women when they didn't give him the attention he wanted.

"That's not true. We worked well together—"

"No, it was more than that," Eric interrupted, his voice shrill. "You're the only one in this godforsaken town who understands me. Just like I'm the only one who gets you. We have a special connection."

Bailey hesitated, as if she was considering her response. At the same time she tugged at the cuff, feeling it slip down half an inch.

"There is no connection, Eric," she argued, deliberately provoking him.

He had the emotional maturity of a toddler. The best way to keep him distracted was to stir his anger.

On cue, his brows snapped together. "Don't say that. We have so much in common. Our work. Our hatred for the small-minded idiots that pollute this town."

"I don't hate the people in Pike," she protested.

"Okay, maybe that's a little harsh, but they're not like us," he insisted. "That's why we belong together."

She shook her head, giving another tug on the cuff. "It's never going to happen, Eric."

"It is." Eric narrowed his eyes. "I've risked too much to have you."

Have her? Bailey shuddered at the possessive claim. Like she was a dog. Or a piece of property.

"Risked what?"

He glared at her, obviously frustrated she didn't know how much he'd jeopardized for her.

"Why do you think I agreed to help Logan?" he demanded, his fists clenching. "I knew you would never look at me as a man until I could move out of my mom's house and have my own place. I needed the cash."

Bailey scowled. "You can't blame me for that."

"I'm not blaming you. I'm explaining why I would do something illegal."

He turned to pace across the broken tiles, as if his emotions were bubbling out of control. Exactly what she wanted, Bailey silently conceded, wincing as she continued to tug at the cuff. Her skin was raw from the scrape of the steel, but she refused to give up.

"Just like you spied on me for a new phone?"

"It wasn't the same thing. That was . . . a mistake."

She assumed it was a mistake because she caught him in the act.

"And kidnapping me?" she asked in overly sweet tones, hoping to keep him off-balance.

He whirled back to send her a frustrated glare. "Why won't you listen to me? It's the only way to keep you safe."

"From what?"

"Dom Lucier."

Bailey resisted the urge to roll her eyes. She was assuming it was her blatant interest in Dom that had sent Eric over the edge.

"Why would you need to keep me safe from Dom?"

"There are things you don't know about him."

"Really?"

"Yeah, really." Eric shoved his fingers through his hair. "He's a suspect in a murder case."

"Murder? Dom?" She stared at him in disbelief. Then, when he continued to stare at her with an expectant expression, she burst out laughing. "That's ridiculous."

"Don't laugh," Eric snapped, striding toward her as his face flushed with anger.

Bailey leaned back, belatedly reminding herself that this wasn't the harmless, goofy Eric she'd assumed him to be. This man had stolen from the residents who trusted him. He'd stalked her, terrorizing her with his texts. And now he'd kidnapped her. She wanted him distracted, not homicidal.

"Eric," she breathed.

"I have proof." He reached into the pocket of his jacket and a sharp fear pierced Bailey's heart. Thankfully, he didn't pull out anything more threatening than a phone. His brow furrowed as he scrolled until he found what he wanted, then, holding it out, he tilted the screen toward her. "See?"

Bailey warily leaned forward, making sure he couldn't see her hands. Then she grudgingly glanced at the phone.

It looked like a news article, although the print was too small to see in the dim light. All she could make out was the headline.

DOM LUCIER
CONNECTED TO MISSING WOMAN

Bailey frowned. Not because she believed this was a genuine news article. Not even for a second. But because Eric seemed to believe it was.

"Where did you get that from?"

Eric straightened and dropped the phone back into the pocket of his jacket. "From our mutual friend."

Bailey blinked in confusion. They had a mutual friend? That seemed unlikely.

"Who?"

"PJ."

Bailey was still confused. "I don't know anyone named PJ."

"You know. From the Murder Club."

"Oh."

Bailey hadn't really paid attention to the names that the players used. They were all fake anyway. She'd remembered them by their specialty. Law enforcement, botanist, accountant . . .

She shook her head. "How would someone from the club even know about Dom?"

"We were discussing the fact that he was in town."

"Why?"

Eric glanced away, obviously trying to hide something. "Because we both suspected he'd come to Pike to take advantage of you."

Bailey studied Eric's tense profile. He was hiding something from her. She was sure of it. But what? Was it possible he'd made up PJ along with the news story hoping to fool Bailey into thinking Dom was some sort of psycho? After all, the threatening texts he'd been sending hadn't terrified her to run in his direction. Was this another crazed scheme to get her to turn to him for protection?

"Well?" He abruptly glanced back at her, as if bothered by the silence. "Aren't you going to say anything?"

She sucked in a deep breath, trying to think clearly. Something that would have been a lot easier if she wasn't cuffed and trapped in a soundproofed bathroom.

"I don't know what you want me to say," she finally conceded. "I certainly don't believe that fake story about Dom."

"It's not fake," Eric snapped.

"Do you honestly believe that Kaden—not to mention Lia—would be friends with a man who was suspected of murder?"

"I trust PJ," Eric insisted.

"A random stranger you met on the Internet?"

Eric licked his lips, his eyes a weird shade of ash in the flickering light. "He's not a stranger," he confessed.

"We've been chatting for over a year. He's the one who invited me to join the Murder Club in the first place." Bitterness laced Eric's words. "He's the one person who actually appreciates how hard it is for me to live in this place, surrounded by inbred jerks who think that milking a cow or driving a fancy truck makes them special."

Bailey narrowed her gaze. Wait. Maybe Eric wasn't making up PJ. Maybe it was Logan. He could have been setting up Eric to not only take the blame for the thefts but for the murders as well. She wasn't sure how, but it made sense.

"Tell me about him."

Eric took a jerky step backward, as if startled by her request. "I can't."

"Why not?"

"I'm sworn to secrecy." Eric held up his hand as her lips parted to ask why. "But I will warn you that he's in a position to know that Dom is a brutal criminal."

She shook her head. He seemed to genuinely believe what he was telling her. Then again, he'd obviously been hiding his true nature for years. She couldn't trust anything coming out of his mouth.

"He's lying to you, Eric."

"No." He made a sound of frustration before he resumed his pacing. "PJ sent the proof."

Bailey resisted the urge to argue. Let Eric think whatever he wanted. The only thing that mattered was that he'd moved far enough away that she could continue her painful attempts at escape.

"What else did he tell you?" she asked, keeping him focused on the mysterious PJ.

"That you're in danger."

"From Dom?"

"Yes." He nodded. "PJ warned me that Dom never stayed in town with his intended victim for more than a couple of weeks. And that he was making plans to leave Pike tonight. He said if I didn't do something quickly to save you, there would be another dead woman in Pike." He sent her a pleading glance. "You see, I had to do something. Even if it seems drastic to you."

Bailey tugged her hand another inch through the handcuff. She'd reached her knuckles. Another tug or two and she'd have her hand free. What she intended to do after that wasn't something she'd considered.

One problem at a time.

"When did he tell you that?" she asked, genuinely curious.

Eric had been sending threatening texts, but he hadn't tried to get her alone. Not until now. Had the mysterious PJ deliberately tried to prod Eric into searching for her? Maybe even kidnapping her?

"Twenty or thirty minutes ago." He shrugged. "I'm not sure. I just know that I got in my car and went looking for you. I had to find you before something terrible happened." He turned to face her, his expression impossible to read. Once again she was struck by the suspicion he wasn't telling her the full truth. "Then I got a call saying that you were at the nursing home. I knew I would never have a better opportunity."

A warning voice nagged at the edge of Bailey's mind. There was something about his words that set off fresh shivers of fear. It was a voice she forced herself to ignore. Right now she had to concentrate on Eric. And how the hell she was going to escape.

"To kidnap me?"

"To rescue you," he insisted.

Eric stepped forward, as if he intended to force her to believe his wild claims, but before he could reach her, there was a dull click and the overhead light abruptly shut off. They were instantly plunged into a darkness so thick it was impossible to see anything.

Fear blasted through Bailey as she struggled to get her hand free. She didn't know what was happening, but she wasn't stupid enough to assume it was someone rushing to her rescue. Or that the electricity had gone out randomly. Assumptions were a good way to end up dead.

Eric seemed equally confused as he muttered a curse and she heard him cautiously shuffle his way through the darkness. She didn't know where he was headed; the sound echoed weirdly through the empty room, but just in case he was searching for her, Bailey lay back and rolled to the side. If he intended to do something to her, she wasn't going to make it easy.

It wasn't until she heard the squeak of the doorknob being turned that she realized he'd gone in the opposite direction. A brief flare of hope surged through her. If he left to check on the electricity, it would give her the opportunity to escape.

The thought was still forming in her mind when there was the creak of door hinges followed by a startled cry from Eric. *What the hell?* She held her breath, pressing herself against the floor as there was a heavy thud, as if something had fallen, followed by the echo of a hard object banging against the tiled floor. Was it Eric? Or the intruder? Impossible to say.

She squinted her eyes as if that could help her peer through the gloom, but before her sight could adjust to the darkness, the overhead light was flicked back on and she was blinking against the abrupt glow.

Her heart desperately wanted to believe that she was being saved, but her logical mind understood that if it was a rescuer, they would be calling out to reassure her that everything was going to be okay.

No. Fear might be making her thoughts fuzzy, but her instincts warned her that she remained in danger. Perhaps even *more* danger.

Tilting her head to an awkward angle, she watched the shadowed form walk toward her with a silent purpose.

Chapter 24

Struggling against the urge to panic, Bailey folded her legs under her and used her shoulders to press herself into a seated position. She didn't know what was about to happen, but she wasn't going to remain sprawled on the filthy floor. She was going to face her enemy on her knees at least.

Plus, her efforts to escape the cuffs had rubbed the flesh from her inner wrists, coating her skin with blood. Painful, but it added a slick coating to her skin that would make it easier to slip her hands out. If she managed to get free, she fully intended to jump to her feet and fight for her survival.

As her eyes slowly focused, she realized there was yet another reason to nurture a ray of hope. The door Eric had closed and she assumed was locked was now wide open. As if daring her to try to escape.

Reluctantly, she concentrated her attention on the man who'd moved to stand directly in front of her.

For a second she was confused. She didn't recognize the stranger in the baseball cap that was pulled low on his head. He was wearing a plain sweatshirt and jeans that would allow him to fade into any local background. Not until a smug smile curved his lips did realization smack into her with enough force to smash the air from her lungs.

No. It wasn't a stranger. The dark curls were hidden beneath the cap and he'd replaced his bohemian style with a good ol' boy vibe, but the piercing green eyes remained the same.

"Thorpe." His name came out as a croak.

"Bailey." He studied her like a specimen beneath a microscope. "Did Eric hurt you?"

Her gaze darted toward Eric, who was crumpled in an awkward position near the doorway. Even at a distance she could see the blood that dripped from a cut on his temple. He'd obviously been struck by something and knocked unconscious. She was going to assume it was the steel pipe that was lying next to his motionless body.

"Yes, he kidnapped me and forced me in here. We need to call the police."

"Call the cops?" He clicked his tongue. "When I went to such trouble to get you here?"

"You . . ." She licked her dry lips. They were so stiff it was hard to form the words. "You helped Eric kidnap me?"

He shrugged. "Thankfully, you made it an easy chore by showing up here tonight. I was worried that Eric would have to grab you somewhere else and bring you to this special room. That might have been too much for him." Turning his head, Thorpe glanced disdainfully at the unconscious man. "He's not the most dependable tool to use, but beggars can't be choosers and I was busy tying up loose ends."

She blinked, recalling Eric's claim that he'd gotten a call to tell him she was at the nursing home. It had to have been from Thorpe.

So did that mean he was also the one who'd killed Nellie and the others? And what about Dom?

Terror blasted through her. A dark, ugly fear that pressed against her like a weight. Suddenly her heart wasn't racing; it was starting and stopping as if it couldn't find the right beat. And her lungs were so tight she couldn't draw in a full breath.

"You were driving the silver BMW."

He nodded. "I knew we were reaching the end of the game when Eric confessed he'd told you that he'd been stealing from the old folks." He didn't sound disappointed. "I spent a couple of hours preparing my surprise for you and then drove around Pike before I finally saw you headed to the nursing home. I knew you would recognize the license plate and follow me." He wrinkled his nose. "I didn't expect you to get out, but I'm nothing if not adaptable. I led your boyfriend away while I called Eric and prompted him to bring you to this place." His expression was taunting. "It all worked out exactly as I wanted."

She struggled to breathe. "Where's Dom?"

"There's no need to worry," he drawled. "He's waiting for you at Kaden's house."

Bailey didn't believe him, but she sensed he wasn't going to tell her the truth. All she could do was hope and pray that Dom was okay.

"I don't understand why you're doing this."

"I know." With a click of his tongue, he reached down to touch her cheek with the tips of his fingers. "I'll admit you've been a huge disappointment. You had such promise in the beginning."

Bailey jerked away from his touch, as if she'd been scalded. In truth, it was like being contaminated with evil.

"The beginning of what?" she demanded.

"Of the Murder Club, of course."

The Murder Club. Regret sliced through her. Every bad thing in her life had started from the moment she'd joined that stupid group.

"You . . ." She was forced to stop to clear the lump from her throat. "You know about the club?"

"I'm a member."

"Oh. Of course," she muttered, the puzzle pieces starting to fall into place. "You're PJ."

"PJ for Poetic Justice." His expression was mocking. "Fitting, don't you think?"

"Fitting for a crazed killer?"

He shrugged off her harsh accusation. "I am most certainly a killer, but there's nothing crazy about me."

"Why?"

"Maybe I should start at the beginning." Thorpe stepped back, as if preparing to begin a lecture. Clearly in his mind he was the teacher and she was the eager student. Even if he did have to kidnap her to have an audience. "With the Murder Club."

"You started it?"

"No, I joined a couple of years ago." The icy façade was banished as a glow of twisted pleasure smoldered in the depths of his green eyes. "It seemed like the perfect way to discover how to commit a murder without getting caught."

The terror humming through her amped up another level. Murder seemed to give him some sort of perverse happiness.

"Seriously?"

"Where else do you have a group of people scouring police reports and newspaper articles while using skills developed from a dozen different careers?" He studied her expression, no doubt enjoying her blatant horror. "If there was a clue left behind, they could find it. Their expertise taught me to avoid all the tiny details I might have overlooked."

Bailey shuddered. He was right, of course. There were few activities where a killer could actually practice before they committed their murder.

"Then you came to Pike to start your killing spree?"

"Oh, it started before then."

She grimaced. It hadn't occurred to her that the murderer had killed before coming to Pike.

"Where did it start?" she asked.

"A small town called Yarrow. Not much bigger than Pike."

"Yarrow," Bailey repeated the name. "Why is that name familiar?"

"Because you solved a murder that was committed there."

"I did?" Shock jolted through Bailey. What the hell? She had never . . . oh. The memory of studying a case when she first joined the Murder Club floated at the edge of her mind. "The elderly woman who died of a supposed heart attack," she muttered, trying to dig up the fuzzy details. "What was her name?"

"Jocelyn Courtland," he smoothly answered. "No one questioned her death. Not until you saw the crime scene photos and pointed out that an elderly woman who suffered from arthritis in her hands would have struggled to open a bottle of wine with an ordinary corkscrew. You were right." He pursed his lips, as if savoring the memory of the murder. "I brought the wine to toast the imminent death of my grandmother. It was an arrogant gesture. And one that might have destroyed me. Thankfully, the cops weren't nearly as observant as you were."

Bailey stared at him in disbelief. "She was your grandmother?"

"And my tormentor." Thorpe stood eerily still in front of her. He wasn't like Eric, who'd paced from side to side as he'd gone from pleading to anger to desperation. Then again, he wasn't emotionless like the psychopaths in movies. His eyes might be devoid of empathy for his dead grandmother, but they burned with an intensity that warned deep inside he possessed a vast hunger that was never sated. A poisonous craving that was destroying him. "It was a shame I couldn't devise a murder that involved a longer time frame and a lot more pain," he continued. "My only comfort was knowing in the end that she realized she was about to die and I was responsible."

The words were deliberately spoken. Not a boast. At least not entirely. But a reminder that he relished the memory of killing his grandmother. And a warning that he wasn't done.

Bailey tugged on the handcuffs. She had to get out of there. If Eric was unhinged, this man was a lethal predator who would kill without mercy.

"Were you the one who brought the case to the Murder Club?" Bailey asked, knowing she had to keep him talking.

When he was done boasting of his triumphs bad things were going to happen.

"More arrogance," he admitted. "I was certain I had committed the perfect crime. But then you pointed out my mistake and I was . . . enchanted." He paused, his gaze sweeping over her upturned face. "I'd finally met a woman who could be my equal. That's why I left you my grandmother's favorite necklace."

Bailey shivered in revulsion. "The pearls belonged to your grandmother?"

"Yes." He looked smug. "I had no idea they would prove to be the perfect clue to Pauline's murder. I brought them to Pike with the intention of handing them to you as a gesture of my admiration."

"Is that why you came here? To give me the pearls?"

"No. That plan was in the works from the minute my grandmother was planted in her grave. The fact that you lived here was just a bonus."

Thank God, Bailey silently breathed. It was bad enough to think that Pike was some sort of magnet for killers. But if she'd been responsible for bringing this lunatic to town . . . How awful would that be?

"Then why are you here?" she demanded; then she remembered his earlier words. "Oh. You're here to write your stupid book about Kaden, right?"

"That was my cover story in case anyone questioned why I was in the area."

"If that was your cover story, why pretend to be an artist?"

He clicked his tongue, his features tightening with annoyance. "Seriously, Bailey," he chastised, heavy disappointment in his voice. "The first rule of becoming a paparazzo is to have a dozen lies prepared to explain your presence while you stalk your victim. If I get caught pretending to be a waiter, I pull out a badge and say I'm an undercover cop. Or a bodyguard. If that doesn't work, I claim that my prey hired me to take pictures and spread them around the tabloids. You'd be shocked how often that happens. Most celebrities truly believe any attention is good attention. I was convinced that the same theory would work for a murderer stalking his kill. And I wasn't wrong, was I? Once you uncovered the fact that I was a journalist and not a reclusive artist, you scratched me off your list of suspects."

She wasn't going to bloat his ego by admitting they had dropped him to the bottom of the list. "So there's no book?"

"Of course there is. And it's going to make me a lot of money."

She stared at him in confusion. "You're making my head hurt."

Thorpe removed his cap and tossed it on the floor, running his hands through his thick curls.

"It's all very simple. I joined the Murder Club to learn how to kill my grandmother. Once it was accomplished I traveled to Pike to complete the second half of my plan. Thankfully, I'd been chatting with Eric

Criswell and he'd mentioned Kaden's upcoming wedding. A perfect excuse to be in town."

"How did you know Eric?" Bailey didn't really care, but Thorpe obviously enjoyed the sound of his own voice and she needed time to get her hands out of the cuffs.

"I occasionally play online video games. One night Eric popped into our group. He bragged about being from Pike, the murder capital of the world. Of course I immediately befriended him. He was the perfect way to learn the latest gossip in town."

"That's why you invited him to be a part of the Murder Club . . ." Bailey's words died on her lips. Eric might have kidnapped her, but he wasn't the one who'd been sending her warning texts. He'd been a pawn in the same game Thorpe had been playing with her. "Did you introduce yourself as PJ after you came to Pike?"

Thorpe shrugged. "Eventually."

Bailey felt a stab of anger that she'd allowed herself to be so easily fooled by the younger man.

"You paid him to spy on me."

"I did."

She frowned as she recalled her brief visit to his room at the top floor of the hunting lodge. She'd seen the monitors. He'd been keeping a constant watch on her without Eric.

"Why? You had a camera on my house."

"The camera was limited. I wanted to know where you were and who you were with after you dropped out of the Murder Club. I couldn't do it myself. I had other priorities. Plus . . ." He hesitated, as if deciding whether to confess the rest of his plan. "I needed to make sure the cops believed he was your stalker. That's why I followed him to Green Bay and bought four burner phones in his name. If they're ever traced, the cops will have all the evidence they need."

Bailey's brain threatened to shut down as fear clawed through her. She wanted to be brave, but the stark knowledge she was facing her own death was overwhelming.

"I don't get it." Bailey forced out the words, genuinely baffled by the way she became the focus of Thorpe's twisted game. "You were spying on me just because I mentioned the wine bottle in an online group?"

"Because we're partners. Or at least we would have been," he said, an ugly edge of jealousy entering his voice. "If Dom Lucier hadn't interfered."

Her mouth was so dry it was hard to speak. "That's why you convinced Eric that Dom was some sort of psychopath?"

His eyes darkened with annoyance. "I sensed he was going to be trouble as soon as he arrived in town. I was at the Bait and Tackle the night he showed up and I could see how you were looking at him."

Bailey continued to struggle with the handcuffs. Thorpe's composure was starting to crack. She sensed he could snap any second.

She had to get out of there.

"Why tell Eric he was a serial killer?" She forced out the question, determined to keep him talking. "Did you think he was going to confront Dom?"

Thorpe glanced toward Eric. "That coward? No. I simply warned him that you would never listen. Not as long as your new friend Dom was close by, whispering in your ear. I insinuated that he needed a way to separate you from the bastard and force you to listen." He glanced back as he raised his hands to gesture around the empty bathroom. "He was the one who suggested that he create a soundproof room where he could keep you safe. Naturally, I assured him it was a perfect idea. I knew we would eventually end up here together."

Bailey kept her gaze locked on Thorpe. She didn't want a reminder that the likelihood of anyone finding her trapped in this abandoned building was close to zero. Or the fact that she was completely at his mercy.

"And now here we are." She couldn't disguise the tremor of fear in her voice. "What are you going to do to me?"

"So impatient," he chided, even as he eyed her with blatant satisfaction. No doubt he'd been visualizing this encounter for weeks. Maybe months. He wanted her to be traumatized. "You're getting ahead of the story."

Bailey swallowed the urge to scream at him in frustrated fury. This was his game. She had no choice but to play it by his rules.

"Okay," she muttered. "You murder your grandmother and then come to Pike to write a book about Kaden, befriend Eric, and randomly start killing people."

"They weren't random," he argued. "What would be the fun in that?"

Bailey's stomach clenched. "Why would you kill them?"

"To punish my mother."

Bailey frowned. "You mean your grandmother?"

"No. My grandmother was already dead."

With a wink, he turned to stroll out of the room, as if

he had all the time in the world. And maybe he did. It wasn't like anyone was looking for her. Not unless Dom was back at the nursing home. A minute later he was returning, wheeling an office chair into the bathroom. Bailey's eyes widened as she took in the slumped form that was tied to the chair. It was an older woman dressed in a bright yellow pantsuit.

Arranging the chair in the middle of the floor, Thorpe grabbed a hunk of the woman's dark red hair and forced up her head, revealing Lorene Donaldson's pale face and the gag shoved into her open mouth.

"This is my mother."

It had been years since Dom had gotten blackout drunk. He'd quickly discovered that the few hours of fun weren't worth the blinding headache and heaving stomach that was inevitably waiting the next morning. But as he grimly clawed his way through the clinging darkness, he couldn't imagine another explanation why his head would feel as if it might explode and his entire body throbbed as if he'd been hit by a freight train . . .

Or a silver BMW.

The memory of the vehicle barreling toward him seared through Dom's foggy brain. Shit. He was no longer worried about a massive hangover. He was worried that he'd died and been sent to hell.

"Dom." A hand grabbed his shoulder. "Dom, can you hear me?"

"Yeah, I hear you," Dom rasped, relief blasting through him. He recognized Zac's voice. Which meant he wasn't dead.

"Open your eyes," Zac commanded.

Dom groaned, too exhausted to make the effort. "Do I have to?"

Zac gave his shoulder a shake. It was small, but it was enough to rattle Dom's aching brain.

"The ambulance is on the way, but I need to know where Bailey is."

Bailey. Dom grimly forced open his eyes, ignoring the pain that throbbed through him from head to toe.

"She's at the nursing home," he said, carefully turning his head to discover Zac crouched next to him wearing his sheriff's uniform and a matching baseball cap. Dom struggled to sit upright. "What are you doing here? I thought you were taking your wife to Madison?"

Zac's hand moved to the center of Dom's back, keeping him steady as he glanced around. The sun was shining brightly overhead, which did nothing for his aching head, but it did assure him that he hadn't been out for long. And he was still in front of the gates that led to Kaden's house with Logan Donaldson's corpse wrapped in a blanket just a few feet away.

The only change was that he was no longer on the hood of the silver BMW that had seemingly disappeared, and there was a deputy in a brown uniform taking pictures of the area around the body.

"Rachel asked her parents to drive her down to Madison," Zac told him. "She has an apartment there, for when she's working out of the cold case office. She knew I'd be worried until I checked out why Bailey called. I'll drive down tomorrow for our appointment." He grimaced as his gaze darted toward the hole in the center of Logan's forehead. "Or at least that's the plan. Tell me what happened."

Dom turned back to the sheriff, quickly telling him about Eric's confession and their trip to the pawnshop, followed by his impulsive chase after the silver BMW.

"Wait." Zac's brows tugged together as he struggled to follow what Dom was telling him. Probably not the easiest task, Dom ruefully acknowledged. His brain was still scrambled and he wasn't sure he was making any sense. "Eric Criswell has been stealing from the residents and Logan Donaldson was pawning the stuff in Green Bay?"

Dom nodded. He'd at least gotten that part right. "Yes."

"Did Eric shoot Logan?"

"I don't know for sure," Dom said, although he had a suspicion of who was responsible. No point in jumping to conclusions. "He was already dead when I pulled into the drive. I know it wasn't Eric who tried to run me over."

Zac looked surprised. "You were run over?"

"Yup. Run down like a deer in the headlights by Kevin Hartford's silver BMW."

"Kevin Hartford?" Zac studied him with blatant concern. As if he was worried he was suffering from a brain injury. It was a concern shared by Dom. "He's dead."

"Yes, but you told us yourself that his car was missing."

"That doesn't make him any less dead," Zac insisted.

"Kevin wasn't driving the car."

Zac's concern changed to curiosity. "Who was?"

"Thorpe." Dom waited for Zac's expression of

shock. Instead, the sheriff frowned in confusion. "Ford Smithson. Also known as Thorpe Curry," Dom clarified. "At least that's the name he uses for his professional career as a paparazzo. Who the hell knows what his real name is."

Zac slowly shook his head. "Why would Ford or Thorpe or whoever the hell he is hit you with Kevin Hartford's stolen car?"

Dom clenched his muscles and forced himself upright. The pounding in his head and his painful bruises weren't going to disappear anytime soon. There was no use sitting on the ground when he had things to do. Starting with beating the hell out of Thorpe Curry.

"I don't know, but I intend to find out," he announced, turning toward the Land Rover that still had the engine running.

Zac grabbed his arm. "Where do you think you're going?"

"To the hunting lodge."

"No way." Zac moved to block his path, his face hard with warning. It was an expression Dom had seen on a lot of cops' faces. Did they practice it at the academy? "You've been injured. You're waiting here for the ambulance."

"I'm fine," Dom insisted, then ruined it as he swayed to the side.

Zac tightened his grip to keep him upright. "You're not fine. You can barely stand."

"I have a headache, a cracked rib, and a few bruises," Dom self-diagnosed the various aches and pains in his body. "I'm not going to the hospital. Not until Thorpe is behind bars."

Zac nodded toward the road, where the sound of sirens echoed through the air. "At least have the paramedics check you out."

"Later. Thorpe deliberately led me into a trap. He was trying to kill me. If he figures out I'm not dead, he's going to try again." Dom clenched his hands, a sudden flare of fear racing through him. "Or he's going to make a run for it."

"I'll deal with Thorpe." Zac touched the weapon strapped to his side. "You get checked out."

Dom wanted to argue. He was the one who'd been lured to this spot and then run over like a piece of trash. But he wasn't stupid. Zac had the gun, the training, and the legal authority to deal with criminals. Obviously he was the best choice to track down Thorpe.

"You're going to the hunting lodge now?" he asked, needing to be reassured that Thorpe wasn't going to escape.

"I'll start there," Zac said. "While I'm doing that, I'll have one of my deputies head over to the nursing home to check on Bailey." He pointed toward the deputy, who was unrolling police tape to block off the area. "Anthony is going to stay and investigate the crime scene. He'll also keep a watch on the house. I want you and Bailey to stay inside with the doors locked. Thorpe isn't going to bother either of you again." Zac stepped back, his expression already distracted, as if preparing his plan to track down and arrest Thorpe. "The ambulance will be here in a minute or two. Stay here and get checked out. Got it?"

"Got it," Dom repeated, without actually agreeing to the lawman's command.

Limping to the Land Rover, he leaned against the side and waited for Zac to return to his vehicle and drive away. He didn't have the energy for arguments. Better to let Zac assume he was going to hang around. Once he was out of sight, however, he jumped in the SUV and swiftly backed out of the driveway.

He thought he heard the sound of the deputy shouting his name, but he never looked back as he gunned the engine and raced back to the nursing home.

Chapter 25

Bailey stared at the older woman with a dull sense of confusion. Dorinda had shared the conversation she'd overheard years ago that'd suggested Lorene was running from her past. But this . . .

"Lorene Donaldson." Bailey forced her gaze toward her captor. "She's your mother?"

"Can't you see the resemblance?" he demanded.

"Not really," she rasped.

"No, neither can I." He released his hold on her head and Lorene's head dropped back to her chest. The older woman wasn't unconscious, but she was obviously in a state of shock. "Not that I'm disappointed. The bitch abandoned me when I was just a child."

"She's the reason you came to Pike?"

"Her and my dear, disgustingly spoiled brother," he agreed.

"Logan."

Thorpe's features twisted with disdain as he stepped away from the slouched woman. As if he wanted space between them despite the fact that he'd kidnapped her.

"Mommy couldn't wait to bail on me, but she was devoted to her beloved Logan." He paused, visibly regaining command of his fraying composure. "At least she was devoted to him until I tainted his precious image."

"What did you do to him?"

"Oh, it was delicious." The disdain vanished as the green eyes smoldered with an icy satisfaction. "It all started when my brother fell in love with Roxanna Novak."

"Who?"

"A college student who is studying nursing in Prague."

Bailey had never heard the name before. Certainly Logan had never mentioned he had a girlfriend.

"Is she from Pike?"

"God no. She's from my imagination." He smirked as Bailey's brows arched. "And made real by the lovely photos I found online of a Swedish model." Lifting his hand, he sent a chef's kiss in her direction. "Tall, blond, and willing to share naked pictures of herself. Logan was in lust from the minute I created my profile and contacted him through the dating app."

"You catfished him," she accused.

"Like a pro." He chuckled. Or at least she guessed that was what it was. It was a weird, wheezing sound. As if he didn't do it very often. "You know what, I *am* a pro. I've spent my whole life pretending to be someone else, haven't I? Until now."

She ignored his boasting. Who cared? "What was the point?"

"To tarnish what I never had," he retorted without apology. "A mother's love."

"By pretending to be naked Roxy?"

"Roxanna Novak," he snapped, as if insulted by her lack of appreciation for his alter ego. "She was not only beautiful, she was also very, very expensive."

Bailey grimaced. "Logan sent her money?"

"Of course. She was a woman." Logan shrugged. "She demanded lavish gifts, assistance to pay for her rent, and even money for her textbooks." He sent a smirk toward the silent Lorene. "It ended up being quite a large sum, didn't it, Mother? Seventy? Eighty thousand dollars."

Bailey belatedly understood. She'd never had an online relationship, but it made sense that it would work like any other relationship. Including the exchange of money. It also explained Logan's growing desperation.

"That's why he started stealing from the residents," she muttered.

"After a little encouragement from me," Thorpe told her, his smirk lingering as he recalled the pleasure of conning his brother. "He'd emptied his bank account and maxed out all his cards, but poor Roxanna desperately needed money to pay for a visa so she could come to be with Logan." He batted his lashes as if he was an actress in a cheesy movie. "I can't express my joy to know he was ruining his life for a woman who didn't even exist."

Bailey shuddered. Logan was an immoral creep for stealing from the residents, not to mention an arrogant idiot, but she almost felt sorry for him. To be so deeply hated by someone you didn't even know existed was awful.

"If you wanted to hurt him, why go to so much effort?" Bailey forced herself to ask as she tugged at the handcuffs. They were stuck at her knuckles, but she was close. "Why not just kill him?"

"Because it wasn't about Logan." He glanced toward Lorene. "It was never about him. He was a meaningless tool to hurt the person who abandoned me."

"Your mother."

Dom pulled into the loading space directly in front of the nursing home, shutting off the engine before slowly crawling out of the SUV. He was running low on fuel, but he wasn't going to worry about it until he had Bailey safely back at Kaden's estate.

Wincing as he limped to the front door, Dom was careful not to take in a deep breath. Eventually he was going to have to get to a doctor and figure out the extent of the damage, but that was another task that could wait. Pressing the buzzer on the intercom, Dom waited for the door to be unlocked so he could step inside the lobby.

He halted and glanced around, expecting Bailey to be waiting for him. Instead, the place was eerily empty. The only person in sight was a sour-faced woman standing next to the nurses' station. Mentally preparing himself to approach the off-putting employee, Dom was thankfully distracted as a tall woman with short, black hair and a familiar face rounded the corner and came to an abrupt halt at the sight of him.

"Dom. Hello again." The woman flashed a wide smile.

"Hi." Dom sifted through the memory of his first night in Pike, when he'd spotted Bailey at the Bait and Tackle with her friend. It felt like a lifetime ago. "Kari, right?"

She arched a brow. "Good memory."

Dom shrugged. "You're Bailey's friend. I hope that means we'll be friends."

"Nice." Kari studied him with an unnerving intensity. "You know, I never thought there would be anyone good enough for Bailey. You might just change my mind."

"I hope so." Dom wasn't just saying what the woman wanted to hear. Anyone who was important to Bailey was going to be important to him. "Do you know where she is?"

"Yeah, she . . ." Kari glanced over her shoulder, her words trailing away. "Oh. She was right here. I'm not sure where she went."

Unease pierced Dom's heart even as he tried to tell himself that nothing could happen to her when she was in such a public place. She was surrounded by her friends and coworkers.

But the past week had taught him one thing: No one was safe in Pike. Especially not Bailey. Until she was standing in front of him, he was going to worry.

"Eric isn't working, is he?" he abruptly demanded.

"No. I haven't seen him."

"What about the Donaldsons?"

Kari narrowed her eyes, her smile fading. "Is something going on? Bailey asked about them earlier."

"Are they here?

"I haven't seen them since Friday. What's going on?" Kari stepped closer, lowering her voice. "You can tell me. I promise not to say a word to anyone."

Dom cleared his throat. In his experience the people who promise not to say anything were the people guaranteed to spread gossip at lightning speed. And while word of Logan's death would soon be making the rounds, Dom wasn't going to be distracted by a thousand questions of what had happened.

"Where would Bailey go to wait for me to pick her up?" he instead asked.

Kari looked as if she wanted to demand answers, but she glanced at his expression and wrinkled her nose in defeat.

"She might be visiting one of the residents, but most of them are getting ready for dinner," Kari said, pursing her lips. "My guess would be the employee break room. Follow me."

Turning around, Kari headed past the nurses' station, her rubber soles squeaking on the tiled floor. Within a couple of minutes they'd reached the end of a short hallway and Kari was pressing open a wooden door. Dom ground his teeth as it quickly became obvious there was only one employee inside the narrow space. A young, dark-haired woman in green scrubs who was seated at the table eating a chocolate bar as she scrolled through her phone.

"Hey, Andrea," Kari said as the woman glanced up with mild annoyance, as if they were interrupting her. "Have you seen Bailey?"

Andrea shook her head. "Nope."

"How long have you been in here?" Dom demanded.

The woman shoved her phone into the front pocket of her shirt. "Ten minutes," she snapped, her face flushing, as if she thought Dom was questioning her work ethic. "No more than fifteen."

"Thanks." Kari sent the woman a reassuring smile before closing the door. She regarded Dom with a chiding expression. "Andrea isn't much of a worker, but she's one of the few aides who are willing to come in on Sundays."

Dom ignored the complaint. He couldn't care less about the staffing issues at Pike Nursing Home. Instead, he pulled out his phone.

"Where else could Bailey be?" he muttered.

"Wait in the lobby," Kari commanded. "I'll look around. She has to be here somewhere."

Dom did as she requested. Kari could complete her search faster without him tagging along, but, more importantly, he'd realized he didn't have any cell service in the hallway. There had to be somewhere in the building where he could get reception.

Entering the lobby, he headed toward the windows, relieved when a bar popped up on the screen. He pressed Bailey's number, listening as it rang, eventually dumping him into voice mail. His gut twisted into a tight knot. Why wasn't she answering? Grimly, he ended the connection and called again. And then again. As if he could force her to answer.

He was still trying when Kari entered the lobby and crossed to stand in front of him.

"She's not here."

"You're sure?"

THE MURDER CLUB 377

"Positive." Kari pressed her hands against her stomach, her expression troubled. "Should I be worried?"

Dom shoved his phone back into his pocket. An explosive terror was surging through him, pumping him with adrenaline. His heart thundered in his chest, a raw urgency to find Bailey making it impossible to stand still.

"There's a deputy on the way," he said. "Tell him that Bailey is missing."

"Missing?" Kari reached out as Dom turned away. "Wait!"

Dom ignored her plea, heading out of the building. There was no way Bailey would have left the nursing home without letting him know where she was going. Which meant someone had forced her to leave.

Limping across the front patio, Dom instinctively glanced around the parking lot, making sure there was no silver BMW lurking in the shadows to run him down. He couldn't rescue Bailey if he was dead.

Not that he knew where or how he was going to rescue her, he grimly acknowledged. But he knew where he was going to start.

The hunting lodge . . .

His fingers were wrapping around the door handle of his Land Rover when his gaze skimmed past the abandoned building next door. He abruptly froze, his breath hissing between his clenched teeth.

There was a car parked behind the nearby dumpster. He hadn't noticed it when he pulled in, but now he easily recognized the rusty vehicle with the back window covered with duct tape.

Eric Criswell.

It couldn't be a coincidence. The creep had to be involved in Bailey's disappearance. Dom forced himself to take the time to send a quick text to Zac; then, with an unwavering determination, he headed toward the side door of the building.

Chapter 26

Bailey wrenched her head back to an awkward angle, meeting the glittering green gaze and mocking smile. She thought she'd heard the muffled ringtone of her phone, but she had no idea what had happened to her purse. She assumed it was at the bottom of the barrel Eric had used to haul her to this room.

At the moment she was more focused on getting out of the handcuffs. Once she was free she would worry about calling for help.

"You're serious?" she rasped as he simply stared at her, as if expecting her to applaud his clever scheme. "This is all about punishing your mother?"

"Exactly. There are two things in this world that Lorene Donaldson cares about: Logan and the Pike Nursing Home," he drawled. "I wanted to destroy both before putting them out of their misery."

Bailey grimaced at the thought of the pain and destruction he'd caused because of his mommy issues. It wasn't like he was the only child who'd ever been abandoned by an adult, she silently fumed.

"Fine. You wanted to punish them. Why hurt anyone else?"

He waved aside her sharp question. "I didn't intend to. Not in the beginning. But then Nellie died and—"

"Did you kill her?" Bailey interrupted, her stomach clenched at the fear this maniac had done something awful to the sweet old woman.

"No. That was God's will," he unintentionally eased her fear. "But I overheard my dear, sweet mother telling Logan that they would inherit enough money to cover his debts if only Gage would conveniently die. So I helped him along."

Bailey breathed a sigh of relief. It was ridiculous considering everything that had happened, and was still happening, but she was happy that Nellie hadn't been murdered.

At the same time she was confused. "Why would you want them to get money when you went to so much trouble to steal it?"

"Logan was foolish enough to share his passwords with Roxanna for his email," Thorpe explained. "I decided to upload the pictures of Gage lying dead on the floor of the lumberyard and send them to Roxanna with the promise he would soon have the funds necessary to bring her to America."

Bailey didn't hide her disgust at the thought of Thorpe taking pictures of a man he'd just killed. Like the corpse was some sort of trophy.

"You intend to frame him for murder," she rasped. "Just as you intend to frame Eric as my stalker."

"Very good." His tone was mocking, as if he was still disappointed she hadn't figured this all out on her own.

"After I arrived I realized it would be much more fun to watch the two of them squirm through a murder trial knowing they'd lost everything. I was even prepared to write a book about their tragic story. A real-life crime thriller. Complete with them committing suicide before they could go to jail. It would have made me a fortune."

She frowned in confusion. "Committing suicide? Both of them?"

"A logical outcome," he insisted. "Once the trial started and I'd decided that dear Mommy had suffered enough, I was going to have Logan write a note claiming they couldn't bear the humiliation before tragically burning the nursing home to the ground, with their dead bodies inside."

Bailey's mouth fell open. It was crazy to be shocked. Thorpe Curry was blatantly evil to the very core. But the mere thought he would be willing to casually murder dozens of elderly people was impossible to accept.

"You were going to burn down the nursing home?"

"It was the easiest way to destroy any evidence." He glared at her in frustration. "But you ruined everything."

"Me?"

"You had no appreciation for my work. You left the nursing home—"

"I was forced to go," she interrupted.

"And you refused to join my private murder club," he continued with his list of complaints. "You were too obsessed with Dom Lucier. That's when I realized I had to do something dramatic to capture your attention."

Bailey searched her mind, trying to come up with the

dramatic gesture he was talking about. A second later a gasp was wrenched from her throat.

"That's why you killed Pauline Hartford?"

He rolled his eyes. "And gave you all the clues you needed to figure out it was me."

Bailey ignored the insult. "Why her?"

"I told you that I needed pictures of Kaden and Lia's wedding for my book and I did. But I didn't mention that I made sure to stay in contact with Kevin Hartford. Even giving him money when he needed a little extra."

"Why?"

"Having access to a local photographer seemed like an asset while I was writing my book. Plus, I knew right away he was a drug addict. They're so easy to manipulate. Over the years I've used them to take care of jobs I can't bribe others to do." His sheer indifference revealed that his lack of empathy wasn't anything new. He'd been using and manipulating people for years. Probably for his whole life. "Still, it wasn't until he mentioned his overbearing grandmother who was making his life a living hell that I decided he would be a perfect victim to include in our murder club," Thorpe admitted.

A perfect victim. Just like his grandmother. Bailey shuddered. He could pretend Pauline's death was part of the game, but she sensed it gave him a perverted pleasure to kill the older woman.

"How did you do it?" Bailey forced out the question.

She didn't want to know the nasty details, she really didn't. But as she shuddered in horror she could feel her knuckles at last scrape painfully past the hard metal. Oh my God. She'd done it! Her hand was free.

Relief blasted through her, but she was smart enough to keep her expression carefully bland as she grabbed the cuff to keep it from banging against the tiles. She had to keep Thorpe distracted as she figured out how to get past him.

"Kevin told me that his grandmother liked to have a few cocktails in the evening, so I set the scene by pulling back the tarp on the pool and then leaving on the lights. Once I was ready I hid in the empty house next door and waited for her to come out and shut off the lights." He paused, disturbing pleasure glowing in his eyes. "One push and . . . bam. She was dead. It was a stroke of luck that Kevin happened to choose that night to come to plead for money. It made him the perfect scapegoat."

She wanted to look away from his twisted enjoyment at the memory of killing a helpless old woman, but she forced her gaze to remain steady. He was going to make a mistake, she silently assured herself. And then she was going to escape.

"You left the pearls at my house," she prompted him to continue with his sick story.

"Ah, yes. I knew you would be smart enough to connect them to the old woman's death."

"Why kill Kevin?"

"I was done with him." His tone indicated that he hadn't given much thought before murdering a man who'd done nothing to him. "And he was another clue in our game."

"A game I told you I didn't want to play."

His eyes blazed with anger. As if her refusal continued to be a source of annoyance.

"Don't worry. It's almost over." Without warning, Thorpe spun around to stand next to the woman slumped in the chair. "First, however, I intend to enjoy some quality time with my mother."

Bailey watched in silence as Thorpe grabbed Lorene by her hair and jerked her head up. Then, with a deliberate attempt to cause her pain, he ripped off the gag and tossed it aside.

"Are you ready to beg for my forgiveness?" Thorpe's voice was harsh, the pretense of icy composure abruptly shattered.

This was the man beneath the mask. The cruel, twisted killer.

Lorene licked her dry lips. "Where's Logan?"

The question had barely left her lips when Thorpe lifted his hand and slapped her face. The motion was almost casual, but his knuckles connected with her cheek with enough force to split open her skin.

"We're not discussing my brother." His fingers tightened their grip on her hair, giving her a shake. "I told you to beg."

Bailey grimaced. She'd never liked Lorene Donaldson, but the sight of her being beaten by her own son was making her stomach cramp with horror.

And worse, they were blocking the doorway, making it impossible for her to make a run for it while Thorpe was distracted.

"Why should I beg?" Lorene remained defiant despite the blood running down her cheek and the furious man looming over her. Bailey might have admired her courage if she wasn't such a bitch. "You'll never forgive me anyway."

Thorpe leaned down, his body rigid with barely suppressed emotion. "Then make me understand. Why did you leave?"

"You know why," Lorene hissed. "Your father was a brutal monster who beat me on a daily basis. And his mother?" Lorene released a sharp, humorless laugh. "She was worse."

Bailey shivered, recalling Dorinda's claim that she'd overheard the unknown older woman being violent toward Lorene all those years ago.

"You're right. They were both monsters. But who was the greater monster?" He leaned closer, the spit from his lips landing on Lorene's bloody face. "The bastards who tormented me? Or the mother who abandoned me to their cruelty?"

"I had no choice." Lorene refused to concede she'd betrayed her oldest child. "They would have killed me if I tried to take you."

Thorpe's face flushed an ugly red. "A real mother would have died to protect her son."

"I had to think of Logan."

A volatile silence filled the room as the words burst out of Lorene's mouth. Bailey instinctively scooted back as she prepared for Thorpe to explode.

He didn't. Instead, he released his hold on his mother's hair and stepped back. As if he didn't trust himself not to strangle her if he stayed too close.

"Of course you did." His features twisted with a feral hatred. "Precious Logan."

Lorene pressed herself back in the leather chair even as her expression remained stubbornly defiant.

"I couldn't save you, but I could save him."

Thorpe's hands clenched, but his lips twisted into a smug smile. "No, no, you couldn't."

Lorene blinked, her courage fading as Thorpe regarded her with a triumphant expression.

"What have you done?"

"What have I done?" Thorpe laughed. "I balanced the scales. I am no longer willing to be the sacrifice. Not for my father. Not for my grandmother. Not for my brother." His gaze swept over his mother with a loathing that was almost tangible. "And certainly not for you."

Lorene released a low groan. Had the awful truth at last smashed through her refusal to admit Logan was gone?

"Is he dead?"

"They're all dead. Except for you." Thorpe paused to allow his mother the opportunity to feel the full agony of Logan's death. Then he stepped forward. "Now it's your turn."

Lorene arched her back, her fear overriding her grief. "No, please."

"Ah, I knew in the end you would plead." There was genuine pleasure in Thorpe's voice. As if he'd been given a treasured gift. "That's all I've wanted. All I've dreamed of . . ."

Bailey struggled to her feet. She didn't know what Thorpe intended to do to his mother, but she knew she couldn't just sit there and watch it happen. Whatever Lorene had done in the past she didn't deserve to be murdered. Besides, once he was done with his mother, Thorpe was going to turn his attention to her.

Better to try to do something while he was focused on Lorene.

Desperately glancing around the derelict bathroom, Bailey searched for something she could use as a weapon.

She was still searching when there was a blur of movement in the doorway and someone appeared. Dom! Her eyes widened as he stepped into the room, his motions oddly stiff.

He was alive, but it was obvious he'd been injured.

"It's over, Thorpe," Dom growled.

Thorpe released a frustrated growl, glaring at the unexpected intruder. "You're supposed to be dead."

"It's going to take a better man than you to get rid of me," Dom taunted, stepping back as he flicked a quick glance in Bailey's direction.

He was trying to get Thorpe away from the open doorway so she could make a run for it.

"Well, I was forced to be a Boy Scout when I was young and we were taught to be prepared for any emergency."

Thorpe tried to match Dom's casual confidence, but it was a brittle act that didn't conceal his unease. He was a tough guy when he was lurking in the shadows or abusing women. He wasn't nearly so brave when he couldn't control the situation. Still, that didn't make him any less dangerous, Bailey realized as he reached into the pocket of his jacket to pull out a knife. With a twist of his wrist, he flipped it open to reveal the wicked-sharp blade.

"I intended to christen this blade with the blood of my mother," Thorpe said, holding up the knife to catch the overhead light. "But I suppose you'll have to do."

Dom took another step back, luring Thorpe toward

the center of the room. "And then what?" he asked. "There's no way you're walking away from this. The sheriff's already on his way."

Thorpe arched his brows. "Do you honestly think I didn't have an escape plan in place?" he scoffed. "My bags are packed and a rental car is waiting for me just down the street, along with a dozen passports and enough money to last me for years." He shrugged. "I'll disappear overseas, and when the time is right I'll return with a new identity and a new life. But first . . ."

Thorpe lunged forward, slashing his arm toward the center of Dom's broad chest.

"Bailey, go!" Dom shouted, dancing away from the blade.

"Don't go far; I have plans for you," Thorpe hissed, his gaze never leaving Dom as he moved to the side, looking for an opening.

Bailey dashed forward, but she didn't head for the door. Instead, she crossed the short distance to where Lorene Donaldson was tied to the chair, her face pale and her eyes wide with shock. Something that might have been hope eased her tight features as she watched Bailey dart around her, as if assuming Bailey intended to untie the ropes holding her in place.

Nothing could be further from Bailey's mind.

She wasn't thinking about escape. There was no way in hell she was leaving Dom to battle a crazed killer. But without a weapon the only way to help was to knock Thorpe off-balance. And she had the perfect means to do that.

Grasping the high back of the chair, Bailey clenched her teeth and shoved it forward with all her might. The tiled floor was broken and littered with shards of ceramic, but desperation gave her enough strength to force the chair forward, and after a few inches the momentum kicked in, allowing her to pick up speed.

It was Lorene's screech of fury at the realization of what Bailey intended to do that alerted Thorpe to the approaching danger. He whirled around, his eyes widening as he watched his mother hurtling toward him.

Bailey never hesitated; she rammed the chair directly into Thorpe even as Dom swung his fist and caught the man square on the jaw.

Thorpe grunted, his eyes rolling back in his head as he toppled backward, landing on the ground with a dull thud. Lorene continued to scream, but Bailey ignored her as she rounded the chair and kicked the unconscious man with enough force to send a sharp pain up her leg.

"Rot in hell, you bastard," she hissed.

Then, with a sob of sheer relief, she walked into Dom's waiting arms.

"It's over," he murmured, holding her close as he pressed his lips to the top of her head.

"Take me away from here," she whispered.

He tightened his hold on her. "Your wish is my command."

Epilogue

It wasn't as simple as Dom had hoped to whisk Bailey away from Pike and the terrible memories that lingered even after Thorpe was arrested. First they'd been delayed by Zac, who'd insisted they stay around and give their statements to his office as well as the Wisconsin Division of Criminal Investigations, who were examining the death of Thorpe's grandmother as well as Pauline Hartford. There was no doubt that Thorpe Curry was going to spend the rest of his life in jail. He'd proudly admitted to traveling to Pike to destroy his family. Still, they needed to tie up all the loose ends.

Then Bailey had insisted on attending Logan's funeral. Even though the Donaldsons had been prepared to destroy her reputation, she'd pointed out that they'd been her employers for years. And that no one else would bother to show up once the rumors circulated through town that Logan had been stealing from the residents, not to mention the fact that he was brother to the psycho killer stalking the streets of Pike. And she'd been right. There had been less than a dozen people surrounding the graveside, where Lorene had stood in silent grief, her icy arrogance shattered beyond repair.

Dom had groused at Bailey's refusal to turn her back on the people who'd betrayed her, even as he'd admired her unwavering loyalty. She would never turn her back on anyone. Let alone her family.

She was special.

And he intended to love and adore her every day for the rest of their lives.

Turning his head, Dom allowed his gaze to skim over Bailey's profile as she soaked in the afternoon sunlight.

They'd arrived in Vegas three days earlier and they were currently seated next to the pool. It was the end of October and the weather had cooled, but it still felt like midsummer compared to the chilled autumn that was coating Wisconsin in layers of frost. It was a delicious indulgence to spend a few hours absorbing the heat and sipping lemonade.

Not that it was all sun and fun. He was in the process of hiring a full-time manager for the pawnshop, while Bailey was busy setting up the new charity she wanted to create. Her work in the nursing home had revealed the need to offer basic legal advice to the elderly, as well as assistance in filing complaints against people and businesses who tried to take advantage of their age. As Bailey said, the more vulnerable a person became, the more they needed a voice to protect their rights.

Lia had already helped Bailey fill out all the necessary paperwork, and between Kaden and Dom, they'd lined up the sort of donors who could get the project off the ground.

For today, however, Dom had insisted they simply relax and enjoy their time together.

Reaching out, he trailed his fingers down her bare arm. "Happy?"

"Hmm. Let me think. I'm drenched in sunshine, lying next to a gorgeous millionaire who spoils me as if I'm a princess." She released a soft sigh, opening her eyes to meet his searching gaze. "It's every woman's dream."

He grasped her hand, lifting it to press against his lips. The movement allowed the sunlight to glitter off the large diamond ring he'd placed on her finger the night before. They hadn't discussed wedding plans yet, but Dom was content with her promise to become his wife. The details didn't matter.

"You're not most women," he assured her. "You don't care about money or finding someone to pamper you."

"True." Her smile softened. "I would love you, Dom Lucier, no matter where you lived, or where you worked, or what money you might have in your bank account." She rolled to the side, her expression somber. "Being with you makes me happy. Waking up next to you makes me happy. And I know beyond a shadow of a doubt that you will always be there for me. No matter what."

"Always," he swore, pressing her hand against his cheek as a warmth that had nothing to do with the sunlight poured through him. He didn't know what he'd done to earn the love of such a rare woman, but he was smart enough to treasure what he'd been given. "I've waited my entire life for you, Bailey Evans."

Her eyes darkened with an unspoken invitation. "And now you have me. For better or worse."

"Forever and ever . . ." he swore in soft tones. "And it still won't be long enough."

Visit our website at
KensingtonBooks.com
to sign up for our newsletters, read
more from your favorite authors, see
books by series, view reading group
guides, and more!

Become a Part of Our
Between the Chapters Book Club
Community and Join the Conversation